HUNTED IN THE HOLLER

A Sheriff Elven Hallie Mystery

DREW STRICKLAND

www.drewstricklandbooks.com

Copyright © 2021 by DREW STRICKLAND

All rights reserved.

No part of this book may be reproduced in any form or by any electronic or mechanical means, including information storage and retrieval systems, without written permission from the author, except for the use of brief quotations in a book review.

This is a work of fiction. Names, characters, places, and incidents are either the products of the author's imagination or used in a fictitious manner. Any resemblance to actual persons, living or dead, or actual events is purely coincidental.

Cover Design by Juan Padrón

For Mom and Dad,
thanks for being there when I need you

JOIN MY READER'S LIST

Members of my Reader's List get free books and cool behind the scenes information to go along with them.

They're also always the first to hear about my new books and promotions going on.

To be a part of the Reader's List and get your free book, sign up at:

https://drewstricklandbooks.com/mail-list/

CHAPTER ONE

The cold.

It's what he hated most.

He'd travelled the world, seen places that ranged from the most elite and expensive exotic locations to a thousand shithole bars in a hundred different countries. He'd seen the best the world had to offer, bright and hopeful, and the dark, seedy underbelly of the worst. Hell, he was part of the worst.

But through all the terrible experiences in the world—including the gut-wrenching food poisoning from eating undercooked pork anus in some sketchy hole-in-the-wall restaurant in Africa, including the thick air and sweat in the steamy streets of Southeast Asia that smelled like hot garbage and vomit, including the loud and crazy way people acted when they were drunk in cities as if others weren't around them—the thing he hated most about anything was the cold.

And now he was in Dupray, West Virginia.

During the winter.

Again.

Dupray wasn't the coldest place he'd ever been. No, that was reserved for a city he couldn't even remember it's name. But that city was in Russia, he was pretty sure about that.

But still, he'd much rather be south of the equator, or maybe even somewhere coastal. He'd avoided Dupray for a while, not having been for a long while. But somehow, he always knew that he'd find himself back in this dreadful town.

The town itself wasn't the problem. After being to so many places, there was only so much the weather could steer his opinion. At the end of it all, it was about the people. And the people in Dupray were what left a bad taste in his mouth.

The way they didn't care for their homes, the way they didn't care to lift themselves out of poverty, the way they blamed anything and anyone for their current situation in life. Suckling on the government teat, collecting their *draw*.

He rolled his eyes at the thought.

If he were honest—which he always was with himself—he used to say it didn't matter. That he didn't judge people. He took care of his business and was done. It wasn't his concern who it was he was dealing with, as long as they found themselves dead and he found himself paid. But when he did that, he was lying to himself. His cares about the person may not have affected how he did his job, but he sure did judge them.

And he was okay with that.

At the end of the day, he wasn't like them. He found a way to not hold himself down, to make his money. It was hard work sometimes, traveling around, but it was worth it. As much as he hated people, traveling the world had led him to finding a few he didn't mind so much.

And the money didn't hurt.

He was sure that he might have more of it than almost everyone combined in the shit hole county he found himself in again.

And he was there to make even more of it.

The man sat in the front seat of his pickup, watching the house across the street. It was the right address, he was sure of it. Early in his career, he had written names and numbers down so he could double-check, but being at it for as long as he'd been, he no longer needed the small reassurances anymore. His mind was sharp as it ever was.

The lights were on in the house. The house was small from the outside, and as he would soon find out, even smaller on the inside. Two bedrooms, from what he could see. A kitchen, single bathroom, and a living room—if it could even be called that.

The houses surrounding it were quiet, a few with lights on, but not many. And even then, nobody seemed to pay attention to anything going on next door or across the street. They had their own problems to deal with, like how to buy their next 12-pack of piss-water to make them forget about their shitty lives.

If they did happen to pop their head out and see what was happening at their dear neighbor's home, well, it would be no big issue for him. Getting caught wasn't on his mind. He was on a few different wanted lists already, so adding some more wasn't no thing. He'd been caught in the act plenty of times before, so it was up to them on how he would deal with it.

He'd never killed anyone who didn't have a commission attached to their name, but if they chose to stand in his way, it would be the biggest mistake of their life and they would never forget it.

Sometimes, it was boring knowing that there was nobody better, but then again, he kept at it. One day, he knew someone or something would catch up to him, and that idea was what kept him going. The idea that someone in the world might just do him in. That he would actually come across someone who deserved to take him down.

He knew it was odd to think that way, but he watched the bodies pile up, one after another, never nervous. Never bothered. Never caught off guard.

It was like fucking missionary-style every day of your life with the same woman at the same time. A little variety would be nice.

He stepped out of the truck, his breath a cloud in the air as he exhaled. He tucked his hands in the pockets of his wool peacoat, already wishing he was done with the job. At least it wasn't snowing, he reminded himself.

He closed his coat tighter around himself as the cold breeze tried to infiltrate underneath. He grumbled and kept his head down as he made his way to the door. The home wasn't in disrepair, but it wasn't anything he would consider well-kept, either. From his research, the man who lived there, Todd Utt, lived alone. Never married. No kids.

It was just the way he liked it. No strings.

The man cleared his throat and ran his hand across his face, stretching his skin so his lips didn't lock up. They were dry and he longed to smother them in petroleum jelly. But that would have to wait until he could settle in for the night.

He lifted his cold hand and rapped on the door with his knuckles. Behind the door, he could hear the television. It was loud enough that he could make out the background laughter on whatever sitcom was being watched. He knocked again, having no tolerance for being kept waiting.

The springs on the recliner inside groaned as the owner inside rose up from the well-worn leather. The man knocked again for good measure.

"I heard ya the first two times," Todd barked from inside. He sounded irritated and half- asleep.

The man on the porch smiled, waiting for Todd to open the door. He shoved his hand back into his pocket, longing to warm his fingers. He could already feel his joints stiffening from being exposed. That was the last thing he needed on the job.

The door opened wide, Todd not even caring to just peek his head out first. Most people would open it just a crack, test the waters of who might be on the other side. Or perhaps there was a dog they were trying to keep inside. Either way, Todd seemingly had no care to do so.

"Yeah?" Todd asked, looking the man up and down.

The man smiled, showing his teeth and faking it big. He wasn't big on the niceties of the world, but knew them well. He had to often use them to get to the places he needed to be, and he'd mastered them well enough that nobody ever suspected otherwise. He just had to know when to turn them on.

"Todd Utt?" the man asked.

"Yeah?" Todd said, unsure who the man was.

Todd was about the same age as he. Somewhere in his fifties, for sure. But his hair was much thinner on top. It still held all its color, unlike his own hair, which had gone mostly gray on the sides. Todd also wore shorts, revealing a large scar on his knee. A solid white line that went straight up and down. In his research, he'd learned that Todd had had an accident when working in the mines some years ago and had to have his knee replaced.

"Boy, I can't believe it's really you," the man said.

Todd narrowed his eyes, a look the man knew very well. It was as if Todd was searching in his memories for a sliver of something that would remember the man standing in front of him. He'd find it soon enough, but really, that would just be a lie. Todd wouldn't ever really remember him, whether he'd truly known him or not.

"We used to work the mines together, shit, maybe twenty years ago," the man said. "I drove a truck in and out, never down in them shafts or nothing."

Todd slowly nodded, still trying to piece it together. "Yeah, uh—"

"James," the man said, holding his hands up as if it should be obvious. He smiled wide, stepping toward Todd as if he'd been invited in. Todd stumbled, but stepped backward, allowing the man inside.

"You remember, don't ya?" the man asked with a chuckle. Projecting confidence toward a stupid man always had a way of working. It was as if they never wanted to be called out on having a failing memory.

James looked around the living room, which was smaller than some bathrooms he'd been in. The television was loud and the lights were off in the living room. The kitchen behind it had the lights on, however. Just as he'd pictured, there was a well-worn chair that sat facing the television. And on the end table next to the chair was an empty beer bottle, a half-full beer bottle, two open packs of Oreos that hadn't been finished, and a pile of wadded-up tissues.

He could see the stages of use that chair had been under.

"Hey, uh, James. I'm sorry, but what are you doing here?" Todd asked.

"Oh, don't worry, I won't be long," the man said, turning around. "I just came to check in, see how things were here."

Todd nodded and slowly shut the door, not latching it completely. "Well, good, I guess. You in town long?"

"Have a job to do, plus see some old friends. Kill a few birds with one stone sort of thing, you know? But not too long."

Todd shifted on his bad knee and back. The man could tell that Todd was nervous, maybe confused, but not sure what to do about it.

"So I was just going to call it a night. Maybe tomorrow we can catch up?" Todd asked, trying to be polite.

The man sighed. "I don't think so," he said. "Tonight is all we've got."

Todd started to get the hint, his face dropping. "James—"

"You know, I wonder something," James said, not caring to hear whatever Todd was going to say. "How did you feel this mornin' when you woke up?"

"What?"

"Was it just regular? Like, another day of pathetic existence, or was there something else? Did it feel off?" James asked. He waited a moment, staring at Todd, studying his face. "I mean, maybe not. It's pretty late at night, so maybe it's more of a few hours' kind of deal. But did you feel like today was the day? That at the end of whatever you'd planned today, you'd find yourself dead?"

Todd stared at James, no longer smiling. No longer feeling polite or needing to use manners. James could see the growing fear in his eyes. Todd never answered him. They almost never did.

"You got a weapon?" James asked, opening his coat to reveal his own pistol on his hip.

"Upstairs," Todd said.

James clucked his tongue, not really liking the answer. "Damn. Don't really want to wait that long to be honest."

"F-for what?" Todd asked.

"To kill you," James said.

"Why would you kill me?"

"Someone out there paid me to. Seems you made an enemy of sorts. Maybe you've been ruffling some feathers, maybe done something shitty," James said with a shrug. "To be honest, I don't much care."

"I ain't that guy anymore," Todd said. "I keep to myself. I don't start shit."

"Todd," James said. "I don't care."

"I don't know you, do I?" Todd asked.

"It really took you up until now to figure that out?" James asked. "Now, I'm a fair man. Usually I like to give someone the option. Draw or die. But since you ain't got a gun on you, well..."

Todd yelled out, which was a surprise to James. That was alright, though, he liked surprises. From a man who seemed so damn confused and daft at putting it together, he sure did come to quite the decision. He didn't run away, but ran toward James.

He lumbered forward, his size like a linebacker's. But from the beer and age, he lacked the speed and finesse to accomplish anything other than putting himself in the line of fire. Not that it would have mattered. Everyone was too slow, when it came to James's work.

James let his coat open fully and he dug his hand beneath, grabbing the pistol that sat on his hip. He pulled it up and put a bullet in the side of Todd's head. The blood and brain splattered against the door behind him. His body fell backward to the floor, blocking the door.

James groaned and rolled his eyes. He knew he should have positioned it so Todd was closer in the living room. He walked to the body, the blood already pooling around his head. Todd's skull was blown out the opposite side of his head, exposing the wet mess of gray-and-red sludge.

James grabbed Todd's feet and pulled him, sliding the weight of his body through the blood across the floor. He moved him just enough so he had clearance to leave. The blood made a large trail across the carpet, but he didn't care. He wasn't trying to make it look like anything other than what it was.

Crime scenes, DNA, motives—all that shit they play on TV, it didn't matter to him. He was wanted almost everywhere he went. But nobody had proof of who he actually was.

He turned to leave, and just as he did, the door drifted open. A woman stepped inside, holding a long gun. She was much older than he was, probably in her eighties, maybe even closer to ninety. The rifle she held was bigger than she was, and she had fear in her eyes.

The man pulled his pistol up, pointing it at her from the side. "Drop the rifle, ma'am," he said.

She turned, but didn't drop it. He could see that her finger was nowhere near the trigger. She stood, frozen in the doorway.

"Ma'am, one more time. Drop the gun. Please," he added. He might have hatred for most people and how they lived, but he still liked to think that he showed respect to his elders. It was the little things that made someone respectable.

The woman shook, but set the gun down, leaning it against the wall as if she hadn't just walked into a room with a dead body. "I heard a gunshot. Thought maybe Todd had blown his head off or got into it with someone," the woman said, shaking. "Who are you?"

"The exterminator," James said.

"Todd's dead?" she asked, staring down at the mess of the man.

"He is," the man said.

"Are you gonna kill me?" she asked.

The man looked her up and down, then holstered his pistol. "No, ma'am. I take great pride in my work, and I don't do it for free."

He walked past the woman, smelling the mothballs and baby

powder scent from her clothes. He stepped off the porch and made his way to his truck. Once inside, he pulled his phone out and dialed.

"Yeah, it's done," James said into the phone, cranking up the heater in the vehicle. He put his hand in front of the vent, his skin burning from the drastic change in temperature.

"Good. I'll send you the names of who is next. If you're this quick, I'd say you won't be here longer than a week," the voice said on the other end. "That's not a problem, right?"

"Not for me. Though a woman did come to check on Todd after she heard the gunshot," the man said.

"Did she see you?"

"Yeah, I'd say so. We exchanged a few pleasantries, more or less."

"Did you kill her?"

"You know the terms. I kill who's been contracted. No more, no less."

"Shit."

"Don't worry. Law enforcement ain't shit. And around here, as far as I remember, the guy's gotta be older than dirt. Might catch a few locals, but he ain't seen nothing like me before."

"No, no, not anymore. The sheriff is different. The last thing we need is him to have an idea of who he's looking for," the voice said.

"Even so, it ain't no skin off my teeth," James said.

There was silence on the phone for a minute. James continued to warm his fingers against the vent, clenching and unclenching them. He knew where this was headed, and he didn't want to step back out in the cold.

"I'm wiring you the money now," the voice said. "Take care of it."

James hung up the phone, then pulled up the app. Sure enough, the money was in his account, just like as he'd been told. He exhaled loudly, and stepped back out of the truck.

He stepped through the doorway and saw the woman still standing over the dead body. It was as if she was transfixed by it. She seemed to be either frozen from the shock of seeing the body or perhaps the man who had made the body that way. The idea of having a brush with death could do a number on someone.

He didn't need to be quick on this one, his gun already pulled. She spun around as soon as he stepped through the doorway.

"I...I thought you said you wouldn't kill me," she said.

"I did, and I meant it at the time. I ain't no liar. I'd normally give you the option to pull, but let's face it, I'd only be wasting both our time. And you've got so little of it as it is."

"But you said—"

"Sorry, ma'am. But you've just been paid for."

He pulled the trigger before she could say another word.

CHAPTER TWO

The sun hung in the air, still halfway from making its way up to being directly above him. Elven tilted his head slightly so the brim of his Stetson covered the ball of fire in the sky, preventing the rays from shining directly into his eyes. The sun and its position was a nuisance for his vision, especially at that moment, but he welcomed the heat it provided.

His Filson tin cloth jacket soaked up the warmth nicely, like a comforting hug by the fireplace. But his nerves were anything but relaxed. Even though it was winter and there was a frigid chill in the air, he felt the band around his hat soak from the sweat gathering on his forehead.

The palm of his hand was placed flat on the grip of his revolver that sat on his hip. He fluttered his fingers against the side, trying to keep his fingers nimble so they didn't seize up in the cold. It was a task he did nearly every day, but this time it was different.

This time, the pressure was on.

Across the field, he saw the outline of a man. He narrowed his eyes, the head a mere black shadow. But it was there, and like it or not, Elven was going to have to take the shot.

He took a deep breath and let it out slowly, waiting for the moment. His heart rate was steady, a trick he'd picked up over the years. Before the big football games in high school, he'd always been on edge. As the running back for the team, the pressure was on him, but he'd learned how to stay calm, to stay focused. The technique was more refined now, but the feeling was still the same as it had been over twenty years ago walking out onto that field.

But this was no high school football game. Back then, those games seemed as if they were all that mattered. That everything in life had led to that moment, and whatever decisions he made would cause them to win or fail. This time, it didn't feel that way. Though he had to admit, being in a quick draw was something that should feel like a life or death moment.

The air was silent around him, to the point he could hear a whistling against his ear. It was faint and he managed to keep the chill from running down his spine. Any sudden movement could cause him to fail.

Then the buzzer went off. It echoed over the field, cracking through the silence like a lightning strike with thunder that followed only a millisecond after.

He watched the figure in the distance, his eyes never leaving its shape. He let his hands do what they did best.

He wrapped his hand around the grip of his revolver and pulled it from its holster. The weight was familiar and comfortable to him, having done it at least a thousand times before. He angled the barrel upward as his arm lifted, and found himself pointing the gun at the dark figure in the distance.

His finger had already been acquainted with the trigger, teasing it as he lifted the weapon. Then, when he was in position, he squeezed.

Everything was step by step. Everything was practiced. Everything was faster than the blink of an eye, but to him, just as he slowed his heart rate, it was as if he slowed time itself.

He felt and saw every step in drawing his revolver until he pulled the trigger.

And then, just as the buzzer had cut through the silence, the explosion of the bullet from his barrel followed. It was a deafening sound, especially in such a large open space that had been filled with silence.

One shot was all he got. One shot, and he knew he had hit his target.

He took a deep breath and watched in the distance, dropping his gun to his side and holstering it. The hot barrel tucked against his leg so he could feel its warmth through the leather.

And just like that, in a split second, the silence was gone.

Screams and shouts came from behind him. He spun around to the crowd and smiled, lifting his hat. It looked as though half of Dupray was out there today.

There were some bleachers set up along the fence that had been long weathered and bowed from decades of butt cheeks, but most of the people stood, leaning against the heavy wood top of the barrier. It was cold, so everyone had donned heavy coats and pants. There were a few who only had on a thick flannel shirt, but Elven knew that those flannels would soon be covered if they got enough snow this winter.

"And that was your very own Sheriff Elven Hallie, everyone," the voice boomed over the same loudspeaker that had buzzed for Elven's signal to fire.

Elven had been going to the Dupray Shooter's Competition for years, held every few years at the Dupray high school. Once he'd made Sheriff, he had debated on whether or not it was appropriate. The mayor—and practically everyone else around him—had basically told him he was full of it and it was a staple for him to be there. Elven played it humble, but really, he liked the attention.

He knew he was a good shot. Hell, he was the best shot in all of Dupray—not that it was a great title to be known by. He hadn't tried his hand many other places, his commitments being to the county and all, but when some out-of-towners came through for the competition, they told him that if he wanted to play the circuit and travel to various competitions, they were sure that he'd make a pretty penny.

Of course, with their being from out of town, they weren't aware that Elven had much more than a penny to his name. In fact, he was sure that anything he made from competitions would never amount to what he already had in his bank account.

But he liked to hear their compliments just the same. The fame itself might be worth traveling around in bumpy trailers and sleeping on uncomfortable mattresses. But as much as Elven loved to gloat and be his cocky self, he also liked to think he was worth more than being a one-trick pony. He was good at what he did in town for Dupray, and he knew he might get more from helping people than he did from showing off.

Didn't meant there wasn't room to show off while in Dupray, though. If the town wanted to cheer him on for his quick draw and give him an award for it, who was he to say no?

His own small entourage was leaning against the wooden posts, having come to see him. He made his way over to them.

"Elven, that was incredible," Madds's voice rang out behind him. Despite her praise, but the way she said the words told him otherwise. She sounded tired and slow. He scanned the crowd, and saw his brunette deputy bundled in a large parka that made her look as if she was drowning in fur. And somehow, she still looked cold. Her teeth chattered as she smiled at him, and he couldn't help but smile back.

He still had reservations about how to act around Madds. His suspicions of her sometimes made it hard to decide his mood. But at the end of the day, she was still his deputy. He wasn't even sure if his hunch was valid. One a previous case, she had given him some wrong information when she'd been sleep-deprived. Who wouldn't have been confused in her shoes?

And if his hunch was valid? Well, he still couldn't figure out what her end game was. It would make no sense for her to lie about anything to do with the last case.

There was also the fact that he hadn't gotten a call back from her previous supervisor in Arizona, which irritated him. With one little phone call, his worries could be put at ease. He decided to act business as usual until he could talk to the guy. After all, Elven knew she was a good cop and had his back. He just needed to follow through to reassure the nagging voice at the back of his head.

She held a single rose in her hand that he hadn't noticed before. When he thought about it, he wasn't sure he'd seen her around before he'd taken his position on the field.

"I've seen you shoot before, but I couldn't believe it. But that timer up there confirms it," Madds said, pointing to the electronic timer that sat at a booth at the side of the field. The timer read 1.72 seconds.

The loudspeaker crackled and the man's voice came on again. "That was one point seven two seconds for Sheriff Hallie. He even hit the target square in the eyes."

More cheers from people, and Elven held his hand up with a smile as if he was at a beauty pageant. In the distance, a boy ran with the paper target that had been across the field. It wasn't a long distance to the target, but to be accurate and quick was something Elven prided himself on.

"You're enjoying every minute of this, aren't you?" Madds asked with a sly smile.

"Just giving the people what they want," he replied. "What's with the rose?"

She shrugged. "Found it on my doorstep," she said. "I guess now we know it wasn't from you. Maybe I have a secret admirer out there." She fluttered her eyes teasingly, and he noticed the bags underneath them.

Johnny came hustling up with two cups of what looked like hot chocolate. He wore a more reasonable coat for the weather, but he'd been in Dupray all his life, which was even longer than Elven, so he was used to it. He handed a cup to Madds, who thanked him before taking a big swig from the steaming Styrofoam cup.

"Hell, did I miss Elven?" Johnny said.

"Sorry to say, but you blink and it's over," Elven said confidently.

"I'm telling you, this year isn't gonna be your year," a voice came from behind Elven.

He turned around and saw Lyman standing on the field side. He was tall and thin, just as he'd always been his whole life. He smiled ear to ear, and wore a gun on his hip that caused it to sag on the side. He looked as if he'd stepped out of a movie, and not one with a big budget.

"What are you wearing?" Elven asked, tapping the huge Stetson on Lyman's head that looked to have been sized up to a watermelon. He wasn't sure he'd ever seen Lyman wearing a hat like this one.

"My lucky hat," Lyman said with a grin. "At least, it'll be lucky after this when I wipe the floor with your time."

Elven leaned back against the fence. "That so?"

"Elven, I tell you, I've been practicing. You wait and see."

"I can't wait to do just that," Elven said.

"You may have the skills and truly be better, but it ain't always about who's better. Sometimes, the other person just wants it more."

"Lyman Starcher is up next," the voice said. There was a small grumble from the crowd along with a handful of shouts and claps.

"That's my cue."

Elven watched as his good friend made his way to the field in clothing that made him look even more ridiculous than he already looked. It was all in good fun, though. Elven knew Lyman wasn't much with a pistol, and that he was going out of his way to put on a show for everyone.

A moment of silence came, followed by the buzzer. Lyman drew his gun, the barrel catching on the lip of its holster. It slid back down and Lyman pulled again, this time clearing the holster. He pulled the trigger when it was pointed toward the target.

Lyman nodded his head, the large hat wobbling atop his crown. He holstered his gun and turned, taking a bow in front of everyone. It was followed by laughs and some cheers. Lyman knew how to make a good joke of himself, that was for sure. He had the confidence of being a buffoon, especially when compared to Elven.

"I think that was over five whole seconds," the voice said. "And not even a knick on the target."

Lyman approached Elven with a smile, shrugging. "I guess it's safe to say you wanted it more."

"Not my skill and talent?" Elven asked. He clapped Lyman on the shoulder and the two laughed together. Even though Lyman was a Starcher, he had always been Elven's friend.

Lyman turned and looked at Madds. His laughter quieted down and he looked away from her. Elven noticed that Madds's eyes diverted as well. Elven had told Madds that Starchers weren't to be trusted, but here he was, yakking it up with one of them. That's probably why she was being so odd, he thought. Plus, she just didn't seem herself in general.

Johnny leaned over the railing. "Hey, Elven, you think you could teach me to shoot like you?" he asked earnestly, his eyes as big as a kid meeting his favorite athlete.

Elven smiled. "I can work with you on shooting, but I can't guarantee how fast you'll be. Tell you what though—you'll definitely hit your target when we're done."

That seemed to make Johnny happy. Elven would have to remember to schedule some time with Johnny. It would be good to help Johnny all around, as he wasn't the most skilled with a gun as it was.

"So is that it?" Madds asked.

"We have one more contestant. A last-minute entry approved by the judges," the voice said over the loudspeaker.

"That's odd. Pretty much everyone who competes has already gone," Lyman remarked.

A man stepped out, wearing jeans and a coat similar to Elven's. He didn't wear a Stetson, but a simple ball cap. It was brown and had no other marks on it, but it was obvious that it was well-worn. The man had stubble on his face. Something about him seemed very familiar to Elven.

"Is that—" Lyman started, but was cut off.

"Dupray's very own Hunter Wallace," the loudspeaker boomed.

"No way," Elven said.

"Who is Hunter Wallace?" Madds asked.

"He used to live in Dupray," Johnny said. "Left a year or two after he graduated high school. He was the most popular guy, quarterback on the football team. Two years ahead of Elven. Basically handed the torch off to Elven when he left."

"Wasn't that like twenty years ago?" Madds asked. "And aren't you like twenty years older than him, Johnny? I mean, unless you were held back...that much?"

Elven chuckled at Madds's terrible job of backpedaling, but he kept his eyes locked on Hunter.

"In small towns, sometimes we don't have much else to think about," Johnny said, almost apologetically.

"And Hunter was more than just a standout student. He was somethin' else," Elven said.

"Oh," Johnny said, leaning over the fence where Madds had balanced her hot chocolate. "You think—"

"Jesus tits, Johnny!" Madds shouted. Elven turned and saw that Johnny had rocked the fence just enough to spill the cup of hot chocolate all over Madds's thick coat. Luckily, it was so dense that the steaming hot beverage didn't burn her. But it left a nasty brown splash all over her front.

"Sorry, Madds," Johnny said. "I'll get you another."

"Don't worry about it," Madds said, trying to wipe herself off. "You missed Elven shoot, so might as well watch this Hunter guy. Hold my rose, I'll go get it myself." She shoved the flower at Johnny.

Madds walked off into the crowd where Johnny had emerged from earlier. Elven turned and looked at Johnny, who looked disappointed in himself. The guy was nothing but kind, but to call him clumsy would be putting it mildly. Elven clapped his hand on Johnny's shoulder, trying to put him at ease as they both turned to watch Hunter's session.

Hunter stood where Lyman and Elven had earlier. The crowd hushed and the buzzer went off. Elven barely had time to see Hunter's arm move, he was so fast. And he didn't even need to look at the timer to know it, but he did anyway.

1.21

Hunter had beaten Elven's time, and even more, he hit the target dead center between the eyes just as Elven had.

There was an audible gasp from the crowd, followed by a moment of silence. Then the crowd erupted in cheers, whistles, and hollers. Elven, Johnny and Lyman just stood in silence, shocked and in awe. Until Lyman spoke first.

"I'd say that he wanted it even more," he said.

CHAPTER THREE

Madds heard the cheers and laughter all around her. She'd missed something big. Of course, she did. Johnny had a way of screwing things up like no one else she'd ever met. Part of her was angry, but he was the kindest and gentlest soul she'd ever met. So she found herself eager to let it go and save the man from her rage.

She'd have to wash the coat or take it to a dry cleaner. Shit, did they even have one of those in Dupray? She wasn't sure she'd seen one anywhere. She hadn't thought much about it, but where she was from, she could find two or three of them on every corner. Funny how different small towns could be from sprawling cities and suburbs.

She made her way through the crowd—one of the biggest she'd seen since coming to Dupray. Johnny had explained to her how the people from neighboring counties and even states would come to participate in the competition. She'd never been to a shooting competition before, but she'd felt the united excitement from the surrounding people and had found herself enjoying it.

Of course, it's being so damn cold was her least favorite part. She wasn't used to it, coming from Arizona. But when she'd found out from the others at the office that it wasn't even the coldest it could be yet, she worried about her decision to move there in the first place. Snow was nice to see on a vacation. Maybe even for a week. But living in it for months on end? Fuck, how was she going to do anything?

She missed the fair weather in the fall and winter, and she didn't mind the blazing-hot summers. But in Dupray, she had cold winters and, most likely, humid summers that she had yet to experience. She groaned, thinking about it.

But she was there for a reason. One, to get away from what she'd left behind in Arizona. She could never go back as long as *he* was still alive. And she was hidden in Dupray, where he would never find her. But even more now, she was in deep with Hollis. And even if she wanted to, she wasn't sure she could get out from underneath his thumb.

She'd thought coming to Dupray was her answer. She'd thought that being hidden in a small town with her extended family around to protect her was for the best. She knew her uncle wasn't the most up-and-up character, but she didn't know just how far his corruption extended. Taking the deputy position, keeping tabs on the happenings inside the sheriff's station, and Elven's investigations—that was where she'd thought it would stop.

Her life in the suburbs surrounding Phoenix, watching stupid reality-TV shows about making moonshine in the Appalachian mountains, had given her a false idea of the crimes her uncle was involved in. Sure, the Starchers did run a moonshine business, and it was just as harmless as she'd thought. Hell, even Elven had let that one slide, unless he could use it to his advantage.

But moonshining had turned out to be the wholesome side of Hollis. Running drugs and murder was the other side, and that's what she knew about. She had an idea that there was even more depth to the crimes that Hollis was—or would be—involved in.

Part of her knew she was naive, lying to herself about *why* her uncle wanted her to keep tabs on Elven. But she told herself it was all going to be worth it. That she would have a line she wouldn't cross, and if it came to it, she would face the consequences of what she'd done, which would amount to little more than probation and a fine, if anything.

But the line, as she'd found out recently, was fluid. She was inching, just a bit, further and further. She told herself it was just one more thing. Just one tiny little extra job for her to do. Like handing over a suspect, never to be seen again. She pushed the thought out of her head, not wanting to think about the torture that man had probably gone through.

When she'd arrived at Dupray, she never had to shoot someone in the line of duty, let alone kill anyone. Now, she'd had to kill a woman in the line of duty, kill multiple attackers to save her life, and, of course, kill a man so she and her family didn't go to prison.

She looked through the crowd in the distance, and saw the face of Abnel Foster. He wasn't really there, seeing as how she'd made sure he would never be anywhere but six feet in the dirt, but sometimes, she still saw his face. The panicked look when he thought he was going to go to jail because of his involvement with her uncle. The realization that he was on his own, so he was backed into a corner and thought playing his only card would save him.

But Madds had made the decision to not let that happen. Abnel had been guilty of many things, but murder hadn't been on that list. Did a man deserve to die for being in deep with Hollis? For doing what he'd had to do to survive? Wasn't she in that same situation?

It was surprising how easy it had been to make the split second call at the time. Just to save herself from jail time, but more than that, she'd found herself more afraid of facing Elven's disappointment. She didn't think she would have such an attachment and admiration for the man before working with him.

She stepped up to the small set-up of tables and tents on the other end of the field. A few people lingered, but most of them were already making their way back toward the field to see whatever crazy happenings had occurred to elicit such a roar. When she reached the table, two women were manning the table in a surprisingly efficient fashion.

"What'll you have?" the blond-haired lady somewhere in her late forties asked. To Madds, the way the woman was dressed, with her jeans and plaid snap-button shirt, she would have guessed her name was one of those two-first-names kind. Like Ellen May, or Bobby Sue.

"Just a hot chocolate," Madds replied, holding out her cash.

The woman looked down at her jacket with a smile and pointed. "I'd say you've had enough. I'd hate to have to cut you off," she said with a laugh.

Ha fucking ha. Madds knew the woman was just being friendly, but she was in no mood for light-hearted banter. Maybe she would have been if she hadn't had to live with the demons she was bearing. But Miss Late Forties, Lame-Joke-Telling, Not-A-Care-In-Her-Fucking-Life Bobby Sue just had to push her, trying to be all cutesy.

Madds shoved the cash at her and took the cup of hot chocolate that sat on the table. She offered a smile, but it was forced, and probably came off looking like a visible *fuck off*.

"Have a blessed day," the woman said, her tone dripping with kindness.

Madds didn't care. Bobby Sue could shove that blessed day right up her—

She stopped in her tracks as soon as she turned around. The crowd continued to walk back and forth through the dirt, but she saw something between people in the distance. But it couldn't be, right?

Another person crossed in front of her and she saw a clearer image.

She dropped the cup of hot chocolate in the dirt. It splashed up, against her jeans, but she didn't care. The burning sensation, followed by the freezing cold temperature that already started to come along, was nothing compared to the icy temperature she felt inside of herself.

The chiseled jaw, the blue eyes, the blond hair that was almost white, and the thin lips that almost disappeared when his mouth was closed.

Her heart picked up its pace so fast, she thought it was going to burst from her chest. Inside, her veins might be ice, but she felt her neck and cheeks go wildly hot. If he had found her, then there was no more hiding.

Her hand went to the gun on her hip and she grit her teeth. He may think he'd finally tracked her down, but she wasn't the same person she'd been when she left. It might be too late for her, but revealing himself now was a mistake he wouldn't live to regret.

She marched forward, pushing through the crowd. The malty scent of beer invaded her nose, what with most of the people already half in the bag. What was a gun show without a little booze, right? But her focus remained the same, and she kept moving. Someone smoked a cigarette nearby and she walked into a cloud of smoke. When this was done, she would have to have one of those herself.

A man bumped into her, laughing as his friends pushed him again. She glanced his way and he turned around, grabbing her elbow, laughing apologetically. "I'm so sorry, miss. My friends are being assholes and we—"

"It's fine," Madds snapped, turning back to where she'd seen that face through the crowd. But he wasn't there anymore. She felt the blood drain from her face, thinking she'd missed her opportunity. She spun her head around and saw the back of his head. That white-blond hair was unmistakable.

She pushed through the crowd, not caring who she ran into this time. She picked up the pace until she was nearly running, shoving anyone out of her way. Then she saw him only twenty feet away. He continued to walk away. He wore a large brown coat and she couldn't tell if there was a gun underneath, but it didn't matter. She was already ahead of him.

"Kurt!" she shouted as she ran directly at him. "Kurt!"

She pulled her gun from the holster and finally caught up to him, grabbing his shoulder with her free hand. She pulled hard, spinning him around. She shoved the gun under his chin, then stared directly into his eyes.

The eyes of a very frightened man.

It wasn't Kurt.

His eyes weren't blue. They were brown. And though he had a chiseled jaw and light blond hair, the man she held was not Kurt.

"Oh my God, please, I don't know what you want," the man pleaded.

A scream came from behind Madds's shoulder. "That woman has a gun!" the voice exclaimed.

"Everyone does!" someone yelled, which was followed by laughter.

Madds was frozen in shock.

"Please," the man said.

Madds dropped her gun, but still held onto him, her left hand a vice on the brown jacket that covered his shoulder. "Where's Kurt?" she managed to ask.

"I-I don't know a Kurt," the man said cautiously. His eyes darted to the gun in her hand, as if he was afraid she was going to put it right back under his chin.

Madds wasn't sure what to do. She wasn't sure how she'd even gotten into this situation. She was so sure she'd seen Kurt, but now she was just threatening a perfect stranger.

"Madds!" a man yelled. It snapped her out of it, and she turned to see Tank. He was easy to spot since he stood taller than everyone else around and was nearly twice the size in muscle. He was on duty and wore his deputy uniform, unlike herself.

"Help, she just shoved a gun in my face, saying something about Kurt. I don't know this crazy woman," the man said.

Madds holstered her weapon and let go of the man. Tank stepped between the two and put his hand on Madds to keep her away from the man. "Are you okay?" Tank asked the man.

"You gotta arrest her!" he shouted.

"I'll take care of it. What I need from you is to walk the other way."

"Are you gonna—"

"Right now," Tank said firmly. The man quickly caught on and did as he was told. Tank watched a moment, making sure he disappeared from sight. When he did, he turned to Madds.

"You okay?" he asked.

"I swear, I thought it was him," Madds said.

"Who?" Tank asked.

"Just...someone," she said, shaking her head. She couldn't tell Tank anything about her past or why she was really in Dupray. "I thought he was a person of interest, but obviously was wrong. When he looked like he was running after I yelled at him, I pulled my gun."

Tank nodded. "I don't think he's going to make a stir about this. Will probably get drunk and be on his way, so there won't be a complaint. When Elven—"

"Don't tell him," Madds implored. "Please."

Tank sighed, looking into her eyes. She didn't know Tank all that well, but she knew him to be good at the job. She didn't know the details, but she was pretty sure he was ex-military. Which branch, she didn't know. He didn't share much of his personal life. But she worried a man like that went by the book, and that also meant reporting to his superiors.

Tank clenched his jaw. "If no complaint comes in, I won't say anything. But if it does, I'll tell it like it is, which is that it was an honest mistake, alright?"

Madds nodded. "That's fair, thank you."

"Just don't let it happen again," Tank said. Madds breathed a sigh of relief when he walked away, but deep inside, she couldn't help but feel like something was going on. That she really had seen Kurt. Had he really been there and she'd missed him?

If he was, then that meant she needed to be ready for anything.

CHAPTER FOUR

Hunter had won the quick draw competition. There were other areas to compete in, but quick draw was the only competition Elven liked to be a part of. Anything involving a rifle, he knew he wouldn't even get close to placing in. He had come to terms that he just wasn't great at longer-distance shooting, especially compared to those who hunted for a living.

Elven wouldn't eat beef because of the way a cow had looked at him once, so there was no way he'd be out hunting down elk.

So he kept to the fast draw, and as much as he thought he played it humble, he'd never expected to lose.

Elven would never let anyone know, but he could admit it to himself—he was a little jealous. His ego could take a lot, but part of him had really wanted to win.

His shot to his ego was quickly forgotten once Hunter had said they would all be at Martin's Bar after the competition. He'd told Elven that he hoped he'd join them there.

Elven had overheard what Johnny had told Madds about Hunter, and he hadn't been wrong. Hunter had been two years ahead of

Elven back in school. Elven had been a cocky sophomore, always upping the ante with the other kids in school.

Hunter, though, had always been better than Elven. He was the seasoned senior who had led the football team. He was kind, and he was popular. But he was also great at everything he tried to achieve. He had inspired Elven to be just like him.

But then, he just up and left Dupray. There were rumors that he'd joined the air force or the CIA, and there were others that had said he was robbing banks across the nation. Others claimed that he'd just hiked into the mountains and never come back.

Elven had never been sure what had happened to Hunter. The only ones who'd had any idea were Hunter's mother and brother, and neither of them had seemed enough to think him dead, though they'd never shared their opinions on the matter. So Elven just figured Hunter had left Dupray because, well, Dupray didn't have a lot going for it for most people.

And now here he was, back as if he'd stepped out of thin air to just be home again. He'd entered a shooting competition to win, and now he was drinking at the same bar, in the same seat even, he'd drank at before as if he hadn't been missing for the last twenty years.

Martin's Bar was busy that night. A few out-of-towners had joined in the celebrations along with the usual crew who found themselves drinking there every night. It was the busiest it got at Martin's, with nearly every seat filled and standing room limited.

The shooting competition wasn't the biggest in West Virginia, but it was the biggest in the southern area of the state. Considering that the states and counties that surrounded Dupray didn't have much else to do, the annual winter shootout was high on the list to attend.

Martin stood behind the bar, pouring at a nonstop rate. He had his long hair tucked into a bun at the back of his head with strands loose across his face. He was at that in-between stage of needing to shave and growing out a beard, and Elven couldn't tell which look he was going for. Beads of sweat gathered on his forehead from running back and forth, trying to take care of the many customers.

Next to him was a blond woman that Elven recognized. Charlene was an old friend of Martin's, sometimes stepping in to help when he had busy events coming up. Normally, Elven would think a woman with such fair skin behind a bar would be something for the drunk and rowdy to harass, but Charlene was different.

She was pretty, her face clear and youthful, but her stature was like that of a linebacker. She towered over Martin, who could not be described as short. Anyone who wanted to mess with her didn't have to worry about Martin having to intervene. Charlene could take care of herself, and everyone there knew it.

Needless to say, Charlene didn't get a lot of flack when pouring drinks.

Elven noticed a crowd at the bar where Charlene stood pouring. She was all smiles at whoever she was speaking to. The man in front of her threw back a shot as the crowd of other men cheered him on. It looked as if he was throwing them back in a line. Elven felt sick just watching it happen.

Then he realized that the man who had drawn the crowd and made Charlene giggly was none other than Hunter Wallace.

Elven couldn't help but smile at how some things may be completely different, but seem like nothing had changed at the same time.

"Ten in a row," Hunter said. "I'd say that's gotta count for something, right?"

Charlene leaned forward, her breasts hanging low over the bar, and puckered up her lips. Hunter leaned forward and planted one right on Charlene's lips. The surrounding group cheered, but before Hunter could pull back, Charlene grabbed the back of his head and kissed him longer. Even more raucous laughter followed.

"Charlene, you and I have got to reconnect before I head out again," Hunter said with a smile.

"I'm not sure you could handle me," she said, obviously flirting back.

"I don't doubt that, but I'm willing to take on a challenge," Hunter said. As if he felt Elven's eyes on him, he turned and saw Elven standing near the doorway. "Holy hell, Elven Hallie, get your rich ass over here."

Elven approached, and when he reached Hunter, he could smell the booze coming off the man in waves. But somehow, he still held himself together really well. The last time Elven had seen Hunter, he would have said he was a good-looking guy. Now, age had treated him even better, giving Hunter the distinguished wrinkles in just the right places to make him look like a rugged Hollywood star.

He had dark black hair with a touch of gray mixed in around his temples. He still wore that same ball cap, now flipped backward after Charlene's excellent customer service. And somehow, he made the holes in his flannel shirt look as if it was a new style straight out of *GQ*.

The crowd of locals, whom Elven knew very well, let him slide in. Hunter stood up from his stool and wrapped his arms around Elven, giving him a solid pat on his back. Elven returned the sentiment. Hunter stood back, and looked Elven up and down.

"Let me get a look at you here, Elven," he said. "Looks like life has treated you well, my friend."

"I could say the same for you," Elven said. "The years don't look like they've been too hard on you."

Hunter shook his head and turned to anyone who would listen. "You guys know that this asshole here was giving me shit when I was a senior in high school. And he was just a little sophomore. He had attitude and confidence, that's for sure."

"If I remember correctly, when it all came to a head, I took one on the jaw," Elven said.

"Me? You're the one who swung first. I just had to put you in your place after that."

"Nearly lost my tooth because of that," Elven said.

"Don't I know it," Hunter said. "Let me tell you, you don't know real fear until Victoria Hallie comes looking for you because her son's perfect smile was under attack."

"You had to deal with her once. I'm the one who had to live with her. If it wasn't for your momma stepping up to her, we both would be regretting that little fight," Elven said.

Hunter laughed. "And we were friends ever since, weren't we?"

"I'd say so," Elven said. It wasn't far from the truth, as they'd been friendly for sure. But he didn't think he was all that close to the man, especially after he'd disappeared. "Though you just up and left without a word to me. Always wondered what had happened there."

Hunter's smile faltered a bit, but he tried to keep up appearances. "Oh, you know how it is," he said, avoiding the topic. "I heard you went on your own expedition out of Dupray for a few years there."

Elven had left and backpacked in many parts of the world, but it was a far cry from disappearing without a word to anyone else. But he decided to drop it for the moment. Hunter was going to be more than drunk once those shots settled in, and it was time for a celebration. Not to give him the third degree.

"Did you know he's the sheriff, too?" a man said to Hunter, putting his hand on Elven's shoulder. Elven looked over and saw that the man was Donnie Price, one of Hunter's old friends from high school. After that, he had worked at the mines that had been owned by Elven's family. Since those had closed, Elven hadn't heard what Donnie had been up to, but he figured it was what anyone in Dupray did—try to make ends meet however they could.

Donnie wasn't a big man, but fairly thin and short. And seeing him again with Hunter reminded Elven of the times he had seen him, more or less, resemble a puppy following its master. Some people just latched onto someone to lead them, for better or worse.

"Is that so?" Hunter asked. "You know, I had worked with ol' Lester for about a year before leaving."

"I did know that," Elven said. "He spoke of you fondly, and like most of us, was disappointed to see you leave."

"Where is that old guy now? Hard to think of him retired and sitting on a porch somewhere."

Elven didn't say anything about Lester. It was hard to imagine the old guy that way, but it's the way he wished he could imagine him. What had happened to him on his last case hadn't been fair, but then again, life never was fair to most.

"So what brings you back?" Elven asked. "Can't be just to show me up at the fast draw in front of the very people I now sheriff."

Hunter chuckled and clapped his hand on Elven's shoulder. "Didn't mean nothin' by it, Elven, but if I come through town, you better believe I'm gonna keep you on your toes." He paused for a moment, then answered the question. "Momma passed."

Elven grimaced. He knew that Hunter's mother had been battling cancer, but hadn't heard the news of her passing. "I'm sorry to hear about that, Hunter. If you need anything—"

"Elven, I haven't seen my momma in almost twenty years. I appreciate you, but I'm fine. Now come on, let's do some shots, you second-place gunslinger!"

Elven forced a smile, but he couldn't help but feel that Hunter was being a little cold, even if he hadn't seen his mother in that many years. Elven didn't have a great relationship with his own family, but he figured there would still be some emotions when it was their time to go.

"Man, you can go fuck yourself!" someone shouted from the corner of the bar, snapping Elven from his concerns about Hunter.

Elven turned to see what the commotion was about. In the corner, one man pointed at another, laughing. The one pointing was large, with a short-sleeved shirt dotted with holes. The other man was half his size and his entire front was soaked with beer. He was holding a half-empty pitcher.

The one who was soaked with beer spun around, looking for who had bumped into him. He grabbed the closest person to him, who was another man that Elven didn't recognize. He was probably from out of town for the competition. Elven did know the man who'd been soaked, though, as well as the one laughing at him.

The pair was Vincent Page and Willie Hutchins. Vincent was the bigger guy, Willie the beer-soaked one. They, too, had worked for the mines that Elven's family had owned. He didn't know them well, but knew enough about them. Now, they worked for the water company, digging ditches for the lines.

They were also known to be a little hot-headed.

Willie gripped the stranger's shoulder with his right hand. He lifted up the half-empty pitcher, ready to smash it across the man's head. But before he could, Donnie Price rushed over and grabbed Willie's arm.

"I'm sorry," the stranger said apologetically. "I was just trying to make my way through and tripped. Didn't mean nothing by it." He was near groveling at Willie.

"Don't pay no mind to this asshat," Donnie said to the stranger.

Hunter leaned toward Elven, rolling his eyes. "Donnie still jumps into a fight the second one starts, huh? Guess things never change." He took another shot, and Elven realized that Hunter didn't much care for Donnie. His attitude and body language said it all.

"Get your hand off me," Willie demanded of Donnie.

But Donnie didn't budge. Willie, in turn, balled his free hand into a fist. Vincent came up behind Donnie, wrapping his large arms around him. Willie swung and connected with Donnie's face once.

Willie pulled back again, but that's when Elven was on him. He grabbed his arm and spun him around, then twisted it behind him. Elven pushed his face down on the closest table to him. A man sat in the corner and grabbed his whiskey before the table shook from the impact.

"Let's cool it down right now," Elven demanded. "I know you may be confused, no uniform and all, but I'm still the sheriff when I'm off-duty."

Elven looked over to Vincent, who still had Donnie in a bear hug. He narrowed his eyes and like a key unlocking a door, Vincent opened his arms, freeing Donnie.

"Now, we've got three choices, all of you," Elven said. "I can take you in for assault, you can go home, or I can buy a round of drinks for everyone if we all just let it go."

Willie was silent, his face still pressed against the table. Finally, Vincent spoke up. "I could go for a drink," he said.

"Smart choice," Elven said, smiling. "How about you?"

"I'll take a scotch on the rocks," Willie said. "Especially if you're buying."

Elven let him stand up and adjust himself. "Glad to hear it. Now, I'll get Martin and Charlene to take the order. I better not have any more of this going on or I will not give you the option next time."

Everyone nodded in agreement and went back to their respective groups. Elven turned to the man at the table who sipped on his whiskey. He seemed unbothered by the excitement. He wore a black jacket and had stubble on his face. He looked to be in his mid to late-fifties, and had a peculiar scar on his face. It stretched from under his chin, cut across his cheek, and ended at his ear.

Elven didn't recognize him at all. But as it was, there were a lot of strangers in town for the competition and Elven hadn't watched all the events to see what he specialized in.

"Apologies for using your table," Elven offered.

The man held his hand up. "No need, Sheriff. I like to see a man take care of business."

"If you want another drink, the next one's on me," Elven said.

"Very generous, but I was just about to leave," he said, drinking the last of his whiskey. He stood and walked by Elven, smelling of cedar chips, whiskey, and a very strong aftershave. He disappeared out the door without another word.

Elven looked over to Hunter, but saw everyone clamoring for his attention again. Elven decided that the party was just about over for him anyway and he needed to get home. Hunter was the excitement for the day, that was for sure. But Elven still had a job to do, and that meant he needed to get some rest to do it.

He left Martin's before the party was too much for him to handle.

CHAPTER FIVE

The show at the bar had been...entertaining. The way a bunch of drunks acted wasn't anything new—in fact, it was a bore—but what excited him was seeing the reaction. First, there was Donnie Price himself at the bar, deciding to break it up when the sheriff was right next to him.

He got the impression it wasn't actually about standing up for anyone, but rather, having the attention drawn to him. To be a hero was something people sought out at times, just for the celebrity of it. And in a small town like Dupray, that could go far with the locals.

But what had impressed him was the sheriff. Off-duty, and able to handle himself well. Some men he'd had interactions with would have gotten into a full-fledged bar fight, but this sheriff had put it to an end immediately. The right amount of force, followed by a choice that he'd creatively come up with. A round of drinks on him.

James smiled, thinking about how costly that bill would be for someone in that town. It might be a full months' wages, if not more. But that didn't stop the sheriff from following through on his word—at least he assumed. The drunk man in the street helped confirm that assumption.

He watched from his truck, keeping his hand in front of the vent that blew hot air, opening and closing his fist as the heat eased his joints. He watched as the man in the road swayed around. His steps were a series of stumbles and fumbles, his legs crossing in front of the other like a moving pretzel. James could see the cloud of fog in front of the target, short exhales that led to small puffs sprinkled in the air.

There were no other vehicles in the parking lot, but there was the one that sat in the alley behind the building. The owner of the bar was still inside, most likely cleaning up and shutting it all down. He had just the right amount of time to finish the job before he was done and would happen upon the man's dead body. None of that mattered to him, but he would like to get the job done so he could get to bed and out of the cold.

He had a long few days ahead of him.

He stepped out of the truck, placing his hand on the butt of the gun. The cold immediately bit into his skin, sinking deep into his muscles and joints. Getting older was a bitch sometimes. But he had work to do.

He knew how it would go down, but he wanted to give the man the benefit of the doubt. He saw the gun underneath the jacket on the man's hip. It bulged to the side, and when he walked, the flap of his jacket swayed loose, revealing the black pistol grip. He'd see if the man had anything on the ball, but of course, he wouldn't. And it wasn't just because he was drunk.

He had no issues killing a drunk man. Honestly, he thought it ridiculous that anyone would intentionally lose control like that. He enjoyed a good whiskey from time to time, but to overdo it was asinine. In his line of work, it could be the last mistake of your life.

Only one streetlight stood in the parking lot, but where the man stood in the road, it was nearly pitch-black. The gravel crunched beneath his boots as if he were crushing potato chips in his hand. His breath was light and his heart steady. James never had any issues confronting a target.

When he got close, he heard the target muttering to himself. It sounded as if he was singing a song. The words were completely lost, but the tune was that of some bluegrass song James thought he had heard before. It was a terrible rendition, of course, and he didn't think the target was even aware that rhythm was a real thing. Because he surely didn't have it.

James stood in the road, facing the back of the target. He took a deep breath and let it out slowly. He was silent, but still, the target stopped singing and turned around. James had seen it before. Maybe it was something to do with the primal nature inside everyone, a return to the lizard-brain days. Or maybe it was something else, something supernatural. But either way, it was as if they could sense that their end was coming. Not everyone had it, but this one did.

"Who are you?" the drunk man asked, his speech surprisingly clear. It was possible that being faced with his upcoming death, even if he didn't yet understand that fully, had sobered him up.

"James," he said, watching the man squint ahead of him, trying to make out any features. But James knew it was too dark to see any detail. He could make out the shape of the man's face across from him, but pressed to give detailed features and he'd have none.

"And what—"

"I don't got a lot of time, so lets skip it," James said.

"I don't know who you think you are mister, but you're messin' with the wrong guy," the man said, opening his coat. James saw the glint of his pistol and smiled.

"Then prove it to me. I think you know why I'm here, even if you are drunk. You can feel it in your bones, can't you?"

James cleared his throat, knowing that he understood. "Should I count it, or—"

The gun went off.

James had pulled, raised, and fired when he saw the target's hand move toward his own pistol. He walked across the street, but he knew the outcome already. He stood over the body, a hole dead center in his head. The drunk had never had a chance to remove the gun from his holster, but his hand wrapped around the grip told James his every intention.

James tucked his gun in his holster and shoved his hand into his pocket, longing to calm the ache he felt at each knuckle of his hand.

"I guess we just pull then," James said, looking at the dead man for a moment more, then headed back to his truck.

CHAPTER SIX

"Thanks for picking me up," Madds said.

Elven glanced over at her in the passenger seat of his Wrangler. She was buttoning her shirt up and he caught a glimpse of the white tank top she wore underneath. A jacket was draped over her legs that she hadn't had a chance to put on yet. Her brown hair was in a bit of disarray and she had a streak of foundation on her jawline.

"Sleep well?" Elven asked.

She pulled the visor down and looked in the mirror. She licked her thumb and rubbed it along the mismatched color, blending the makeup in, then tossed her hair so it draped evenly over her face.

She turned to him, heavy bags underneath her eyes that she'd tried to cover up with concealer, but they were so bad that no amount would help.

"That obvious?" she asked.

"Just seems like you were tossing and turning all night, or just rolled out of bed. Couldn't be sure which," Elven said.

Madds sighed as Elven drove. "My car being in the shop isn't helping. I'm sure that bill isn't going to be cheap."

"Who'd you end up taking it to?" Elven asked, but he knew what the answer would be.

"Took it to Wade," Madds said sheepishly, confirming his suspicion.

Unless someone wanted to make a trip hours away to the edge of the county where David Hershey lived and worked on farm equipment, occasionally supplementing his income with a few cars here and there, the Starchers were the only ones around who could take care of it. Especially since making that deal with Oliver and Jeff on their new dealership.

"At least it was Wade and not Corbin," Elven said, as if it made any real difference. The two brothers worked together most of the time.

Madds nodded. "And I had the worst nightmare. Every time I'd fall asleep, I was shooting out of bed again."

"Hopefully, I wasn't in it," Elven said with a smile.

Madds didn't seem to find it funny. "There's only one way I see you in my dreams, and it's definitely not a nightmare," she said, her mouth forgetting to pass her thoughts through a filter first.

She quickly covered her mouth, her eyes wide.

Elven laughed out loud, caught off-guard by her sudden admission. "I'd say sleep deprivation doesn't suit you. Not unless you want to share all your secrets." He shot her a wink.

"I did not mean it the way it came out," Madds said, trying to backpedal.

"So how did you mean it then?" he asked.

"Just that—oh shit, I don't know. I can barely think straight. Where are we going anyway?" she asked, making an obvious change to the subject.

Elven let it slide, but kept that tidbit of information she'd spilled so he could poke fun at her later. "Got a call from Meredith that a body was found. Figured I wouldn't make you find your way to the station and we could head there together."

"Where?" she asked.

"Downtown, right outside Martin's Bar," Elven said.

"Weren't you just there last night?" Madds asked.

He nodded. There wasn't much else he knew, and as soon as they saw the body and assessed the situation, he could make all the assumptions he wanted. But for now, he had to keep his speculations at bay. He didn't even know who was dead, or if it was related to anything that had happened at the competition or the bar. Either way, he still had a bad feeling about it.

CHAPTER SEVEN

It was still early in the morning, the sun barely peeking out over the horizon. They'd find themselves in the magic hour of the morning in a few minutes, but for now, it was still fairly dark. Elven held a flashlight to aid with the darkness, as there was only a lone streetlight on the corner where Martin's Bar was located.

Elven had parked his Jeep at the back of Martin's Bar where the streetlight stood, but the body was about a hundred feet away, outside of the area that the light was able to reach. The parking lot was completely empty and there wasn't so much as a single chirp from a bird. It was eerily quiet.

Elven scanned the parking lot, then the street. He could see a lump in the road, the dark shape of the body right in the center where lines had once been painted that were now long faded. As he circled around with his flashlight, there was nothing else. Not a single person in sight.

"Who did you say called this in?" Madds asked, rubbing her arms.

"I didn't. Meredith never offered it up, either. Probably should have asked," Elven said.

Madds shivered next to him, the sound of her chattering teeth cutting through the awful silence. "It's b-bizarre," she said.

"Madds, you gonna be alright out here?" Elven asked, concerned about her low tolerance for the cold.

She nodded. Or may have been more shivering. Either way, she seemed to want to stay. "J-just need to get used to it. I might need to shop for a warmer coat."

"I'd say so," he said, looking at her outfit. She wasn't wearing the giant parka that drowned her in the fur lining. Instead, she wore a jacket that looked little better than a windbreaker. Elven didn't even think he would be comfortable wearing something that thin, and he'd grown up in Dupray. "What happened to the jacket you wore at the competition?"

She exhaled, a huge cloud of fog flowing into the air. "For warmth, I wish I'd worn that. But I'd never be able to reach my gun if needed. And as it is, it's creepy out here, so I'd rather have mobility. Besides, I gotta get it cleaned after the hot chocolate debacle."

He nodded in agreement. "True, but I just hope you don't freeze out here. Can't have your fingers lock up from the cold if you plan on pulling the trigger."

The two stood in silence, still unsure of what to do. Nobody was up and out in Dupray yet. In a few hours, there would be a scene for sure, but Elven was still perplexed by the fact that nobody was standing around the body. Surely nobody had called it in and left the scene.

"Hold on a sec," Elven said. "Hold this a minute." He turned to get into his Jeep after handing Madds his flashlight, and grabbed the radio off his dashboard. He clicked it on. "Hey, Meredith, have you called Martin to get him out here?"

The radio crackled and Meredith's voice came on over the radio. She sounded pretty chipper for being in the office so early, but then again, she had always been an early riser for as long as he had known her. "Already did it, Elven."

"And who'd you say called this in anyway? I can't—"

"Elven," Madds said. Her voice sounded stressed with concern.

Elven set the radio down and looked over to where Madds stared. From behind the building of Martin's Bar, a figure stepped out. It was too dark from where they were to make out any features of who it might be, but by the looks of him, he wasn't small.

Elven stepped out of the Jeep and pulled the revolver from his holster on his hip. The shadowy figure approached and Elven lifted his gun, pointing it straight at him. A cold breeze picked up, but Elven was too focused to even feel it.

"Identify yourself!" Elven commanded.

"Sheriff?" a familiar voice called out to him.

"Madds," Elven said, and she finally worked the flashlight Elven had handed her. She truly was off today, and he would need to talk to her about trying to get some sleep. The last thing he needed was her being too sluggish when they needed her fast reflexes.

The beam of light shot across the lot, revealing a bearded face on the other end. Elven let out a sigh of relief and saw that it was just Tony. He seemed off, but Elven couldn't place it. Most of the time, he would think the man was drunk, being that his history in the community was just that. A town drunk.

"Tony, everything alright?" Elven asked.

Tony walked cautiously toward them. His gate was soft and slow, as if he was afraid of the sound of his own footsteps. The light stayed on his face, and Elven noticed his eyes were bloodshot. He shook his head and shivered.

"I called it in," Tony finally said.

"What are you doing out here?" Elven asked, unsure what to think. Tony was usually a gentle man. Often drunk, but never violent.

"I-I was headed into town for Frank. He asked me to pick up some items this morning before I headed in to help on his farm," Tony said. His words were clear, if not a little shaky.

"And you found yourself here at Martin's Bar?" Elven asked.

"I ain't been drinkin', Elven. I swear it. Been sober ever since you found me at ol' Dority's farm. He's got me doing jobs still since fixin' up the chicken coop I messed with."

Elven eyed him, and he had to admit, Tony did not seem drunk at all. While Elven may have always known him to be one, he had seen the change in Tony after the chicken coop incident at Frank Dority's farm. What had seemed a big screw-up on Tony's part had actually had been one of the best things for the man. Elven was happy to see it. Tony was a kind man, just wrestled with his own demons like everyone else.

"Honest to God, Elven, I ain't—"

Elven holstered his revolver and held up his empty hand. "I believe you, Tony. I'm glad to hear you're on the wagon and gettin' work. Better than most people."

"I know it," Tony replied.

"So what can you tell me here?" Elven asked, motioning toward the body in the road.

Tony shook his head. "I don't know. I just was drivin' and saw him in the road. I pulled over to take a look and saw he was dead." Tony shivered, but not from the cold. "I ain't never seen a dead man before."

Elven looked around again, the parking lot empty except for the three of them and Elven's Jeep. "You said you drove? Where's your vehicle?"

Tony pointed to the alley that he walked out of. "Around back."

"Why there? Why not right here in the lot?"

Tony looked around, adding a shrug. "Not sure if you noticed, but it's damn eerie out here. I ain't gonna hang out alone with a dead body. Besides, what if whoever did this is still out here watching?"

"Did this?" Elven asked.

"You ain't seen the body yet?" Tony asked.

Elven shook his head. And with that, he headed for the body. Being in the center of the road, a small part of him had assumed the victim had been hit by a car—maybe had stumbled out drunk and been clipped, but Elven was proven wrong when he, Tony, and Madds all made their way to stand over the body.

The man's legs were twisted backward. It looked as if he'd fallen dead right there in that spot. His coat was open and a gun sat on his hip. It was still holstered, his hand on the grip. The gun wasn't odd, considering half of Dupray carried one, and probably even more after the shooting competition the previous day. But his hand being near it meant he'd probably had the intention to use it. And he wasn't mangled, the way he would have been if a car had run him over. No, there was only a single wound.

A bullet hole, dead center in his forehead. A single line of blood trailed out of it, down the side of his head and around his cheek.

Elven winced, recognizing him. Madds turned to see the look on his face.

"You know him?" Madds asked.

Elven nodded. "He was here last night with Hunter and the rest of the competition celebrating." It was more than that, though. Elven had known him a lot longer than just from the bar the previous night. The victim had worked for his parents at the mines, and before that, he'd been friends with Hunter, going back to his teenage days.

The dead man was Donnie Price.

CHAPTER EIGHT

"Elven, fuck," Martin said, staring at the body of Donnie Price in the middle of the road. Martin had shown up, half-dressed and groggy from being woken up so early in the morning. His long hair had been tucked into a messy waterfall of a knot at the top of his head. In his line of work, he was wired to be a night owl, which meant anything to do with the early hours of the day was foreign to him. He let out a long yawn.

"I'm sorry," Martin offered, looking back at Elven as he realized the yawn may not have been in good taste. "I ain't being callous, I just only got three hours—"

"It's fine," Elven said. "Nobody's judging you."

Martin nodded, his eyes drifting back to the body. "I didn't see anything last night."

"Nothing at all? What time did you leave the bar?" Elven asked.

"I mean, probably three in the morning," Martin said, his face twisting into a sorrowful expression. "Donnie could be an asshole sometimes, but he didn't deserve this. I doubt he even had any cash on him. He ran a tab that he barely kept up with when he was here."

Elven nodded. It was true—Donnie wasn't well-off. But it also wasn't a robbery. The seven dollars in his wallet that was tucked in his back pocket proved that. And they didn't bother to steal his gun. This was just a cold, hard murder for reasons Elven couldn't figure yet.

Elven looked over to his Jeep where Madds sat with Tony. She spoke with him, but he figured there wasn't much he could offer as help. He'd only rolled up on the body, not seen it go down. But Tony was in a bad way, having seen the body. His knee bounced at a rapid rate and he rubbed his hands over his face. Sometimes, people could spook after seeing one, and Madds was great at calming and consoling them. Elven hoped so, because Tony had come so far in his sobriety. The last thing he needed was to find his way to the bottom of another bottle after this.

"I-I gave him rides home sometimes," Martin said. "He was the type to close the place down, but he also didn't have a car. Came here with someone and outstayed them—this time, Hunter and the others. I figured when he wasn't out here, he got a ride with someone else. Maybe hitched."

"Did he ask you for a ride this time?" Elven asked.

Martin nodded. "Stepped outside so I could close up. He was pretty drunk. But when I got out here, I took a quick look and didn't see him in the parking lot. Called out for him, but no answer. It wasn't the first time he found his way home. He didn't always want to wait so long, I guess. I'd been left waitin' around for him, not knowing he'd gotten another ride, so I learned not to stick around if he wasn't out here. I didn't think to look in the street. It's so damn dark out here, I didn't know he'd be, well, right there."

"You didn't hear anything? A gunshot?"

Martin shook his head and pointed to his left ear. "I'm nearly all deaf in this ear, and I can tell the other is givin' up the ghost sooner than later. To offset it, I play the music pretty loud when I'm in the bar by myself. The most I might have heard is what sounded like a muffler backfire. Didn't think it was a gunshot."

Elven watched Martin run through the night's events in his head.

He was fishing around, trying to see if there was anything at all that could help. Elven could tell that he wasn't hiding anything, but he still had to ask.

"You two didn't get into it, did you? Exchange words or anything like that?" Elven asked, watching his eyes.

Martin's pupils stopped moving from his previous mind search, and stared directly at Elven. "Elven, that ain't me, and you know it. If I draw on a man and put him down, it's for a damn good reason. And even so, you'd be the first person I'd call. Besides, I'd never in a million years make that kinda shot." He pointed to Donnie's head, where the single bullet had taken him out.

"Fair enough," Elven said, knowing Martin was telling the truth. He wasn't a murderer, though he did know the man to have had to shoot a man or two in his day. But never dead, and as he said, the first person he called was the sheriff. However, all those times were before he'd gotten the job.

"What about those guys last night?" Elven asked.

"Which ones? It was a bit of a full house after the competition."

"Vincent Page and Willie Hutchins. Vincent's the bigger guy, Willie's the—"

"Yeah, I know 'em," Martin said.

"They come here often?"

Martin nodded. "Oh yeah, they tie one off after work. Every day. Like clockwork really."

"Last night, they were ready to exchange fists over a spilled pitcher. Is that also like clockwork?"

Martin hesitated, then shrugged. But he didn't seem very confident.

"Martin, what is it?" Elven asked.

"Look, they get into it sometimes. They get drunk and rowdy. I mean, really, they're assholes and loudmouths, but that's it."

"Why'd you hesitate?"

Martin sighed, pinching the bridge between his eyes. "Look, there was one time that Vincent got into it with a guy and took it outside. When the guy hit harder than Vincent thought he could, Willie hit him in the back of the head with a crowbar."

Elven narrowed his eyes down. "How long ago was this? I don't remember a call coming to the station about that."

"That's because I didn't call it in. Elven, you know I can't call you down here every time someone has too much to drink and causes problems. Shit, you'd never be able to investigate things like this," Martin said, gesturing to the body. "When I heard what was goin' on outside that day, I took care of it. Grabbed my shotgun and chased them off. Told them if they ever did somethin' like that again, I'd ban 'em for life."

"And that fight they were ready to start? The one that Donnie came in and got involved with? Would that count as a permanent ban?" Elven asked, lifting a brow.

"It stopped before it got bad. Nobody was hit with a crowbar."

Elven looked at the body in the road. "You're right about that. Then again, who needs a crowbar when you've got a three fifty-seven?"

CHAPTER NINE

Madds and Elven had loaded up Donnie's body in the back of Elven's Wrangler. Luckily for them, he kept a tarp back there for that very purpose. It wasn't the ideal situation, but the road where Donnie lay was heavily used when driving in and out of the downtown area. If they left Donnie out there, roping it off as a crime scene and waiting for Phil to show, it would cause a huge stir in the town.

If Elven thought it necessary to rope off the scene, he would have. But he and Madds had walked the area with their flashlights before moving Donnie, and they'd come up empty-handed. Nothing of use was there. The only thing they had was Martin telling them that he may have heard a gunshot...or a muffler backfire.

The single piece of evidence they'd found was a lone shell casing in the road. Elven picked it up with a pen and slid it into a small bag to hand to Phil, along with Donnie. But he wasn't confident that there would be much of anything on it. Pulling a print off a casing was one thing, but matching it to any sort of database was another. In Dupray, that database was a book with inkblots on squares. The preferred search tool of choice? A magnifying glass.

And since Elven didn't have the patience to do it, and didn't want to waste valuable manpower on something that was such a shot in the dark. Johnny usually was the one to scour the books. His track record was zero for a thousand, or something like it anyway.

No, Elven still dealt with a crime scene as delicate as possible, but in Dupray, if he wanted to get to the bottom of things, it was pure detective work.

Madds kept glancing to the back of the Jeep from her seat. The backseat, where he usually held the drunks and anyone else being arrested, was empty. The body of Donnie Price was in the cargo space in the back.

"You alright?" Elven asked.

"Just seems a little, I don't know, insulting? At least a bit odd, don't you think?" Madds asked.

Elven shrugged. "If it was me, I'd rather take a ride in the trunk than be out in the open for everyone to gawk at. Wouldn't you? If you'd rather, we could have asked to use Tony's pickup and put Donnie in the bed of the truck."

He looked at Madds who shivered. She didn't seem alright. Another additive to his unfounded suspicions. But maybe it was nothing. It was obvious she wasn't sleeping well, which she'd confirmed to him. He didn't know if he should be worried yet, or if it was going to truly cause problems in her work.

"Those nightmares really took their toll, didn't they?" Elven asked. "You gonna be alright?"

She blinked a few times. "Yeah, I'll be fine. Just thinking about how I want my dead body transported around town gives me the shivers. I don't like to think about that."

"Ain't nobody owed anything but one thing in life. We all have to face it one day or another," Elven said.

"I'm hoping for later. But more than anything, I hope I deserve better than the back of a Jeep when it comes," Madds added, looking around. "Where are we?"

Elven had pulled his Jeep into a large construction zone. The zone wasn't so much as anything being built, but more dug up. A huge space of land that sat next to a neighborhood of rundown homes had piles of dirt in various places, located right next to ditches and troughs dug into the land.

He parked his Jeep next to a beat-up Nissan truck. The half they could see was caked in dirt. The only clean spot on the vehicle was the door handle. The other trucks in the makeshift lot looked similar.

"Gonna interview a couple of guys who were at the bar last night," Elven said, but before he could step out of his Jeep, the radio crackled on. It was Meredith.

"Hey, Elven, you anywhere you can get to Blythe Lane over in Jolo?" she asked.

Elven considered for a moment, scrunching his brow. He grabbed the receiver and held it to his mouth. "A bit far away now, then I got to swing by Phil's to drop, uh, something off. After that maybe, but I figured I'd be on the other side of the county for a bit. Can it wait?"

"I don't know. This girl on the phone sounds real shook-up. Think she might be havin' a panic attack or somethin'. Can barely get much information from her 'bout what even's goin' on."

Elven held the radio for a moment, thinking. Even if he dropped everything and headed that way, he'd be at least an hour until he reached Jolo. And he'd be toting Donnie around for longer than he intended. "I think Tank and Johnny might have to handle this one."

"Will do, Elven."

"Just keep me posted if I need to head that way later," he said before finally stepping out of the Jeep.

Madds followed him in a hurry. She ran around the side of the vehicle, stopping Elven. "We aren't taking Donnie's body to Phil first? Christ, Elven, I really don't want to ride around with him all day. It's morbid."

Elven smiled. "Madds, we don't have all day to spend driving back and forth places. Phil's is all the way across town, but Vincent and Willie are right here. We'll stop at Phil's after here. If they had anything to do with it, I don't want them gettin' wise and running off."

Madds didn't look happy, but Elven knew he was right. The more time they spent driving was time to let the case go cold. And they'd keep the questioning short.

"But he's gonna start stinking your Jeep up. He'll bake in there," Madds protested.

"If you feel any heat in the air, I'm sure you'll be the first to let me know it. Not sure if you were aware, but when it ain't running, that Jeep's practically an icebox," Elven said, still taking note of her sour face. He grabbed her shoulder and looked in her eyes. "If Donnie starts complaining, we'll head out immediately. You got my word on that." He smiled before making his way to the piles of dirt.

A breeze kicked up some dirt from the loose piles that had been dug, flinging it against his mirrored sunglasses. In the distance, he could hear the chatter from people in the ditches behind the small mountains of dirt they had created. Before he made it the full way, a man came jogging his way.

"Excuse me, can I help you?" he asked, clipboard tucked underneath his arm.

Elven turned, laying eyes on the small, but round man. He wore a light jacket, possibly thinner than Madds's. But he didn't seem to mind, likely used to the winter conditions.

"Oh," the man said, slowing when he neared Elven. "Didn't know it was you, sheriff. What can I do for you?"

"I'm here to speak with Vincent Page and Willie Hutchins. It's my understanding that they work out here," Elven said, having gathered the information from Meredith when he'd been at the crime scene.

The man looked at the clipboard, muttering to himself as he did. "Vincent Page, Vincent Page...oh, right here," he said, his finger hitting the clipboard. "C'mon, I'll take you to him. Just watch your step."

Elven stole a glance at Madds, who was close by, then followed the man with the clipboard. There were various holes and ditches dug into the ground. Far more than he would have expected from the makeshift parking lot with so few vehicles. They navigated through the labyrinth of dirt piles until they settled next to one, no different than the others.

Except this one held both the men that Elven was looking for. Vincent was down in the ditch, his feet resting on a pipe as he leaned against the dirt wall, smoking a cigarette. Willie drank from a water bottle, wiping sweat from his forehead. Even in this cold weather, the work they did was hard enough to make them perspire.

"I'll see if I can find that, uh, Willie, you said?" the man with a clipboard asked.

"Already have," Elven said, motioning to Willie.

"Oh, right. We get so many people show up for a day or two, never to come back. I can't keep track of everyone. Digging ditches ain't glamorous and it don't pay well. But if the guys that can fix the water lines had to dig 'em up, it would cost at least three times as much. At least this way, there's work for those less skilled," the man said, unapologetically.

"Aw, shit," Willie said, noticing Elven. "I thought you was gonna leave us alone. We didn't even hit anyone last night."

The man with a clipboard lifted an eyebrow, curious about the situation. Vincent smacked Willie on the shoulder. "Shut up, you idiot," he grunted.

"I need to talk to you both about last night," Elven said.

Vincent looked at their supervisor, then back at Elven. "Can we do it somewhere else?"

Elven nodded, leading both of the men away from the work area and back to his Jeep. On the way, Madds's foot slid near the side of a ditch and she nearly tumbled into it, but Vincent grabbed her arm, preventing her from doing so.

"Thanks," she said, her cheeks growing red from embarrassment.

"Don't mention it," Vincent said.

When they reached the back of the Jeep, Elven stopped. The supervisor holding his clipboard was out of earshot, but that didn't prevent him from staring at the four of them. Some people just couldn't mind their own business. All the other men in the ditches didn't seem to have that problem as they had given them less than even a handful of glances as they'd passed by.

"Alright, tell me what happened last night," Elven said.

Vincent and Willie exchanged glances, as if they were confused, then turned to Elven again. "What do you mean?" Vincent asked. "We drank the round you bought for everyone. Had another pitcher. Then went home."

"Yeah, and we left a nice tip for that Charlene, too, when she gave us those drinks. Two dollars," Willie added. "That's like..." he held up a few fingers trying to count. "Shit, like twenty percent or somethin'."

Vincent nodded to confirm.

"Glad we got to the bottom of that," Elven said sarcastically. "I mean, what happened with Donnie Price?"

"Who?" Vincent asked.

"The guy you bear-hugged last night when he stopped Willie here from throwing a punch at that other one," Elven said.

"Shit, that was Donnie Price?" Vincent asked. "Didn't catch his face since I was behind him, or I was too drunk." He shrugged. "Typical, though."

"Why do you say that?" Madds asked.

Vincent shrugged. This time, it was Willie's turn to talk. "He likes to think of himself as this white knight or some shit. Coming in, saving the day. Bunch of horse shit, if you ask me. I've known that guy for a long time, on and off anyway. He likes to think of himself as some savior, stepping into fights when he got nothing to do with it."

"Sounds like that might not be a bad thing if he was breaking them up," Madds remarked.

Vincent shook his head. "But he wasn't. It was just an excuse to fight. Never was friends with the guy, but we had mutuals. From what I hear, he was an angry cunt."

"This angry cunt," Madds repeated. "You get into other fights with him? Or just this one?"

Both of the men shrugged, but didn't offer an answer.

"The deputy asked you a question," Elven said, backing her up. "It should be easy to know who you get into a fight with."

"Look, I don't know. Yeah, maybe. But we get into fights with a lot of people, alright? Nothin' serious or nothin'. Just blowin' off some steam with other assholes," Vincent said.

"Just blowing off steam? Like the guy you cracked over the head with a crowbar, which made Martin chase you off with a shotgun?" Elven asked.

"Sounds to me like Donnie isn't the only angry cunt around here," Madds chimed in.

Vincent shrugged his large shoulders again. "We ain't done nothin' like that again. Martin said we couldn't drink there anymore if we did. Fuck, I ain't drivin' all the way out to Wolf Tavern. Bunch of asshole bikers drink there."

Elven couldn't help but smile. A bunch of bikers did drink there, and Elven knew if Vincent and Willie ever threw down with them, they would be getting a dose of their own medicine. Men in those clubs had each other's back.

"What's this about anyway?" Willie asked, stepping in. "Is Donnie talkin' shit about us? Cause I tell ya, if he is, I'll let him have it. He wants to fight me one on one, I'll do it. I don't need Vincent there to give a beat down."

"No, he ain't talkin' about anyone anymore," Elven said.

"Good," Willie said. "I outta find him anyway and give him that fer just for you comin' down here and hasslin' us."

"No need," Elven said, growing irritated with each word Willie uttered. He opened the back of the Jeep, revealing Donnie's body on the tarp. "You got beef with him, you let him have it."

Willie and Vincent stared in disbelief. Willie, the big talker he was, backed up a few steps with a horrified look on his face.

"Not much for words now, are you, Willie?" Madds added to Elven's delight.

"Shit," Vincent said. "What the hell happened to him?"

"Well, I'd say he took one too many bullets to the head," Elven said.

"Willie, want to count how many bullets that is? We can wait," Madds dug in.

"We-we ain't had nothin' to do with that," Willie said, finding his voice again.

"I don't know," Elven said. "You seem to have a big problem with the guy. Talking a big game and all. Maybe you already went and sought him out after the bar scuffle last night. Donnie was bigger than you, and he stopped you once. But he was a lot drunker at the end of the night, and it's one thing to catch a fist. Another to catch a bullet. What do you think, Madds?"

"Sounds like Willie here had motive. Maybe even more than Vincent," she replied.

"Me?" Vincent asked. "I didn't have anything to do with it. I went home right after leaving. Ask anyone. M-my old lady, she'll tell ya. I slept on the couch cause I was so drunk she didn't want me in bed. Besides, I can't even own a gun after my felony charge eight years ago."

Elven nodded, then turned to Willie. "Sounds like Vincent has an alibi, which we will check. Including what that felony was for," he said, lifting his eyes toward Vincent to drive the point home before bringing them back to Willie. "What about you? Anyone to corroborate that you didn't double back your way to Martin's?"

Willie went searching in his head, his eyes running back and forth over the ground. He was panicking inside, and Elven knew it. At this point, by the way the men were acting, he didn't believe they did have anything to do with Donnie's murder. But he had to make sure. And he liked to see them panic after the amount of trash-talked they'd just done.

"My landlady," Willie said, lifting his hand like a kid in school with the correct answer. "Had to piss so bad, I couldn't make it inside and watered the bushes outside her window. Didn't know she'd still be up and see me, though." Willie twisted his face into a frown. "Old

Lady McCarthy really laid into me about it. But she'll tell ya, I got there well before Martin's even closed."

"Some big man you are. Getting into fights at the bar, cracking them over the head with a crowbar," Madds said. "I bet that old lady is vicious."

Elven chuckled. He knew Linda McCarthy, and to be fair, she wasn't someone whose bad side he'd want to be on. In a way, he felt a little bad for Willie after hearing his story.

"But she'll tell ya, I was home. I ain't killed nobody," Willie said, sounding defeated.

Elven closed up the Jeep, putting Donnie out of view. "Any ideas who might have then?"

Neither of them offered a person up. "The guy was an asshole," Vincent said. "But we didn't want him dead. If you knew him at all, you'd know he probably made a lot of enemies, being the way he was. Hell, even his friends didn't like him. Just about anyone could be on that list."

CHAPTER TEN

Johnny felt his heart race as they pulled up to the address Meredith had given them. He wasn't usually first to a scene, though he still wasn't sure what the scene was. Meredith hadn't given Tank or him a lot of information, saying something about a woman being too hysterical. So to him, it sounded pretty urgent.

And usually, that was something Elven handled.

But Elven had his plate full at the moment, dealing with a dead body over by Martin's Bar. Johnny had been to scenes before, ones with plenty of dead bodies, and even sometimes where a gunshot might happen, though never directed at him. But as always, someone had been there first.

His mind ran through all the what ifs. He immediately went to thinking he'd have to draw his gun, maybe shoot someone. He'd never had to use his gun in the field before and hoped he could handle it if it came to it. If the woman was hysterical, was someone breaking into her home? Was she currently in danger? If so, was she already dead? Had they been too late?

He tried to shove the thoughts from his mind, his hand shaking as he reached for his seatbelt. He'd never been great with nerves, and that's all this job was. Sometimes, he wondered how the hell he ever got into the position to begin with. But he knew that answer.

He'd cleaned the station so many times—vacuuming the carpets, mopping the floors, and attending to any other messes that had needed his attention. After all, he was hired as the janitor when he'd first set foot in that building. But along the way, he'd found himself admiring the work the police did. Looking at the men in the uniforms with respect and awe when they were able to solve crimes and take care of the community that he loved so much.

Of course, it had all been a dream then, but when the position had opened up, he'd considered telling Lester, the sheriff at the time. But of course, how ridiculous would that be? The janitor becoming a deputy? He'd seen the work they did there, and there was no way he would ever fit in.

But it was Lester, the kind-hearted, old fatherly figure type who had approached Johnny with the idea. Johnny had laughed as if it were some crazy joke. But Lester didn't laugh. In fact, Johnny still clearly remembered what he'd told him.

Laughing at yourself is a good thing, but don't let it get in the way of what you're actually capable of. If you keep telling yourself you ain't cut out for the job, then you never will be. Instead, ask yourself why you think you ain't cut out for the job. And then force yourself to answer.

Johnny wasn't sure exactly what it had all meant at the time, but when he did ask himself, there were some answers. But none of them that were good enough to not try. And then Lester had hired him. The old man had seen something in him that he wasn't sure he ever did himself.

Maybe Johnny wasn't great with nerves, but the rest of the department was. Johnny was better at other things, like heart, as Lester told him. Sometimes, he really missed the old guy, but he saw bits of him in Elven and, at times, was reminded just why he looked up to someone much younger than himself.

"You alright?" Tank asked from the driver's seat. His eyes were on Johnny's hands, which were still quivering.

Johnny cleared his throat, steadying himself. "Yeah, you know me. Not always cut out for the unknown."

Tank nodded, pity in his eyes. Tank was a good friend to Johnny. He was another man Johnny looked up to, always able to stand his ground in some very troubling situations. He was the exact opposite of himself, hardly ever talking about his feelings, whereas Johnny didn't have to talk about them—he just showed them. But even though they were at opposite ends, they still had each other's back.

"Just breathe easy. We don't even know what we're looking for yet. But from out here, it seems fairly safe," Tank said, trying to help Johnny.

Johnny looked out the window at the row of houses. The houses were all small, of course, no smaller than his own home that he shared with his mother. Two bedroom structures with a living room and kitchen, from what he could tell. Each home had a small porch made from wood. They weren't expensive homes, but they weren't trailers either. To have one meant that whoever lived in them most likely had a job. Probably one that didn't pay much, of course, but enough to make some ends meet.

The two deputies stepped out of the heat of the truck into the crisp cold air outside. Johnny scanned the area, seeing a few icy patches in the road. It was already dropping below freezing, and it would be any day now that they started to receive the calls of vehicles skidding into the frozen, muddy sections of the roads. The deputies weren't exactly roadside assistance, but it was also one of the things Johnny usually took care of when the station was called during the winter, letting Elven and Tank take care of the more urgent issues.

He turned to ask Tank the address they were supposed to be, but just as he did, he saw a figure running up to them on the driver's side of the truck.

"T-Tank," Johnny said, scrambling to pull his gun from its

holster. Of course, he had the leather strap snapped around the gun and was unable to pull it out in time.

Tank hadn't been facing the right direction and was surprised when he turned around. But instead of being attacked, the figure wrapped their arms around Tank.

"Oh my God, thank you, thank you, thank you," the woman said.

Johnny was able to see that the figure was a small woman. Her face was buried into Tank's midsection so he couldn't make out her face. She had curly blonde hair and was very short—at least compared to Tank. Compared to anyone else, she might just be called short.

Tank held his hands up, not knowing what to do. "Uh, yeah," Tank said. "Hey, uh, Johnny, can you?"

Johnny smiled and headed around the side of the truck, feeling calm again now that the woman was alright. Tank was a good man, a good husband, a good father. He was well-equipped to handle himself in a fight, and never really complained about much. Johnny also knew him to be an ex-marine, though Tank rarely talked about his military history. But just as Tank wasn't great with his feelings, he was also not great with relating to people.

The woman squeezed tighter, and Johnny could see the panic set in on Tank's face. He couldn't help but chuckle even more. He knew Tank would much rather be in a standoff, guns drawn, than have to deal with a stranger hugging him.

"I was really scared," the woman said in a muffled voice, her face still buried in Tank's shirt.

"Uh, miss? Can you please, um, we're here and ready to help, but you need to let go," Tank said, unsure of what to say.

She pulled away and looked up at the large, muscular man she was practically groping. Johnny could finally see her face and stopped in his tracks. She was beautiful. She had rosy cheeks, which made those blonde curls stand out even more. A few freckles dotted the skin under her blue eyes. She even had one single freckle at the tip of her nose that looked as if she had accidentally poked herself with an uncapped pen.

"Okay. Now what seems to be the problem?" Tank asked, still holding his hands above her, desperately wanting for her to let go of her own volition.

"It's my neighbor," she said. "I hadn't heard from her, and it's Tuesday. We always check in on Tuesday with each other. She likes to…"

"Yeah?" Tank asked.

"Hello," she said, this time directly to Johnny.

"Miss," Johnny said, holding a hand up to tip his imaginary hat. He realized how stupid he looked just then and felt his cheeks heat up with embarrassment.

But instead of rolling her eyes or completely ignoring him, she giggled. To Johnny, it sounded the way butterflies made him feel when he saw them. It was almost magical. Johnny found himself smiling wider than he thought his cheeks could even stretch.

Tank cleared his throat. "So this neighbor, what happened?"

The woman, who looked to be closer to Elven's age than Johnny's, glanced up at Tank, letting her arms finally fall from Tank's waist. He exhaled in relief and stepped two paces backward as if to keep it from happening again. But Johnny only moved closer to her.

"Right. Katherine, my neighbor, she didn't come over. Now, I know she's older and might not be up for visits all the time, but I felt the need to check in on her, you know? It ain't breaking the law if I walk into her house uninvited is it? I just wanted to make sure she's alright," the woman said, her tone pleading as if she was going to be in trouble.

Johnny stepped even closer and grabbed her hand. Her skin was soft and warm, cutting through the harshest of cold. "It's alright, we ain't gonna arrest you. Sounds like you were just bein' a good neighbor," Johnny said, his tone calm and steady. He even surprised himself that there wasn't even a stutter or crack in his voice. "I'm Johnny."

She smiled, shying away slightly, but never letting go of his hand. "That's a nice name. Makes mine sound like I came out of the fifteen hundreds or somethin'."

"Oh, Johnny's about as simple as it comes," Johnny found himself saying. "C'mon, yours can't be that bad."

She kept her mouth shut, but in a cute way. Her eyes betrayed her and they told Johnny that she wanted to tell him her name, and so much more.

"Miss," Tank said, cutting in with his no-nonsense tone. "I'm gonna need your name since you called us out here."

Her face soured at Tank. "Bernadette."

"Last name?" Tank asked, writing it down on a small pad he'd pulled from his back pocket.

"Hensley. Bernadette Hensley," she said, obviously unhappy. Johnny wasn't sure if it was because of her name or because she didn't like the way Tank's bedside manner was more than lacking.

"I think that's a great name. Matches you swimmingly. In fact, I'd go so far as to say you're just as cute as a button," Johnny said, finding a newfound confidence in his words. His heart was beating fast and he couldn't seem to stop talking. He questioned if he was making a fool of himself.

She giggled again. "Well, Johnny. You can call me whatever you like as long as you call me."

Johnny matched her giggle, creating a pair of giggles between the two of them.

"What the hell is going on here?" Tank asked impatiently, but nobody paid him any attention. "Alright, look, you called us out for something and I'd like to know what it is."

Johnny glanced at his partner and saw the irritation on his face. Most people had that look on their face when dealing with Johnny, but this seemed at another level. Johnny pulled himself away for a moment and stood tall.

"Right, Button—er, I mean, Bernadette. You said you went into your neighbors house?" Johnny asked, trying to keep his tone professional.

She nodded. "But she wasn't in there. Her door was unlocked, though. I checked every room. Her car's there, but I ain't seen her leave." She pointed to the green Oldsmobile on the side of the road. It was surprisingly clean, and the paint on it had hardly any issues for a car that was twenty years old.

"So then you called us?" Johnny asked.

Johnny watched her shake her head, her blond curls catching the sunlight, making her look like an angel. "No, I figured she went over to Todd's house. She sometimes makes him a lasagna. He's a single guy who doesn't eat too well, considering. I used to think something was going on between those two, but I think she just wanted the company, like she did with me on Tuesdays."

"Sure," Johnny offered.

"And that's when I saw it," she said.

"Saw what?" Johnny asked. But Bernadette started to cry again, tears rolling down her cheeks. She shook her head, trying to talk, but the words just wouldn't come. "It's okay, it's gonna be okay, alright? Here, come with me and sit down here."

He wrapped his arms around her back, leading her to his side of the truck. She smelled like freshly baked apple pie and that moment when the leaves start to fall at the beginning of autumn. He opened the truck door and sat her down, facing him.

"You sit here and take a moment, alright?" Johnny said. "Tank and I will go check out the house, can you point me to Todd's?"

She pointed to the white house with an screen door that had been left ajar. "Good, that's good. If you hear anything, you get on that radio, alright? Meredith is on the other end and she'll get you all sorted."

"You make sure and be careful, alright?" she asked.

"Always," Johnny said, sending her a wink, then stood up. He turned to Tank, then something caught his foot and made him stumble forward. His cheeks flushed red with embarrassment, and thankfully, Tank grabbed his shoulder before he fell on his face. Johnny stole a glance behind him toward Bernadette, who held a look of concern on her face, but didn't laugh. He smiled nervously.

Tank and Johnny made their way across the road toward Todd's house. As soon as Johnny had pulled away from Bernadette, he felt the dread settle in again. The fear of the unknown. What she'd seen in that house must have been pretty bad to shake her up, but he also thought since she was alright, nothing still posed a threat there.

But they couldn't be sure.

They climbed the steps up the porch and walked the small wooden platform, checking the few corners they could. They didn't see anything out of the ordinary.

"Should we go around back?" Johnny asked.

Tank shook his head, pulling his gun. "I'm gonna need you covering me here if anything happens, but don't worry. I don't think it will."

Johnny nodded, pulling his own gun, this time, no issues getting the snap undone on the leather strap. Tank pulled the screen door open with his free hand. Johnny grabbed it from him and saw the wooden door underneath was also open ajar.

Tank pushed it with his foot, easing it open. The hinge creaked as it slowly drifted inward. Tank stepped inside, and Johnny stepped behind him. Tank made it about five steps inside, then grabbed his nose. Johnny followed shortly after.

The smell was horrible. It was worse than the time he'd left four pounds of ground beef out on the counter. He'd forgotten to load it in the cooler after grocery shopping when he'd taken his mother up to the lake for the weekend. It had been a hot summer, and the two days in the warm house had amped up the decay. It had taken a whole month until he could no longer smell it in the house.

But this was different. It wasn't a hot summer. And it wasn't just four pounds of ground beef on the counter. He turned to his right, and nearly emptied his stomach right then and there.

"Oh, God," Johnny said, seeing what lay before him.

CHAPTER ELEVEN

Elven had taken Donnie's body to Phil Driscoll's funeral home after speaking with Vincent and Willie, much to Madds's relief. He noticed that she no longer fidgeted in her seat as much since stopping at Phil's, but she still wasn't the same as her usual perky self.

There was no use for an autopsy, though Elven figured Phil might do one anyway. Maybe it had been a slow week for the old guy, but he'd made the excuse about making sure there was nothing else hidden that Elven hadn't seen. Elven had let the old guy have his way, though he'd considered telling him that a bullet to the head didn't need much else to assist with a murder.

He'd kept his comments to himself, however.

Next on the list of things to do was go see Hunter. He was one of the last people to see Donnie, plus, being his friend and all, Elven felt he should break the news himself. Donnie didn't have any next of kin. He didn't have a big family to begin with, but Elven was aware of an uncle who had succumbed to stubbornness and a leg infection. And he had a brother who had swallowed the wrong end of a shotgun two years back.

Elven reflected that Hunter's coming back was probably the happiest Donnie had been, considering how close he and Hunter had been back in the day.

The old house that Hunter had grown up in was just as Elven had always known it. Glenna Wallace was a woman who took pride in everything she did. She was always active in the community for as far back as Elven could remember. She spent a lot of time in her garden behind her home that bordered the forest, always making sure that whatever she didn't sell at the farmer's market, she donated to those in need. Even though he knew the Wallaces to not have a lot of money, like most in Dupray, Glenna never would have let it stand to have her house presented as less than it was.

A home that was cherished and appreciated by its owner.

But he also knew that in the later years of her life, things hadn't gone so well for her. He'd heard she had cancer, but she still powered on, not letting it stop her. Her son Noah had helped her, picking up as much slack as she would allow. But in the end, well, it was as he'd told Madds earlier. Nobody was owed anything but one thing in life, and sooner or later, it would come for them all. In Glenna's case, it was the former.

It always was when it came to good people.

"So you knew them well?" Madds asked as they made their way out of the Jeep.

"The Wallaces?" Elven asked.

"Yeah. Hunter and his mom?" Madds asked.

"I guess you could say that. When Hunter left, his brother Noah had a lot put on him because of it, but he took it in stride. I'm not sure Glenna ever really got over Hunter leaving. We chatted here and there over the years, but never about Hunter. Once he was gone, it was like he'd never been here in the first place."

When Elven set foot on the wooden porch, not a single creak came from the old boards. He smiled, thinking about how he'd remembered seeing the old woman down on her knees, replacing planks, repainting them white, and scrubbing them down if they ever were dirty. The house had to be three times as old as he was, and yet, it felt newer than just about everything else in the community.

"That's gotta be hard," Madds said. "Nobody knows why he left?"

Elven shrugged. "If they did, nobody was talking about it. I suspect Glenna knew. Maybe Noah, but maybe not. Sometimes parents hide things from their children when they think they're doing the right thing."

"Didn't you ask him when you were at the bar last night?" Madds asked. "Seems like it should have been the first thing that came up, right?"

"Madds, you ever spend any time with a group of guys? You think we're sipping on mimosas, having a deep, yet delightful, conversation about our feelings on our past decisions? On what made us leave town and not tell anyone about it, when most likely, that answer has something to do with something extremely personal?"

Madds sighed. "You're right. It's the three *B's*—beers, boobs, and belching."

Elven smiled, giving her a curious look.

She shrugged. "I had a brother. Oh, and don't forget seeing who can tap the other's nut sack without flinching first."

Elven couldn't help but laugh that time. "I guess you've found out the secret of men. But you make that nut to a ball and it's the four *B's*. Just a little insider tip for you." He shot her a wink.

"I am taking notes," Madds said with a wry smile.

Elven knocked on the door, noticing again that not a single hinge rattled or shook against the frame. Another cold breeze blew past them and he could feel Madds shiver right next to him. But she was putting up with the cold a lot better than when they'd first started the day.

The door opened, and Hunter stood with a smile. He wore jeans, but no shirt, and Elven noticed just how fit he looked. He remembered Hunter had been an athlete in high school, just like Elven, but he looked to be all muscle now. He wasn't big like Tank, but he was cut. Like he'd spent a lot of time in the gym, trying to look that way.

"Oh, wow," Madds said audibly.

Elven turned to her, grimacing. Her cheeks grew red with embarrassment, but Hunter didn't seem to mind. He laughed at the two.

"Elven Hallie—I mean, Sheriff Elven Hallie, I thought that was you," Hunter said excitedly, like a neighbor welcoming his best friend.

"The emblem a big giveaway?" Madds asked, referring to the sheriff's label on the side of the Wrangler.

Hunter shook his head. "Nah, ain't nobody else in Dupray confident enough to drive a Jeep. It's all pick-up trucks and whatever else that don't cost more than five thousand dollars."

"The Jeep is practical for where we live," Elven defended. "Know anything else that's gonna get up in those hills?"

"Yeah, an ATV," Hunter replied dryly. "Come on in, don't be standing out in the cold. This little lady looks like she's about to freeze her nipples right off." Hunter stopped talking, mouth wide open as if he'd just stepped on her toe. "I'm sorry, miss. I just get a little excited around this guy that I forget my manners."

Madds shook her head. "It's not rude if it's the truth," she said, pushing past him before she had to wait any longer.

Hunter laughed. "I like her."

"She's got a way with people," Elven said.

Hunter turned around, leading Elven into the house. Elven noticed immediately the scars on Hunter's back. There were two jagged marks down his left side and one on his right that was the size of a half-dollar, its color red and white. It reminded him of a bullet hole, but there wasn't a spot on Hunter's chest to match that would have been the exit wound.

Hunter's living room was almost as he'd remembered it. A couch sat close to the door, and if it moved one inch closer, the door would slam into the armrest. The television was across from it, and a coffee table the TV and the couch. On the far wall, he remembered a set of two armchairs, but they were gone. In their place was a hospital bed with a stripped mattress. An empty IV stand sat next to it.

"Somebody sick?" Madds asked.

Elven cleared his throat, realizing he'd forgotten to tell her about Glenna's passing. "Uh, Madds, Hunter's mother, Glenna, passed recently."

Madds eyes went wide, and again, her cheeks flushed from embarrassment. Elven frowned. He knew he'd be hearing about that one in the car.

"I am so sorry. My condolences," Madds offered.

Hunter laughed. "Nah, don't sweat it. You didn't know. Ol' Elven here obviously forgot to let you in on that bit of info, didn't he?"

Hunter had a way of letting someone off the hook easily. He might have been putting it on Elven, but Madds looked a little less panicked. "Sorry," Elven said to them both.

"Guess momma was too stubborn to stay in a hospital," Hunter said, his eyes lingering on the bed for a second or two. He grabbed a black shirt off the couch and pulled it over his head. "But that was just like her."

Elven nodded. He knew it would have taken a disaster to get Glenna to leave her home. Not even a little thing like cancer would have done it. She was a strong, stubborn woman, even in the end.

"Like I told Elven the other day, though, I ain't seen her in years. And I ain't talked to her either in the same time. Hate to be cold about it, but neither one of us knew who we were in the end," Hunter said.

Elven did think Hunter was being cold about it. They may not have known each other for the last twenty years, but the first half of life was one of life's most important parts. There had to be some part of him that missed the woman who had raised him.

"That ain't all you came for is it?" Hunter asked. He watched their faces and cocked his head in curiosity. "What's up?"

"Well, I hate to say it," Elven said. "But Donnie Price was found dead this morning."

Hunter didn't flinch. He seemed to consider Elven's words for a moment, scrunching his brow in thought, then released the tension and shook his head. "Damn, that's a shame."

Now it was Elven's turn to cock his head in curiosity. Hunter didn't seem fazed at all by the news. Of course, other than last night, he knew that Hunter hadn't seen Donnie for about as long as he'd seen his own mother, and her death didn't seem to bother him much, either.

Something was different about Hunter. He just seemed...off.

"That's it?" Madds asked, breaking the silence. "Elven told me you two were pretty good buddies back in the day."

Hunter nodded. "The key part of that being *back in the day*."

"You two seemed pretty chummy last night," Elven said.

Hunter shrugged. "Look, we were friends way back twenty years ago. Kinda like you and me, Elven. But tell me, if you found out I'd died, how broken up would you be? I mean, don't get me wrong, I don't wish the man dead or nothin', but it's just one of those things where you think on it a moment, shake your head, say that's a shame, and move on. Ain't it?"

Elven supposed he was right, but nobody really talked that way. Where was the compassion, the empathy, or at the very least, feigning sorrow? Then again, maybe he didn't know Hunter all that well anymore.

Hunter sighed. "Between you and me, Donnie was always kind of a jerk. Back then, we were friends, but he was the type to do something annoying as hell, then laugh as if it was a joke that everyone was supposed to think was funny. But it wasn't. He liked the attention."

"That's an understatement," a voice said from around the corner. The three of them turned to the direction of the hallway and saw a man enter. It was Noah, Hunter's younger brother.

Noah had similar features to Hunter. His nose was sloped in the same way, his eyes were the same color, and his lips had the same dimples at the corners when he smiled. But he was also different in many ways. He was at least eight inches shorter than his brother, his physique was hardly there at all—his shirt loose where Hunter's would hug at his muscles—and he was much paler than him.

"Noah," Elven said with a nod.

Noah reached a hand out to Elven and shook with him. "It's good to see you, Elven."

"I'm sorry to hear about Glenna. She was a good woman," Elven offered.

Noah smiled, almost to the point he was doing it to swallow down the emotions that were wanting to bubble up from deep inside him. "Yes, she was. She always held you in high regard, too. You were one of the few people Hunter knew that she liked. Believe me, that's sayin' a lot."

"I don't doubt it."

"You gonna be at the funeral?" Noah asked. "It's on Thursday, down at Phil Driscoll's. Pastor Magner is gonna speak."

"I wouldn't miss it," Elven said. He turned to Madds, ready to introduce her, but she beat him to the punch.

"Madds," she said, grabbing Noah's hand. "I'm—"

"Elven's new deputy," Noah said. "I've heard some things about you already."

"Hopefully nothing too bad."

"Just that you took out a handful of burglars over at Driscoll's funeral home by yourself. Never would have thought you'd look, well, like you do."

Madds smiled, but didn't seem to like the attention by the way she seemed to shy away.

"And then there was Cathy, too," Noah added.

"Convenience Cathy?" Hunter asked. "Shit, I used to steal forties from her back in high school." He turned to Elven. "Oh, that ain't gonna get me arrested now, is it?"

"I think the statute of limitations is over for that one," Elven said, then turned to Noah. "You said something about Donnie?"

Noah shrugged. "Yeah, that him being described as a jerk was an understatement. The man was a straight-up asshole, then and now."

"Have you seen him lately?" Elven asked.

"Here and there. I tend not to hang out with dickheads like that. I always hope that men like that start to calm down, that getting older makes them realize that just pissing people off while laughing isn't really the attention you want. Nobody thinks it's funny. But some just never do."

"I remember the way he treated you back then," Elven said. And it was true. Donnie had picked on those who hadn't been as popular as he was. Even Hunter's own brother hadn't been off-limits to him.

Noah nodded. "Like I said, the guy never changed."

"Last night, when you left the bar, did anything seem off to you?" Elven asked Hunter.

Hunter shook his head. "It got late, the party was dwindling, and I decided to come home. Donnie said he was gonna stay and close the place down. He was pretty lit, but he's a big boy. And unless things have changed, Martin runs a tight ship."

"Nope, that's still Martin," Elven added.

"That's the last I saw him. Just a few others in the bar, but nobody I'd know," Hunter said. "Nobody he got into it with either."

"What happened to Donnie?" Noah asked.

"Found him in the middle of the road. Caught a bullet between the eyes," Elven said.

"Damn," Noah said.

"And what about you?" Elven asked to Hunter.

"What about me?"

"Once you left the bar, where'd you go?" he asked.

Hunter narrowed his eyes. "You thinkin' I killed Donnie?"

Elven shook his head. "I'm not thinkin' anything yet. Just trying to get the whole story." The way Hunter had acted with the news really didn't leave Elven feeling good. It was as Vincent and Willie had said—even his friends might be his enemy.

"And I told it to you. You know me, Elven. If I was gonna kill someone, I sure as shit wouldn't kill one of my friends."

"Thought you said he wasn't really a friend, though."

"You—" Hunter stopped and glared at Elven, gritting his teeth in frustration. Elven really didn't think Hunter had anything to do with it, but with everyone saying how awful Donnie had been, and Hunter not seeming too surprised, he couldn't rule it out. Adding pressure was sometimes the best way to figure someone out.

"Not sure how good of a sheriff you are, but from here, it doesn't look like a good one. You're grasping at straws," Hunter said.

"You're not too far off. Just seems that a man comes back to town, can shoot like nobody I've ever seen, and then his friend, who has nothing positive said about him, is found dead from a single bullet. In the pitch-dark, possibly half in the bag himself, you'd have to be incredibly lucky—or incredibly skilled—to make that shot."

Hunter looked none too pleased, but Elven wanted to see how he'd react. He had absolutely no proof in blaming Hunter, but he would keep pushing.

"Just because a man is an asshole, don't mean I'm gonna go around killin' him for that. Hell, if that were the case, half this county would be dead," Hunter said.

"You still didn't tell me where you were last night," Elven said.

Hunter stared Elven down, the corner of his mouth twitching like he wanted to deck him.

"He came home and was here the rest of the night," Noah said.

Elven broke his staring contest and looked at Hunter's brother.

"He was drunk, couldn't get his key in the door, so I had to get up and let him in. I was just glad I didn't have to clean up any puke. Had enough of that with momma and the chemo," Noah added, and Elven felt a sudden twinge of guilt.

"What time was that?" he asked.

"Maybe a little after twelve. Then I watched Hunter fall face first into the bed and pass out without another word. His damn snores could wake the whole county, so I know he didn't leave."

"And you were here all night?" Elven asked Noah.

"Yeah," he said with a shrug. "What, am I now a suspect 'cause I spoke up?"

Elven shook his head. "You said it yourself. Donnie wasn't nice to you."

"So I kill him some twenty years later?" Noah asked. "And on top of that, I'm a crack shot to get someone between the eyes?"

"Don't need to be when your brother is," Elven said.

"You know, Elven. This is not quite the welcome I thought I was gonna get, especially from you. Whatever good graces my momma might have held you in, they're all gone. She ain't here no more," Hunter said, his voice too menacing to ignore. It was time to go.

Elven turned around and walked out the door. Madds followed behind quickly.

"That took a sudden turn I didn't expect," she said. "What the hell was that about?"

Elven shook his head. "Something just doesn't feel right. Hunter isn't telling the whole truth, and maybe it ain't about Donnie, but there's something he's hiding."

"I thought he was your friend," she said.

"It's like he said. It's been twenty years. Can you really know someone after that long?"

CHAPTER TWELVE

After leaving Hunter and Noah Wallace's home, Elven had radioed over to Tank and Johnny. They were both at the scene to where they'd been called out, and in fact, it was worse than anyone had realized before they'd headed out. Tank told Elven and Madds that they both needed to come out and take a look.

So that's just what they did. Madds didn't feel the need to push Elven's questioning of Hunter anymore. He was fairly good at reading people, of course, unless it was Madds—a fact that she was grateful for. So if he felt the need to push it with Hunter, she trusted his instincts were right. Besides, she had her own problems on her mind.

She couldn't stop thinking about what had happened at the shooting competition. She could have sworn that she'd seen Kurt there. Maybe he'd lost her in the crowd and she'd mistaken the other poor guy for him, but she felt in her bones that he was there. Watching her. Waiting for the right moment to strike. She shuddered at the thought.

Elven drove the Jeep over to the scene and pulled up. As soon as they arrived, they both noticed that Johnny seemed pretty upset.

As well as the woman, assuming she was the one who had called it in.

Tank stood on the porch of the house next to Johnny, whose truck was parked nearby. Tank didn't seem troubled, but he wasn't smiling. Madds had known him to keep his emotions to himself—hell, the guy had taken buckshot to the gut and had barely mentioned anything about it later. But it was obvious that he wasn't pleased.

When they stepped out of the Jeep, Elven pointed to the weeping woman sitting off to the side of the house. She was sitting on the curb —well, perhaps curb was being generous. It was more like a slab of concrete that had been left there from a project that had never been finished. There was no sidewalk there. Only dirt that had been trampled so much, there were now paths.

"Go see if you can talk to her," he said to Madds. She gave him a look, and he sighed. "It's not that I don't want you with me checking out the scene. You're better with people when they're upset. I need your help here. Tank has seen everything and can walk me through. We can fill you in later."

She accepted his orders, even though she did want to see what the fuss was about. And she knew that Hollis would want to know what was going on with the case, if there was anything to tell. She would need to check in soon to make sure whatever had happened in the house hadn't been due to one of his concoctions. She also needed to see if there was anything she needed to steer Elven away from as far as the Donnie Price case.

Being Hollis's eyes and ears in the department was difficult when he didn't keep her in the loop on what all he had his hands in.

Madds went to the crying woman on the slab. The first thing she noticed was she was very pretty, if not a bit odd. Maybe that was unfair to think of someone, but something just felt different about her. She couldn't place it, but it was there. She looked normal on the outside, but Madds wondered if there was something else to the woman that wasn't tucked inside the heavy coat she wore. There was a sixth sense tugging at her. She also found herself feeling a bit

79

envious of the way she was bundled up so much, she looked like a prairie dog poking its head out of a hole.

"Miss, I'm Deputy Maddison Clark," Madds said. "Mind if I sit down with you?"

The woman moved to the side, nodding her head. She wiped her nose with a tissue. "My name's Bernadette," she said.

"Alright, Bernadette," Madds said, sitting. Immediately, she regretted it. The half of her ass that didn't sit where Bernadette had previously covered was ice-cold once it touched the concrete. She grit her teeth and put up with her now-numb asscheek.

"I know things like this happen," Bernadette said. "It's just, I never thought they would happen to me. To my neighbors, you know?"

Madds nodded, still not knowing what had happened in the house. "What did you see?"

Bernadette shook her head. "Nothing, really. I mean, nothing about whatever happened. But after, I saw what had happened to them. Katherine and Todd had been in there, and now they're both dead. Both sh-shot."

Bernadette turned to Madds and hugged her tight. Madds could smell the hairspray she'd used on the curls that had looked so perfect, along with the vanilla-scented perfume she'd used. "I'm sorry you had to see that," Madds said.

Bernadette pulled away with a smile. She motioned toward the house, into which Elven had already disappeared. "I'm just glad that handsome officer is here now."

Madds laughed. Elven was always so cocky about the way he looked, yet people just had to keep reminding him about it. She would have to keep Bernadette's words to herself, unless she wanted his head to get even bigger than it was.

"Yeah, he has a way, I suppose," Madds said.

"Is he single?" Bernadette asked.

Madds swallowed. She felt some strange emotion bubbling inside of her. She immediately felt defensive, and wasn't quite sure why.

Elven was her boss, and at the same time, the person she was supposed to keep an eye on. Nothing more.

But she couldn't help the way she felt. Which was...jealous.

"Uh, I mean, I don't know if he's your type," Madds said. "Elven is a complicated man. Being the sheriff and all, he's pretty busy anyway."

Bernadette laughed. "Oh, God, not him. That man is prettier than I am. I can tell a lot of work goes into that look. Pretentious much?"

Madds laughed out loud. Maybe she wouldn't be keeping this comment to herself after all. Elven being called out for being the way he was—well, that was just funny.

"I meant the deputy," Bernadette said.

Madds lifted her eyebrows. She'd never thought of Tank as much of anything more than a co-worker. The man was all business, but if she were pressed to look at him differently, she supposed that maybe he could be handsome. If you were into that sort of type, anyway.

"Tank? I'm pretty sure he's ma—"

"No, Johnny," Bernadette clarified.

Madds stopped talking. She blinked twice at the woman in front of her. She was beautiful, but Madds couldn't shake that something felt odd about her. And now she knew why.

"I just think he's the cutest man I ever laid eyes on, don't you think?" Bernadette asked.

Johnny stepped out of the house after having gone in with Tank and Elven. He grabbed his gun and examined it. The magazine fell out of the bottom as he fumbled around. It clattered to the deck and he quickly scooped it up, looking around to make sure nobody caught him. Of course, when Madds locked eyes with Johnny, he gave a nervous laugh, then jammed the magazine back in and holstered his weapon.

She turned to Bernadette with a wide smile. "Johnny is absolutely available. In fact, I think if you were to ask him, he would be more than happy to take you out."

"You think?" Bernadette asked. "I mean, I don't know. Being a deputy, he's probably real busy. And it's such a distinguished job, ain't it? Having to wear a uniform and all."

Madds smiled, trying to contain her excitement. Inside, her mind was running with the thoughts about how cute Bernadette was, and how Johnny might actually get laid. For every Adam, there was an Eve. She even had a moment where she'd forgotten all about the idea of seeing Kurt.

"I'll go talk to him, don't you worry," Madds said, giddy about playing matchmaker. Bernadette smiled as Madds got up and made her way up the steps of the house.

"Hey, Madds," Johnny said.

"Pretty hard today, huh?" she asked, seeing that Johnny was still a little shaken.

He nodded. "Sure is."

"You know, that woman over there, she's pretty shaken up, too."

"Oh, Bernadette?" he asked, perking up when saying her name. Madds couldn't help but smile. "Yeah, she was pretty upset when we got here. Nearly had to pry her off Tank."

"I think she'd be better off with you talking to her."

"Me? Oh, nah. You're better at consoling than me."

"I really think you should," Madds pressed.

He considered a moment, biting his lip. "I can't do that. She... well, she's too darn cute."

Madds felt like squealing.

"Ain't she?" he asked.

"She's definitely a cutie," Madds said. "And I think she might think someone else here is cute, too."

He laughed. "Oh, everyone likes Elven," he said, making the same mistake Madds had earlier.

Madds grabbed Johnny's shoulder and looked him in the eye. "Johnny, God love you, but sometimes you're a little too dense for your own good. It's not Elven." She poked him in his soft chest. "Get your ass over there and talk to that woman."

Johnny's face grew a slight shade of white at the thought. "It was one thing when she needed help, but now, just to talk? About what?"

Something caught Madds's eye, just over Johnny's shoulder. There was movement that looked like a person. Whoever it was, they wanted to stay out of view, but they were doing a piss-poor job of it. Almost as though...they were trying to stay out of anyone's view, except Madds's.

She stepped around Johnny, patting him on the shoulder, half-listening now. "Whatever comes to mind, Johnny. You'll do fine," she said, dismissing him. Her mind had snapped away from matchmaker and back to the job. Or something like it. She felt the need to hunt down whoever was out there, poking around.

"I gotta check something," she said before running down the steps of the porch, leaving Johnny to make his own decision about talking to Bernadette.

CHAPTER THIRTEEN

Elven noticed that Madds had left the porch, heading across the road to where a few other homes sat. It didn't bother him, and didn't raise any flags for him that she was searching the area. She was a capable cop, if not a little distracted lately. She could handle herself.

But what did pique his curiosity was when he looked through the window and saw the witness sitting next to the road. No longer was she crying, but laughing. He moved a bit closer and saw that Johnny sat with her on the slab of broken concrete. The two seemed very chummy, and Johnny, more confident than he'd ever seen the man before.

"What is all that about?" Elven asked Tank.

Tank came over to the window and spotted Johnny sitting next to the woman, whose name, Elven would later learn, was Bernadette. Tank let out such a loud groan, it was as if he was in agony. Elven looked at his deputy, but saw no reason for concern.

"Don't even get me started," Tank said. "The day has been bizarre, I'll tell you that much."

Elven turned back to the pair outside, watching Johnny make

some motions with his hands and Bernadette laughing as though she'd been told the funniest thing she'd ever heard. She grabbed his shoulder as she did.

"Huh," Elven said, never remembering the last time he'd seen Johnny entertain a woman. Or really, talk to a woman other than Madds, Meredith, or his own mother. Good for him, he thought, before pulling himself back to the crime scene.

"That woman," Elven said. "She said she didn't see anything?"

Tank shook his head as he walked to the bodies. Elven followed.

The door had been closed, according to Tank's notes from Bernadette. And she hadn't moved anything as soon as she'd seen what had happened.

And what had happened...well, it was a mess.

Katherine, or rather, her body, lay on top of Todd Utt's body. Her head had a single hole in between her eyes, but the back of her head was blown out. Brains, bits of skull, and clumps of hair littered the dining room table, which was straight ahead from where Elven stood. Both bodies looked as though they'd been there for a few days before being found.

"She must have been shot at close range," Elven said. "Inches away. The force of the gunshot would have been so much to create the explosion out the back, like you see."

Tank nodded in agreement. "I saw that a few times overseas. Between a scared recruit rounding a corner and firing a round point-blank. Even saw a Haji so scared, he ate his gun."

Elven looked at Tank, who rarely spoke of his time in the military, and narrowed his eyes.

"Sorry, old habits," Tank said, referring to his slur.

Elven ignored it and went back to the case, not having time to scold Tank for his word choice. Tank wasn't wrong about the crime scene, but Elven didn't suspect the woman had shot herself between the eyes. It wasn't the spot that came naturally when shooting oneself in the head. Besides, there was no handgun around.

Her body lay on top of Todd Utt's. Elven had known Todd

himself. Most everyone in Dupray had history that went back decades or longer. Todd had been the assistant football coach at the high school. He was a mean son-of-a-gun when he wanted to be—though Elven, being who he was, had never had that side of Todd's aimed directly toward him. Todd had also picked on those who couldn't hack it during practice, and Elven had never been that guy.

And when football season wasn't happening, he'd worked at the Hallie mines.

Todd had a bullet hole in the side of his head. Right through the temple. But it hadn't been shot close range. His brains were splattered on the wall and door, but when Elven moved Todd's head to the side, he saw it wasn't as high of pressure that had exploded out the other end.

"I don't think he was shot here," Tank said. "There's a long streak of blood down the door, then on the floor as if he was dragged."

Elven nodded. "If he was in the way of the door, I'd say whoever did this wanted to get out that door." He pointed to the front door, where the bits of brain clung to the wood.

"Phil is gonna hate this one," Tank said. He wasn't wrong. Phil was going to have a full house soon. With Donnie, and now the two bodies in front of him, it would be a busy week for the old guy.

"So why the two of them together?" Elven asked, more to himself than directly to Tank. But his deputy answered anyway.

"Maybe they were shackin' up together," Tank offered. "Either Todd or Katherine had a spouse that got jealous. With the body moved, we know it wasn't murder-suicide."

Elven nodded, working it through his head. He didn't think someone as old as Katherine was shacking up with anyone. At least, he didn't want to think she was.

"Didn't you say the neighbor told you both of them lived alone? And it doesn't explain the rifle," Elven said, pointing to the gun leaning against the wall. "There's no blood on it, yet it's right in the way where Todd's brains would be covering it. So it was put there after he got shot. I think Katherine came in after, saw something she wasn't supposed to, and took a bullet because of it. I bet if we check Katherine's house, we'll find a spot that fits that rifle perfectly. Maybe even Bernadette out there would be able to vouch that it was Katherine's."

"Who would want to kill Todd Utt?" Tank asked.

Elven shrugged. He hadn't heard what Todd had been up to for some time. After the mines closed and Todd had stopped driving equipment up the mountain for the Hallies, Elven had lost track of him. There had been about ten years that Todd could have gotten into some trouble.

"You checked the rest of the house, right?" Elven asked.

"Every corner," Tank said. "The place is a sty, but nothing looks tossed. From the looks of it, I don't think Todd had anything worth stealing anyway."

"So this was targeted," Elven said. "Who do you know that goes to kill someone, looks for a headshot instead of center mass, and nails it in one shot?"

Tank shook his head. "Other than a professional?"

Tank had said just what Elven was thinking. "It seems too good to just be a lucky shot, doesn't it?" Elven asked.

"What about Donnie? You said he was shot between the eyes, right?" Tank asked.

Elven nodded. "Wasn't gonna search the whole woods for another bullet, but only found the one shell in the road. One shot, between the eyes. Pitch-black out."

"Think they're connected?" Tank asked.

"Can't say for sure yet, but seems too coincidental," Elven said. He was already trying to think of what the two men could have been into that would elicit a professional hit. And he knew where he was going to have to look.

The records of the mines. And if any of that information was still around, it would be at Elven's parents house.

CHAPTER FOURTEEN

Madds crept around the house across the street from the scene of the crime. This house was in much more disrepair than any other home in the area. She thought it was abandoned, by the look of it. The siding was falling off, and the small fence that bordered the property had fallen over from being half rotted out.

She kept her hand on her gun, ready for anything to pop out. Her mind immediately went to Kurt, and how she knew she had seen him at the shooting competition. Was he following her again?

If he was, why? Why would he not come after her when she was alone? Her heart raced, knowing he was around. She could just feel it.

She rounded the corner, but saw nothing. Just a dirt field that had weeds growing intermittently in it. She could hear a mumbling, then peered into the window she stood next to and saw the television was on inside. So much for the building being abandoned.

She turned back to the field, but just as she did, she saw a large pipe coming at her face. It smacked her right in the nose and the pain surged through her whole face.

"Goddammit!" she screamed as she grabbed at her nose. She

lifted her gun, but all she saw were black spots wherever she looked. The pain was too much, and she fought to not topple over.

But then, instead of being attacked, she heard footsteps running away from her, moving.

The motherfucker was trying to run.

She heard the direction they were headed and bolted toward them. She could see the ground in front of her and the sun at the top, but there was still a large black spot in the center of her path. Slowly, as she continued to run, the spot shrank until it was little more than a speck.

She could finally see the features of the person she chased. The person who had attacked her. It was a man, and he wore a ball cap that covered most of his hair. But she could see underneath that it was blond. The white-blond hair she knew too well.

"Stop!" she called out. But he didn't stop. "Kurt, stop! I will shoot you in the back, you motherfucker!"

He kept running. She raised her gun as she ran, but she couldn't get a clear shot at him. If she stopped, she would, but shooting him in the back wouldn't satisfy her. She wanted to look him in the eyes when she pulled the trigger.

One thing she did have was her speed. She forced her legs to move faster, to push harder, until she closed the gap between them. When she could just graze the edge of his shirt with her fingertips, she pushed on her heels and lunged forward.

The two hit the dead grass beneath them, tumbling forward. She felt his head hit hard into a patch of dirt, a groan of pain escaping his mouth. She pushed herself up, grabbing at his head as she did. She pulled hard and he yelped louder.

"Kurt, I swear to God, I'm gonna fucking kill you!" she shouted.

She spun him around and lowered her eyes to his. She forced the gun into his face, pushing hard against his nose.

"Madds!" Johnny yelled, running toward her.

She looked at Johnny from over her shoulder, keeping a firm grip on Kurt beneath her.

"I'm sorry, I'm sorry," Kurt pleaded.

"Johnny, stay out of this, I got it!" Madds yelled, intending to end it right then and there, even if it cost her.

She turned back and looked at his face. Her vision had cleared, though her nose still pulsed with pain. But when she looked, she realized that it wasn't him. It wasn't Kurt.

"She's gonna kill me, man. Help!" he pleaded to Johnny.

The man had a goatee with a soul patch on his bottom lip. His hair was bleached out, but his beard was dark black. He had brown eyes and a look of panic on his face.

"Madds, what are you doing?" Johnny asked, finally catching up to them. He placed a hand on her shoulder.

"He, I mean, I thought he was—"

"She's crazy, man. Kept calling me Kurt or some shit. I swear I didn't have nothin' to do with them people that got killed over there," he said. "I was just curious what was happening when I saw the police lights."

"Where is Kurt?" she asked.

"I don't know no Kurt," he said.

"Madds, put the gun away," Johnny said, his tone calm.

She shoved the gun in her holster and pulled her cuffs out. She clamped them behind his back and he hollered again. "What you doin' that for?"

"You still hit me in the face, you asshole," she said.

"I thought you was gonna shoot me," he said.

"I don't give a shit. Assaulting a deputy is serious," she said, lifting him off the ground when she stood. "Thanks, Johnny."

Johnny nodded, still looking concerned. She didn't blame him—so was she. She thought for sure she'd had Kurt this time. But now, she was beginning to question everything, including her sanity.

CHAPTER FIFTEEN

HE'D BEEN ALL OVER THE WORLD, AND SOMETIMES NOTHING changed.

It wasn't always about killing someone who was difficult. A lot of the time, it was just finding them. Sure, people could be guarded. That wasn't really an issue, not for him. He could wait, lure, or bulldoze his way through whatever obstacles his target created for him. That wasn't the difficult part.

But it was when someone so small and unknown by most—usually a target who had no celebrity, no sort of profile—decided to go missing. Well, that was the most difficult.

Most people were stupid about it. Credit cards that left a paper trail, smartphones that pinged, an internet trail. Hell, there was one guy who had gone into hiding, but still posted on Instagram daily. If the beaches in the background weren't enough to point the way to him, the location attached to the image file surely did the trick.

But a small target in a shithole like Dupray was different. There were no credit card trails, no smartphone pings. He wondered if his target actually wanted to go missing or if he was just a broke hermit.

Either way, finding his last target was proving a real chore for him. And until he did, he'd be sitting around Dupray for a while.

So that's what he did. Sit in Dupray. Right in the diner known as Hank's. He'd been there before, years ago in that other lifetime he rarely thought about. But from what he could remember, not a whole lot had changed at the diner.

The stools at the counter were the same, if not more worn and cracked. The booths looked as if they'd never been reupholstered, the tables never touched up. He didn't remember the floors or walls as well, but by the look of them, they may have had a fresh coat of paint at most. Fresh, meaning in the past decade.

The only thing that had changed was the staff. Well, maybe not so much. There was waitress whose name tag pinned to her ample breast read "Rhea." Her cheeks were rosy and her attitude chipper. She wasn't the same woman he'd seen in his previous life, but she fit the same age as whoever it was had been there before.

In a way, everything about the place had been perfectly preserved in time.

If that were the case, then that would hopefully go for the recipes as well. And that meant he was in for a treat.

Rhea slid a plate in front of him, and even though she'd told him that the apple pie was her favorite, he opted for her second favorite pie—pecan pie. It wasn't that he didn't like apple pie, but that he just had a special relationship with pecan.

"I know you said you'd pass on the á la mode, but I put a scoop of vanilla in a bowl anyway. Wasn't sure if it was a taste or a lactose thing, or you just didn't want to spend the extra, but this way, you can decide. And don't worry, there's no extra charge. I just wanted to see your face when you tasted it," she said, extra bubbly.

He narrowed his eyes at the pie. It looked as if a bit of steam still wafted from it. The steam floated over the bowl that was slightly iced over, keeping the ice cream inside extra cold. He cut into the pie, then dipped the same fork into the ice cream. He shoveled everything into his mouth as Rhea stood by with a knowing smile.

The flavors flooded his mouth. The ice cream was cheap, and not as creamy as it could be, but it didn't matter. The sugary taste of vanilla mixed with the sweet and salty custard of the pie to make for an amazing combination. It was one of the best pies he'd ever had in his life. It almost made coming to Dupray—and suffering through the cold—worth it. Almost.

"Is that bourbon?" James asked, his mouth still half-full of pie.

Rhea smiled. "There's a distillery out in Berkeley County that makes moonshine and bourbon. Hank gets it straight from them. Says he won't get anything else."

"Hank might just be a genius when it comes to pie," James said, shoveling another bite into his mouth.

"I'll pass that along."

"Thank you for the ice cream," James added. "You were right."

"Been here long enough that I should know what I'm doing," she said.

"How long exactly?" James asked.

Rhea shrugged. "Didn't grow up here, but came through from Kentucky when I was sixteen. Didn't have much in my pocket, but Hank gave me a job. Been here ever since."

"Didn't feel like leaving? Once you saved up, I mean?" James asked, truly curious.

"Nah. Home wasn't that great to me. Hank's been good. The town in general, too. People don't got a lot of money, but overall, they're kind. I make enough to be content, and at the end of the day, that's all that matters to me. Plus, I'm good at the job."

James pointed his fork at her, hovering over his plate. "That ain't no lie."

She smiled wide at the compliment. "You let me know if there's anything else I can get ya."

"Actually, I do have a question," he said. "Don't mean to be rude, but sixteen doesn't seem as if it was yesterday."

She laughed. "Is that your way of sayin' I'm gettin' old?"

"No, miss," he said. "But it does seem like you know the town well enough and the people in it."

"I've seen most of the town's faces walk through those doors, sure."

"I'm lookin' for a fella, name's Amos. You know him?"

"Sure do," she said without a blink.

"Happen to know where he's at?"

He could see in her face that she was reluctant to say anything. Most kind people in smaller towns were that way to strangers, even amid friendly banter.

"I understand not wanting to give a stranger his address, but I just had something to give him. Maybe he comes in here or hangs out at some other place? Pool hall or fishing spot?"

Relief seemed to settle over her face. He knew the mention of trying to find him at a public place versus home would be enough for that, especially after the chat they'd just had.

"There's Dylan Amos and his daddy Michael Amos. Honestly, I wouldn't even know where either one lives these days. I ain't seen 'em in a couple months. All I know is Michael lives up in the hills somewhere and I think his son takes care of things for him. Pops in from time to time on supply runs."

He nodded. That wasn't a whole lot to go on, which was disappointing, but he didn't fault Rhea for it. At least the diner hadn't been a total waste. The pie, and talking to Rhea, had been a delight. The woman impressed him. She worked, and was happy with her work. It was hard to find that kind of ethic and loyalty these days.

"Hey, Tubs, you gonna hang out down on that end all day, or you gonna take our order?" a man said from the other end of the counter.

James looked their way, seeing a tall man who looked to be about twenty pounds overweight himself. He sat with a smaller friend who looked to be missing those same twenty pounds his friend had on him. The small friend smacked the bigger one on the shoulder.

"You can't say that, man," he said, but he was laughing the whole time.

Rhea frowned, her demeanor shifting from proud and happy to defeated. Definitely sadder. James had noticed that Rhea wasn't someone to be described as thin, but she was a very pretty woman, inside and out. He'd only spoken to her for a few minutes, but he hated seeing someone like that take on that sort of flack.

She grumbled and rolled her eyes. James wasn't sure if she was trying to get him to commiserate with her or if she was speaking to herself, as if it was her only way to get through the day. "Jason Rowe and Nick Myers. Yay. Just the spot of sunshine I needed." Her voice was dull and fatigued.

She walked off and attended to the men, taking their orders. But the entire time, her shoulders slumped over. She gallantly tried to smile, but he could tell those guys just weren't letting up on her.

He could have sworn he heard one of them oink like a pig. They both continued to laugh as she walked away, limply putting a ticket in the window for the cook.

James got up from his seat and walked down the counter. The men didn't seem to notice his approach, but he stopped right beside them. The two of them smelled like sweat, dirt, and a hint of manure. Their clothes matched the look, as if they'd not washed for three days.

"Excuse me," James said. "But I was talking to that lovely waitress there and it seems to me that you're hassling her. Can I ask why?"

The larger man scoffed, looking James up and down from his barstool. "What's it to you? We're just having a bit of fun. Ol' Rhea there can take a joke. She don't need you comin' to her rescue."

"Yeah, Pops. Rhea knows we just jokin'."

James considered them a moment. He didn't care they were trying to tell him he was old. Hell, sometimes he felt that way himself. It didn't mean he couldn't whoop their asses if he wanted, though. But he wasn't trying to start a fight.

"She's doing her job, and doing it well, I might add. You can't get service like that just anywhere. You boys don't know how good you have it here. Maybe you should give her a break," James said, pulling his long coat back to reveal the butt of his revolver.

Both of them caught it, their eyes glancing for a split second, then back to James's face. They didn't seem worried, but their attitude did shift.

"Whatever man, just go back to your fuckin' pie and leave us alone," the bigger guy said.

James stayed for a moment longer, staring at the two men. They turned back to the counter and didn't say another word. When he was satisfied, he turned and walked back to his half-finished pie.

Rhea brought the two men a couple glasses of water, setting a straw next to each cup. The smaller guy muttered a "thanks", but the bigger guy said nothing. It wasn't the most polite interaction, but it was much better than the last one James had witnessed. That was satisfaction enough for him.

She headed back his way and let out a sigh. "I appreciate it. But I don't need you fighting the battles for me."

James nodded. "Didn't mean anything by it. Just appreciate the job you do."

She smiled. "Thank you. Did seem like you scared them for the moment. But knowing them, they'll just be back at it tomorrow. Nick, the smaller guy, he ain't so bad. He just follows Jason around like a lost puppy. If he had a different friend, he might even be a decent man. But there ain't no savin' Jason. He been sour since the day he was born. Only thing that'll change that is a bullet," she said.

James lifted an eyebrow. She quickly covered her mouth and gasped.

"Oh my, I apologize. I shouldn't say those things to anyone, let alone a man I just met. You probably think the worst of me now."

James shook his head. "Far from it. Never apologize for saying what's on your mind. Believe me, I've heard a lot worse." He shoveled the rest of the pie into his mouth.

"Still," she said. "The pie's on me today, mister."

He shook his head. "I won't hear of it. I don't do handouts. You work hard, and I can pay. It's how the world works." He pulled out his wallet, but she placed a hand over it.

"Consider taking a stand for me the pie payment," she said, her eyes earnest.

He held onto her smile, her hand touching his, then tucked his wallet away. "Fair enough."

He knew he'd find his target sooner than later, but for the moment, he had time to kill.

CHAPTER SIXTEEN

The scene had been a rough one. Two dead bodies in the house. Bernadette a crying mess. Madds taking a hit to the face by some guy. And the case was just as confusing as ever.

But somehow, Johnny seemed to be happier than Elven had ever seen him. The man appeared to be walking on clouds.

"I ain't do nothin'!" the man with the bleached hair and goatee screamed.

Madds shoved him in front of Meredith's desk and back to the hall that led to the jail cell. She was in a sour mood, and Elven couldn't really blame her. She had two pieces of tissue shoved in her nose. She'd tried to clean up with a bottle of water by the car, but her skin was red and a large smear of blood remained on her cheek, trailing from her nose.

"You hit a cop in the face, asshole. Now you get to simmer in it," she said, shoving him all the way down the hall. She twisted his arm and he yelled in pain. It wasn't anything too harsh, so Elven let it go. Madds would get over it soon enough.

"Eventful day?" Meredith said, pausing as the man screamed louder, then the sound quickly fade away. The cell door slammed hard, and Elven knew he was no longer in danger from Madds.

"Eventful, but fruitless," he said.

"And what about you, Johnny?" Meredith asked. "You look like you just won the lottery with that grin plastered on your face. You gonna quit us and head to Bora Bora?"

Meredith's hair was curled up and extra springy today. She wore red lipstick that matched her blouse. She was always well put-together, her appearance nothing less than professional.

"Ain't like that," Johnny said.

"Johnny here met himself a girl," Elven said with a grin.

Meredith's jaw dropped. Then she smiled wide. "Johnny, I cannot believe it. You'll have to tell me all about her. What's she look like? How old is she? Does she work?"

Meredith fired off questions faster than Elven thought Johnny could even think of them. But he didn't answer any. He twisted his face, cutting in.

"Sorry, Meredith. I'll tell ya all about her, but I gotta talk to Elven first," he said.

She frowned, disappointed not to get the good gossip, but she nodded. "I'll be here when you're ready to spill the tea. That's what the kids say these days."

Elven stood next to the table at the back where the coffee pot sat, half-drank. Johnny came up to him.

"What's up?" Elven asked.

"It's about Madds."

Elven was all ears. He hadn't seen the interaction go down himself, but he'd heard a little. But it seemed Johnny was troubled about more than just a friend getting hit in the face. And given his recent good fortune meeting Bernadette, it must have been serious.

"Look, I don't want to get her in trouble, but something seemed off about her," Johnny said.

"How so?" Elven asked, knowing he'd been thinking that same thing about Madds lately.

Johnny shrugged. "Like I said—"

"Johnny, you're a good man. A good friend. You won't be getting her in trouble. If I think it's nothing, then I'll say it. But if there's other things at play, I need to know."

He nodded at Elven's words. "I didn't see the start, but I heard her scream, so I ran after her. Elven, let me tell you, when I found her on top of that man, I swear, I thought she was gonna kill him. She had her gun shoved, barrel touching his face.

"Now, I ain't sayin' he didn't deserve to be scared or that he shouldn't be in a cell. But Elven, she was scary. Like there was something else goin' on in her head. As if something had possessed her."

Just then, Madds entered the room, her brows knitted together. She glared at the two men.

"Johnny, if you got a problem with me, then you say it to my face," she said, marching toward them.

Johnny immediately slumped over. He wasn't sure if he was worried she was going to attack him or if he just felt guilty for disappointing her. Elven stepped in front of the man, his hand raised.

"Just hold up," Elven said.

She stopped, taken aback. "I wasn't gonna hit Johnny, Elven." She looked over his shoulder. "Johnny, you know that, right?"

He turned. "I don't know what to think, Madds. I'm sorry, I really am. But when I saw you out there, I...well, I got scared."

"You had your gun in that man's face?" Elven asked.

She widened her eyes and threw her hands up in front of her, pointing to her nose. "Look at my fucking face, Elven. He blindsided me with a pipe. Might even have broken my fucking nose. I saw red immediately. Hell, I didn't see much of anything at first, 'cause I thought I was blind for a minute. But you care that I pulled my gun on someone who attacked me?"

"I'm just making sure that you didn't use excessive force. If you're saying you didn't, then I believe you. But if Johnny comes to me and says he got scared and was worried about you, then I need to ask. If I go check on that man in there, am I gonna find him any more roughed up than when we brought him in?"

"Oh, fuck you, Elven. I twisted his fucking arm and he's crying like a baby. You can go check on him all you want. He's just fine," she said, pulling the tissue from her nose. It came out in large blood-covered clots.

He nodded. "Alright. Go clean yourself up and take the rest of the day off."

She scoffed, looking at Elven as if he'd just called her the worst word in the book.

"Go see Phil, make sure nothing is broken. I've seen a guy get a nasty septal hematoma before. Trust me, you don't want that," Elven said.

Madds grit her teeth.

"Madds, what I'm asking you to do ain't unreasonable. You know that. This isn't a punishment. Go get checked out, then relax. You've had a rough one. You told me yourself you haven't been sleeping well. Maybe you can get some rest."

Madds seemed to lighten at those words, but she was still none too happy. He couldn't control how she felt, but he hoped she could see it with a much clearer mind after getting some rest.

CHAPTER SEVENTEEN

He knew she was angry, but he didn't care. She was off her game and was going to get herself—or someone else—hurt. She badly needed the rest.

Elven shut the door behind him when he entered his office. He thought about everything he knew about Madds again. She'd shown up at his office without much in the way of a past. Sure, Meredith had done her legwork, and Madds had worked out well on the previous two cases. But lately, she'd been way off the mark.

He could chalk it up to lack of sleep. And to be fair, she'd been through a very tough case with Spencer Caldwell and Abnel not too long ago. Killing someone was never easy, and she'd had to do her fair share of it when fighting to survive and save the lives of those around her.

But that nagging feeling about her was back. The one that ate at him and made him call her previous department weeks ago.

Why hadn't they gotten back to him yet?

He slumped into his chair, exhausted at the day he'd just had. The day that was still going strong. He let out a sigh as he tried to talk himself into it. And out of it.

He felt that curiosity he always needed to satisfy. Part of him was worried he was going to be right about Madds. That she had a secret she was hiding. That maybe she didn't cope well and lost it easily. Really, it could be anything. And he'd been working side by side with her, having zero idea about her history.

Then again, he was also worried he was going to be wrong. That if he got a hold of her supervisor, they would wonder why he'd ever decided to call. They'd tell him the stress of a new environment, coupled with the job she'd had to do, could be what was causing her to act differently. And then, he'd feel awful for ever doubting her.

Either way, he was going to feel awful.

But he would feel worse if he didn't follow through with what his gut was telling him to do.

He pulled out her resume again, remembering their conversation when she'd been hired.

Mesa. It's close to Phoenix. In fact, we usually just say Phoenix, but on a resumé, I figured it was best to put the actual department down.

He pulled the name of her supervisor from the list of references. Sergeant Edward Garcia. There was a phone number next to his name, but he decided to just call the department and see if he was in. A quick search on his computer told him the non-emergency line for the department, as it had the last time he'd called them.

He lifted his phone, holding down the hook switch. He stared at it for a moment, then dialed.

The phone rang once, then was picked up.

"Mesa, PD," the voice said.

Elven cleared his throat. "Yeah, hi, this is Sheriff Elven Hallie. I—" he paused for a moment. The last time he'd called, he'd asked to speak to someone about Madds, but had never heard back. Maybe there was something they didn't want him to know about her. Well, if that was the case, then he'd end up in the same position he was before.

"Sheriff?" the voice asked.

"Sorry," Elven said. "I need to speak to Sergeant Edward Garcia."

"What's this concerning?"

He'd thought not mentioning Madds was the best idea, but he hadn't thought about what reason he could supply instead if he was asked. Truth be told, he didn't think they would even ask.

"Uh, about a case he was working that I think I'm dealing with here in my department."

"Which case?"

Jeez. They really wanted to know everything, didn't they?

"About a double homicide. A couple, they still haven't caught the guy," Elven said, thinking there had to be an unsolved double homicide in a place as big as Madds had made it seem. He wasn't really lying, either. He truly was dealing with a double homicide, and Katherine and Todd might have been a couple, for all he knew. But he was pretty sure it had nothing to do with anything Sergeant Garcia would know about, so maybe he was lying after all. He swallowed his guilt down, knowing it was for the best. "Look, is Sergeant Garcia in?"

"I'll patch you through now. Hold on, Sheriff."

Thank heaven, Elven thought.

There was no Muzak while he waited, but instead, a narration of things that the police department did for the community. It was a very calm, male voice that told him all about the outreach programs and the officers who cared about keeping their city safe. That was followed by a quick message about emergencies and when it was appropriate to call 911.

After listening to the message twice, the phone picked up. A loud, phlegmy hack echoed from the receiver, followed by a cough.

"Garcia," the man said.

"Sergeant Garcia?" Elven asked.

"Yeah, this is Eddie."

"You're a hard man to get ahold of," Elven said. "This is Sheriff Elven Hallie of Dupray County, West Virginia."

"West Virginia? Hell, I don't know how any of my homicides or their suspects might have ended up there. Which one was this about again?" he asked.

"Actually, it's not really about that. Don't get me wrong, I've got a homicide here, but that's not the connection to the case," Elven said.

"What can I do for you, sheriff?" Garcia asked, his voice edging on irritation.

"I've got a new deputy here. Well, she's not so new actually. Been here a few months. Maddison Cook."

Sergeant Garcia laughed, the rock-hard tone in his voice loosening up. "Madds? Shit, how'd she end up all the way out in West Virginia?"

Elven let out a sigh of relief. He wasn't sure what he was expecting. Maybe some resistance talking about her, or perhaps a soured response to her name. But when Garcia chuckled, it seemed to put him at ease from his worst thoughts.

"So you're saying you know her?" he asked.

"Sure do. I was her supervisor for a few years. I'm pretty sure I spoke to a woman some time ago about her. Didn't remember where exactly it was, but now you calling—"

"Yep, she's out here in Dupray County," Elven said. "That was my secretary."

"Wow, what's the weather like out there? She hated the cold. Bitched about it all the time out here, and I mean, we're talking the forties on a bad day in winter."

Elven laughed. "Sounds like not a whole lot has changed. Except it's a lot colder than that here."

"I bet. Glad to hear she landed on her feet, though," Garcia said. "Was sad to see her leave."

"Actually, that's something I wanted to talk about. She's been having a bit of a hard time lately. And—"

"Wait, you said I'm a hard man to get a hold of," Garcia said, cutting in. His tone wasn't so jovial now, but inquisitive.

"That's right."

"No offense, but I'm here all the time. Truth be told, the older I get, the more I enjoy being in the office. I'm probably the easiest person to get on the phone if I'm not in a meeting or helping an interrogation. When your secretary called me a few months back, she called my direct line. Did you just call the general department line?"

Elven shifted in his chair. He now felt something was off with Sergeant Garcia. He wasn't sure why it mattered which line he'd called. To be honest, hearing that Meredith had called a direct line was something he would have to question later. For all she knew, it could have been anyone on the other line. But calling the department line ensured that the caller would get the real person he or she was looking for.

"I left a message with the clerk, whoever she was, to have you give me a call back," Elven said. "Said it was directly about Madds. Since it had been a few weeks and I still hadn't heard back, I called again just now."

Garcia paused for a moment. He was still there. Elven could still hear his breathing, except it was a bit more labored. Even a bit more frantic.

Garcia cleared his throat again and swallowed audibly. "Goddammit Sheriff."

Elven wasn't sure he heard him right. Garcia's voice was barely above a whisper, yet heavy.

"Sergeant, is something wrong? I'm not sure I understand what's going on. Is—"

"Sheriff, I have to go before something else gets fucked. But I suggest you talk to her about why she left when she did," Garcia said. And then, the line disconnected.

Elven sat, staring at the phone a moment. He wasn't sure what he was supposed to do with the conversation he'd just had. One moment, the man had been laughing with him about his deputy, and the next, he'd been acting as though Elven had outed him as having proof of some government conspiracy.

The phone began to let out a howler tone from being off the hook for too long. Elven slowly lowered it back into the cradle and shook his head.

Whatever his worries had been before, that conversation had not put them at ease.

CHAPTER EIGHTEEN

As difficult as Dylan and his father Michael Amos were proving for him to find, Jason Rowe was not.

James had pulled his truck around the back of the trailer, parking it were no one could see it from the road. The trailer sat on a piece of land that looked huge, though he wasn't sure where the property line actually began. By the looks of the place, it went on for a ways with the amount of junk that was placed throughout it.

Inside wasn't much better. After breaking the lock on the door—a task that was simple to do, but reserved for when he was sure the mark wouldn't notice—he set foot in the cramped trailer. The first thing he noticed was the smell.

It was a combination of gym socks, old milk, tobacco, and stale farts. He turned his nose, opting to grab the tin of Skoal sitting on the table by the door and hold it under his nose. The tobacco scent, he could tolerate long-term. The rest of the smells, he preferred to keep at a minimum.

The place was a mess. Not only were dirty clothes piled on the couch, leaving a single space to sit on directly across from the television, but there were also petrified half-eaten remains of food practically glued to paper plates littered across the floor. It looked like some college bachelor's delight. But Jason looked to be at least twice the age of someone in college, and James was sure that the man had never even opened a book once finishing high school. If he'd even done that.

No, James had already made up his mind about who Jason was. Perhaps he'd been popular, of sorts, when younger. He could garner a crowd for whatever asinine things he did at school, and even think he had friends because of it. But as time went on, Nick had been the only one who'd lasted, and that wasn't because of anything Jason did. It was more because of what Nick had going on in his life—or rather, what he lacked in his life.

James was no therapist, but he knew he had Jason's personality narrowed down by the interaction at the diner. And now, the inside of his trailer.

James looked around, trying to find a spot that was clean enough to sit. He settled on the small folding stool tucked away in the corner. It was red and had a handle on it, meant for the elderly when they had nothing else to sit on in the shower.

After a while, he heard the sound of a vehicle pull up. He didn't bother looking outside. He figured Jason didn't have many visitors. The worst case would be that Jason didn't actually own the shitty land his trailer sat on and the landlord came by to try to collect however many months' rent Jason was behind. If that was the case, James could easily explain his way out of it without flashing his gun.

But when the key slid in the door and the handle turned, James knew he had nothing to worry about. Just as he'd expected, Jason never even noticed that his lock had been broken. The handle would have turned without the key. To be honest, James was more surprised that the door had been locked in the first place.

But he supposed that even a shitty place like this trailer Jason lived in could have something that could be stolen. In a place like Dupray, someone's trash was another's treasure.

It took Jason exactly seventeen seconds to notice that something was off. First, scratching his crotch, he whistled a tune that James didn't recognize. Then he tossed his keys on the counter. They slid toward the sink, knocking a glass and making a cracking noise. But it was when Jason went to grab his tin of Skoal that he finally noticed something was off.

Jason's eyes rose from the table where James had taken the tin, and locked his gaze with James's own. James was sitting in the corner, leaning over the handle of the stool. Jason didn't move. He just froze, his hand still on the table as if waiting for the tin to materialize at any moment.

"You think yourself as some kind of badass, don't you, Jason?" James asked, making his voice low and gravelly.

There was a long pause. "Y-you can't be in here," Jason managed to say. "How'd you get in?"

"You're a stain. On this world, on this town. And believe me, that's sayin' something," James said.

Another pause as Jason tried to make sense of things. "Did you follow me here?"

James smiled. "I was here before you, so think about it."

Jason rummaged through whatever little brain he had in his head. His eyes went back and forth, trying to make sense of the situation. "I ain't afraid of fighting you," he managed to say.

"Yes, you are," James said, looking him straight in the eye. And he was right. Jason could barely keep eye contact, and whenever he did, he quivered.

"Look, man, I won't bother her again. I swear it, alright? That's what this is about, right?" Jason said, and James was surprised that he went straight to it. That he didn't mouth off anymore, and went right to pleading. Perhaps Jason saw something in him that knew he was serious. That knew that the man in front of him was one who should not be fucked with.

"I know you won't," James said. "That's why I'm here."

Jason's eyes widened. "No, I mean it. Hell, I won't go near the diner. You don't have to do this."

James stood, shrugging when he was fully upright. "It's too late. I get paid, I do the work."

"Y-y-you got paid? To k-kill me?" Jason asked.

James let out a sigh. "I'll be honest, I ain't never accepted a slice of pie as payment before. But damn, if that wasn't the best pie I ever had. I'm really glad she pushed me into getting the á la mode."

"You can't. Please. I'll pay you more. Whatever you want. I got money—"

"You ain't got shit," James said firmly. "Besides, it's already been done. When you made the decisions you did at the diner, you set in motion something that brought us both to this very point." He pointed to the floor as he said it to add emphasis. "That waitress is good at her job. You gotta respect someone who works for their living and enjoys doing it. She'll be better off without you. She even says that little friend of yours will, too. So really, think of it as you doin' everyone a favor."

Jason's eye went all over the room, seemingly searching for a way out of it. James knew thinking wasn't his best suit.

"On your hip," James said.

"Huh?" Jason asked, his mouth open.

"It's the best I can do," James said, pointing to the revolver on Jason's hip. "I'll give you the chance. You draw that gun, pull the trigger before I do, and kill me. Well, then I guess I can't do nothin' about it, can I?"

"Y-you'll draw before me," Jason predicted, as if he could see the future.

"That's the idea, but I'll count it down still. After I say one, I'm gonna pull my gun, whether you try or not. Choice is yours."

Jason's breathing grew short and shallow. His forehead was beading with sweat, even though there was hardly a difference between the cold outside and the cold inside the trailer.

James set the tin of Skoal down. "Three. T—"

The gun went off, leaving a small ringing silence in the air. James sighed as he watched Jason tumble backward. His back slammed against the wall and he slid down until he was in a seated position on the floor. His head cocked to the side, eyes still open. A single hole went through his cheekbone and out the side of his head. It looked as if the bullet had curved inside his skull and exited at a left turn.

The asshole had his hand on the gun, half pulled from its holster. He tried to draw early.

"It's always the dickheads who can't face their mortality that jump the count. The same ones who like to push people around to make them feel big." James squatted down close to Jason's face and saw the blood trickle down his cheek like a morbid teardrop.

James flexed his hand, feeling his joints ache as he did.

"Fuck, was aiming between your eyes. This damn cold just ain't for me anymore, is it?"

He waited for a moment in the silence, never hearing an answer, then stood up.

"Damn, son. You took so long to answer when alive, I thought you still was."

CHAPTER NINETEEN

Madds was nearly frozen by the time she reached the house. She tried to wrap herself up on the long walk, but it was no use. Her jacket hardly had any use against Dupray's level of cold. She couldn't wait to get her big parka back on. Now, since she had the day off, she kicked herself for not picking it up from her motel room first.

She would have taken a taxi straight to the house, but after Elven had made it very clear that word travels fast in Dupray, she opted to be dropped off at the garage. Her car was there, still being worked on. But the walk between the garage and the Starcher house wasn't too long. Just long enough for her to regret the decision.

But at least she had the cover of saying she was checking in on her car. Besides, nobody would suspect her of being in with Hollis and his family. Also known as her family. Not that anyone knew it, and sometimes it didn't feel that way to her either. She was still an outsider, even if she shared some of their blood.

She reached the large house on its vast piece of land. She knew that Elven had always had it out for Hollis, and on the surface, she thought the things he said about Hollis were true. Hollis always presented himself as doing good for the people in Starcher Hollow and in Dupray. But really, he was a criminal. She knew this well.

But there was something else about him she couldn't figure out. Elven didn't just have a lawman's hatred for a criminal, but there was something deeper. Like a history she couldn't figure out. Maybe it was just due to years of being around it—around him. Maybe that's all it was, but something told her it wasn't.

What she did know, though, was that she was too damn tired to figure any of it out at that moment.

She let out a long sigh when she reached the back door of the house. She'd taken the extra precaution of walking around the large building so if any prying eyes were glued to the door, she wouldn't be seen just walking in as if she owned the place. She might just be paranoid, but the last thing she needed was Elven and the rest of the guys at the station to suspect her of anything else.

It was bad enough that they thought she was losing her mind.

The door was locked, but that was no problem for her. Hollis had given her a key after the last case she'd worked for him. That cover-up job had apparently earned her some respect and trust from him, not that she cared. Being in his good graces was one thing. She'd rather not be on his bad side after seeing what the man was capable of. But did she really want to be respected by him? For being disreputable?

Her mind was all over the place, worrying about Elven, Hollis, Kurt, and just about anything else that had the opportunity to poke at her and keep her from getting any rest.

She stepped inside the home, feeling the heat from the furnace, and couldn't wait to close the door behind her. As soon as she did, though, she did not expect to be met the way she was.

Immediately, a dog ran up to her, barking her head off. She bared her teeth, growling low, lowering her head down as if she was ready to pounce. Madds pushed her back against the door, surprised at the sudden noise. The dog was black and big. It looked like a pit bull, or something like it.

She didn't normally judge a dog by its breed, but when it was big, mean, and ready to attack, that's when she got worried.

Her hand wrapped around the handle of her gun from reflex, but she never had to pull the trigger. A whistle echoed in the house, making her ears ring from its high pitch. The dog immediately backed down, and started whimpering toward the direction the whistle came from.

"She's family. You better recognize that," Hollis warned the dog as he walked down the hall and into the main living room where Madds waited.

She stayed glued to the door as the dog walked away, tucking her tail between her legs as she did. Eventually, the dog lay next to a chair on the carpeted floor, resting her chin on her paws while staring at Hollis.

"You can come on in, she ain't gonna bite ya," he said.

"Nice dog," she said.

"Corbin's addition," Hollis said. "She's a mean ol' thing when she wants to be, but don't let that fool you. She's a sweetie underneath that bark."

Madds cautiously walked into the living room closer to Hollis, but kept her hand on her gun. The way her heart was pounding, his reassurance was the only thing keeping her from having a full-blown panic attack.

Hollis was carrying a Mason jar filled with tea. He sipped it gingerly as he looked her over. He wore a long-sleeved plaid shirt tucked into jeans. He held a cane, which was a bit off-brand for him. He was a big man, both physically and figuratively speaking as a figure in town. For him to carry a cane made him seem old and frail. Sometimes, she forgot that he was somewhere near sixty.

"Don't mind the cane," he said. "I mostly use it around the house in the winter. The cold gets to my knee much worse this time of year." He lifted his leg and stretched it, showing her he was still mobile.

There was a long pause as she thought about what to say. She didn't even know where to begin. With her mind in a fog and her worries coming to the surface, it was all too much. Her lip quivered just thinking about it.

"Maddie, what seems to be the problem?" he asked, putting his hand on her shoulder. The gesture didn't go unnoticed by her, and she realized she was truly grateful to have someone that seemed to care.

"I feel like I'm fucking losing it," she said, holding back tears. "Kurt is here. I know he is. I saw him. I fucking swear I saw him." Her voice was bordering on a whisper as if she was trying to convince herself and not Hollis.

"Kurt? Your ex?"

Madds nodded, but didn't say anything. She sniffled, keeping her emotions at bay as best she could.

"Tanya," Corbin called out from somewhere in the house. "Tanya, where you at?"

The dog's ears perked up at the sound of her owner. She turned her head toward the hallway, where Madds saw Corbin bumbling his way toward them. He was just as big as Hollis, but less gray and more agile. His overalls were clipped on one side while the other hung loose. He wore a goofy smile as he carried a doll in his hands.

"There you are, girl," Corbin said. "Look what I got you." He tossed the soft, fabric doll to the dog. She instantly scooped it up in her jaws, and began to chew on it.

"Corbin, you mind giving us a minute?" Hollis asked. "Your cousin is having a difficult day today and needs my assistance with something."

Corbin looked at Madds and laughed. "Don't blame her. She's probably all fucked up 'cause she's gotta follow Elven's tight ass around all day. I bet he clenches those cheeks so tight 'cause he wants to keep the stick up there."

Hollis turned and glared at his oldest son. "You got a delivery to get to, don't you?"

Corbin frowned. "It's gonna take me all night," he protested.

"Then you better get to it sooner than later," Hollis said, staying firm no matter what Corbin would say.

Corbin grumbled, but did as his father told him. "I'll be back, girl," he told Tanya. She didn't seem to notice and continued to play with her new chew toy.

Hollis turned his attention back to Madds, his face and smile back to its soft, nurturing ways. Normally, she would say he was good at manipulation and reading people, but right then, she was grateful for it. She wanted to be taken care of for the moment.

He placed both his hands on her arms and she felt stable for a brief moment. "You need to calm down, alright?"

She nodded and swallowed hard.

"How would Kurt know you're here?" Hollis asked.

She shook her head, and this time, tears fell from her eyes. "I-I don't know. But I know he's here."

"And you say you saw him?" he asked, wiping away a tear from her cheek.

"Yes. Maybe. I mean, I don't know," she admitted. "I keep seeing him, but he's never there. It sounds crazy. I think I'm losing my fucking mind."

Hollis pursed his lips, studying her. "You look beat. When's the last time you slept?"

She blinked, trying to remember. "Days? I don't know. A week maybe? It's on and off. Never anything substantial. I can't fucking sleep because he's out there, hunting me down."

Hollis put his smile on again, and this time, it told her he was there. That he cared. And that he was there to take care of things. That was something not even her own father had ever been able to do for her.

"You're gonna lay down in the guest bedroom, alright? Get some rest. Can you do that for me?"

She shook her head, exhausted. She wanted so badly to get some sleep, to let her mind rest, but she just didn't believe it was possible.

She couldn't stop thinking about Kurt and how she swore she had seen him.

"Maddie, if he's out there lookin' for you, ain't no way he can get to you in this house, you hear me? You saw what happened when Tanya there saw someone she didn't know. And believe me, if they ain't family, I ain't pullin' her off. Besides, I'll be here and so will your cousins. And that's *if* anyone would even think of finding you here," Hollis said, genuine compassion in his voice.

He made a lot of good points. But there was one she still worried about.

"What if Elven—"

"Elven won't be around here. And if he comes by, I'll lead him away. Your car ain't here, right? So no reason for him to think you are. You need to stop worrying and let me take care of it, alright? We will find this asshole and he will never bother you again," Hollis said. "That's part of the deal we made, wasn't it?"

She nodded. "I just never had this much stress on me before. It's all so much."

Hollis looked at her compassionately. "I put a lot on you, so that's on me. The last case was a bit much to handle and I shoulda seen that. But you did good and you kept this family safe. So now, I will keep you safe."

She let out a sigh of relief and wrapped her arms around Hollis. He held off for a moment, taken aback by her sudden embrace, but then he wrapped his arms around her. She felt safe in his arms, feeling like a baby being cradled by her father, being told everything would be alright. It had been so long since she'd had that true feeling of family.

CHAPTER TWENTY

There were a lot of questions Elven had about Madds, but at the same time, they didn't add up to much more than a hunch and some strange interactions. His real focus needed to be on the case at hand. He had three people dead, all killed by someone who knew exactly what they were doing. Madds's acting strange was anything but top priority for him right now.

It was a bit of a stretch, but if Elven's theory of Katherine being murdered because she'd walked in at the wrong time held water, then that meant the last connection between Todd and Donnie was the last job they shared.

The mines owned by his parents.

The main provider of work in Dupray had been Hallie Mining Company, but that had closed almost ten years ago. Dupray was never a mecca for wealth, but there was a stark difference in the town between when the mines were open and when they were closed.

Population had dwindled each year, while it seemed the county had slowly deteriorated. There was rarely anything new that was ever built, and even when it was, Elven hardly saw it occupied. The car lot that was being built by Jeff Hawkins and Mayor Meeks hadn't opened yet, but Elven had his suspicions that when it did, it wouldn't be long until it became just another ghost town. Not a lot of people had money to spend on new vehicles.

Those who stayed usually stayed out of habit. Sure, some businesses were owned and patronized, but they were hardly sustainable at the current levels. Elven knew the only thing that could change things was a big boost to their local economy in the form of a large workforce hiring. Digging ditches for water lines, selling a used car once a month, and liquor sales would hardly achieve that.

He also knew that his parents wouldn't be the ones to do that. Their opinion of the very people who'd helped build their empire was so low, it disgusted him to know he shared the same name with them. He didn't blame people who hated the Hallies, but he tried everything he could to separate their opinion of his parents from their opinion of him.

But sometimes, he had to make nice with his parents. After all, they were family. And on occasion, he needed their help for a case.

Which is exactly why he found himself on their property.

He wished he could just run up to the door like any other house he'd known, but that would have been too informal for his parents. Part of him didn't blame them. With the amount of money they had, and the hatred most of the town had for them, they needed their protection.

So instead, he rolled his Jeep up to the small booth in front of a gate that sat at the edge of the Hallie property. It was a small guard booth with just enough room for one person to sit, read, watch television, and pretty much waste eight hours at a time until the next person relieved them from duty.

It appeared that today, Edgar was on duty. Elven had known Edgar for about seven years. He'd been hired after the mines had closed, and he was from one of the neighboring counties whose name Elven couldn't recall. Edgar was in his sixties and was retired law enforcement. However, he didn't look like he was in his sixties as he still took care of himself, his shoulders giving Tank's a run for their money.

From what Elven could see, Edgar enjoyed the work. Or at least, the pay that came attached to the work. Edgar was nothing but friendly whenever Elven came around, which was a rare thing, but Elven had never seen the man without a smile on his face.

"Elven, what brings you by today?" Edgar asked, looking up from his tablet.

Elven couldn't help but mirror Edgar's infectious smile. The answer would normally be obvious, except that he was pretty sure Edgar knew the relationship between he and his parents was more than just tense.

"Oh, just popping in for a visit with the parents," Elven lied.

Edgar smirked, then narrowed his eyes. "I may be retired, but I still pick up on bullshit when I hear it. Besides, you're a terrible liar."

Elven chuckled. "Guilty as charged. I'm working a case and need to see if I can find some old employment files from the mines."

Edgar leaned in, his interest piqued. "Is it those murders I heard about?"

"Already heard about them? You don't even live in Dupray," Elven pointed out.

Edgar shrugged. "This old guy can still sniff out a case."

"Nothing concrete yet," Elven said.

"If you need some back-up, I'm your man," Edgar said. "Don't get me wrong—retirement is nice, and I'm making more money sitting in this box than I ever did from the city. But damn if I don't miss a little excitement from time to time."

"I'll keep that in mind if something comes up," Elven offered.

Edgar pushed a button, rolling the gate open for Elven to pass through. "Try not to stay too long," Edgar said. "I'd hate to see that attitude sour up on me."

Elven nodded and drove onto the property. The house was set back a ways from the main gate. He couldn't even see it from where he was on the road. The path wound up a long road that went uphill, somewhat like Elven's own home. Except this driveway made his look like a back alley.

The Hallies practically had their own private national park inside their gates. Once Elven drove into the trees, he felt as if he was in the middle of a forest. Of course, this forest had cameras at every turn, leaving no space unseen by the eyes of security at the house.

After a short drive through the trees, he exited out to an open area that looked up a hill. The house sat at the top of the hill, giving it a view of everything beneath it. From there, he knew he could see out for miles. It was a beautiful view, one that cost more than just the dollars to build it, but also the homes of the people who'd been in the way. He'd heard that his parents had purchased old family homes, just to tear them down so they wouldn't have to be seen by them.

His parents, Victoria and Alvin Hallie, would never accept the sight of poverty in their view. Elven was sure it took them a serious amount of cash to buy someone's property that had been passed down to generations, but then again, it was only a serious amount to the people that money had been given to. To the Hallies, it was no different than ordering take-out. A minor expense for their convenience.

Elven took the switchbacks up the hill toward the house. The switchbacks were steep in sections, but that was the price to pay for luxury. It was nothing his Jeep couldn't handle and he quickly made it to the top. Just as he would at the country club, he pulled into a parking spot off the side of the house, even though an attendant waited outside, ready to take over that task for him.

Elven knew how good he had it with his near mansion-like cabin in the woods. He tried not taking it for granted, though some days he probably did. But it was true that the Hallie property he stood in front of made his place look like a shack in the woods.

The house cast a large shadow over the land, dwarfing everything beneath it. He could count the floors going up—there were four of them. And while that was only one more floor than his own home had, he knew how far down inside the mountain the Hallie house went. He also knew that along with the protection, money, and elitism came paranoia. The basement was filled with various panic rooms. Some were made for safety from intruders, and some were made for lasting years after disaster.

He stepped toward the door, passing the female attendant who was dressed in a wrinkle-free pantsuit. He wasn't sure who she was, as she was most likely new to the job. But he was sure that the background check done on her had been extensive.

"Hello, Mr. Hallie," she said, friendly enough.

"Sheriff Hallie, but Elven's fine," he said.

"My apologies, Sheriff Hallie," she said. "I'm Annabelle. If you need anything, please feel free to ask. Mrs. Hallie is coming to see you."

He looked Annabelle over. She was in her late forties, and her style was much too proper for his taste. But that's what he was sure his mother demanded of all her help. "And my father?"

Annabelle's eyes betrayed her for a brief moment, her mouth following by twisting downward at the corners. "Mr. Hallie, well, he is home. He is aware you are here."

Elven smiled. "Don't sweat it. I know how he is."

She seemed relieved, though she didn't try to commiserate with him. He walked through the door, taking his hat off his head.

The inside of the house was even bigger than it looked from the outside. The main room was large and open, the ceiling vaulted as high as the roof. No separate floors were above them—that was for the rest of the home. As Victoria had always told Elven, first impressions were the most important. And the first impression that was left when entering the home was nothing less than spectacular, if not pretentious.

As large and grandiose as the house was, it was just that. A house. He would never describe that house as homey, being that there was hardly any love in the structure. It was nothing but cold decor and money wherever one looked. Growing up in that house, he could count on one hand the times he had felt comfortable in it. It had left the belief in him that there was more to life than just accumulating money.

Further back, he knew the house twisted into various wings that any stranger to the house would easily get lost in. But he didn't intend on venturing further inside. He wanted to make this visit as short and to the point as possible.

"Elven, my dear boy, this is a lovely surprise," he heard the familiar voice of his mother echo from somewhere in the house.

He spun around, trying to see the direction she was coming from. His eyes finally settled on the third hallway to his left. His mother's heels clicked against the marble floors. It was just like her to not be comfortable in her own home either. Appearances were everything to her.

She was still a lovely woman on the outside. She worked out with a personal trainer every day to keep fit and spent a lot of time at the indoor pool they had in the east wing of the house. On top of that, the money spent on various skin creams and the occasional touch-up surgery had more than served their purpose. She could pass for his older sister.

"Hi, Mom, I was hoping—"

"Don't tell me this visit is about work," she said with a frown.

"Afraid so."

She sighed. "I should have known. All work with you, isn't it? Just like your father."

He clenched his jaw, hating when his mother told him that. There might be similarities shared between him and his father, just as with anyone else who valued their job, but beyond that, he was nothing like the man.

"That dreadful job of yours," she went on. "I just—"

"Can we not do this?" Elven asked. "It's going to be a long drive back to Dupray and I'd like it if we could have a pleasant—and brief —visit."

She smiled coldly. "Fair enough," she said. "What can I help you with?"

HUNTED IN THE HOLLER

"I need to look into some people who used to work at the mines for you. Donnie Price and Todd Utt?"

Victoria frowned, not a single wrinkle forming on her Botox-injected face. "Unless they were on the corporate team, I'm afraid I wouldn't know who they are."

Elven nodded, figuring as much. "I was hoping you would still have files from then. Any sort of disciplinary measures that HR had to deal with maybe?"

"Disciplinary measures?" his father's familiar voice echoed from the fifth hallway coming from his right. Elven turned to see the old man making his way toward them. He seemed thinner than Elven had last remembered, but still had a permanent scowl on his face.

"Alvin, dear. I didn't think you'd be coming," Victoria said.

"Avoid seeing my son in my own home? What kind of a man do you think I am?" he asked.

Elven had a few answers to that, but he kept them to himself.

"So what's this I hear about you wanting some files on the mining employees?"

"Sounds like you're up to speed," Elven said.

"If anything happened on management's watch and it was reported to us, we would have immediately fired whoever it was who'd caused problems. Can't have those hillbillies running things into the ground. You let them get away with something, they'll take advantage—like that," Alvin said, snapping his fingers. "Useful tools they are sometimes, but a means to an end. Awful people I do not miss dealing with."

"You never had to *deal* with them," Elven said, sharply. His mother could admit the truth at least. But his father acted as if he'd been at the mines daily, speaking to the very people who had made him his money. And acting like they were so far beneath him? Elven tried to hold his tongue, but he couldn't.

"Why are you even still here?" Elven asked. "Both of you? If you hate the people in this county so much, why live in it? Go to New York or LA. Maybe somewhere overseas, where more people like yourselves would be. That way you wouldn't have to be around such *awful* people."

Victoria grumbled, but didn't respond. "Then I wouldn't see my favorite son," she said. Elven was an only child, so she was trying to be cute with her wording. But he figured if they did have another son that leaned more toward their values, Elven truly wouldn't be the favorite. "Maybe if you decided to come with us to one of those places, we would consider it."

She spoke as if it was a real option to be put on the table. "Why don't you?" she pressed.

"Because these people—the ones that you think are so beneath you—they are my people."

Alvin shook his head, still scowling. Victoria looked as if she was about to have a heart attack from hearing such derogatory things.

"Look, it's late," Elven said. "Just point me in the direction of the files and I'll fish them out myself."

Victoria relented. "Annabelle will take you to the storage room where we keep them."

"Thank you," Elven said, turning toward Annabelle.

"And Elven," Victoria said. He looked over his shoulder at his mother. She had a genuine smile on her face that he could have sworn creased her skin at the edge of her cheek. "It is good to see you."

CHAPTER TWENTY-ONE

Penny walked through the living room of her home. She was looking for her daddy to see what he wanted for dinner. She knew he was probably craving macaroni and cheese, a favorite of his, since it had been about a week since she'd made it last. And if she was going to do that, she'd need to go to the store and pick up more milk.

She took care of most of the meals for her and her family. Her mother had used to take care of that chore, but had taught her everything she knew about cooking before her untimely passing. Nobody had asked Penny to take over the role, but she just fell into it naturally. Her mother had been the glue of the family, and she' tried to hang onto those things her mother did that had kept them all together.

Hollis was a strong leader for her and her brothers, but if it was up to him, they'd be eating Hungry Man dinners every night in front of the television. Eventually, Penny knew the family would start to fall apart, no matter how much he tried. For someone who had a way with words, and manipulating them to get what he wanted, he didn't seem to grasp what was the real communication and love between them all that kept the family together.

"Daddy?" she called out toward the hallway.

There was no answer. Tanya, Corbin's new dog, came trotting into the room. Penny squatted down and pet her, rubbing her cheeks. "You know where he is?"

Tanya didn't respond, only kept licking Penny's hands. Penny smiled, liking that there was a dog in the house, even if Corbin did try to make her meaner than Penny knew she truly was. She'd make sure to give Tanya lots of attention and love so she didn't pick up too many of Corbin's traits.

Penny stood and headed down the hallway toward her father's room. The hall was narrow from being built a handful of generations before. Over time, the family had expanded with new additions to the home, but the original pieces were all still there, making a drastic impact when walking through the house. Hollis had always said they needed to hold on to the past and remember what their family had been through so they could pave the way for the future.

She passed by the bathroom, and then the guest room that opened on the left. The door was closed, which was odd. But perhaps it was closed to keep Tanya out, though her father loved dogs and, growing up, if her mother had ever locked her childhood dog Bruno out of the house, Hollis would holler at her and let the poor guy back inside.

She opened the door and poked her head inside. "Daddy?" she asked.

Hollis wasn't inside. Instead, she was surprised to see her cousin in bed. But what surprised her even more was the gun that she saw pointed at her face.

Madds's eyes were bloodshot and she looked panicked. Penny stood, eyes wide, her legs frozen. Madds blinked twice, then let out an exhale, dropping the gun.

"I'm sorry, I—I thought you were someone else," Madds said, breathing heavy.

Penny relaxed. "You okay?"

Madds nodded, but to Penny, she didn't look okay. "Hollis said I could rest here."

Penny stepped inside, closing the door behind her. She saw Madds's clothes on the floor, her tan uniform shirt and a pair of black pants. Her holster sat on the nightstand, where Madds shoved her gun back inside. She wore a white undershirt, but her legs were covered by the bed's blanket.

"Sorry I bothered you," Penny said.

"It's alright, you didn't know. It's been a rough few days, I guess," Madds said.

"You know, we haven't talked much since you came to town. I can't believe it's already been a few months," Penny said. "It's been a long time since there's been another woman around."

Madds smiled. "Not sure if you mean that as a good thing. Not trying to step on your territory or anything."

Penny shook her head. "It's a good thing. Ever since momma passed, it's just been me and four boys. And I do mean *boys*. My brothers are grown-ass men and you'd think they could take care of themselves, but if it weren't for me, they'd never have clean drawers or eat another vegetable in their life."

Madds laughed. "I can see that from Corbin, but Lyman and Wade, too?"

Penny sat on the bed next to Madds. "Oh, God, they're the worst. Corbin might be a bit dim, but you put food in front of him and he'll eat it till their ain't nothin' left. Lyman and Wade like to have opinions on things, like criticizing how much seasoning is on their food. Wade can't have his green beans touching his creamed corn or he'll throw a fit. Lyman comes up with some random ideas that he ain't gonna eat anything green one month, then the next month it'll be orange. Like he's on some fast he read off some hippie internet blog."

Madds laughed. "Who would have known?"

"How momma ever put up with it all is amazing. That woman was a saint, I tell you."

"I wish I could have known her," Madds said. "I remember

coming out for the funeral. I was so little, but I remember seeing you and thinking you were so cool. I got stuck with a brother, but wished I had a sister."

Penny smiled. "I remember you, too. You were that little girl following me around when I was an attitude-filled teenager. I was so mean to you because I was irritated by my new little shadow."

"I never noticed you being mean. I was just happy to be around you."

"Well, I'm sorry still. And you know, I always wanted a sister, too. So you being here is a nice change," Penny offered.

Madds smiled. "It's been a long time since I've had family around. I wish we could have been closer growing up. I wish we could be closer now."

Penny took a deep breath and let it out slowly. She felt the same way about Madds, but she also felt something else about her being there. She paused for a moment, then just said it.

"What you're doing to Elven ain't right," she said.

Madds obviously wasn't expecting to hear that. Her smile slid off her face. "It's your dad's idea. I'm just going along with it. You say it's not right, but you don't feel the need to tell him. How are you one to judge me?"

"I don't cross Daddy, but he also knows better than to ask of me anything like that. I stay out of his business. Daddy respects that. Haven't you noticed that me and Lyman are still in his good graces, but we don't get involved? And how we're still friends with Elven?" Penny asked. "You could do the same if you wanted."

"Not for what I need from Hollis, I can't."

"And what is that? To be in hiding? To have protection? Cause I still ain't figured it out and you don't seem very forthcoming with that information." Penny grilled. "Look, you're still family. Above anything else, whether it be spying on Elven or needing protection, Daddy stands for family. No matter what you decide."

"You say that as if it is true. I might be family, but I'm not his daughter or son. I'm not even the favorite niece that was always around. I'm damn near a stranger. And I don't have some secret history with Elven for Hollis to respect." Madds's tone was turning from defensive to angry. "What's up with that anyway? Why do you care enough to stick your nose in my business? What, were you high school sweethearts or something? 'Cause it sure as hell seems to me that maybe you're jealous of how close I'm getting to Elven."

Penny glared at her. She may have started with the questions, but Madds was making it personal. "It's different with us. Something you wouldn't understand."

"Well, since you're keeping your nose out of your daddy's business, maybe you can start doing the same with mine. 'Cause right now, his business is my business," Madds shot.

Penny stood up and stormed toward the door. She turned back at Madds before leaving. "I did say I wanted a sister before. I just didn't realize she could be a catty bitch." She slammed the door, leaving Madds alone in the room.

CHAPTER TWENTY-TWO

Elven sat on the floor, surrounded by boxes of files. He had various papers piled around him in no specific order. When he went through one stack, he'd place it to a different spot, then start on the next. The sun had dropped some time ago, and now, he worked under a single floor lamp that managed to illuminate nearly the entire room.

He'd found a section of boxes of employee records. Then he'd found a good five-year time period when he was sure that Todd and Donnie had worked at the mines. As much as his mother had pestered him to stay for dinner and continue working at their home, he refused, instead loading the boxes in his Jeep and taking them home.

Annabelle had helped him load the vehicle, but when he arrived home, unloading them was all on him. He didn't mind, as physical labor had a way of making him feel accomplished. Like he was getting real work done and narrowing in on whatever he was looking for in the case.

Yeti, his white Great Pyrenees companion, approached as he worked diligently on the floor. He wandered into the room, sniffing at a few of the stacks next to Elven before lying next to his master, resting his head in Elven's lap.

"You alright, Yeti?" he asked.

Yeti just cocked his head, glancing up at his master. Elven smiled and scratched at Yeti's ears, which sent the dog rolling onto his side, enjoying the attention.

Elven sifted through another folder and finally came across some names he recognized. It was a carbon copy of disciplinary action issued by someone in the HR department. They had signed it, along with Donnie Price, Todd Utt, and two other men. Printed next to the signatures were the names Michael Amos and Jerry Farnham.

There were two papers, which said there were incidents of miscommunication and workplace tension without going into specifics. Elven couldn't help but laugh.

"Workplace tension? Miscommunication?" he asked, Yeti whimpering in response. "Nice corporate-speak. What does that even mean?"

Underneath the papers was another page that had one signature. This time, it was only Michael Amos who'd signed. It was a pink slip. Notice of termination due to workplace harassment. On the slip, it mentioned a physical altercation between Michael Amos and Jerry Farnham.

There was a second pink slip issued the next day, but this time, there was no signature. Jerry Farnham had been terminated for not showing up, and not notifying anyone of his absence.

After that, Elven could find no other papers for Donnie Price or Todd Utt, but as far as it looked, neither one of them had been terminated. At least, not in the same time frame.

He would have to check in on Michael Amos and Jerry Farnham. He had their last known addresses from when they'd worked at the mines on the paperwork, which, of course, was at least ten years old. But in Dupray, if they'd stayed, there wasn't a whole lot of moving within the county.

He yawned, petting his furry friend, who was now nearly asleep in his lap. Given the amount of time he'd spent in the room and the windows being pitch-black outside, he knew it was pretty late. Checking on the addresses would have to wait until the morning. He needed to get some rest if he wanted to see whether he was worth anything in the morning.

CHAPTER TWENTY-THREE

Penny rolled over, waking from what felt like a deep sleep. It was dark out, and she could hear nothing more than the usual nighttime sounds of the house. The refrigerator hummed from the depths of the kitchen, and there was the constant flowing white noise in the background that she knew was the river. On quiet nights, the sound carried up from below the hill where their house sat.

She swallowed, and felt the dryness in her throat. She reached for the bottle on her nightstand and opened it, feeling a quick splash against her tongue. But there was nothing more now. The bottle was empty.

She cursed herself for not filling it before lying down. But she'd been preoccupied, thinking about Madds sleeping in the room down the hall from her own. It really didn't bother her that her cousin was sleeping in the house, but after their argument, she wasn't sure how she felt about the woman.

She put her bare feet on the wood floor, feeling the furnace blowing heat directly onto her feet. She always had the vent angled slightly to the left so the floor would be warm when she stepped out of bed. The clock across the room beamed its red lights, showing 3:24 AM.

She sighed and made her way out of her room. She wore pajama pants that sagged from her hips as the drawstring was so old, it would no longer tighten around her thin waist. The cuffs of the pants dragged along the floor, sweeping at the hair and dander left by Tanya.

The hallway was just as warm as her bedroom—one of the benefits of it being a narrow space. But when she stepped into the living room, the temperature dropped noticeably. It wasn't enough to warrant her putting any more clothes on, but she did shiver slightly, wrapping her arms around herself and rubbing the fabric of her pajama top.

Her feet felt the shag of the rug, and she held out her hand so she didn't bump into her father's recliner, which he kept next to the back door. It was his favorite spot, but she felt it didn't fit well in the position. Of course, there was no talking him out of it. So after many nights of doing the same walk through the dark, only to bump right into it, she'd learned to keep a hand out to keep from doing it again.

The kitchen was just ahead, the breakfast bar low enough to let her look straight in. But something stopped her. Out of the corner of her eye, she could see movement in the other recliner. The one that didn't stick out like a sore thumb. It rocked forward and backward, ever so gently.

She moved her eyes in her head, not daring to turn her neck. And that's when she saw a man sitting in the chair. He held a raised gun, pointed directly at her.

"Wh-who are you?" she asked, her voice barely a whisper.

He smiled, the hand not on his gun reaching down. Tanya, the dog that was supposed to be so mean toward intruders did nothing but lap up the stranger's attention. He pet the top of her head, then scratched behind her ears as if he was her master.

"An old friend," he said, his voice low, but not quite a whisper.

"What are you doing here?" she asked, still frozen in place. Her heart raced.

He watched her for a moment. She could feel his eyes crawling all over her body, as if searching her for something. "I've got work in town."

"What kind of work?"

"The killing kind."

She swallowed, feeling her throat close up, dryer than ever. "I can scream," she said. "M-my daddy and brothers will be out here."

That didn't seem to bother him. Instead, he just smiled.

"There's a sheriff's deputy in the other room. All's I gotta do is yelp and she'll be out here," she said, remembering the gun she had been met with when she'd entered Madds's room.

"Oh, I know all about who is in this house, deputy and all," he said. "Such an interesting dynamic here, that's for sure. But girlie, you scream, and it won't end well for any of them, you hear? Now, I don't wanna shoot anyone. I prefer to shoot just those on my list. And right now, there's only one more name on it."

His list? Penny's heart beat so fast she it felt like one long pump. "Am—am I on it?"

He stood up and walked toward her. Tanya did nothing but watch as he did. Penny could feel his presence getting closer and closer. Like the air between them was compressing, bringing nothing but tension and pressure between them.

"You ain't on it," he finally said.

"Is anyone else that's here?"

He shook his head once. "Not yet anyway. But things can change fast, I suppose."

"What do you want?"

He was behind her now. So close, she could smell his aftershave and the scent of burnt leather. He exhaled, and she felt the air from his nose blow against the back of her neck. "Wanted to see how the family life was. Just to stop in, check on an old friend, I guess."

"Did you? Wh-who is it?"

"Someone from another life. Like I said, things change fast. Time moves on, even after the dead. But I find that ghosts tend to linger."

Penny shook as he brushed past her. She looked and saw him move toward the back door, not turning to face her.

"Have a good night, Penny," he said, then stopped and lifted his hand. "Oh, I'm gonna borrow this." He scooped the key off the end table and jingled it in the air. Tanya lifted her head at the noise, watching him.

He left the house, letting the door ease shut. And then he was gone. As if the interaction had never happened. Penny shook and took three steps into the kitchen before she collapsed, her back against the cabinets.

Tanya followed her into the kitchen, her claws clicking against the tile. She looked at Penny curiously and lay her head on Penny's lap. Penny tried to calm herself, but it was no use. Instead, she sobbed to herself while holding onto the dog.

CHAPTER TWENTY-FOUR

Elven sat at his desk, fidgeting around. He had the files on top of his desk that contained the information for Jerry Farnham and Michael Amos. He had planned on visiting them early that morning, but he was waiting for Madds.

He glanced at the clock, seeing it was already nine-thirty in the morning.

Madds was late. Not only was she late, but she was *very* late. It wasn't like her, at least, from what he knew of her.

He was beginning to think that maybe he didn't know all that much.

Going through the events of the day yesterday, he had sent her home to get cleaned up, checked out, and get some much needed rest. Perhaps she was still sleeping, which he could let it slide.

He picked up his phone and called her. The phone rang once before going straight to voicemail, which was a standard unpersonalized message from the carrier. Apparently, she had never set a message up herself.

He stood up and walked around the desk, hesitating to open the door. He looked around, surrounded by most of Lester's things. He hadn't redecorated all that much, still not feeling it was completely his office yet. But he also liked to hang onto his old mentor's memory. Like Lester was still there to offer a helping hand and guide him.

He could think of a talk he'd had in that very office with the man. One that had been a turning point for him, getting him to think long and hard about if he truly wanted to be a deputy. He was grateful for that moment, and always thought he could do the same for someone else down the line.

He finally pulled the door open and leaned into the hallway.

"Hey, Tank, you busy?" he called out.

Tank made his way out of his office, his shoulders just barely clearing the frame. "What's up, Elven?"

"Madds isn't answering. After last night, I'm a little worried. And after what Johnny had seen and with her acting that way, what do you think? You notice anything off with her lately?"

Tank shuffled his feet, his eyes averting anywhere but Elven's own. "I, uh—"

"Tank, what is it?" Elven asked, feeling there was something his deputy wanted to say.

Tank sighed. "I wasn't gonna say anything, but you're asking. I saw her pull a gun on someone."

Elven nodded. "I know, Johnny told me. She got hit in the face—"

"No, Elven. This was before. I saw her do it at the shoot-off competition," Tank said apologetically.

"What? Why didn't you say anything?"

"Because I didn't want her to get in trouble. I figured it was just a miscommunication or something. I didn't think that she was gonna do it again."

"And what was the reason? Did the guy hit her, go after someone? What?"

Tank shook his head. "I have no idea. She just kept asking about Kurt. The guy had no idea what she was talkin' about, and Madds said it wasn't him. That she saw it wrong or something. I'm sorry, Elven."

Elven was angry, but he had to remember that Tank was just doing his co-worker a favor. He'd been on the receiving end of those favors a few times as a deputy himself, when he'd done something stupid and worried that Lester would find out about it. Nothing serious, but Tank was always there for him.

"Like I said, I didn't want to say anything. She asked me not to, but after hearing she was gonna blow someone else's head off yesterday, well, I was wrong to keep it from you," Tank said. "I don't know what's goin' on, but it seems odd."

Elven clapped Tank on the shoulder. "You're a good man, Tank. Don't worry, though. We'll get to the bottom of it."

That was a promise Elven intended to keep, as soon as he could get a hold of Madds.

CHAPTER TWENTY-FIVE

The sun shone on her face. The birds chirped right outside her window. Her body ached as if it had been through a full week of torture. Her muscles felt sore all over and her neck had a crick in it.

But more than anything, she actually felt rested.

She rolled over in the bed, the yellow sheets crumpled at her feet. The comforter, however, was piled and folded over herself. She sprawled out, letting out a long yawn, relishing in the moment.

Eventually, her body started to unlock, stretch, and release all the tension. She must have been in such a deep sleep that she'd ended up in a very uncomfortable position. It didn't matter to her, though. For the first time in days, she felt like she could think clearly.

Madds sat up with a smile, glancing out the window. The blinds were open and she could see the grass field that led down a slope to the river. It was a beautiful view with a few trees, which she would later learn were called a Tree of Heaven. She let out a nice, steady exhale, ready to begin her day.

And that's when she remembered where she was.

The view from the motel had no view like the one she had now.

HUNTED IN THE HOLLER

She remembered the feeling of Hollis's fatherly tone, settling her nerves. And then, his offer to stay in the house, and of course, her agreement to it.

Immediately, her restful state, her ease of attitude, her focus changed to panic. Her first thought was that someone would have seen her at the Starcher property, entering and not leaving until the morning.

What if Elven had seen?

But that was ridiculous, right? How would Elven have seen her go there? The last she saw, he was in Dupray proper, and Starcher Hollow was a bit of a drive. He couldn't be everywhere in the county at the same time. Dupray County was a pretty big stretch, after all.

No, he wouldn't have seen her. And to be honest, she doubted anyone at all would have seen her. She'd covered her tracks by walking, and it wasn't like anyone had been staking the place out.

If they were, she'd have known about it. Her not being kept in the loop on something like that meant she had a lot bigger problems than just being seen with Hollis.

She took a deep breath, calming herself down. There was no reason to panic.

At least, that's what she told herself.

Her thoughts on that flipped as soon as she saw the clock. 9:35 a.m..

"Oh, shit!"

She quickly stood, not caring about the sudden change in temperature from leaving the covers. The last thing she needed to worry about was being cold when she was over two hours late to work. She pulled her shirt on, buttoning it quickly, then picked up her pants from the floor and jumped into them, cramming the end of her shirt into the waistband before buttoning the fly.

She shoved her holster onto her belt and stepped into her shoes before running out the door.

She didn't have time to look for Hollis and check in. To tell him how much she appreciated being looked after and how she'd been able to get some much needed sleep. No, now her mind was on what she was going to tell Elven. It should be easy enough—he had known she was sleep-deprived, so oversleeping wouldn't be that bad.

But she still didn't want to give him any more reason to dig into her business.

She ran past Tanya, who gave her nothing more than a glance. The dog looked tired, as if she'd been up all night. But Madds didn't bother to take a closer look.

She ran out the door, never noticing Penny still on the floor of the kitchen, wide-awake and shaking.

Elven was gearing up to leave the station. Part of him wanted to head straight to Jerry Farnham's place and let Madds figure out she wasn't needed on the job if she didn't want to be there. But really, that was just him being stubborn.

Everyone was allowed to have bad days and mess up from time to time. Heaven knows how many times Johnny had screwed the pooch on a case, only to be welcomed back at the job as if nothing had happened. Of course, he was scolded or instructed as was seen fit, but at the department, there seemed to be no limits on how much a person could get away with.

So why was he being so hard on Madds?

His gut feeling was mostly why. That he didn't know something, and she was keeping whatever it was from him. And maybe there was a little bit of something else. That he'd grown close to her, and her keeping whatever it was to herself was tantamount to telling him he wasn't important.

Important enough to tell him? Or that he wasn't important enough to her?

Either way, it was stupid. He was being stupid. Wasn't he?

And what if it wasn't her dropping the ball by being late? What if she'd had an accident, or something else had happened to her? He owed it to her to check on her, to make sure she was okay before jumping to any conclusions about her intentionally keeping things from him.

He grabbed his Stetson from the edge of his desk and carried it with him on his way out the door. And just as he set foot in the hallway, he heard the front door to the station open. It sounded like an elephant stampede rushed into the station.

"I'm sorry I'm late," Madds said, out of breath.

"Darlin' where've you been? Elven ain't too happy," Meredith said from the front desk. "You better go talk to him now."

Part of Elven was relieved. He didn't want anything to happen to Madds. She was his friend, and an important part of the station. To be honest, he was glad she'd walked in the doors back when the Sophia Hawkins case had started those months ago. He could hardly remember having to split the workload between just he, Tank, and Johnny.

But now, he was even more concerned. With Madds fine, that meant she had screwed up. It was time to find out what was going on with her, and then he could figure out how to handle it. He was prepared to give one of his classic speeches about the job, work ethic, and how others were counting on her. He'd given that to Johnny a few times, and if he thought back far enough, could remember a handful of those same things being told to a younger version of himself by Lester.

Madds entered the hallway, looking a mess of herself. Her shirt hadn't been buttoned all they way to the top and looked as if she'd pulled it from the dirty hamper. Her hair could use a few strokes of a brush and her make-up, no matter how little she wore, still seemed smudged and worn.

Even with the messy look, he did have to admit that she looked a lot better than when he'd seen her yesterday. Her nose had a nasty bruise at the bridge that spread onto her cheekbones. But underneath her eyes were far less dark. She was no longer toting around a pair of out-of-town bags there.

"Elven," she said, still out of breath.

"My office," he said, his tone stern.

She walked behind him, her head hung low, looking as though making the walk of shame out of a college dormitory the morning after a wild party. He held the door open for her as she walked by him. She smelled differently than usual, and there was something about her scent that was so familiar to him. He just couldn't place it. Whatever it was, it made him think of his younger days. Old memories of better times.

She sat in the chair in front of his desk. Elven took a quick look down the hall, seeing Johnny and Tank in the doorways to their offices, watching the scene unfold. As soon as they saw Elven, they both acted as if they'd been examining something in their hands. Elven rolled his eyes and closed the office door behind him.

"Alright," he said as he made his way to his desk. Instead of sitting in his chair, he leaned against the corner in front of her. "What's going on?"

"I'm sorry, Elven. I overslept," she said.

He nodded. "Is that it?"

"What else would it be?"

He shrugged. "You've been off."

"I'm fine, Elven, I swear. I haven't been sleeping well, but I slept last night and now I'm clear-headed. Ready to do the job."

"Why haven't you been sleeping well? Is it because of the last case? I may have overlooked it, thinking you'd be fine. But it was stressful. You had to fight for your life, and in the end, you ended up saving mine. I'm sure your religious history and being at the church when it happened had to do something to your head, right?"

"No. I mean, a little yeah. But it's not that. I just—"

"I called your old supervisor," he said, deciding to just lay it all out. The guilt of his own gut feeling had been eating at him. She wasn't the only one with a conscience, and maybe it was just best to get it all out there.

"You what?" she asked, surprised.

"It's clear you haven't been yourself. You have to see that. Not sleeping, then the incident yesterday."

"He hit me with a fucking pipe in the face!"

"And you're supposed to use necessary force. If Johnny hadn't come along, you might be in a cell for blowing some guy's head off who'd been running away from you," he said. He paused a moment, thinking about his next words. "Tank told me what happened at the competition."

Her eyes went wide, her mouth agape.

"Don't be mad at Tank, alright? I grilled him to see if he noticed anything wrong with you. He felt it was something he needed to share, especially after what happened yesterday. From what he said, nobody attacked you that day and you still took it too far with them," Elven said. "We're worried about you."

Madds clenched her jaw, trying to come up with something. "How'd you get ahold of him?" she finally asked.

Elven cocked his head, unsure what she meant.

"My supervisor. I assume you mean Sergeant Garcia, right? Did you call his personal line?"

He shook his head. "I phoned up the department."

Madds's breathing became shallow. She swallowed hard.

"Madds, why does that matter? What is going on?" Elven asked once again, sick of feeling he was being kept in the dark. "Who is this Kurt you keep asking about? Both Tank and Johnny told me you kept saying that name."

Madds shook her head.

"Madds, you need to talk right now. If you want to have any chance of staying in this department and me helping you, you have to give me something."

She sighed, the tension releasing from her shoulders and she held up her hands. "Kurt is my ex-husband. Or current husband, I guess."

"You're married?" he asked, stunned.

"Separated. Apparently not far enough, though. Tried filing for divorce, but..." she waved her hand, letting the sentence trail off. "That's not even the important part."

"Alright, then what is?" Elven asked, still reeling from the surprising news.

"He's why I came out here. Why I left Arizona. He was a cop, or, still is, I think. We had a tepid relationship, really. I mean, don't get me wrong—at first, it was great. But then as time went on, he became distant. Meaner, too. I figured he was cheating on me. Hell, he may have been, for all I know, but that wasn't what I found out."

Elven folded his hands in front of him, listening.

"I found out he was in on some things less than legal. Some of them minor, but some, well, nothing that a cop should be doing, that's for sure."

"Like what?"

"Skimming on the side. Letting dealers slide on his watch. That kind of thing. I didn't know what to do with that information at first, sort of. I just told myself I was wrong. I was in total disbelief, really. I mean, I couldn't be married to some sort of drug-dealer landlord, right?"

She laughed, as if still finding it ridiculous to say.

"But it was a lot worse than that. When I found a big wad of cash, I got suspicious. So when I followed him and saw his little side hustle, I decided to take it further. Kept tailing him. He was in way deeper than just letting some assholes deal on his watch for some extra cash. I overheard the conversation he had with someone, the men he met with. He was the goddamned entry point."

"The entry point for the drug supply?"

Madds nodded, eye brows lifted. "For the area at least. He was working directly with the cartel straight over the border."

Elven narrowed his eyes. They had drug problems aplenty in Dupray, and the cartel wasn't unheard of pretty much anywhere you went. But he didn't have much of an issue with them in Dupray, as far as he knew. Most of the time, he had to deal with some meth labs and overenthusiastic Oxy prescribers.

"Did you tell anyone? Your superiors?"

"Of course I did. But I had no proof. And when I brought it up, I was met with a lot of hostility and questions. Kurt's reach had tainted some key points in the department. I mean, don't get me wrong, not everyone there was in on it. But one or two people was all it took. And who could tell who was or wasn't part of it? When I tried talking about it, my complaints fell on deaf ears, at best. At worse, well, word got back to him. My word against his, and he'd been well-liked for ten years before I came around."

Elven felt himself get heated. She had kept a huge secret from him, and now it was causing a lot of problems. "That's why you wanted to come to small-town Dupray? So nobody would think to look for you here? I'm sure we're too far behind the times for some city girl like yourself to be searched for. Just some hillbilly town for you to get lost in, right?"

She shrugged. "At first, I thought that way, I guess. But Elven, I like the job. I like Dupray. I never had a boss like you before. I didn't think—"

"That's right," Elven said. "You didn't think. I asked you point-blank when you took the job. But when you didn't want to share, I said that whatever those reasons are better not come back to bite us in the backside, you remember that?"

Madds nodded. "But Elven—"

"And now, I've got some ex-husband coming for the woman who witnessed something he didn't like. And he's in bed with the cartel? Wow, Madds. That really doesn't seem like you're keeping up your end of the bargain. This is going above and beyond biting us in the backside. For all I know, I could have some of the cartel in my backyard because they're lookin' for you."

"Maybe if you didn't go snooping around and call my old department, we wouldn't be here right now. You think anyone would have found me if you hadn't tipped them off with a fucking phone call?" she fired back.

He stared her down, thinking he was going to grind his teeth down to nothing if he kept clenching his jaw. "Gun and badge," Elven growled, not waiting for any more excuses.

She looked at him, her face falling. "What?"

"I wouldn't have had to go snooping if you'd have been upfront with me."

"As if you would have hired me in the first place," Madds said. "Tell me I haven't done a good job for you. Tell me I haven't done everything you asked. You said it yourself—I saved your life before."

"Things have changed," he said. "Now I've got to worry about you, your past coming for you, and all the while, I've got some professional killing people in my county. For all I know, you brought that down on us."

"Oh, fuck you, Elven," she spat, standing. She threw her gun and badge on his desk. "Here, take it. Now I have no authority, and no protection if anyone is coming for me. You happy?"

"Madds, you're paranoid. You've stuck your gun in two men's faces you thought were your ex, and they weren't. Next time, someone may not be there to stop you from pulling the trigger, and I cannot have that on my conscience."

She laughed in disbelief. "So much for opening up. Telling the truth so you could help me. Right? Guess I was right not to say anything. I'm on my own."

She left the office before Elven could get another word in.

CHAPTER TWENTY-SIX

"Holy shit, it looks like a tornado swept through here," Lyman said with a yawn.

He stepped into the hallway, stretching his arms in the air. He'd decided to get some rest that day, not that he really had much to do in the first place. His father didn't ask much of him on most days, knowing his relationship with Elven. But from time to time, there was something he needed to do for the man. Just nothing that would be too far on the wrong side of the law.

Corbin took care of that, which is why he still hadn't returned to the house. "Deliveries" is what Hollis called them. And sure, that was probably the case. But what exactly was being delivered, Lyman didn't know. If it was anything more than moonshine, he didn't want to know.

He made his way past the guest room, where the door was open. He peeked inside, seeing that Madds was long gone. And on top of that, she'd left the room a right mess. The comforter had been thrown to the floor, the sheets were still tangled on the mattress. Even the chair by the door had been knocked over. His cousin had apparently been in quite the hurry to leave.

He sighed, knowing the secret he had to keep from Elven. He didn't like to think about keeping that kind of information from his best friend, but it was all part of the tangled web of lies and deceit he had to be in because of who he was. A Starcher. His family had to come first. Elven, no matter how good of a friend he was, had to come second.

But there were still lines he wouldn't cross that Hollis knew. As long as Hollis respected those, he kept the secrets.

Lyman made his way through the living room, stepping around the stupid chair his father liked to sit in. Its placement was such a nuisance, but it was Hollis's house, so it was his rules. As if that mattered—even if it hadn't been his house, Hollis would find a way to still make it his rules.

Tanya lay on the tile floor of the kitchen, her backend sticking out from behind the counters. Her tail wagged and he smiled at the sight. Even if she was Corbin's dog, Lyman was glad to have her in the house. He liked animals, and it had been too long since they'd had one around.

"What are you up to, girl?" Lyman asked her. He bent down to pet her, then rounded the corner and saw her head in Penny's lap. Penny didn't look at him, but stared straight forward.

"Penny?" he asked.

She looked as if she'd been crying all night, but now, she had nothing left to form a tear. Her eyes were bloodshot and she looked frozen in place. He squat down next to her and grabbed her face with his hand.

"Penny, what happened? Are you alright?"

Her eyes turned to him and she managed to shake her head. Her lip trembled and the tears came again. Lyman grabbed her head and wrapped his arms around her, bringing her into her chest. He slid to a seated position next to her.

"It's gonna be alright," he said to her, confused. Then he shouted out to his father. "Hollis!"

Tanya barked toward the hallway, adding emphasis to Lyman's calls for help.

"I'm comin', I'm comin'," Hollis called out from deep within the house. Lyman watched as his father entered the hallway and hobbled his way toward them with the help of his cane.

"Dad, somethin's wrong with Penny," he said.

Hollis hurried up the best he could, concern all over this face. When he saw Penny on the kitchen floor, he squatted down next to her, holding the edge of the counter as he did. His knee creaked and popped as he reached their level.

"Penny, honey, what happened?" Hollis asked.

She pushed her head up from Lyman's arm, still crying. Lyman could feel his shirt now wet with her tears. Hollis placed his hand against her moist cheek and wiped a tear from underneath her eye.

"S-someone was here. Last night," she said, voice quivering.

Lyman watched Hollis's face turn to confusion. He still looked compassionate, but Lyman felt the same way. How could anyone have been there last night?

"He said he was checking in on someone. Knew all about Maddison bein' a deputy. She brought him into this house, I know it. Said he had some list of people to kill."

"Did you see him?" Hollis asked.

"A man. I think he had a scar right here," she said, pointing to the bottom of her cheek. "It was dark, and I was scared, Daddy. He said something about time moving on. Ghosts lingering? It didn't make no sense to me."

Hollis closed his mouth, his eyes darting as if he was in deep in thought. "What else?" Lyman asked when Hollis didn't say anything.

He could feel Penny shrug in his embrace. "He was polite, but I could tell he was meaner than hell. Didn't touch me or nothin', but he took the keys to the truck," she said. "Daddy, I don't want our cousin here. That man was somethin' dark, and if that's who she's runnin' from, I ain't gonna have nothing to do with him."

Hollis remained quiet. Lyman gave him a nudge, hoping he'd have something to put Penny at ease.

"Yeah, that's fine, honey," Hollis finally said, as if he was brushing her off. "Don't worry, he ain't coming back here."

Lyman studied his father. He didn't know what was going on, but he could tell that Hollis knew more than he was letting on. There was something else happening, and he wasn't sure if it was tied to Madds or his father.

CHAPTER TWENTY-SEVEN

After the little showdown with Madds in his office, he needed to get back to work. Keeping his mind on the job was a good way of not overthinking his decision to put her on leave. He knew he'd been angry, and maybe had taken it a bit farther than he should have, but in the end, the job was what mattered. And if she couldn't do it, then she shouldn't be on the case.

He had two agendas on his list for the day. Interview both Michael Amos and Jerry Farnham. Whatever information he garnered from them would decide his next course of action. But until that happened, he wasn't sure really where to go. Connecting them to the altercation at the mines was his best bet. Two of the four men involved were now dead, so if his hunch was right, there might be one more body coming.

He chose Michael Amos first, seeing how he was the one first let go from the mine. If Donnie and Todd were his friends, then it would make sense that Michael might be the next target. Seeing to Michael's safety was the most important.

The last-known address he could find, which matched the one from his employer history, was also the closest to Dupray. Of course, "close" in Dupray didn't mean much. Anywhere was at least an hour away, especially given how the address was some rural route that led into the hills. It wasn't too far into the Appalachians to the point he'd worry about running into those who didn't like folks from town, but it was far enough that he needed to be cautious.

Most people who lived far out of town by themselves took their protection seriously. And a lone vehicle on their property was most likely out of the usual.

The road to the property was so rocky, it was amazing any vehicle had ever made it up that way. Lucky for him, his Jeep could handle some of the most rugged terrain. The tires splashed in a few mud puddles along the way, and even though it hadn't rained recently, the vegetation that surrounded the road was extremely moist.

The final stretch of dirt to where he could see the top of the home was so steep, he worried about backsliding on the wet ground. His tires were new enough that he was confident the tread would hold him down. But if he felt like he needed, he would pull over and hike the rest of the way.

After a few gear shifts, he didn't need to put the Jeep off to the side. One conveniently placed rock jutted up from the ground, letting his tire grip it enough to give him the last push to crest the hill where a lone shack sat. Beyond the shack, the road tapered off until he could see a thicket of trees.

There was absolutely nothing up here. Saying that Michael Amos was a bit of a hermit was probably an understatement.

He stepped out of the Jeep, noticing immediately that the air was much thinner at the top of the hill. Maybe it was in his head, but he was colder and shorter of breath. He cleared his throat audibly, wanting to let Michael know he was there.

"Michael Amos?" he called out. "I'm Sheriff Elven Hallie, coming to ask a few questions. I want to make my presence known to you that I only have a few questions about something going on in town that I do not think you have direct involvement in."

He didn't know Amos, but he knew men like him. Stepping onto their land was a good way to get oneself shot. But some of those reclusive types also knew the law enough to get away with it. He thought if he made his intentions known, he could avoid any conflict.

The shack was small enough that if someone were to hike through, they could miss it completely. It blended in with the surrounding forest that was already half-dead due to the cold. There were two doors on either side of the windows, blinds covering both from the inside. There was no porch, but a set of stairs that went up three steps. The ground was flat enough that next to the stairs sat a weathered, splintered rocking chair.

The door swung open and a man came out holding a rifle. "Hallie, you say?" he asked. His beard was bushy. His clothes looked a little old and had small holes in various places, but were surprisingly clean.

"That's right," Elven said, showing his hands. "Just had a few questions. You Michael Amos?"

The man spit a long stream of tobacco-laden saliva to the side. It stretched about two feet before disconnecting from his lips and smacking against the dirt floor. "You related to them Hallie Mining folks?"

Elven sighed. "My parents," he grumbled.

Michael gave him a once-over, and set his rifle against the wall. "My daddy was a rotten sumbitch, too. Whatchoo wanna know?" He sat on the steps, his bony knees poking up to his chest.

Elven put his hands down and smiled. It wasn't often that being the son of his parents had a good impression on people. Especially when the general opinion of them was less than stellar. But life could be unpredictable.

"You're Michael Amos? I was expecting someone a bit younger," Elven said. For Michael having worked at the mines, and being involved with Donnie and Todd, he seemed a lot older than Elven had expected. The man looked seventy.

"That's me," he said. He started to hack and cough. After a few heavy breaths and growls, Michael worked up a wad of phlegm. He spit it off to the side, much like his tobacco. But this spittle wasn't brown—it was black. "Got some kinda lung disease now. Working the mines ain't a healthy line of work, as I'm sure you know. That kind of thing ages a man, I suppose."

"Have you heard about Donnie Price and Todd Utt?" Elven asked, broaching the subject cautiously. He didn't know what the man knew about or the last time he'd even been in town. He wanted to see his reaction to get a read.

"Those assholes?" he laughed. "Shit, I ain't seen them since I worked for your parents. What they been up to?"

"Dead," Elven said. "Both of them."

"How?" Michael asked, not bothered by the news.

"Shot in the head."

"Well, like I said, ain't talked to them in some time. Truth be told, other than my son, I ain't talked to many people these days. Shame to hear, though."

"I was trying to tie it together, their murders," Elven said. "Most I could come up was the mining job. That's why I came to see you."

"Seems reasonable," Michael shrugged. He was fidgety, but not in a suspicious way. His neck creaked a few times and he had a tic that pulled his mouth up now and again. Elven wondered if he had some other undiagnosed illness along with the lung disease.

"I came across a report in your files about Jerry Farnham."

Michael laughed. "Sheesh, Sheriff. You done gone back a ways, ain't ya?"

"It's my job."

"Is old Jerry back, then? Ain't seen that fella longer than the other two."

"I have a feeling you know more than that, don't you?"

Michael shrugged, and gave another head spasm. "Back then, we used to talk some shit."

"About?"

Michael waved his hand and turned his head, as if finding something more interesting in the woods. But he still spoke. "Something about one of Donnie's friends. Some guy that Todd had coached or somethin', I think. You know that Todd was an assistant coach at the high school?"

Elven nodded. He'd been on the football team himself, so he remembered Todd. Not everyone had liked him. He was a bit hard on the guys, but never on Elven. Maybe it had something to do with Elven being good at his position. Or, more likely, his last name.

"Me, Donnie, and Todd were buddies at work. Donnie was younger, but Todd liked him and I liked Todd. So we talked a lot. They drove the equipment up the mountain, where I'd take it and bring it down in the shaft. We'd see each other every day."

"What about Jerry? What did he do?"

Michael laughed. "You mean besides stir up shit? Fuck if I know," he said, chewing, though Elven wasn't sure if anything was really in his mouth anymore. "Guy was a bit of a cock. Then again, we all were."

"So this friend of Donnie's, the one that Todd had coached, you remember his name?"

"Mmmm," Michael said, chewing at the bottom of his lip. He twisted his head into the air as if he just saw a bird swoop over him, but there was nothing there. He looked at the ground. "Some hot-shot kid. Cutter? Shooter? Fuck, if you hadn't noticed I ain't so good with the memory. Can't even remember the last time I changed my underwear."

"Hunter?"

Michael clapped and pointed at Elven, though he kept his eyes at the ground. "That's the one." Michael inhaled deeply, sounding as if someone was dragging a fishhook down his throat. A coughing fit came on suddenly, and he doubled over. He opened his mouth and slowly let the saliva fall out in thick strings. A black and bloody mass of gunk followed it in a splatter at his feet.

"You ever see a doctor? Get that checked out?" Elven asked, concerned by the sight.

"I ain't got any money, and I don't go to town much, if you don't remember."

"If you file some paperwork against the mines, I'm sure the mining company will have the money and insurance to take care of you," Elven said. It was the right thing to do, even if it cost his parents money. It wasn't like they'd notice anyway.

Michael waved his hand again. "I don't need no fuckin' handouts. Don't need to be taken care of. Especially not by those assholes. B'sides, ain't nobody gonna pinpoint where this shit came from. Smoked for all my life until six months ago when I started chewin'. I've made my bed. It's my problem to deal with."

Elven could appreciate someone not wanting to burden anyone or not wanting to accept a handout. Then again, he also hated to see someone risk their welfare because they were too darn stubborn. But it was like Michael said. It was his problem to deal with.

"What were these things Jerry was sayin'?" Elven asked, focusing back on the case. "About Hunter."

"Fuck if I know. Even if I heard, I ain't gonna remember. All I do remember is he was sayin' somethin' the others didn't like. They was my friends, so I joined in with the hazing. Jerry was a fucktard."

"So you had no idea, but because your friends didn't like it, you participated in getting into a fight with him?"

"Ain't never been called a smart man," Michael said, shrugging.

"After you were fired, what happened to Jerry? He never showed up for his shift the next day."

Michael shrugged. "Got fired 'cause I threw a punch on the clock. After that, Todd and Donnie took me for beers that night. They said they were gonna take care of it for me. Beyond that, fuck if I know."

"So this *taking care of it*," Elven said. "You weren't there to help?"

"Nope," Michael said. "But from what I hear, that hotshot Hunter guy was gonna be."

CHAPTER TWENTY-EIGHT

Madds was angry, there was no doubt about that. She felt like Elven had really let her down. All the talk about helping her, opening up, being there—that was all a bunch of talk. But should she really have expected it to be any different?

What right did she have to expect Elven to have her back? Sure, she was double-crossing him by being in Hollis's pocket, but he didn't know that. And just when she was wondering if it was the right thing to be doing.

If anything, this little spat they had really opened her eyes to who was truly in her corner. Push came to shove, it wasn't gonna be Elven.

But Hollis was different. He'd surprised her with his nurturing ability, his compassion, and his readily available help.

Maybe there was something to being part of the family after all.

She sat in the passenger's seat of Johnny's old, beat-up Dodge Dynasty. She was pretty sure it was a 1991. From the outside, she wondered how it ran, but the inside was in surprisingly good condition. Except, of course, for the paneling underneath the window that was peeling off and wavered with each bump of the road. Johnny had volunteered to give her a lift since her car was still in the shop.

She made her way back to the motel room. She'd been staying there for a few months now and really thought it was time to find her own place. Of course, without knowing how long her leave of absence would be—if it didn't turn out to be a permanent thing—she wasn't sure she would have the money for anything.

"I don't really know what to say," Johnny said from the driver's seat. "Don't be too mad at Elven, I guess. He cares about you. I know it. He's just angry."

Madds looked at Johnny before stepping out of the car. Johnny was a good guy, and loyal to Elven. He was too innocent to be mad at, so she didn't want to drag him into anything. Instead, she leaned over and gave him a hug. At least he was a friend, trying to be there as best as he could.

"Thanks for the ride, Johnny," she said.

"Of course. You need anything else, you give me a call, alright?" he said. "I got plans tonight, but if I need to, I'll come on by."

Madds smiled. "Plans? With that girl we met the other day?"

Johnny smiled wide, his cheeks growing red. "We're hittin' it off pretty well."

"Thanks, Johnny. Don't worry about me. I'll be fine," she said, stepping out of the old vehicle.

He nodded, giving one last smile before driving off. She headed up the path to her room that faced the street, glad that Johnny hadn't waited. She wanted to have a bit of alone time before hitting her head against the pillow. Even though she'd slept like a rock, she knew there was still a lot more catching up on sleep to do.

She pulled her key out of her pocket and looked at the door. There was one thing about the door she hadn't noticed until now, standing out against the dull-green color.

A single red rose was tied to the doorknob with a piece of string. It was beautiful and full, not a single sign of wilt. It was just like the one she'd gotten a couple of days ago, but this time, there was something else. Attached to the rose was a white card with her name written on the outside.

She looked around, trying to see if anyone was around, waiting to see her pick it up. But she was alone. The only sound she heard was from a few doors down, where the television had been left on in one of the rooms. She was pretty sure there was a long-term tenant there, considering there was hardly anyone who visited. But she'd never seen who stayed there, despite that the TV was always on.

She turned back to the rose and picked it up. She smelled it, wondering who would have left it. And who would know she was staying there.

When she opened the card, her curiosity turned into dread.

There was a little smiley face drawn next to the words that read: *Missing you.*

CHAPTER TWENTY-NINE

The conversation with Michael had been interesting, to say the least. From the way the man had spun it, it sounded as if Todd and Donnie had done something nasty to Jerry. And for his not showing up to work the next day, Elven had a lot of questions. For Jerry, and for Hunter.

But Jerry was next on the list. He needed to hear it from the man first before he went and accused Hunter of anything again. After all, if Jerry had nothing bad to say, then there was nothing to see Hunter about. Maybe he was barking up the wrong tree with his questions.

He hoped that's all it was.

Jerry Farnham's last-known address was at a house out in Jolo. It wasn't a part of a neighborhood, but it was nothing like Michael Amos's residence. It was in a town, about four miles away from a Gas 'n Grab, which looked to be mostly grab and very little gas. One lone pump sat out front, looking as if it had been built in the sixties. The store behind it was enough to walk into, but looked as if the floor plan mimicked a hopscotch template in size and space.

Between the Farnham residence and the Gas 'n Grab was

nothing but an empty stretch of road that went up and down, continuing well past the house when he reached it.

He pulled the Jeep up next to one of those cars for toddlers. It was red on the bottom, yellow on top, with a space underneath so the kids could "drive" the car like Fred Flintstone. On the side of the kid's car that faced his Jeep, someone had apparently scribbled all over the side with permanent black marker. The other side was pock-marked, full of line-shaped holes. The kind that a knife stabbed into plastic would make.

The sun was getting low. A day of driving all over Dupray could easily eat up time. Sometimes, the cases just inched along when following leads all over the county. But it was work that needed to be done.

As soon as he stepped out of his Jeep, the door to the single-wide trailer flew open. By the sheer force of the screen door smacking against the wall, Elven worried it would knock the rickety building clean over.

"I ain't done nothin' wrong," a woman protested before Elven could speak.

She was thin, her skin wrinkled and drooping from her bones. She had almost no muscle mass that he could see. By the look of her, she was somewhere in her fifties, but from her condition, Elven figured she was probably closer to her forties. She wore a shirt completely inappropriate for the weather, her shoulders and arms completely exposed, though that didn't seem to bother her.

In her arms, she carried a baby, looking about a year old. The kid, a girl by her long hair and hair bow, gave a distant stare. That's when Elven noticed the scars up the woman's arm that started at the crook of her elbow.

"I pee in a cup and check out clean during every visit from my parole officer," she said, giving Elven a lot more information that he was there for. "So you got no business coming here to harass me."

"Ma'am," Elven said. "I'm—"

"I'm thirty-nine years old. You ain't gotta 'ma'am' me."

Elven knew drugs were hard on people, but thirty-nine? Wow. And to have such a young kid? How could her body even handle that, given her condition?

"Apologies, miss," he corrected. "I'm here to see if Jerry Farnham is around."

She cackled. "Jerry? Shit, you about fifteen years too late if you wanted to ask anything from him."

"Is he dead?" Elven asked.

"Hell if I know. He just ain't been around. Wouldn't doubt it, though. One day, he was here, then one day, he wasn't. Never even came back for his shit."

"Are you his girlfriend?" he asked, cautious to not say "wife" since he didn't see a ring on her finger.

"What the fuck do I look like to you? We ain't all money and sunshine here, but I ain't down for that backwoods shit. He's my brother," she said, waving her arm around. The kid in her other arm bounced around without changing her vacant expression.

"And what's your name?" Elven asked.

She considered him a moment, deciding if she should tell him or not. In the end, she must have figured that she'd told him enough about her that he could call up a parole officer and find out. "Lindsay. Lindsay Farnham."

"And where were you when he never came back? Did you file a missing person's report?"

"Was in rehab. My third time," she said. "Don't know shit about where he went. And no, I didn't file a report. We weren't exactly close."

"But he lived here?"

"If you could call it that," she said. "He slept here. Sometimes anyway. We had separate lives."

"Even though you're family?" he asked, knowing himself that family wasn't always close.

She shrugged. "All's I know is he came to see me in rehab. Which is fuckin' hilarious since he always said he wouldn't set foot in the place, so I knew he had somethin' important to tell me. Said he had some sort of information that was gonna turn the town upside-down or somethin'. That he was gonna get some sort of status. Fuck if I know what that means."

"And he hasn't contacted you since?"

"No, he ain't called or nothin'." Lindsay scooted the girl up in her arms, nearly dropping her. Again, the girl gave no expression.

"Miss, if you'd want to set your daughter down, that's fine. Or if you'd like—"

"She ain't my daughter," she said with a laugh. "My granddaughter."

Elven blinked in disbelief.

"I got her fine, she don't mind. My daughter's workin' down at the grocery, so I watch little Elsie here. Keeps me entertained. We like to watch that one show with the people that marry other people. Them wives and sisters, you know the one?"

Elven shook his head, genuinely having no clue. And thankful he didn't. If he had to watch hours of it a day, well, he could see why Elsie had that look on her face.

"To be honest, I don't give much of a shit what happened to Jerry. He's the reason I got hooked on the shit. Been to rehab four times, jail once. He didn't use himself, not that I know of. Just got his good ol' sister on the junk, the asshole. Him leavin' was the best thing to happen to me. Gave me less excuses to use."

Elven nodded. "Thank you for your time."

"Hey, if you do see him, you tell him to stay the fuck away, alright? I don't need him comin' around fucking up my life again. I just got it back," she said.

"If I see him, I'll make sure to pass it along," Elven said before turning back to his Jeep.

CHAPTER THIRTY

THE NEXT DAY, ELVEN SKIPPED THE UNIFORM. THE MORNING started early for him, as it usually did. His house was quiet on top of the hill, and Yeti was his only company. He enjoyed that time with his dog. It gave him time to clear his head for the day ahead.

But the day ahead wasn't the usual. He wore a suit, ready to pay his respects to Glenna Wallace. Her funeral was scheduled that day, and even though he had left things a bit rocky with Noah and Hunter a few days back, he still planned on going for her sake.

They had invited him, after all. Of course, that was before he had all but accused Hunter—and even Noah—of killing Donnie. But when did he much care about what anyone else thought?

When he arrived, he saw that a large portion of the town of Dupray was there, gathering outside Phil's funeral home, conversing and people filtering inside slowly. He quickly pulled his Jeep around back, finding a spot easily. Most people parked out front along the road, but Elven had a standing spot for his frequent visits.

He went inside, waiting a moment for a chance to see Glenna. The casket was open and only one woman stood at the casket. When she was done, he took his turn to step up.

The body didn't look like the woman he knew. It was always that way with a body-viewing. No matter how skilled or talented the funeral home, Elven could never imagine that they'd be able to match the life inside of the person. They just ended up sculpting a far cry from the original deal.

Her hair was brushed out, and in places, he could tell she was wearing a wig. After the chemo treatments, he imagined that she'd lost some of her hair. She was much thinner than he remembered her, but then again, he hadn't seen her in some time. Their bed was in the living room, which was a new development from the last time he exchanged words with her. There was a lot of lost time he could never get back.

But it was still Glenna in front of him. He didn't need to say anything out loud. He just thought of the times she'd been there for him in high school. The times she'd been a mom of the football team, and more of a mom to him than his own mother had been. He smiled, thinking about how she'd treated him no better or worse than anyone else on the team. He couldn't have gotten away with anything when it came to her.

And he respected her for it. Eventually, she did treat him differently, but only because she'd actually gotten to know him. Not his name.

The world needed more people like Glenna Wallace. He was sad to see her go.

"If everyone would be seated, we'd like to get started," Pastor Magner said with a smile. He lightly touched Elven on the back and whispered to him. "Good to see you here."

"Wouldn't miss it," Elven said. He turned to see Hunter and Noah sitting in the front row. They both glanced at him and Elven offered a nod. They returned the acknowledgment. At least not all bridges were burned, he thought to himself.

He made his way to the back of the room, where the chairs were lined in rows. A hand waved Elven down as he searched for an empty spot. He made his way toward the back and smiled at the woman wearing a tight, black dress with lace on the shoulders.

Penny had saved him a seat.

CHAPTER THIRTY-ONE

ONCE LUKE MAGNER HAD FINISHED THE CEREMONY AND everyone had stood, saying whatever they had to say, they closed with a prayer. Noah seemed upset, having been unable to make it through his portion of the eulogy. The tears had choked him up and he'd had to sit down again. Pastor Magner had escorted him back to his seat next to his brother, who only sat there, unfazed by his brother's emotions.

Hunter had been asked to speak, which he did. To Elven, Hunter's speech seemed odd. Hunter said a few words that felt... empty. More than anything, Hunter seemed bothered by having to be there more than the reason he was there. Was there truly no love shared between the two just because so much time had passed?

Glenna was a good woman for as long as Elven had known her. It was hard to believe that someone could be that estranged from a mother, especially a loving mother like Glenna. As rocky as his relationship was with his own mother, he didn't think it was that bad.

But it wasn't his to judge, he supposed.

After the prayer, Elven turned to Penny with a smile. He was glad that she had been there, and not just to save him a seat. She looked incredible, reminding him of the old days, back when she'd been more outgoing. It had been a while since he'd seen her in something that accentuated her figure. These days, when he saw her, she seemed so shy.

"What?" she asked as he watched her for a moment too long.

He shook his head. "Just haven't seen you in a long time."

"You've seen me plenty," she said, tucking a strand of hair behind her ear, bringing that timidity to the forefront again.

"Not the Penny I used to know."

She twisted her mouth and hung her head low. He didn't think his comment would offend her, but apparently, it was the wrong thing to say.

"I'm sorry, I didn't mean anything by it," he said quickly.

"No, it's okay. I just..." she closed her mouth and bit her lip.

Something seemed different about her, and not in a good way. She may not be the old Penny he knew anymore, but she was also acting different from the more recent version of herself. She seemed nervous. Cautious, even, as if something bad had happened.

"Penny, is everything—"

"Look at the two of you," a man said, interrupting them. Elven turned to see Noah. His suit fit a little loose around the shoulders and his tie was undone. He was no longer crying, having collected himself well.

"Hey, Noah," Elven said, standing. "I'm really sorry about your mother."

He nodded. "Appreciate that," he said, then turned back to Penny. "Momma would love to see the two of you together. Just like old times, right?"

Penny shifted on her feet, obviously uncomfortable. Elven didn't really like to talk about the past, especially when it came to Penny. But Noah wasn't himself that day, and he was just alluding to better days, so Elven didn't blame him.

"Noah, I think I'm gonna go chat with Hunter. Again, my condolences," Elven said. "Penny, good to see you."

He turned and locked eyes with Penny as she watched him walk away. She quickly turned to Noah as he stepped into Elven's place. There was a line over by Hunter, most people wanting to offer their condolences and probably ask the man where he'd run off to all this time. So Elven hung in the back, out of sight from Noah and Penny, but still in earshot.

"Mama always liked you," Noah said to Penny.

"She was a good woman," Penny replied.

"If you weren't with Elven, she'd have wanted you to be with Hunter. I know it. And you know that meant somethin' 'cause nobody was good enough for him when it came to her," Noah said with a laugh.

Penny laughed along with him, and Elven could remember the days when that wasn't a foreign thing to hear. Hearing it brought joy to him, along with sadness.

"That was always the thing, right? Me and Hunter. Or me and Elven. Like people were placing bets."

"Well, I was always too shy to make a move," Noah said.

She laughed again and he could hear the smile in her voice. "You shouldn't have been. You've become a very handsome man. Who knows, if Elven wasn't in the picture, you might have had a shot," she said.

Elven couldn't tell if she was being polite or genuine. It didn't matter much to him, but he didn't know Penny to string someone along.

"He ain't now, right?" Noah asked.

There was a long pause. Finally, Penny spoke. "I'm really sorry about Glenna."

Elven hung his head, feeling just a little bit relieved, even though he had no right or reason to be jealous in the first place. He noticed Hunter finally had a moment to breathe from the crowd, and he took the opportunity to speak to the man.

"Elven," Hunter said. His tone wasn't morose, but defensive. After their last talk, Elven couldn't blame him.

"Hunter, my condolences," Elven said.

Hunter nodded. His suit fit much better than Noah's. He kept his tie fully knotted. "Thanks for coming," he said, turning away.

Before he could leave, Elven grabbed him by the elbow. He couldn't resist and had to ask him. "Hunter, I had a question."

Hunter looked at Elven, waiting for him to speak.

"What do you know about Jerry Farnham?"

Hunter's eyes flashed, as if he recognized the name, but he recovered quickly. "Jerry Farnham? Who's that?"

"He used to work at the mines with Donnie and Todd. Also, Michael Amos."

Hunter clenched his jaw and stepped into Elven's personal space. "This is about your case? You've got some fucking nerve coming into my momma's funeral and accusing me again."

"I ain't accusing—"

"How dare you, Elven Hallie," Hunter said, his voice raising. People began to turn their way, curious at the new commotion.

"Whoa, what's going on Hunter?" Noah asked, stepping between the two.

"The *sheriff* here has some more questions about his case. Wants to know something about some guys I ain't heard of."

Noah turned at Elven, and stared him down. "My momma loved you, you know that? Like you were her own son."

Elven noticed Hunter grimace when Noah said it.

"You come in to ask questions at her funeral now? Hell, she ain't even in the ground yet. She's right over there. You wanna ask louder so she can hear you?" Noah asked, his voice rising to a yell. Not a single person in the funeral home was looking elsewhere.

"I apologize. I just needed—"

"Fuck you, Elven," Hunter yelled shoving his brother to the side. He threw a right hook that landed right across Elven's jaw. Elven took it and didn't reciprocate. He grabbed at his mouth, now throbbing in pain.

But that wasn't enough for Hunter. He came at him again,

throwing a left punch. It landed hard against Elven's chin. He took that one too, but when the third fist came, Elven wasn't going to just stand there.

He ducked the right hook that time and grabbed at Hunter's midsection. He wrapped his arms around Hunter's waist and the two of them sprawled into the rows of chairs. Everyone ran to the sides as the wooden folding chairs went falling. Elven felt his head hit the edge of a chair and his body take a hard tumble on top of another one, the leg jutting into his ribs. Hunter got it even worse as his back went first into the pile.

"Get off him!" Noah yelled, jumping into the mess of chairs. He jumped on Elven's back, pounding his fists against what felt like his kidneys. Elven reached above him, grabbing Noah's head and flipping him over onto the floor in front of him. Noah let out a groan as he landed.

Elven continued to struggle with Hunter, but eventually, they managed to separate from each other, scrambling backward on the pile of chairs.

"Boys, stop this," Luke Magner tried telling them, as if he were in Sunday School again with the kids, breaking up a fight. Except the kids were three grown men.

Elven put a hand up on a chair, lifting himself up. He could feel that his ribs were bruised from the fall. Hunter looked no better, his face bleeding at the lip from catching the edge of a chair the wrong way. When Hunter lifted himself up, though, Elven saw his jacket hang open.

Just beneath his jacket on his hip was Hunter's revolver. And Elven watched Hunter's free hand move toward the pistol grip.

It's gonna be that kind of fight, he thought. He dug his hand beneath his own jacket, where his revolver sat. It wasn't the most aesthetically pleasing look, but it was the one that offered him the most protection. He'd found that after taking the job, he didn't go much of anywhere without his gun, even funerals. And now, he'd been vindicated in his decision.

The two stood up at the same time, and Elven pulled his revolver out. When he locked eyes with Hunter, he saw he'd already had his drawn.

Not a single word was said. It was so silent, Elven thought he could hear a cockroach fart.

Everyone stood frozen, watching, waiting for something to happen.

"Pulling a gun on an officer of the law?" Elven said. "I let the punch slide, out of respect for Glenna, but this is crossing the line."

"If I wanted you dead, you'd have a bullet in you and bleeding out on the floor before you could have wrapped your finger around that trigger. And you know it, don't you?" Hunter asked. "You're the one come in here and disrespected my momma, accusing me of stuff you ain't have any idea about."

"Don't talk to me about disrespecting that woman. You're her son and can't even muster up a single tear for her. It's obvious to everyone in here that you don't have a single emotion for what's going on. If I were a stranger on the street, I'd have no idea you ever lost your momma."

Hunter squeezed his hand against the grip on his pistol and Elven witnessed his knuckles go white. He kept his cool, ready to pull the trigger if he had to.

"Hunter, put the gun down, son," Pastor Magner said evenly, trying to step in between them.

"Pastor Magner, I got a lot of respect for you, so you best stay out of the way. Elven and I got somethin' to settle," Hunter said.

"I can't—"

"It's fine, Pastor," Elven said, keeping his eyes locked on Hunter. Luke Magner swallowed hard, but he didn't step in the line of fire.

"Just admit it, Elven. You're jealous of me, ain't ya? Sure, you may have all the money and name to get whatever you want. You even have the fuckin' balls to think you're so good, bein' the sheriff. But you know you never were the best. That I was always better. You even went so far as to claim my momma almost as your own."

"Stop this!" Penny shouted. "You're supposed to be friends!"

"Oh, Penny," Hunter said. "We never were. Not really. Might have been friendly, but Elven here only was because he knew I'd be graduating. That his day would come and he'd be top dog on the team. At the whole school. Ain't that right? Shit, when I left town, I bet it was the best day of your life."

Elven squeezed his hand against his revolver. He could feel a pound of pressure weighing on the trigger. Hunter kept running his mouth, talking as if he knew everything about Elven. He knew just the way to get under his skin.

"Hunter," Noah said. "Put it down. Elven ain't all bad, you know that. It's what Momma would have wanted."

Hunter bit his bottom lip, still holding the revolver. Finally, he dropped his arm. "Alright."

Elven swallowed hard, thankful he didn't have to pull the trigger. And a little bit of him was afraid that even if he had needed to, Hunter was right. About everything.

"Hands in the air," Elven said. "You're under arrest. Both of you."

Hunter rolled his eyes and dropped his gun to the floor before putting his hands up. Noah followed along.

"Elven," Penny said. "You—"

"Penny, stay out of this," Elven barked. "I'm taking them down to the station for assaulting an officer."

He brought his cuffs out and wrapped them around Hunter's wrists, which were now behind his back. Everyone watched, but nobody said anything. Elven wanted to think he was making the right decision. He had thought Hunter was somehow involved in the murders, but at the same time, everything about arresting them at their mother's funeral felt wrong.

He rarely felt embarrassed, but right then, something in his gut said he was making a big mistake.

CHAPTER THIRTY-TWO

MADDS SAT AT HANK'S DINER IN THE BOOTH NEAR THE DOOR. She had been able to sleep decent enough again, though the rose outside her motel had left her with a lot of questions.

Missing you.

The note had been in a neat handwriting she didn't recognize. Though to be fair, it seemed whoever had written it had taken their time to do so. Probably going out of their way to make sure their handwriting wasn't anything she'd recognize.

Which led her to one question. Had Kurt really left it there for her?

She had been so paranoid, seeing him in places that had turned out not to be him, but blamed the lack of sleep. This time, she had concrete proof of his presence.

Proof of what? That someone sent her a rose?

Shit, maybe she just had a secret admirer with poor timing that landed. But what were the odds of that happening? Especially seeing as how she didn't have a lot of friends in Dupray outside of work.

Tank was happily married, so he was out of the question. He didn't seem the type to step out on his wife, not when he was so professional. And she would have suspected Johnny, except now, he was smitten with Bernadette.

She laughed thinking it could be Elven. Would he practically fire her, then rush to leave her a rose on her motel room door? Doubtful.

Madds didn't think she'd find any answers in the different options running through her head, but it still bothered her. She was lost, and she knew that the possibility of her ex finding her was real. She just couldn't help but think he was fucking with her. It was definitely something he would do.

"Excuse me?" a man said, approaching. Madds snapped out of her head, looking up at him. He looked to be in his late forties with a warm smile on his face. He was handsome, in an older, messy-haired sort of way. He didn't wear an apron, and she'd never seen him in the diner before.

She sighed, thinking she was about to get hit on. Even though she was twenty-six, and probably too young for the guy, she knew that didn't stop everyone. She wasn't wearing her uniform, but instead, was wearing a blouse that showed more cleavage than usual. She wished she'd kept her coat on, but instead, it sat next to her in the booth.

"Yeah?" she asked, already putting up defenses.

"I'm sorry, I don't mean to bother you. I just, well, it seemed like something was wrong and I wanted to make sure you were alright," he said, his smile creasing the skin around his eyes.

She watched him and his eyes never dipped below her face. She'd read him wrong. There was compassion in those eyes, and it seemed he truly was concerned. She felt guilty that she went into defense-mode immediately. This whole Kurt thing was really messing with her.

"I'm fine," she said. "I appreciate you asking though."

He nodded. "You remind me of someone who's not around anymore. If someone had asked her if everything was alright, I feel like she might still be around. See something, say something, right?"

She nodded, knowing that was true, but feeling sad for whoever he was referring to. "Thank you."

"Well, I'll leave you be then. Gotta get to work. Sorry to have bothered you."

"Don't be. Have a good day," she said, letting the man leave.

She smiled, being reminded of a simple thing like kindness. If anything, the interruption had been very welcome. And part of her thought she was being stupid about being so paranoid about Kurt. She was under Hollis's protection, right? And, as she'd seen, Hollis wasn't someone she would want to mess with. If Kurt did show up, he'd be the one in bad shape when Hollis got a hold of him. Maybe everything was going to be fine.

From behind her, a man cleared his throat, then she felt a tap on her shoulder. She sighed, thinking the See Something, Say Something guy was back. Even if he'd had good intentions, maybe he thought her reciprocated kindness was an open invitation to get her number. She just couldn't win.

"Hey, I don't mean to be rude," she said, starting to turn around.

"Then don't be."

Madds froze. He walked in front of her, and then around to the other side of the booth. She watched him slide into the booth right across from her. He smiled, looking her over.

It was Kurt.

He was sitting right in front of her. She glanced around, the few patrons in the diner still going about their meals. This was the real world. Not a dream. If she could move, she would have pinched herself, just to make sure.

But she didn't think she needed to.

The details were all there. His blue eyes that seemed to look straight into her, knowing all her thoughts. The blond hair that was so light, it was almost white. And the smile across his face. The one that stretched above a firm jaw line, lifting higher at the right side than the left so it made his head look tilted.

It was Kurt, alright.

Her heart picked up the pace. They were in a public place, so she didn't think he would try anything so brazen as to grab her, or worse. But she didn't want to take any chances. Her hand crept to her belt, and that's when she remembered that Elven had taken her gun. She cursed him in her thoughts.

"What's good here?" he asked, grabbing the menu from under her hands. He lifted it, mouthing the various items on the page.

She kept her eyes locked on him, but didn't say a word. She was afraid her voice would betray her. It would show all the holes in her armor that her face hadn't already. A small tremble, maybe a crack in her voice, or worse, tears streaming down her face. She tried to remain strong, stubborn, and show him that he had no control over her anymore. Even though that was an obvious lie.

He shrugged. "Guess I probably won't be here long enough to eat," he said putting the menu down. He looked back into her eyes. "I've missed you, Maddie."

"Don't call me that," she managed to eke out.

"What's that?"

"Maddie," she said, this time a little firmer. "Don't call me that."

He laughed. "You never had a problem with me calling you that before."

It was true. She'd hated when most people had called her that, but Kurt had been different. When they'd first met, he'd said the nickname she loathed, but she found herself aching to hear it pass through his lips again and again. It became a term of endearment. But eventually, just like their relationship, it had soured and been tainted by all the other names that had been passed through those lips that he'd chosen to call her.

"I was worried when you didn't come back," he said, his face more serious. "Scared, actually. I looked for you everywhere I could think. Shit, I even went to your sister-in-law's place. She said she hadn't seen you since your brother went missing, though. A shame, she's a nice lady. I had no idea where you went."

"Should have stopped looking," she said.

"I did," he said. "At first, those cartel boys were tense, which meant, so was I. I was so paranoid everywhere I went. I checked for bugs in my house, wires on my friends. You know, I would even drive around streets three or four times just to spot if I had a tail. Every time I heard a noise outside the door, I thought it was the FBI or the DEA come to take me away." He shook his head. "But nothing. That's when I realized that you weren't coming for me. You were just as scared as I was."

She thought about saying something, but kept her mouth shut. Kurt could talk when he wanted, and nothing she would say was going to stop him from telling her whatever story he had.

"I told them you were dead," he said with a sigh. "Hated to do it, but it was the best thing to put everyone at ease once I realized you had no ill intentions. They bought it, which is good, 'cause you know how those Mexicans can be when not everything goes to plan. And then, I got comfortable. Relaxed. I really did. Don't get me wrong, it wasn't the same without you, but I bought into the lie and just decided that you were really dead."

He chuckled again as he picked at the corner of the menu where the laminate had peeled away. The chuckle was more of a memory response than anything being truly funny. "I even went through a short period of mourning over you."

"So why didn't you stay there? Keep up with the lie?"

He stopped fidgeting with the menu. "Because one day, some asshole sheriff called the station. He was wanting to talk to Garcia, which wouldn't have been bad if he'd actually gone straight to him. But of course, that didn't happen. Instead, Eric picked up the phone. And Eric, come to find out, was feeding information to the Mexicans, sort of keeping tabs for them on what came in and out of the station so they could decide if anything was important to pursue.

"And let me tell you, hearing that Officer Maddison Cook was alive and well in a shithole place called Dupray was of great interest to them."

"So what?" she asked, trying to hide her growing alarm. "You're here to kill me? Prove that you're loyal to them?"

Kurt twisted his face into confusion, dropping the facade of knowing everything, of being too smug for his own good. "Maddie, who do you think I am?" he asked, his voice bordering on genuine compassion. "I know I may not have been the person you thought you married, and that it was obvious we were growing apart. But I'm not this monster you've made me out to be. You're all in your head."

"What?"

"I came here because I miss you. I mean that. I came to take you back home. Now there doesn't have to be any secrets."

"To what? You can't be serious?" she asked. "What about being worried I'd turn you in? What about the cartel knowing I'm not dead, that you lied, and that I could turn on them?"

"Don't get me wrong—they weren't happy to hear that you weren't dead. But that's on me, not you. They have to put some trust in people, knowing they won't turn them in, all the time. And you not saying shit to anyone—other than Garcia, of course—goes a long way."

Madds shook her head in disbelief. This is not how she ever expected a meeting to go if Kurt ever did show up.

"Look, I know you're apprehensive. But I'm telling you, this is for the best. We can go back home, you can have your job back, even. You don't even have to be involved. Just look the other way. You don't want to stay in this shithole, do you? You can be a real cop again."

"One on the take," she shot back. Though, she knew that's exactly what she was in Dupray. What Kurt was asking her was far less than she had to do in Dupray.

Kurt shrugged. "Think it over. If you do, you'll realize it's the best way. And before you get into your head about anything else, I hope I've made you realize I want nothing more than to just be with you. If I wanted you dead, I wouldn't have come to talk."

He stood up and walked to her side, leaning down and kissing her on the forehead. She felt his lips against her skin. A part of her remembered the few moments that were good that they'd had together, but overall, she just remembered the way she'd felt when she'd found out about him.

As soon as he was out of the diner and far out of sight, she hopped up from her seat and ran the opposite direction.

CHAPTER THIRTY-THREE

MADDS BURST IN THROUGH THE BACK DOOR, FORGETTING HER earlier paranoia about checking her surroundings before doing so. She'd gotten a lift from a friendly man, driving a truck with a bed full of chickens. She didn't know him, and wondered if it was the way she'd dressed to have prompted him to pick her up, but she didn't give a rat's ass. If he wanted to stare at her tits, so much the better as long as she made it as far away from Kurt and to the safety of Hollis's home.

When she'd entered the room, Tanya looked up from the floor next to the recliner in the center of the room. She growled, baring her teeth at Madds, but didn't rush her. She'd learned a little since meeting Madds, but not enough to still get defensive.

"Shut it, Tanya," Madds snapped, this time not bothered by the dog's presence. She was ready to throw down with the mutt if need be. There were more important things right now than some dog with an attitude problem.

Nobody was in the living room or the kitchen. No TV was on, and the house was eerily quiet. No breakfast remains or the sounds of lunch being made. Not a glass of sweet tea on the edge of the end table by the chair.

"Hollis?" she called out. "Penny, Lyman? Anyone here?"

She had seen an unfamiliar red truck out back. It was pulled around, just at the edge of the house. But with all her cousins living there, she didn't know what kind of company they kept. For all she knew, Corbin or Lyman had a girlfriend who had come by. But when she thought about it, she hadn't seen any other vehicles. Hollis, Corbin, and Lyman's trucks were all absent. She didn't know what Penny drove.

Either way, she wasn't sure anyone was home.

"Hollis?" she called out again, making her way down to through the hallway. Even if she'd been sleeping there and had been told she was family, she still felt uneasy in the house. She hadn't gotten used to the smells, still feeling as if she'd stepped into a stranger's home. A stranger who cooked different foods, used a different laundry detergent, and just didn't have the scent she was used to.

She passed the open rooms, seeing that hers was still the same way she'd left it before. Lyman, Penny, and Corbin's rooms were all empty as she passed them by. At the far end of the narrow hallway was Hollis's room. The door was open halfway, but she couldn't see anything from where she stood.

When she reached it, she debated on knocking, or perhaps asking for him again. But instead, she pushed the door all the way open. The room opened up, much bigger than she'd thought it would be. It looked to be even bigger than the living room. There was a bed centered in the room, with one side of the mattress more noticeably sunken in than the other.

She stepped inside, still feeling awkward doing so. Entering someone's bedroom uninvited felt like an invasion. To her right, the room broke off into a smaller room, where the doorway had, too, been left open. Except this time, she saw Hollis sitting behind a desk. He stared down at it with a card in his hand.

"Hollis?" she asked. He looked up, startled to see her. How he hadn't seen or heard her earlier was baffling, but by the look on his face, he'd been deep in thought.

"Maddie," he said, his voice distant. "What, uh, what can I do for you?"

"You alright?"

"Fine," he said. "How about you? You look like somethin's on your mind."

She could say the same about him, but she wasn't there to talk about his problems. She needed help with her own. She walked into his office, standing in front of the desk.

"Kurt is here," she said. "This time, it's real, and I know it. He found me at the diner."

"Are you alright?" he asked, focusing fully on her. "Did he attack you?"

She shook her head, still in disbelief. "He just sat across from me at my table and talked."

"Talked? Why would he just talk? Was Elven with you?" he asked. At first, it sounded like an odd question, but when she thought about it, it wasn't an unreasonable ask. A man who was strapped with a gun and wearing a sheriff's badge would probably help avoid an attack. But she hadn't told Hollis about what had happened between her and Elven.

"No, Elven isn't really talking to me. He pulled me off the case," she admitted. "More than that, actually. I may be fired."

"What case?"

"You don't know? There were some murders in town," she said with a shrug. "Figured you would have heard all about it."

He shook his head. "Tell me."

"Some guys got shot. Elven thinks it might be a professional from the way they were killed."

"Why didn't you tell me about this?" Hollis said, his eyes growing wide. He seemed way more concerned about the case than her ex being in town.

"I didn't think it was a big deal. Three dead that we know of.

Each was shot in the head, with one bullet. He has some idea that it's this Hunter guy that came into town recently, but I don't know anything about that." She watched his face grow a deeper shade of red with each word she uttered. "Why's it matter?"

He stood, nearly the color of a tomato by the time she was done. "It matters because that's what you're paid to do. You keep me in the loop on everything. That was the fucking deal. You hear me? Letting something like this slip by without a thought could have cost us our lives, don't you understand?"

"Hollis, I'm sorry. I was too worried—"

"About your little problem, yes, I know. I've heard all about Kurt and his little chat with you. But if you don't do your fucking job, keep your end of the deal, then why the hell should I do mine?" he spat.

"I'm sorry, I—"

"Shove it, you ungrateful bitch. I let you into my home, took care of you like you were one of my own, and this is how you repay me? I'm done with your sorries. I need to get to the bottom of this," Hollis said, walking around his desk and shoving past her.

"What about Kurt? What about keeping me safe?"

"I don't give a shit. He sat and chatted with you. Doesn't sound so dire to me. Meanwhile, I've got a fucking hit man on my hands that you don't seem to give two fucks about. If I've got to handle my own problems, then so do you."

He stormed out of the room, not bothering to take his cane with him. She watched as her last hope of dealing with Kurt abandoned her.

CHAPTER THIRTY-FOUR

It was a quiet day at the station, though most days were quiet in the station. Not a lot of trouble came through except the occasional drunk and disorderly that, more often than not, Elven let sleep it off without so much as a write-up.

But today was even more quiet, seeing that Glenna Wallace's funeral had taken place. Meredith had known the woman, and while they were more likely acquaintances, Meredith had considered her a friend. They'd exchanged more than just pleasant words, and sometimes would visit the farmer's market together, chatting about her boys and swapping humorous, and sometimes horror, stories about their late husbands.

But that had been years before the cancer had been discovered. Meredith had told Glenna exactly how she felt about her, so there were never any doubts. Ever since her husband had passed, Meredith had made sure to never let anything go unsaid. She was straight to the point, and made sure Glenna knew that she valued their time together and that the days at the market would never be the same again.

So when it came time for the funeral, Meredith saw no reason to go. There was no reason to say goodbye when every time she saw someone, she'd made sure to say goodbye as if it was the last time she'd see them. At her age, if she spent time going to funerals, she'd never find time for the rest of her own life.

That's why she stayed at work, hanging out with Johnny and Tank, and letting Elven pay his respects. She'd much rather spend time with a closed book like Tank and a goofball like Johnny than with a room full of crying people.

She stood up from her desk and made her way over to the back table where the coffee pot sat. Next to the mugs was a box of donuts. She opened it up and saw that all were left were two double chocolate. She sighed, shaking her head.

"Hey, Johnny," she called out toward the hallway. She knew Johnny wasn't going to be up to anything. Unless Elven had given him a task, he was probably clicking around on his computer, playing a game of solitaire. "Did you eat all the Boston cream?"

There was no answer, but she could hear the creak of the springs in Johnny's chair as he released them from the pressure that his ass had applied. Footsteps came toward her until she saw his face.

"No, Meredith. I swear, I didn't eat it," he said. She was inclined to believe him, considering that a smear of jelly was at the corner of his lip and his chin was dotted with powdered sugar.

"Tank?" she called out.

Another creak of the chair, and Tank was in the hallway. He moved his mouth to the side. "Sorry, Meredith. Didn't know you wanted it."

She sighed, shaking her head. "You'd think you boys would know by now that I like the Boston creams."

"I can run and get another one for you if you really want," Tank offered.

He was a good man, and she wasn't really angry. It was more of an inconvenience than anything. She picked up the double chocolate and took a bite. "Don't worry about it, sweetie," she said, remembering she was the mother of the office, and with that came love. And she did love the men in that station like her own boys.

The front door opened, and in walked a woman with curly blond hair. She was shorter, not too thin, but not overweight either. More curvy than anything else.

"Can I help you?" Meredith asked, swallowing the bite of donut. She approached the woman, who looked to be her early thirties. "Did you need to report something?"

She smiled wide, showing a row of perfectly white teeth. She looked like she was one of those models on the magazines showcasing home decor. "Oh, no. I'm just here visitin'."

Meredith rolled her eyes. It didn't happen often, but from time to time, someone younger and less familiar with the Hallie name would show up and want to chat to the handsome sheriff. The poor girl had even brought what looked to be a picnic basket.

"I'm sorry," Meredith said. "Sheriff Hallie, or Elven, depending on how he introduced himself to you, isn't here. I can take a message if you'd like." She thought this woman didn't quite fit the mold of one of Elven's girlfriends. She'd picked up on a lot of things over the years working with the men, and Elven's type had been one of them. He much preferred brunettes, but as his last female companion had proved, he was no stranger to branching out, either.

The woman laughed. "Does every woman that works in this office have a crush on the sheriff or somethin'?" she asked. "No offense, but how can that man date someone when he obviously loves himself more than anyone else?"

Meredith let out a belly-shaking laugh. She laughed so hard, she grew afraid she wasn't going to ever catch her breath. She wiped a tear from her eye. "Oh my Lord," Meredith said, fanning herself.

"Button?" Johnny asked, turning around after examining the last double-chocolate donut in the box.

Meredith glanced at Johnny, seeing a stupid grin come over his face. She turned back to the pretty woman in front of her, surprised to see a matching grin. "There he is," the woman said, her voice bordering on giggly.

"Button?" Meredith asked no one in particular.

"'Cause she's cuter than a button. Meredith, this is Button—er, Bernadette," Johnny said.

"Hi," Meredith said, still fanning herself. Surprise came over her that the pretty woman, Button, was there to see Johnny of all people.

"Nice to meet you, Meredith," Button said. "Johnny, I packed you a lunch. You haven't been eating donuts all morning, have you?" She put her hands on her hips and pouted.

"I still got room for whatever it is you packed me," Johnny reassured, giving Button a peck on the lips.

Meredith couldn't stop smiling at the sight. In all her years, she'd never seen Johnny so smitten. And she'd never seen a woman react the same way to him. She couldn't be happier. Johnny was a good man. A little clumsy, sometimes dim, but his heart was bigger than anyone else's she knew. It had taken just the right kind of person to also see that in him.

"We've been talking every day since meeting a few days ago," Johnny said. "Goin' out every night."

"Sometimes staying in," Button added with an eyebrow lift.

"Button," Johnny said in a hushed tone, embarrassed.

Meredith looked at the two of them together. "I am so pleased to meet you, Button."

Tank stepped up to the trio and clapped his hand on Johnny's shoulder. "I'm really proud of you, Johnny."

Meredith had never seen Johnny so proud, so happy, and so much the best version of himself. A good woman to spend time with, praise from a good man and co-worker. Now, all he needed was to get laid and he'd be a brand new man.

Before she could get any more details about the relationship, the phone rang. "Hold on a sec," Meredith said as she picked up, slightly irritated by the interruption. "Dupray County Sheriff's Department."

A man was frantic on the other end. She nodded, trying to listen.

She got his name—Nick Myers. Then came his address, and she proceeded to ask him what he was calling about.

"It's my friend, he ain't answering the door. I can see him on the floor. Oh, Jesus, he ain't movin'. There, holy shit, he's been shot. His head's all blown out the back."

CHAPTER THIRTY-FIVE

James sat in his motel room, his gun laid out in front of him. He was at a dead end, and trying to think of his next move. He seemed to get his best ideas when he was cleaning his gun. It had a way of keeping him focused, allowing him to clear his head as he did something with his hands. Sometimes, an idea would just land in his lap.

But finding this Amos fella was going to be difficult at this point. He could try to ask around, but if they were like Rhea, he figured not many people knew Amos. And those who did know him, well, they might have some questions for him, such as why he was looking in the first place.

He held the bore brush and dipped into the small vial of solvent. He picked up the unloaded pistol with his left hand, looking down the barrel, and fed the brush into it. He did a few swipes with the brush when the radio crackled to life. He set his gun down, trying to listen and see if anything was worth his time.

A woman's voice came on, and when she said the word "sheriff", he decided he should listen. He sat up from the chair and headed to the radio in the corner that sat on a small table. He cranked the knob gently, turning the volume up.

"Elven, I got a guy just now called and said his friend's been shot," the woman said.

James lifted the corner of his mouth into a half-smile, knowing that Nick had found his buddy Jason.

"You think you can swing by? It's out a ways," she said.

"Can't do it, Meredith," the man said, who James figured was the sheriff. "You'll have to send Johnny and Tank."

"Everything alright?"

"Oh yeah. Just bringing two down to the station to get booked."

"Who?"

"Noah and Hunter Wallace."

"Elven!" Meredith exclaimed, her voice shifting to a scolding tone. "Weren't you all just at their momma's funeral?"

"It's not my doing," the sheriff—Elven—said.

"Like hell!" someone shouted in the background.

"They're gonna sit in a cell. I already called Michael Amos down, too. I want to get to the bottom of this whole thing."

James's ears perked up at the name. He chewed the side of his cheek, thinking.

"Michael Amos? Ain't seen him in a long while. He still able to drive?"

"His son Dylan is giving him a ride down. This way, we can all have a little chat together."

James smiled. Cleaning his gun always had a way of making his mind clear and the idea would fall into his lap.

CHAPTER THIRTY-SIX

Hollis sat in his recliner in the living room, staring at the wall. He had a glass of sweet tea next to him, but hadn't taken a single sip. The ice had melted down until it was just small afterthoughts of cubes. The condensation on the glass had created a ring in the wood that would ruin the finish. But the stain on the table was the farthest thing from his mind.

He rubbed his leg, the cold locking his joints up worse than ever. It was his burden to bear from a stupid mistake long ago. Long before Elven had stepped into his first job as a deputy.

Back when he'd known the man, James Smith.

Most days, he would forget about him, but on days when it was coldest, when his knee would act up the most, he would always think of the man.

The door opened, and Corbin walked in. It was just the person he was hoping to see, though "hope" wasn't quite the right word to use in this situation. Not when someone like James Smith was in town.

Corbin reeked of manure and sweat. He'd tracked dirt in the house across the rug on the floor. At least, Hollis thought it was dirt, though he smell of cow shit on him might be evidence it wasn't. But that was a conversation for another day.

Corbin squat down as Tanya ran up to him, her tongue greedily licking at his face. "That's a good girl, did you miss your daddy?" he greeted her in a high-pitched voice.

Hollis cleared his throat and Corbin turned around, not having seen his father upon entry. "Oh, hey, Daddy. Didn't see you."

"Figured as much," Hollis muttered.

"Shit, that run was nothin' but bullshit. First, when I get there, they ain't have any idea where to load the goddamn cases. Then they act like they want me to do it. Fuck, you wouldn't think that I been drivin' out there at least four times by now. You better call down to Billy and tell him I ain't givin' them an orientation next time. They better know who they're dealin' with," Corbin said, running his mouth as if he hadn't done a terrible thing.

Hollis stared him down. "That's important to you, right? Stayin' in line, makin' sure people respect you. The chain of command, so to speak."

Corbin shrugged, obviously confused. "Guess so."

Hollis nodded slowly, taking it in. "That's good. That's real good. Then I'm sure you'll be supportive of my decision to ask you what the fuck it is you got your hands into?"

Corbin stopped petting Tanya and knitted his brows together. "Daddy, what are you talkin' about?"

"You tell me," Hollis said. "Someone came by a couple nights ago."

Corbin held his hands up in a shrug. "People come by here all the time."

"Not like this. Not inside my house, standing next to my daughter and scarin' the livin' hell outta her!" Hollis yelled, now standing over his son.

"Daddy, I-I...Tanya was here, she shoulda—"

"Oh, yeah, she was downright ferocious. Not even a goddam

peep from her as he stroked her head like she was his own," Hollis said. "Don't go blamin' that dog, neither. This was your fuck-up."

"I don't know what you think I did. I wasn't even here!" Corbin protested.

"Don't you take that tone with me. You went into my goddamn book didn't you? *Didn't you?!*"

Corbin didn't say a word. The fear of God had apparently been put in him.

"You know, I didn't ask Lyman about this. Didn't even think to ask Wade. You know why?" Hollis asked. Corbin shook his head, his bottom lip trembling. "'Cause they ain't a couple of dumbasses. No, that's reserved for a fuck-up like you, ain't it? It just reeks of your hands all over it." Hollis waved his hand in the air for emphasis.

"I-I..."

"You might be willing to get your hands dirty in all this business, but you're dumber than a fucking rock. That's how I know it was you."

Hollis stared down at his son, who stood up. Corbin had grown taller than himself over the years, his shoulders and build bigger than his own. But the way he hung his head showed Hollis that Corbin knew who was still in charge.

"I met some guy in a bar," Corbin began. "He was upset about somethin'. Spoutin' his mouth off about some guys that done him wrong. Said he had the means, if he could just find someone to help him. Wanted to make them pay."

"Who was he?"

Corbin shrugged. "I ain't never seen him before. I mean, maybe, but why would I remember some asshole? Told him I'd get the name of someone good to help if he'd give me ten grand. Like a finder's fee, you know?" he asked, trying to get Hollis to acknowledge even the smallest of his achievements.

"And you pulled this name?" Hollis asked. He threw his hand toward his room in a fit of anger. "Out of all them fuckin' names in that book, you picked this one?"

"I-I remember when I was a kid, you'd spoken about this James guy like he was some sort of hero to you. Someone who would always come through. You said he's the best. I figured this fella who paid me better get what he wanted. I was just offerin' good service is all."

Hollis shook his head. "So now you're thinkin' like your brothers. Wanting to provide good service, wanting to be a real businessman, is that it?"

Corbin kept his head low and offered a sheepish shrug.

"Boy, you've no idea what you brought down on this place."

CHAPTER THIRTY-SEVEN

Elven locked Hunter and Noah in a cell together. Johnny and Tank were gone on the call Meredith had taken. Not that it mattered. Elven wanted to see them to their cell himself.

Hunter shook his head and plopped down on the bench against the back wall. Noah, however, approached the bars.

"Elven, I don't know what you think you're doin', but this ain't right and you know it," Noah said.

"What ain't right is pulling a gun on me or physically attacking me," Elven said.

"You started the whole thing. I was just trying to get you off my brother."

Elven shook his head. "Noah, you'll be out in no time, I'm sure. Your brother, however, he might not be, depending."

"Depending on what?" Hunter asked, lifting his head.

"On what kind of information I get from you."

"Elven, I knew you were full of yourself, but I never thought you were this fuckin' stupid before," Hunter said, rolling his eyes. "Guess things can change a lot, can't they?"

Meredith entered the room, clearing her throat. Everyone turned their attention to her. "Elven, Michael Amos is here."

"Meredith, this ain't right. You know it ain't," Noah said. "You were always good to my momma and she was to you, wasn't she?"

Meredith held her tongue, but Elven could see in her eyes that she was struggling. He turned to Noah. "Noah, sit down and shut up. I won't ask again."

"What are you gonna do?" Hunter asked. "Now you threatening to beat him to get him to shut up? Maybe you are just like your daddy, after all. This job is just a power play, ain't it?"

Elven marched to the cell, glaring at Hunter, but kept his mouth shut. Hunter was just trying to get a rise out of him, and it was working. Elven turned, leaving them to sit alone while he followed Meredith down the hall.

"Elven, I don't know what's gotten into you, but you're scaring me," she said. "This ain't you. Something is off, and it's not a good look on you."

"Meredith—"

"Before you say something, just remember that I still care about you, Elven. That me tellin' you this is from a place of love. And that I will not tolerate any attitude thrown my way. You hear me?"

He took a deep breath and nodded. He paused for a moment before answering. "I appreciate your concern, Meredith. And maybe I'm not fully myself right now. Bein' lied to while someone is murdering citizens of my county ain't what I call a good time. It's good of you to say something, but I'm still the sheriff. I'm still working this case. And if I think it's necessary to arrest those boys at their mother's funeral...well then, that's just how it goes." He paused again for a moment. "If you feel that you no longer have the stomach for this job, then I will understand. Are we clear?"

Meredith took his words in. She may not have liked it, but she nodded. "Yes, Sheriff."

He walked into the lobby where Michael Amos stood waiting. He was twitchier than when Elven had visited him at his shack in the woods. His hair was a mess, and each time he creaked his neck to the side, the hair on his right side flipped up and floated back down gently, only to be repeated with each tic.

Behind him, another man stood. He was around Elven's age, possibly a year or two younger. He seemed more together than Michael.

"Michael, thank you for coming," Elven said.

"I ain't been to town in forever. My son Dylan had to bring me," he said.

"Appreciate you takin' the time," Elven said to Dylan.

Dylan shrugged. "No problem. You need me with him, or..."

"No, I think your father can handle himself. He's not in trouble and I just want to have a chat with him and another man. Don't worry, I'll keep an eye on him."

"Good, 'cause I'm jonesin' for a cigarette. Didn't want to smoke in the car, considerin' his lungs and all," Dylan said, though Elven didn't think he had any real idea how bad a shape Michael was in.

Dylan walked out the door, pulling a pack of cigarettes from his pocket while Elven led Michael down the hallway toward the cell.

"W ELL, this isn't the dumbest thing you've done," he said to himself. "But it definitely ain't the smartest."

James found himself sitting in the truck he'd stolen from the Starcher residence. He smiled, thinking about the look on Hollis's face when he realized who was back in town. And on top of that, to borrow his truck. He almost had a good chuckle at that alone.

But the truck was also necessary for other reasons. At some point, he knew the red truck he'd stolen would be reported, or at the very least, spotted on one of his many errands. He was actually surprised it hadn't been mentioned when the call came in about Jason's dead body being found. Then again, Nick hadn't seemed like the sharpest tool in the shed. Even if he'd seen the truck when leaving the diner, the man probably hadn't put together who was the one that had put a bullet through his buddy's skull.

And Hollis was the perfect mark for stealing a car. He wouldn't be quick to call the sheriff about it, and once he figured out who had done the stealing, he probably wouldn't be in a rush to find the truck with him in it.

Getting under Hollis's skin was just the icing on the cake.

He immediately thought of the pie back at Hank's Diner, reminding himself he'd have to grab a slice on his way out. This was the last job, and he was finally going to get out of miserable, cold Dupray. Even worse, a storm was forming, with the clouds collecting overhead. He could get his job done and be gone just in time for it to get even colder.

He watched the front of the station patiently, knowing that the man he wanted was inside. The two deputies had gone out to see the dead man he'd left in the trailer, which made his job even easier. He didn't know how many other people worked the station, but by the size of it, it couldn't be many. He evaluated the situation, seeing that there were two unmarked cars out front, plus the Jeep with the Dupray County Sheriff's Department emblem on the side.

Knowing one of them was Amos's vehicle, that left two others, assuming nobody had carpooled or parked elsewhere. He knew he could make it in and out, killing his mark. He just didn't want to make any trouble out of it. He had no problem shooting anyone who needed shooting if they were in his way, but avoiding it was always easier.

He just needed to plan.

And that's when his plan unfolded right before his eyes.

He watched the door open, and Dylan Amos stepped outside. He wore a heavy jacket and cupped his hand around a cigarette. Soon after, he was puffing away at the stick. He leaned against the sheriff's Jeep and looked up at the sky.

James couldn't help but let a smile slip across his face as he stepped out of the truck.

CHAPTER THIRTY-EIGHT

"So this is Hunter?" Michael asked, sitting down in a metal folding chair across from the jail cell. He looked at Elven and pointed at Hunter.

Elven nodded.

"Who the fuck is this guy?" Hunter asked, crossing his arms in front of him.

"He's the only one who might have information about Jerry Farnham. I mean, other than you, that is," Elven said, watching to see if there was a reaction.

Hunter tensed up at the mention of Jerry, but he rolled his eyes, trying to play it off. Elven wasn't sure what that meant, but there was something there.

"I got fired from the mines for punching that motherfucker," Michael said. "He was talkin' shit about you."

"I don't even know you, asshole," Hunter said. "I don't need some old-timer sticking up for me about something that I've got no idea about anyway."

Michael chewed at his lips as he cycled through his thoughts. "I was friends with Donnie Price and Todd Utt."

"Todd Utt?" Hunter asked. "The fucking assistant coach back at my high school? Elven, what the fuck is this even about?"

"It's about what happened to Jerry Farnham. It's about why someone is in town killing folks who had something to do with whatever went down between the five of you," Elven said.

"Well, whippy shit," Hunter said. He laid on a thick sarcastic accent. "Looks like you dun cracked the case, Sheriff." He turned to Elven, serious again. "Really, Elven, this is dumb. I don't know this fucker. Todd was the dickhead coach at our high school I didn't even like that much. Donnie was my friend—"

"That you don't seem to have much love for," Elven interjected.

"Big fucking deal. So what? You think I killed them, because what? They were sticking up for me? So now what? Am I supposed to kill this Michael asshole next?"

Michael paid no attention to Hunter, but turned his attention to Noah. He squinted his eyes and cocked his head. "This one, you look familiar."

"Me?" Noah asked.

Michael nodded, his head shaking as he did it.

"What'd you say your name was?" Noah asked, leaning against the bars.

"Michael Amos," he said.

Noah squinted, seemingly trying to remember. Then he leaned back and smiled. "Oh shit, you're Dylan's dad, aren't you?"

Michael nodded. "That's my boy."

"Yeah," Noah said, shaking his finger. "We played together when we were kids. I think I only saw you once back then."

"You's that scrawny friend of his, right? I's busy at work. His momma had him most the time."

"How is he? I ain't seen him in a while," Noah said with a smile.

"Good, he's out there. Drove me over."

"Assuming I'm out of here, I'll have to say hi. Can't believe Dylan's still around," Noah said.

"Great goin' Elven," Hunter said. "You set up the world's worst fucking reunion here. Case closed."

Elven furrowed his brow, irritated that he was getting nowhere with this conversation. Hunter was right. It did seem to be a waste of time.

And then, before he could ask any more questions, four gunshots rang out in the air just outside the building.

CHAPTER THIRTY-NINE

Elven rushed past Meredith, who was fine. She was down below her desk, but the gunshots hadn't come from inside the station. They'd come from outside. In situations like this, he'd instructed her to get out of the way in case someone ever came in. Of course, he was also pretty sure she kept a gun in her purse that she put by her feet underneath the desk.

"Stay down!" he shouted to her as he ran out the door.

He was immediately hit with the smell of cigarette smoke. It invaded the cold air as it filled his lungs and he coughed, putting his arm over his face. He spun around, trying to take in the scene of what had happened.

In the distance, a truck sped off. It wasn't just a passerby, either. By the way the tires peeled out and the exhaust clouded in the air behind it, whoever was driving was running from the area. But the truck was also familiar. More than just familiar, he knew the vehicle to a T. The years of seeing it, keeping an eye on it, there was no mistaking that truck.

It was Hollis Starcher's vehicle.

Elven turned, grabbing his keys from his pocket and ran to his Jeep. As soon as he rounded it, he stopped. Dylan Amos was on the ground, his head leaning against the front tire. He'd been shot in the head, and there was a splatter of blood against the paint on his Jeep. His eyes were open and his mouth hung low. In his hand, a cigarette still smoldered between his fingers.

He hopped into the Jeep, leaving the door open and grabbed the radio. He held it to his mouth and clicked the button. "Tank, you there?"

He noticed dark storm clouds coming together in the distance. A storm was coming.

After a moment, Tank picked up. "Yeah, Elven, what's up?"

"I need you to look for Hollis's truck. It's headed west of the station. Whoever is in there just killed Dylan Amos in the parking lot."

"We're halfway to the dead body call."

"Then turn around. You'll see him soon coming your way."

"You on his tail?" Tank asked. "Want to try to box him in?"

Elven stuck the key in the ignition and fired up the Jeep. "I'm—"

He stopped talking when he glanced toward the back of the vehicle outside. The tire was completely flat, the side wall blown out. Then he realized that Dylan had one bullet in him, but he heard four gunshots. He stepped out and walked to the other side of his Jeep, seeing the two other tires that Dylan wasn't leaning against. They were both blown out, holes in their sides.

Elven grumbled and reached across the seat, grabbing the radio.

"No," he said. "Gonna be hung up a minute, so the two of you are on your own until I can make it there. If you can stop him, then I can catch up. Otherwise, I'm headed straight to Hollis's."

"Got it," Tank said.

Elven stepped back out to see Michael walking out of the station. The twitchy movement on his face settled into a grimace. "Dylan?" he asked. Then a groan came out of his mouth and he dropped to his son. "Aw, hell, Dylan?"

Elven had locked up Hunter and Noah and had brought Michael in, thinking that he was protecting someone and stopping someone else.

But instead, something else was going on, and Elven was on the completely wrong path.

CHAPTER FORTY

Elven pulled up to the large house that he'd known well. Just like Hollis's truck, he'd been to the house quite often. Before and after he'd become a law enforcement officer. On the way in, he hadn't noticed the truck that had sped away from the station, but he hadn't checked around the entire property, either.

As much as he wanted to believe Hollis had murdered Dylan Amos back at the station, he didn't see it being true. Hollis was a lot of things, and Elven knew he had it in him to kill a man. But he wasn't one to do something so direct and be caught in the middle of the day doing it. If he wanted Dylan dead, he'd have made sure there was nothing to tie him to it, along with making sure he was in a very public place, far away from the scene of the crime.

There was also no way he'd use his truck for a job.

Elven stepped out of the Buick he'd borrowed from Meredith. It wasn't his ideal mode of transportation, and it smelled like overpowering perfume with a dash of cucumbers. But it had four tires in good condition. He hated asking her to borrow it, but as she pointed out when handing the keys over, he had bought it for her in the first place

—not that he'd told anyone around town about that, or tried to hold it against her.

He appreciated Meredith's hard work, and when her husband had passed, she didn't have a lot left to her. So when she needed a vehicle to get to work when her car had finally broken down to the point it wasn't worth fixing, he'd taken her to buy one, no questions asked. No guilt passed. And nothing expected in return.

In the end, he was grateful that she'd let him borrow the car instead of having to finding three replacement tires. That would be a chore for when he got back. Besides, Phil was headed by to pick up Dylan Amos anyway, so Elven would have had to move his body.

And as much as Elven didn't want to be callous, he had someone more important to deal with right now.

Elven stood and knocked on the door. He put his hands on his hips as he waited. Dealing with Hollis in the past, he' expected there to be a bit of a wait, maybe because Hollis thought he was important enough to make others wait. Maybe one of his sons would answer the door and give Elven a bunch of grief for being on their doorstep.

But the door swung open after only a few seconds, and Hollis stood before him.

Elven took a step backward, realizing he was nearly toe to toe with Hollis. The man looked different. His composure wasn't the well-rehearsed gentle man he liked to tote around town. Instead, he seemed older. Less put together.

"Elven," Hollis said without a smile.

"What's with the truck, Hollis?" Elven asked.

Hollis shrugged, but it was half-hearted. The man looked tired.

"I see there's a new one around the side," Elven said, referring to a red truck he didn't recognize that poked out from the corner of the house.

"What of it?" he asked.

"I've got a dead man in my parking lot. Just shot no less than an hour ago."

"Sorry to hear, but I don't see why you're at my doorstep."

"I can appreciate that, except that your truck was seen fleeing the scene of the crime."

"Seen by who?" Hollis demanded.

"Me. I watched your truck speed away, leaving that dead man lying against my Jeep."

Hollis chewed his tongue for a moment. "My truck was stolen," he finally admitted.

A cold breeze came by and Elven wanted to step into the heat of the house, but Hollis blocked the way, and he wasn't about to ask Hollis to let him in. "Something is going on Hollis. What is it? What do you know?"

"Elven. Always thinkin' I'm in on whatever crime it is you're investigating. I just told you my truck was stolen."

"And that's one of the many things that come off as odd to me. Who in their right mind would steal from you?" Elven asked. "And even stranger, you let him get away with it."

Hollis took a deep breath, holding it a moment. Finally, he sighed. "Alright Elven, I'll level with ya. I ain't got nothing to do with this one, that's the God's honest truth. I mean it. But this man you're lookin' for...I know him."

Elven narrowed his eyes and felt the anger building inside of him. He should have known that Hollis had his hands in this somehow. "You know him and you expect me to think you ain't a part of this?"

Hollis held his hands up, defeated. "Believe me, I wouldn't have invited this man to Dupray. Not for anything, you hear me? He's deadlier than anything you ever seen. If he's killin' people, that means he's been paid. Paid well. Ain't nothin' gonna stop him until he completes the job. Your best option is to stay out of his way and hope you ain't on that list."

"Stay out of his way?" Elven asked. "It's my job to protect and serve the people of Dupray."

"This one's bigger than you, Elven. Hell, it's bigger than me, too. Do not get in his way."

Elven was dismayed by Hollis's admission. He was a big man,

with a big head to match. Not a lot scared him, but Elven could see it in his eyes. Hollis was petrified.

"I got two deputies goin' after him right now," Elven said.

"Elven, pull them off," Hollis said. "Those men ain't prepared for anyone like this. Even that jarhead you got for a deputy. Let this one go, I mean it. I ain't meddling with this one."

"How do you know him?"

"This guy and me, we go way back. Had taken some work that he was on, too. Ever since then, I made it a point to stay away from anything he was involved with. He ain't like you or me. He's got his own set of rules, and there ain't no breakin' them."

"So what? Let murders happen in my county and have this guy skate?" Elven asked.

Hollis shook his head. "I heard he had one last name on his list. If you say someone was shot outside the station, sounds like the list is complete. I don't want to see anything happen to you. What you decide from here is your choice, but Elven, let this one go."

And as if on cue, thunder kicked up in the distance.

CHAPTER FORTY-ONE

"Elven," Tank said. "We got him. His truck is about five miles off the road down Yara Way. There's a building over here, looks abandoned."

Tank waited as he held the radio. "Elven, you there?"

Thunder cracked overhead and lightning flashed in the distance. "Shit, I don't know if it's a connection issue or if he ain't by the radio."

Johnny watched Tank stand and debate in his head. He picked something from his teeth, digging his tongue under his upper lip. Another clash of thunder came, and Johnny nearly jumped at the sound.

"I think we should wait for Elven," Johnny said. He really didn't want to go inside and look for the guy. He knew Tank was thinking the opposite, but then again, Tank was a brave man. He'd seen a lot of action in his military days, and he'd never been afraid to stand up to anyone before. Hell, the guy had even been shot.

Johnny, however, was nothing like that.

Tank clapped his hand on Johnny's shoulder, drawing his attention "Johnny, I know what you're thinking, alright? Don't. We're gonna be fine. We've both trained for this—he's just some asshole. I'm sure you've got some image in your head about some western shootout, but it ain't gonna be like that. I'll take the lead, you just back me up. We'll cuff the asshole and it'll be all over, alright?"

Johnny shook, still not sure. His stomach growled in response. He always got hungry when he was nervous.

Tank smiled, which was rare when he was in the zone. "You've been practicin' your shooting with Elven. I'm sure you've gotten a lot better. And we'll get you a snack after this, alright? What's your go-to snack when you get home?"

"N-nachos," Johnny said.

"Good man," Tank said. "Nachos are easy, right? Even better when someone is there to help make it for you. Throw some chips and cheese together, microwave it, boom. Easy. Just think of it like the nachos of a takedown."

Johnny found himself nodding. Tank had a way to make it seem so damn easy. But as much as Johnny wanted to think of this as the nachos of a takedown, he could count numerous times that he left the microwave too long and burned the cheese to the plate. He knew he could screw up the easiest of tasks.

Tank started to move toward the abandoned building. It was a large wooden structure. At some point in its life, it had been a barn, but that had been at least five years ago. The roof looked to have caved in at the corner. One door was closed while the other flapped open from the strong wind that suddenly picked up.

Tank put his back against the wall and looked at Johnny, who followed suit. Each of them pulled their weapons out, and Johnny's hand trembled. Tank reached over to Johnny, placing his own hand on Johnny's and locked eyes with him.

"Just follow my lead," he said.

Johnny took a deep breath, smelling the rain in the air. There was a cleansing coming, and Johnny wanted to be home before the downpour.

Tank spun toward the open door and rushed in. Johnny followed behind, trying to keep his breathing steady, trying to not think of all the ways he could mess this up.

Inside, the barn was bleak. It was dark, except where the hazy light came in through the roof. The cloud coverage was making it even more difficult to see. Moss grew at the edges of the roof where the rain had soaked into the exposed wooden beams.

On the ground was a stack of old wood. It had been piled there at some point, probably before being abandoned, and now the planks were warped and useless. Dust floated in the air, shining at the small rays that passed through the clouds.

In the center of the barn sat a black car. It was a four-door Ford Taurus with a few dents in the bumper. At the front of the car, the barn door was wide open so it could be driven out. Tank gave Johnny a single nod and lifted his gun. He worked his way to the left side of the car and Johnny stayed on the right side far back enough, just inside the doorway.

"Stop right there," a voice said from Johnny's left. He turned his head and saw a man dressed in black. His gun was raised, pointed at Tank. Tank froze where he stood.

"Sheriff's department," Tank said, slowly turning.

"Don't do that," the man said. Johnny stood, his gun in his hand, but pointed at the dirt floor he stood on. He wanted to pull it up, but he stood frozen as the man kept his gun on Tank.

"You don't want to do this," Tank said. "Just put your hands up and we can make this easy."

"I ain't gonna freeze. I ain't gonna put my hands up," the man replied. "But I will give you a warning, though. Put your guns down now. I got no list with your names on it, so I got no reason to shoot you unless you give me one."

Tank stood for a moment and Johnny just watched it unfold. He was waiting for Tank's lead to do something. And what shocked Johnny the most was that the man had shoved his gun in his holster, no longer pointing it at Tank.

Johnny took the opportunity to raise his gun, narrowing his sights on the man in black. But his hand shook and he froze. His gun was pointed at the man, and it didn't seem to bother him one bit. The man flashed a glance toward Johnny, a slight uptick to the corner of his mouth, but returned his eyes toward Tank.

"I can see you ain't gonna listen," the man said with a frown. "I really hate to do this to a man of the law who ain't on my list. But it wouldn't be the first time."

"Tank," Johnny managed to say. He wanted to say that the man's gun was no longer raised, that Tank could turn around. But something in his throat hitched and he couldn't bring himself to it. Something inside him told him that if he did, his friend would be dead.

The man considered Tank as he stood there, his gun still up, pointed at nothing. It was as if he was truly pondering his next step, toying with Tank. Why had he holstered his weapon? And even more, why could Johnny not pull his own trigger?

"I'm telling you now, deputy," the man said.

"The next words out of your mouth better be 'yes sir', followed by the gun on the ground," Tank said. "I did two tours in Iraq, motherfucker. I ain't scared of someone like you."

The man in black sighed again. Johnny watched his chest inflate, then deflate. He shook his head as Tank slowly turned around.

"Looks like you're one lucky son of a bitch," the man said. Tank continued to turn, and Johnny thought the man might actually give up, but instead, there was a glint in his eye.

"Johnny, now!" Tank yelled.

But Johnny didn't move. He stood shaking, his gun trembling in his hands.

Tank spun around quickly, diving to the side as he fired his weapon. At the same time, Johnny watched the man as his hand gave a hint of a flutter, and suddenly, it was raised. He had his gun in his hand and his arm extended toward Tank, and the muzzle flash escaped from the end of the barrel. Thunder cracked at the same time the gun went off, creating an echo of blasts all around. The man's gun, the thunder, Tank's gun.

But the man stood, still pointing his gun toward Tank. Or at least, where Tank had been standing.

The rain started to pour down, entering through the caved-in roof. It fell over the man, soaking him almost immediately. Johnny felt the ice-cold rain over his skin, still holding the gun locked on the man. He would have loved to blame the rain, but it was nothing other than fear. Johnny, still frozen, watched as the man walked toward Tank, who was now on the ground. The top half of him fell so that Johnny could see him poke out from behind the Taurus.

Tank yelled out in pain and Johnny could see him scrambling on the floor, his shoulder covered in blood. His arm was above his head, lying on the ground. His gun was at least two feet away from his hand.

"Johnny!" Tank yelled. But Johnny couldn't move. He'd just watched his friend take a bullet. The man who made everything look so easy. The one who was so brave, he practically laughed in the face of danger. And now, he was the one on the ground bleeding while Johnny let it happen.

The man walked toward Tank, his gun pointed directly at his head. Johnny felt his lip quiver, unable to do anything to stop him.

Eventually, the man stopped, feet spread over Tank's body as he writhed in pain. "What were you? Marine?"

Tank grit his teeth and yelled from the pain. From the frustration. From being bested, and his partner doing nothing to stop the man who now pointed a gun at his face. Johnny knew he was a joke. He'd just never come to terms with it before.

"Figured as much," the man said, his voice calm. "I got a lot of respect for you. All the shit they make you do, yet you do it. You do the job you signed up for." He snorted through his nose, then spit out whatever he'd come up with out his mouth off to the side. "If you hadn't figured it out yet, that's why it's just your shoulder. Through and through, or close to anyway. Once you're stitched up, you'll be right as rain."

The man smiled, holding his empty palm out like to collect the cold water that flooded down over them. "I fucking hate the cold," he said. "Don't be too hard on yourself for this. You never had a chance, though I am impressed you got that shot off. Just got no aim to back it up. Take it easy for at least a week, soldier."

"Fuck you," Tank said through a clenched jaw.

The man smiled down at him, then turned to Johnny. He let out a laugh and holstered his gun. He took a few steps toward Johnny. Johnny found the strength to face him, his gun still pointed directly at him. The man just walked his way, closer and closer, as if he was out for a Sunday stroll, until the barrel of Johnny's gun was poked directly into his chest.

Johnny began to shake. Every limb he had trembled, and he began to feel the warmth of his piss run down his leg. It was a stark contrast from the cold rain pattering down on him.

"Y-y-you gonna kill me?" he managed to stammer.

The man let out a *hmmm* as he looked Johnny up and down. He smiled when he saw the obvious trail that led down from his crotch. "Give me that before you hurt yourself."

He placed his hand on Johnny's gun, gently lowering his hand. He took the gun from Johnny's grip, but Johnny was lying to himself—he practically couldn't wait to hand it over to him.

Johnny continued to stand in front of the man, looking into his eyes, seeing the devil himself. "I don't work for free, and you ain't worth the price of a bullet anyway. I told you neither of you were on my list. Now, go tend to your friend and call the sheriff. Probably an ambulance, too."

Johnny couldn't hold it back anymore and felt the tears mix with the rain on his face. What was happening right now?

"You got a wife, girlfriend maybe?" He looked Johnny up and down. Johnny's breathing was shallow and he didn't know what to say. "You ain't queer, are ya? I ain't prejudiced or nothin', you just don't seem the type," the man said, his eyes still so empty behind them. Still so cold. Everything he said was matter-of-fact, so casual, as if he hadn't just killed a man and shot another. "Come on, I ain't gonna bite."

"G-g-girlfriend," Johnny said. "J-just met a few days ago."

The man pursed his lips and nodded, giving his approval. "Good for you," he said, poking Johnny in the chest. It wasn't hard or menacing, but it didn't make Johnny any calmer. "I want you to do me a favor, alright?"

Johnny stared at him, having no piss left in his bladder to expel down his leg anymore. He nodded, no longer knowing what were tears and what was rain.

"Once the ambulance comes and takes your friend to the hospital," he said, holding a finger up at Johnny's expression. "Remember, he's gonna be fine. Once he's there, I want you to go to that woman that took pity on a dolt like you. The one who doesn't mind wastin' her time, holding that clammy hand of yours, havin' to wipe her palm on her pretty dress cause you ain't got the confidence in yourself to think someone as pretty as she is would be with you. Assumin' she's pretty, of course, but I find most women are, in their individual ways. I want you to take that woman in your arms and kiss her. Then fuck her until neither one of you can feel your legs anymore. And when you're done, and your pecker is beggin' to surrender, I want you to remember that this day, that this fucking moment, the one right here, is when your life changed."

The man stood, his nose nearly pressed against Johnny's. Johnny could smell a hint of sweetness mixed with old milk. But none of it mattered, he was too focused on the man's words, on the idea of dying.

"I'm sure you'll cry about it," the man continued. "That you felt you shoulda done better. That you could have been a man and stood up to me. That if you was anyone else, you would have pulled that trigger. But let me tell you, if you were anyone else, that feeling I want you to experience, the one where you can't feel your legs and your cock is floppier than a balloon that's lost its air? That would be the feeling' you'd have the rest of your life. Cause while I ain't gonna work for free and kill ya, I sure as shit wouldn't let you outta here without takin' a bullet in your spine. And you wouldn't be able to fuck that woman, or anyone else for that matter, ever again."

The man poked Johnny in the head, and Johnny knew it like he knew how to make a plate of nachos—this man owned him, and there was nothing he could do about it.

"You're gonna let everyone down around you, you know that, don't you? Friendly or not, if you can't do what you're called upon, you ain't worth shit. Maybe you should consider a different profession," he said. "Ever thought of being a janitor?"

With that, the man laughed and walked way. He stepped over Tank, who was still in pain and didn't try to go for his gun. Even Tank knew that he'd been offered his life from that man. The man slid into the driver's seat of the Taurus, turned the ignition, and drove off before Johnny could convince himself to move his legs.

As soon as he was gone, Johnny collapsed to the ground, managing to find the strength to crawl to Tank. The ground had gone soggy, his fingers sinking into the mud. When he reached Tank, he bawled, apologized, and most of all, remembered every last word that man had told him.

CHAPTER FORTY-TWO

The sheriff's station had been a clusterfuck as soon as Elven had run off. He'd left, but not before letting Meredith have the keys to the jail. Once Phil had gotten there to help with Dylan Amos's body, she let Hunter and Noah out. The two of them stayed to help Phil load the body up, Michael hollering about his son the whole way.

"Elven let us out?" Hunter asked.

Meredith nodded. "Radioed over and said it was obvious this wasn't you. He even said he might have been wrong, but you didn't hear that from me."

Hunter was in no rush to laugh. Not with there being a man shot dead only moments before. And he also wasn't in a rush to give Elven any credit. He'd admitted he was wrong only when it had blown up in his face in the worst way. And he hadn't even admitted it directly to him or his brother.

"I'm sorry about your mother," Meredith offered. "And I'm sorry about the added grief."

Hunter held no grudges against her, and it seemed his brother didn't, either. Meredith was a good woman, doing her job. And according to Noah, she'd been a good friend to his mother, which he supposed might count for something.

Once everyone had left the station, Meredith had even given them a lift to Phil's to get their truck that had been left during the funeral. Phil had offered to squeeze them into his vehicle, but Noah didn't seem too keen on spending time with the dead body of his old friend, and Hunter didn't want to be in the car with Michael as he cried over his son. So they waited for Meredith.

After a quiet ride, they'd taken their truck back home. Or to Noah's home anyway. Hunter might have grown up in it, but he didn't feel like he had any claim on it now. Not since he'd been gone for twenty years. Not since he left for the reasons he did.

He wasn't sure he'd feel welcome there ever again.

Back at the house, exhaustion set in, and he could tell it was the same for his brother as well. They both had their ties completely loosened around their necks, and their sport coats were shrugged back on their shoulders. Noah opted to unbutton his shirt a few buttons so his undershirt was exposed. He threw the keys on the table next to the couch and stared at the empty hospital bed for a moment.

Hunter cleared his throat. "Hey, I'm uh, sorry about Dylan."

Noah cocked his head to the side and turned around, a confused expression on his face. "What?"

"What you were sayin' to Michael. You were his friend, right? I know you said you ain't seen him for a while, but still, I'm sorry. It's hard losing a friend," Hunter said. He hadn't seen his brother in a long time, so he didn't know what to say. He was trying. But it didn't seem like he was connecting very well.

"Dylan Amos?" Noah said as if he couldn't believe what he was hearing. "Fuck off, Hunter. Just drop the brotherly love act, alright? I know you don't fucking care about me."

Hunter was shocked. His brother wasn't known to stand up for himself much, but then again, he was a different person from the high school graduate he'd left behind.

"That ain't true, Noah," Hunter said.

"You don't know shit about me," Noah said. "If you were a good brother, or hell, just a brother at all, you'd know that he and I were friends when we were eight."

"I've missed out on a lot, I know—"

"When we were *eight*, Hunter. You were still here, but you were too busy being the great Hunter Wallace. Better than everyone. Better than your own fucking brother. Too good to see that by the time I was in middle school, Dylan Amos was too popular for me, too. Story of my fuckin' life apparently. He told me he didn't want to hang out with losers anymore right in front of the whole goddamn school. Cause that's what I was, a loser. I was laughed at for weeks because of it."

Hunter looked at his brother, seeing the hurt and pain in his eyes. Even now, after all these years, he held onto that. "I'm sorry, Noah. I just—"

"Yeah, I bet you are," Noah said. "You know, most brothers would have seen me cryin' every day. They would have done something. Stood up for me. Gone to beat the motherfucker up. But you did nothing. You just let it happen."

Hunter didn't know what to say. He could see the vein in Noah's forehead bulging as he shouted at him, and tears welling up in his eyes. His mouth was practically frothing. It seemed he'd been holding it all in for twenty years for it to burst out now.

"You had your own life to live. The one that was so fucking great. The one that had all the popular kids wanting to be around you, so you couldn't bother to stand up for the little guy, even if the little guy was your own blood. And then your life was so fucking great that you decided to just up and take it out of here. Just leave me and momma because you were too good for this place. You were too good for us."

"Noah—"

Noah turned and stormed off, leaving Hunter alone in the room. He really had missed out on a lot, and there was nothing he could do now to make up for it.

CHAPTER FORTY-THREE

Elven made the drive to the hospital that was at the edge of the county. It was a long trip, but one that needed taking. Johnny had called him immediately after calling the ambulance. He was rambling about Tank being shot and the guy that had been so fast with his shooting. Elven didn't know what to make of it exactly.

The nurse at the desk had pointed him in the direction and he was able to find the room himself. The hospital wasn't very large, so it was hard to get lost. But it could still be confusing with the commotion of the nurses and doctors hustling about, along with his own emotions pulling at him to make sure both his deputies were alright.

When he entered the room, Tank lay in bed with his eyes closed. He was hooked up to an IV drip and a machine that beeped softly. The lights were all off, except for the one above the entry point where he stood and the bathroom light in the corner. The door there was only opened a crack, most likely so if Tank had to go, he could stand and find his way there.

Elven was confused about why he had all the machinery hooked up to him.

"They had to do surgery," Johnny said from the dark corner, as if reading his mind. He turned and saw him lean forward, his face closer to the light. His eyes were red and puffy. He'd been crying. A lot.

"The doctor said the bullet had exited out the back, but that they needed to get in there and stitch up some artery or tendons or something, I don't know. Said it was really minor, but still had to be done. He spoke so fast, I didn't know what he was sayin'."

"Surgery seemed to be done really fast, so that's good," Elven said.

Johnny shrugged. "I didn't notice."

Elven sighed, seeing Johnny such a mess and Tank out of commission. "I'll call Sandra. I'm sure Tank's wife is going to give me an earful for this."

"I already did," Johnny said. "And yeah, you're right. It was an earful."

Johnny was usually pretty happy wherever he went. Like an ignorant idiot at times, but now, he didn't have a hint of joy in his voice at all. He was broken. Defeated. Like there was nothing left in him.

"She's on her way, but had to drop the kids at the neighbors or something," Johnny added. He paused, turning to Tank. Elven saw the bandage covering the man's shoulder. He wore a gown, but the entire right side of his upper body was exposed. "This is my fault, Elven."

"Johnny," Tank grumbled, his voice groggy and dry. Tank's eyes fluttered and he turned his head. Johnny stood up, eyes wide and went to the bedside. "Am I dead?"

"No, you're gonna be alright, Tank," Johnny said, grabbing his hand.

"Thank God," Tank said. "I was about to be really disappointed if the first face I saw when I got to heaven was your ugly mug." He smiled and followed it up with a laugh.

"It ain't funny," Johnny said. "I'm so sorry, Tank. I should have done something. I should have—"

"Johnny, stop it. This ain't your fault, you hear me? I remember everything that happened, and if you'd done anything different, you'd be lying in the bed down the hall in worse shape. We both know it."

Johnny shook his head. "Even if it's true, it don't make me feel any better."

"Did I hear you called Sandra?" Tank asked.

Johnny nodded.

"Shit, Johnny. That's punishment enough for whatever you think you deserve. I'm sure you'll get more of it next time she sees you, too. I'm surprised you survived *that*."

"Glad to see you're okay, Tank," Elven said, cutting in.

"Elven. This guy, man, he's somethin' else. He's got something dark inside of him, and I've never seen someone draw so fast. The fucker holstered his gun like it was some sort of game. I had my gun up, ready to shoot, and he still got me," Tank said in disbelief.

Tank confirmed what Hollis had told him. "Well, as much as I hate to say it, I think he's gone. I heard he had one more on his list, and Dylan Amos rounds that out. I don't think we'll be catching him before he blows town."

"Good riddance," Tank said, his head shifting on his pillow. He closed his eyes for a moment, then opened them, but they began to droop again.

"You get some rest," Elven said. "We'll step outside."

Tank nodded as he drifted off to sleep. Elven took Johnny out to the hallway, where the lighting was harsh. He could see Johnny's face even better. He looked in worse shape than Tank.

"You're just gonna let him go?" Johnny asked.

"I don't like it, but he's got no reason to stay in Dupray anymore. I'm sure he's halfway out of town already."

Johnny nodded. "Good, I guess. Wouldn't want to put you in that position anyway. And with me as your only back-up."

227

Elven grabbed Johnny's shoulder and shook him until he locked eyes with him. "Johnny, you got Tank here. He's gonna be alright. There's nothing else you could have done, you understand?"

Johnny shook his head. "No, I don't. I know what I am to this department. I'm a joke. I'm the guy that bumbles around, knowing nothin' about nothin'. The guy no one wants to show up when they call something in, and if he does, I'm met with sighs and eye rolls. Lester hired me all those years ago 'cause he was desperate. I took it because I thought it was what I wanted, that it would make me somethin' I was never gonna be. But I never shoulda been hired. I don't belong here. At best, I fuck everything up. At worst, I'll get someone killed."

"Johnny," Elven said, but it was no use. Johnny shoved past Elven and ran down the hall. He was out of sight by the time Elven could turn around.

THE RAIN CONTINUED to pour down. It had been pouring from the entire drive away from the hospital to the very porch he sat on. Johnny was soaked through and freezing cold. But none of it bothered him. In fact, he welcomed the cold. At least it numbed everything in his body, except of course, for the one thing he wished it would numb.

He was torn up inside as he stared out into the darkness. A house across the street had its lights on in one room, and he could see the television flashing in the other room. Every so often, the darkness would shift to a blue light, then back to darkness, followed by another flash of blue with each scene that changed on the show.

He couldn't get the words out of his head. The ones the man had left him with.

You're gonna let everyone down around you.

Johnny swallowed. He wanted to believe that wasn't the case.

That maybe he was just a gentle soul, like his mother had always told him. That he was a loyal friend. A good man. But deep down, the man was right.

Wasn't he?

Johnny listened to the rain pattering down on the ground next to him, the thunder cracking in the distance. He wasn't worth shit, just like the man had told him. Straight and to the point. At least someone had the decency to tell him. Not like Elven or Tank. They tried to be his friend, to make him feel better. But he didn't deserve to feel better.

The light next to the door clicked on and the door swung open. Button poked her head out, looking around, and then saw Johnny there, soaked head to toe.

"Johnny?" she asked, stepping out into the rain. "What're you doin' out here?"

She walked up to him and he couldn't bring himself to look at her. He stared forward, feeling sorry for himself. He just wanted to be close to her, but didn't want to have to face her.

"You're gonna catch pneumonia out here. My Lord, Johnny, your lips are blue. You're freezing."

She knelt down to him and grabbed both sides of his face in her hands. Her skin was warm against his frozen cheeks, slowly bringing the feeling back to them. "Johnny, what's wrong? Talk to me."

She dipped lower until his eyes were locked onto hers. And as soon as he looked at her squarely, he lost it. His lips quivered, and he wailed. The tears poured down again.

She grabbed his face, standing and wrapped her arms around him. He sobbed into her, smelling her perfume, feeling her warmth.

"Johnny, what's wrong? You're scaring me," she said. "Come on."

She pulled at him, and he let himself stand. Her hair was soaked and her teeth already chattering. He felt awful bringing her out into the cold like he had. But he was grateful for her. He was glad she had come out to save him. He looked into her eyes and leaned forward.

He met her lips with his own. She tasted like raspberries and vanilla. Her warmth flooded into him and he wrapped his arms around her. He broke their kiss and buried his head into her shoulder while she held him, her hand on the back of his head.

After a moment, she pulled at him, and he followed her into the house.

CHAPTER FORTY-FOUR

Elven found himself at Martin's Bar after a long day. Even after Johnny had taken the earful from Sandra over the phone, she'd still had it in her to rip Elven a new one when meeting him at the hospital. Lots of talk about responsibility, family, ego, and disappointment was involved. It was quite the conversation. Well, "conversation" might not have been the right word. Usually that involved two people talking, and this was definitely one way.

Once she'd said her peace, though, she calmed down and saw Tank. Elven watched as she prepared to do the same with her husband. The poor guy had just been shot, and now he was going to have to suffer through even worse.

Elven smiled when he saw Tank quickly close an eye when he saw his wife. Can't yell at a guy resting after surgery, Elven supposed. And his tactic worked, but Elven couldn't help but think it was a risky move. She'd just stew and bottle it up until he woke, and then the explosion might be even greater.

But Tank was used to it, so he would let the man decide his own fate. Besides, he loved her for a reason, and her caring enough to be that worried about him showed Elven that she felt the same about Tank. He was glad Tank could have someone stay with him.

And that's when Elven headed home. He'd planned to get some rest, put the day behind him, but his mind was still all over the place. Getting rest was going to be a tough sell, and his mind could be a stubborn one sometimes. That's when he saw the lights calling to him from Martin's Bar. It looked no different than any other night, but with the day he had, he was drawn to the bar like a moth to flame and pulled in without thinking of it.

It was noticeably quieter inside than most days. The storm was enough to keep people away, but perhaps with Glenna's funeral, the fight that ensued, and now, the very publicly known murders, everyone had decided to take it easy. To stay inside and keep to themselves.

Of course, he couldn't help but laugh to himself when he saw who sat at the bar.

Hunter Wallace.

He just couldn't get away, could he? He had screwed up massively, and now he had to face it directly.

Hunter sipped on a small glass that had three ice cubes in it. The brown liquid in it was nearly gone, barely lining the bottom. Hunter threw the last of it back, then hunched over the bar. He raised the glass toward Charlene, who came by to take it from him.

"You alright, sweetie?" she asked.

"Oh, yeah, I could just use another," Hunter answered.

She threw the old ice in the sink and refilled it with more whiskey and fresh ice, placing it in front of him. She leaned over, her breasts front and center. "You know, I was a little disappointed when you didn't call. Maybe tonight, when I get off work, we could—"

"I appreciate the offer," Hunter said. "I've just got somethin' on my mind, so please, don't take offense."

She leaned back and smiled. "None taken, honey. I know it's been a rough day for you. But I'll take a rain check, alright?" She winked, and he raised a glass to her.

Elven slid next to him in the empty stool. "Always had a way with the ladies. I see that hasn't changed."

Hunter turned to Elven, looking over his shoulder. He turned back to his drink. "You here to arrest me again? For some new charges this time, or still for that shit you started at the funeral?"

"You gonna pull a gun on me?"

Hunter shrugged. "Haven't decided."

Elven strummed his hand on the bartop. "I guess I owe you an apology. For a lot of things. I was wrong."

Hunter sat up and looked around. He spun his head around dramatically, as if he was searching for something.

"What?" Elven asked.

"Oh, just seeing if anyone else was around to confirm this. Ain't nobody gonna believe that Elven Hallie came to apologize to me," Hunter said. "He's too full of himself, he doesn't think he's ever wrong."

"I suppose I deserve that," Elven said.

"You deserve a lot more than that," Hunter shot back.

"Fair enough," Elven said. "But I'm tryin' here, alright? So will you let me say my piece or are you just gonna give me flack the whole time?"

Hunter lifted his hand, palm up, encouraging him to continue.

"I was wrong about you. I should have known that. The last I saw you, you were a good man. That kind of thing doesn't change too much. And you were right."

"Holy—"

Elven glared at him.

"Sorry," Hunter said with a smile.

"I may have had a bit of jealousy when I saw you. I mean, you came into town out of nowhere and blew my little competition away like it was nothing. Getting the girl like it ain't a thing," he said, motioning to Charlene. "It just reminded me of all those times you were better than me. It's stupid, I know. Hell, I was stupid. You just made it seem so easy, and all the time, I had to worry about people being the way they were to me 'cause of my name. My parents. Their money. You didn't have any of that. You just had everyone's respect for being you."

Hunter sat, the two of them in silence for a moment. Eventually, he spoke. "You're right. You are stupid," he said with a smile. "But you aren't that wrong. A lot of time passed, and believe me, I've done some real shitty things in my past. Not knowin' anyone, needing money, good with guns. You can put it together, I'm sure. But some things I done, I wish I could take back."

Elven nodded, knowing he had his own demons.

"But you know, eventually it worked out. Found my footing, got a good job. Settled in a place out in Texas doing trick shots at a gun show." He chuckled. "Sounds corny, but it was fun. Pay was decent and I was good at it. I even found someone. For a while anyway"

"What happened?"

Hunter shrugged. "Sometimes people grow apart, I guess. Ain't nothing either one of us did. Just life, right?"

Elven nodded. "Hard to imagine you actually settling down, though. You were always playing the field. I was just grateful in high school you didn't set your sights on Penny."

Hunter laughed. "Nah, that girl had eyes for you only."

"So did you meet her at a strip club? Was her name Diamond or Jezebel?" Elven asked with a laugh, trying to figure out the type of woman who would have made Hunter content.

Hunter played with his glass, the condensation pooling around the bottom. He looked at Elven. "His name was Pete."

Elven wasn't prepared for that. He looked into Hunter's eyes, feeling he could see into the man's soul. There was pain inside.

"He was a good man," Hunter said. "I guess I lied when I said it wasn't anything either one of us did. It was me. I know it."

"What happened?"

"He wanted to meet the family. Shit, I met his, so it made sense to him. His mother was nothing but kind. His father was a good man, accepting and everything. But I didn't understand it. I told him we couldn't come here, not together. Dupray ain't the most progressive place. Eventually, after a lot of pestering, he finally told me I wasn't comfortable enough being who I was. And that if I couldn't accept myself, then neither could he."

Hunter took a sip of his whiskey, then set the glass back down.

"But you weren't wrong," he said. "He was a stripper when we met."

Elven burst out laughing. "I knew you always had a type."

Hunter nodded. "That I do. That I do."

Elven slapped Hunter on the back, remembering at one point, he'd had a friend in the man. He wished he hadn't been so jealous and stubborn.

"Jerry never showed back up to work because he caught me," Hunter revealed. "More than that, I made a pass at him."

"How'd you know him?" Elven asked.

"Met him at a party. I knew he was a dealer, but figured it was just a fun thing he did at parties. I'd been drinkin' and thought he was hinting at something. Obviously, I misread the signals. I was still new at it, confused at what was goin' on in my head. So that little attempt was met with a fat lip and bein' called a faggot. I was left even more scared and confused, but this time, I was worried everyone would find out what I was. This dirty secret inside of me, at least, that's how I was made to feel at the time.

"So Donnie told me he'd been talkin' shit about me at the mines. Mouthin' off about me being gay. They, of course, didn't believe him. Who would believe that Hunter Wallace was a cocksucker?"

Elven cringed at the word, but it was Hunter's story.

"So he and Todd Utt set him up to come out in the woods. That's when I met them there. We took turns, but I did most of it. Beat the living shit out of him, then I stuck a gun in his face and told him if he didn't leave, if I ever saw him again, I'd shoot him dead wherever he stood. Donnie and Todd practically had to pull me off him 'cause they thought I was gonna kill him."

"Would you have?"

Hunter sighed. "I don't know. Maybe. I do know I meant what I said though, and that's what scared me. I ain't proud of it, Elven. What I did. I just didn't know what to do back then. I could barely look at myself in the mirror. Not accepting who I was, pretending to be something else. In the end, by doin' all that, I was turning into something worse."

"So that's why you left?"

Hunter nodded. "I couldn't be myself, and I couldn't be this other person."

"Hunter, that's not true. I would have—"

"Oh, fuck off, Elven. Yeah, maybe you wouldn't have given a shit. You're a decent person. Hell, I'm sure there's a handful of others around that are, too. But you know Dupray. There's more than a few shit heels here to make life miserable. Besides, it wasn't about them. It was about me."

Elven didn't have much of an answer to that. Hunter was right, and at the end of the day, Elven had never had to deal with that. The worst thing he'd dealt with was being judged because he had money. That was a lot different than being hated for who you were.

"You know, Elven. You may have been jealous of me, but I always envied you. And it wasn't because of the money. You're a good man. And even though you got shit about who your parents were, you stayed here in Dupray. I bet you dollars to donuts they hate you takin' on this job, too. Am I right?"

Elven nodded.

"You looked them in the eye and told them you don't give two shits about what they think. And I can see that you actually care about the job. You're too damn cocky for your own good, maybe. But I look up to you. I'm glad to know you, Elven Hallie."

CHAPTER FORTY-FIVE

His getaway vehicle had been stashed where he didn't think anyone would see it, and it wouldn't have if the two deputies hadn't caught up to him. But it was no matter. One was likely in a hospital bed and the other one didn't have the stones to follow up on trying to catch him. If the sheriff knew what was good for him, he'd stay out of the way.

But he still felt the need to stop back at his room. He had a small place rented at the edge of town. He paid cash so as to not leave a trail. It was a dump of a place, but then again, everywhere in Dupray could be described that way.

At the room, he had a few items, like an extra gun, a stash of cash, snacks, and spare clothes. He kept most of his things in the Taurus, in case he didn't want to head back to the room. But also kept extra items in the room in case he needed an emergency spot to hunker down in. They were all things he could live without on the chance he needed to blow town fast, but he didn't feel it was necessary . Nobody was going to be coming after him, and he liked to collect his things for the next job.

It was all just precaution and old habits. At this point in the game, he'd only ever needed to use the stash once in his career. And that was back when he was still fairly green, working with those less skilled than he was.

He jumped out of his Taurus and ran to the door, ducking underneath the canopy outside his motel room door. The rain was so heavy that all the drying he'd done in the car had been for not as the short run he'd just done had soaked him again. He cursed himself and fumbled with the key in his pocket. His hands were stiff from the cold and he couldn't wait to leave town.

Just as soon as he slid the key in the door and turned the handle, his phone rang in his pocket. He shut the door behind him, blowing on his hands to warm them up, then grabbed his phone.

"James," he said.

He did a quick check of his room, making sure nobody had been there. He'd left explicit instruction to the front desk to not let anyone in to clean the room until he checked out. He figured they'd be happy with less work, and he'd leave them a big tip anyway. He tipped the front desk clerk well enough to also keep an eye on any strangers around.

"You still in town?" the voice said on the other end.

"The job is done. My business is none of yours now," he said, ready to hang up.

"Hold on. I've got another job if you're up for it."

James sighed, looking out the window. It was wet and cold, and he hated everything about it. But he was being hired to do another job. Could he really be mad?

"What is it?" James asked.

"Two more," the voice said.

"I was looking forward to relaxing a bit," James lied. He never relaxed. He enjoyed places where people relaxed, but he was always working. Always on call. It's what he enjoyed the most. "That last one was a bit of a recluse. Hard to find."

"I'm sorry that it was too much trouble—"

"Nobody gives me trouble. It was easy," James said. He didn't want anyone to think he was complaining, or that he couldn't handle something. There was no one better than him.

"Alright," he said. "I'll pay whatever the price, if you want the money."

James bit the side of his cheek, lifting his revolver from his hip. He replaced the two bullets in the cylinder he had fired earlier.

"I'm listening," he said, snapping it back in place.

CHAPTER FORTY-SIX

Hunter walked into Noah's house. After all, that's what it was now. He figured it had been passed down to Hunter in his mother's will, but then again, he didn't know. He'd never taken a look at it, and he didn't have any intentions of claiming anything as his.

Noah stood over the hospital bed that sat in the living room. He had the mattress stripped and piled into the corner. He worked on folding the bed up, dropping the sides down and squeezing it together so it became half the size.

Hunter walked to him, his head light from the booze.

"Let me help," Hunter said, grabbing at the wheels to unlock them.

"I don't need your help," Noah said, his voice on edge.

Hunter didn't stop. Instead, he continued to walk around the bed, pushing on the side of the wheels that said *unlock*.

"I said I don't need your fuckin' help," Noah said, shoving his brother. Hunter fell back against the wall and held up his hands. He looked at his brother's face and saw his eyes filled with rage.

"Noah," Hunter said, deciding what to say next. It was already clear he was just trying to help, but it was also clear that Noah wasn't having anything to do with him.

"I've been doing this for the past year without anyone's help, you know that?" Noah asked. "When the insurance brought it by, they showed me how to do it. We couldn't afford a nurse at the house, so I did everything. I took notes, but after the second time doing it, I didn't need them, either."

"Okay, Noah, I—"

"But that's not it, Hunter. It wasn't just folding up a bed and setting out some sheets. It got bad in the end. I'd have to walk her around, and then when she was too weak I had to wipe her ass. I would carry her piss and shit across the living room to dump it in the fucking toilet. There was no nurse here to run a catheter. It was all me. As if we had any fucking money for that, Hunter. It was all me."

Hunter stood looking at his little brother, seeing that his anger wasn't really directed toward him. It was directed at everyone and everything around him. He was angry with the world. With the circumstances he'd been thrown in.

Noah held up a hand and let it drop to his side. His demeanor shifted and his shoulders slumped. He was exhausted.

"If you're here for the life insurance money, you can just leave already," Noah said.

Hunter hadn't even thought about any insurance money. The only thing he'd thought about was the house being worth something, but he wasn't even there for that. It was Noah's now, and he could do whatever he saw fit to do with it.

"I didn't come for money," Hunter said. "Is that what you thought?"

Noah laughed bitterly. "Good, 'cause there ain't none left."

"I came to make sure my little brother was alright. To pay my respects to momma," Hunter said. "I didn't come here to make you angry."

Noah shook his head. "Whatever, Hunter. Looks like you did what you came here for. Momma's in the ground, and I'm fine."

Hunter walked to his brother and stood in front of him. He was still a good foot taller than his little brother and he thought about when they'd been boys. They'd wrestle around and Hunter would easily win. He'd grab him in a headlock until Noah would surrender.

Hunter wrapped his arms around his brother's head, pulling him in. But it was no headlock. He hugged him close, forgetting what it felt like.

"I'm so sorry, Noah. I was a shit brother when I was here, and then I left you alone. I've done nothing but let you down."

Noah pushed away from his brother. "And you think a few sorries are gonna make me forget any of that?"

Hunter shook his head. "No, I don't. And I can't expect you to ever forgive me. But I'm proud of you."

Noah was ready for a fight. Hunter could see it in his eyes. But then something changed. He looked taken aback.

"You're what?" Noah asked.

"Proud of you. I really am," Hunter said. "The way you stuck by Momma doing what you had to do. I know I left you alone, but you were the right one to take care of her. Momma always favored you."

"Bullshit," Noah said. "You're the all-star. The good-looking one, the athlete, the confident one. You were momma's favorite. She lost something the day you left. Don't fucking tell me I'm the favorite."

"But she still kept going, didn't she? If you were the one who'd left, she'd never recover. You're the better son and I know it. The thoughtful one, the smart one. I think she could see a lot of what a good man was gonna be in you. And so can I. I envy you, Noah. I've always looked up to you."

"To me? You sure as shit didn't show it," Noah said. "Always standing by as that fucker Donnie Price would pick on me in high school. You'd just laugh as he pushed me, trip me, make a fool of me in front of everyone."

Hunter nodded. Noah was right—he'd never stood up for him. "You always knew who you were. You never tried to be something you weren't. Instead, you opted to stay that nerd, enjoying your classes, reading, and playing with those little connect toy thingies even though people would make fun of you. You might have had it rough, but you didn't let it change you. I could never have been that guy. I never was."

"And what did you have to change?"

"Everything. I never had that self-identity. And because I couldn't accept who I was, how could I expect Momma to do the same?"

Noah's chin quivered. "Why'd you leave? Why'd you leave me and Momma all alone? Why'd you do that to us?"

A tear ran down Hunter's face to match the one on Noah's. "Because I couldn't take staring back at everyone, living this lie of who I was supposed to be. Everyone here expected great things from me. Everyone looked at me as this kind of savior of Dupray, like I was some second coming to save them from themselves. I couldn't take that kind of pressure. And Momma was better off without me. You were, too."

Noah grit his teeth. "That's not true. All of this, you're fucking lying to me."

"No, it's true. I always looked up to you, my baby brother. I'm sorry for everything you had to go through while I was here and when I left. For me not to stand by you, there's no forgiveness. I just thought I was supposed to go along with everyone else, pretending to be this person. I love you, Noah."

"Shut up, shut the fuck up," Noah bawled. "Why now? Why are you telling me this now, you fucking idiot?"

Hunter wrapped his arms around his brother again. Noah beat his fists against him, but Hunter held tight this time. Eventually, Noah stopped beating and just sobbed against Hunter's chest.

"It's gonna be okay, Noah. It's gonna be okay. I'm so sorry," Hunter said, stroking the back of his little brother's head. He never realized how much he'd missed his brother until he held him in his arms.

Hunter felt Noah tense up in his grasp, then looked up at him.

He pushed backward from Hunter, his eyes wide. "Hunter...you need to go. You need to run—now."

Hunter furrowed his brow, trying to make sense of what Noah was telling him. "What?"

Noah pushed at him. "Go now. Take my truck if you need. Just get the hell out of here as fast as you can and don't stop runnin'."

Hunter saw something in his brother's eyes that told him everything. It sunk deep inside him. "Noah, what happened? What have you done?"

"I'm sorry, Hunter. I'm so sorry."

Hunter grabbed his heavy coat from the side of the couch and slipped it on, heading toward the door. He got to the doorway, ready to leave, then stopped. He turned back to his brother, seeing the look of sheer terror on his face. Tears were running down his cheeks like a broken faucet handle.

"I love you, Noah. No matter what," Hunter said before turning and walking out the door.

CHAPTER FORTY-SEVEN

The storm raged as Hunter drove down the road leading out of Dupray. He disappeared from the lights of town, letting the darkness wrap around him like a warm blanket. It was always easier to run. Easier to hide. Easier to leave everyone and everything behind.

Just like he'd done all those years ago.

But he never thought about the pain he'd caused when he'd done it. And the feeling he was left with was worse than if he'd just faced his fears to begin with. Twenty years of his life was gone because he hadn't been able to stand up for himself.

He missed his momma. The care and love she provided, and even her worst years in the end. He hadn't been there for her, and it ate him up inside. He wished he could take that back. He wished he would have been there to clean up her vomit, to bathe her, to show her that he loved her.

But he couldn't.

All he could do was change for the better.

He rolled up on a sign that was cracked, the paint fading away from years of sun and rain. His headlights illuminated the front. He could make out the words, faintly outlined in the center.

NOW LEAVING DUPRAY COUNTY

Just like he'd done twenty years ago.

He stopped the truck and let it idle, listening to the raindrops against the roof. Against the windshield. Nature's ticking clock, edging him to make a decision, telling him time was running out.

He slammed his hands onto the steering wheel and yelled, letting out everything he'd been holding in. All the things he wished he would have done before.

He checked in the passenger's seat, confirming his gun was there, and spun the wheel, hitting the gas. He turned back toward Dupray.

He'd been running most of his life, and now he was done. If someone was coming to kill him, he'd face it head-on. And he'd show whoever was coming for him that they were making the biggest mistake of their life.

CHAPTER FORTY-EIGHT

The thunder was so loud, it nearly shook the house as Elven lay in bed. The rain washed over the window, creating a terror-inducing shadow as lightning flashed behind it. Yeti jumped down from the bed and tucked his head underneath the bed frame, but he was too big to squeeze his whole body in.

Elven continued to lay, his eyes barely open. His mind was still running over the day's events, but exhaustion was taking over, with the help of the booze he'd drank. He hoped to be asleep in no time.

A storm like the one Dupray was having always helped him sleep better. Outside would be a mess once it cleared up. The road leading down from his house would probably have to be checked for fallen trees and mud slides, but it was worth it for the peace the night would give him.

He absentmindedly pat the bed, hearing Yeti's whimpers. The poor dog did not seem to think the storm was calming.

"C'mon, boy," Elven said, his voice fading away as he slowly slipped away. "It's okay."

After a while, Elven closed his eyes.

Yeti barked.

Elven shot up, his eyes wide. He'd been right at the edge of being asleep, or maybe he had slept. He wasn't sure, but it seemed that time had frozen and jumped at the same time. His heart raced and he looked around in the dark room, the rain still coming down hard.

Yeti growled and let out another bark.

"What is it, Yeti?" Elven asked.

Yeti scurried his paws against the wood floor and nudged his nose against the door. Once he got it open enough for him to squeeze through, he ran out of the room.

Elven rubbed his hands against his face and sighed. He wasn't in the mood to deal with Yeti's fear of thunder. If the dog wanted to cuddle in the bed, then he could. If he wanted to hide instead, then so be it. But if he was going to bark all night, Elven wasn't going to put up with it.

He slid out of the bed, stark-naked. He kept the house warm enough that the blanket on the bed was overkill. Clothes would be more so.

Yeti barked again, followed by a growl. This time, Elven heard it directed at the front door. That was a lot different than just his fear of the storm.

He grabbed his pair of jeans from the hamper in the corner and slid them on. The last thing he was going to do was run someone down in the rain with his tackle berries dangling. The way word spread in Dupray, if he was gonna be offering up indecent exposure, he sure as hell wouldn't do it when it was freezing out.

He grabbed his gun from the nightstand and walked toward the front door. Yeti continued to growl.

"What is it, boy?" Elven asked.

A flash of lightning lit up the kitchen and living room through the large uncovered windows behind him. Ahead of him, he could see a figure through the small window in the center of the front door.

A loud banging occurred that could not be confused with thunder. It rapped against the door at a frantic pace. It paused for a quick moment, only to continue again. This time, it pounded even louder.

"Good boy," Elven said to Yeti, offering him a quick pet on the head with his empty hand. Yeti looked up at his master, almost smiling at the attention, then reverted to guard mode.

"Elven," the voice yelled. "Elven, you in there?!"

Elven stood next to the door, his shoulder against the wall as he looked at the handle. "Who is it?" he called out.

"Noah Wallace, you gotta help me," he said, his voice strained and raspy.

Elven motioned with his hand for Yeti to stand down, which he obeyed immediately, planting his backside on the floor. But the dog never took his eyes off the door.

Elven opened the door, hand squeezing the grip of his revolver, ready to lift it if need be. Noah rushed inside, soaking wet. He wore a small jacket that offered little protection from the elements and his lips were blue because of it. But that seemed to be the last thing on Noah's mind.

"Elven, we gotta help him," Noah huffed, out of breath.

Elven peeked out the door, seeing no vehicle. "How'd you get up here?" he asked.

"I drove, but my truck couldn't make the road. It got stuck and I ran the rest of the way," Noah said.

"Noah, you're freezing. Let's get you dry and—"

"Elven, there's no time, don't you hear? We gotta help Hunter!" he shouted, flailing his arms.

"What's wrong with Hunter? Is he down the road?"

Noah shook his head. Elven hadn't noticed from the rain and the darkness, but when another strike of lightning came, his face showed all the signs that he'd been crying. "He's after him, he's after him," he panted, still out of breath.

"Who is after him?"

Noah paced in front of Elven, manic and making no sense. "I didn't know. I didn't know, Elven. You gotta believe me." He locked eyes with Elven, and deep inside his gaze, Elven could see he was begging for forgiveness.

Elven grabbed Noah by the shoulders. "Noah, you need to take a deep breath and calm down. Can you do that for me?"

Noah nodded, doing as Elven had asked.

"Good. Now, what is going on?" Elven asked.

"I never knew the reason Hunter left. I thought I knew him, but I didn't. My brother loves me, but, I—I didn't know. And now it's too late."

Elven narrowed his eyes. "Noah, what happened? What did you do?"

Noah closed his mouth, his eyes trying to say what his mouth couldn't. Finally, he parted his lips and the words came out. "I ordered the hit."

"You?" Elven asked.

"He's going out there right now. I told him to run, I did. Told him to get out of town. He knows a fight's coming. One he ain't prepared for. But it's Hunter."

Elven knew what Noah meant. Hunter might have been running from himself, but he never ran from a fight. And he was just as cocksure as Elven, if not more. Hunter would be confident he'd win, but from everything Hollis had told him, and everything he'd seen himself, Hunter would be meeting his own death.

"Please, you have to help. He's my brother," Noah pleaded.

Elven ran to his room to throw clothes on. He came out, shirt half-buttoned and jacket thrown over his shoulders. "Shut up and get in the Jeep."

CHAPTER FORTY-NINE

Hunter sat in the middle of the field, the water soaking him through. He kept his hands in his pockets, keeping his joints from locking up on him. He was freezing, but his mind was so focused that his teeth didn't chatter.

The field was a pool of mud, the grass dead and covered. His pants were soggy, but he didn't care. He had a lot of memories on that field. It was the very place he'd thrown the seventy-nine yard pass to win the game that had put them in the finals his senior year of high school. He'd been tackled into the dirt, the grass, and the mud more times than he could count. He'd ran back and forth over the field in drills, practice, and games so many times that if he'd done it on a treadmill, the motor would have burned out.

It was also where he'd had his first kiss. Touched his first breast. Vanessa Hutchins, if he recalled correctly. Which now made him chuckle at the thought. Always good with the ladies. Apparently, the secret to that was to not care at all. He was surprised nobody had ever figured him out.

But there were a lot of memories on that field. And it was the first place he'd come to when returning to Dupray. Besting Elven at the shooting competition in front of everyone. He was a good man, Hunter had to admit. But he did take a little pleasure in putting him in his place.

And now he waited. For whatever was to happen to happen. He knew he was good. Better than that really, but if it came to it, he'd rather die than run again.

The lightning cracked in the sky, and across the field he saw the shape of a man. This was no target to hit when the buzzer went off. This was the real deal.

"Your brother didn't say where you'd be," the man shouted over the rain. "But by the way I seen you shoot before, I figured it might be out here."

Hunter stood, his pants clinging against his skin from the mud. The man across from him wore a black hat that formed a waterfall off the side of his face.

"You know me?" Hunter shouted back.

He nodded. "Seen you down in Texas, doin' those trick shots a handful of times. You put on a good show. Also heard about some other dealings you had around there. Seems we may have run in similar circles. For a moment anyway."

"What's your name?"

"James."

Hunter snarled. "Then James, you know I'm faster than anyone I ever came across. I don't want to kill a man, but if it comes down to me or you, I'll do what it takes to stay standing."

"You ain't never come across me, son," the man said. "Those shows you put on are a lot of fun. I once saw you shoot four bottles with one bullet, and you damn near made it look like you curved the shot. Still haven't figured out that one."

Hunter stared him down, his heart racing.

James shrugged. "Guess it's like those magicians then. Never share their secrets. Y'know, I went to the bar once down there after a show and you actually bought me a drink. You were one of the few people there who wasn't so high on himself, but gracious. Really made me appreciate the job you did. A man who practices to get better, who enjoys his work—well, that's someone to respect."

"Then why do this? Why try to kill me?"

"That's the way the world works," James said. "I get paid, someone dies. No other way around it. In the end, we all finish up in the same place. Life's too short to worry about liking someone enough to not want to put them in the ground."

"I feel sorry for you," Hunter said, shaking his head. "That ain't no way to live, mister."

The two of them stared at each other for a moment, the rain splashing in the puddles around them. Hunter's feet sunk in the mud, planting him where he stood.

"You ready?" James asked.

Hunter had never been more ready in his life.

He went for his gun, watching the dark figure across him do the same. He brought his gun up, one eye locking across his barrel and down at James.

They both fired.

CHAPTER FIFTY

"Talk," Elven demanded as he floored the gas pedal. His Jeep careened over the puddles in the road, but he righted the wheel, keeping the Jeep from losing total control. The three brand-new tires he'd put on were gripping the road as they were supposed to. He had his high beams on, but all he could see in front of him was a wave of water, washing over his windshield.

Not another soul was on the road.

Noah sobbed, but Elven grabbed his shirt, pulling him toward him.

"Cut the sob act and tell me what you did," Elven barked.

"Nobody ever respected me here," Noah said between sobs. "My momma, she always wanted me to stand up for myself, but I—I just couldn't. Didn't know how."

"So you paid someone to kill people for you?"

"I was at the bar drinkin' after Momma died. I barely remember anything, but Donnie was there and slapped me so hard I was seein' stars. Some big guy was there and saw it all happen. He looked familiar, but like I said, I was wasted. Donnie just laughed. I started crying, not just because of Donnie, but because of Momma. When Donnie left, I was mouthin' off about how I hated that fucker so much. Then the big guy said he knew someone that could help. Could take care of my problems if I wanted them gone."

"What did he get in return?"

"Paid him ten grand for the information," Noah said.

"A hitman, Noah?"

Noah nodded. "After what they all did to me, and Dylan stabbing me in the back when we were kids. Sayin' I was a loser, everyone laughing at me. It sticks with you. Then Donnie, always picking on me, getting laughs from everyone, even my brother. He never changed. He just got older, but was the same asshole he always was."

"What about Todd?"

Noah scoffed. "Coach Utt? The guy that was workin' the mines at the same time as gettin' paid a hundred bucks a week to help with the team? Someone who was supposed to keep kids' interest at heart? That asshole was one of the worst. He liked to think he was still young, still cool and connected. Relivin' high school 'cause he was just a piece of shit like the rest of us."

Elven remembered some of the stories from the team. Todd had liked to work the other guys on the team hard, but at the end of the day, he did favor some of the more popular guys.

"He was on some power trip. I got locked in the locker room one day after PE. One of Donnie's jokes. Left me there naked and alone. I was bangin' on the door, hoping someone would come by to let me out. Finally, Todd found me. He walked in the office, saw me through the window. But instead of lettin' me out, he laughed at me. Then he held up a finger and I thought he was gettin' his keys to unlock the door. But when he came back, he had the whole girls' volleyball team with him."

Noah sat in silence, Elven said nothing.

"You can imagine their reaction," Noah said.

Elven felt sorry for Noah. Noah had been picked on a lot through school, even had seen it once or twice himself. He'd never done the bullying toward him, but he probably could have done more to stop it.

"I'm sorry, Noah," Elven offered. "But none of that can excuse what you did."

"They ruined my life, Elven. I ain't never had anything but fear, hatred, and evil struck down upon me. The only one who never made me feel that way was my momma, so when she died, I got that life insurance policy paid out. I made them all pay for how they treated me."

"And now? What about Hunter? What would your momma think of you now?"

Noah hung his head. "I made a mistake," he said.

"You're sick, Noah. You should have spent that money on a therapist or gotten out of Dupray. Anything other than this. What they did to you ain't right, but you had other choices."

"I don't even know where to start looking for Hunter," Noah said, staring into the dark abyss outside the Jeep.

Elven grit his teeth. He would have to deal with Noah later. He wanted to arrest him and throw him in a cell, but right now, that was at the bottom of the list. He had to get to Hunter before it was too late.

"I know where he is," Elven said, heading to the football field.

CHAPTER FIFTY-ONE

Hunter stood, his hand steady. His heart was calm, even, slow. He took a breath, staring across from him, the weight of his gun familiar and comforting. The air was tinted with the scent of sulfur, bordering on metallic. The smoke was quickly driven away by the relentless raindrops hammering down.

Hunter took a deep breath, squinting his eyes, searching across him in the dark. Between the pitch-black night and the haze of the rain, he couldn't see James.

Until the lightning struck.

James still stood, right in the same spot he was before. It looked as if he had his hand raised, holding at his neck. Hunter lifted a corner of his mouth, knowing he must have hit him. There were no rules now—he just needed to fire again, and James would be dead.

Hunter felt a sudden pinch at his chest when he took another breath, feeling the need to cough. It was warm and thick, the feeling climbing from his throat as he did. He wiped at his mouth, and on the back of his hand, he saw blood. It washed away with the rain.

He went to fire again, but his hand was weak. The revolver dropped from his hand, unable to bear its weight any longer. Something was wrong, but his mind hadn't yet caught up with what was happening.

It wasn't until his legs went weak and he felt the immediate need to sit, that the realization set in. He grabbed at his coat, feeling the warm blood pouring out of his chest. It ran down his body, soaking into his clothes as it did, and washed into the mud.

He took a quick glance, his hand finding the entry point. There was a hole about the size of a quarter on the left side of his coat. His finger poked deeper and found that the hole continued through the coat and into him. He had no idea if that's where it stopped or if it exited out the back, but by the way he was feeling, he figured it didn't much matter.

He fell backward, splashing into the pooling water, his face being pelted by the raindrops. He took a breath, but it wasn't easy this time. It was labored, like sucking soda through a straw that had been littered with holes. He kept trying to suck the air in, but the more he did, the harder it became.

The rain stopped hitting his face, but the storm continued. Hunter focused and saw James standing above him. He could see him now that he was close enough, making out the details of his face. The scar at the side of his cheek. But there was no smile on his face. He wasn't there to gloat.

James held his hand at his throat, and Hunter thought he saw a red line of blood streaming from under his hand.

"That's the problem goin' for a headshot in this kind of weather," James said, his voice hoarse. "Small target, low visibility, the elements can do funny things to someone. Not to mention the target moves. Ain't like the gun shows, is it?"

Hunter shook, now feeling every bit of the cold infiltrating his body. It was worse than the weather, something that no blanket could satiate. He tried holding on to anything to keep him grounded, even clutching at the words coming out of James's mouth.

James cocked his head and looked closer at Hunter's wound. "I missed your heart, I'm sure. You'd be dead now if I hadn't. But by the looks, maybe blew open your aorta. I'm no doctor, but in my experience, you've got three minutes."

Hunter swallowed, his vision closing in. The darkness growing closer and closer, until all he could see was the man who had done this to him standing over him.

"I—I—I ain't n—never been outd—drawn," Hunter said.

James nodded. "Guess all it takes is once. We both know that. Hell, I may need a stitch or two, which is more than I can say about anyone I ever stood against."

Hunter stared at him, listening. He had hardly any energy to say another word.

"Gotta be honest," James said. "If anyone had a shot, I was hoping it'd be you. I'm afraid now that age is gonna catch up to me, I'll die of something as mundane as a heart attack in a shitty motel room, or worse, catch a bullet well past my prime from some asshole that just learned to use a gun." James shook his head. "One minute, you're the best, and then life don't even have the decency to send someone better to do the job. Guess I ain't owed anything else."

Hunter felt the life slipping from him. His vision closing in even more, the darkness wrapping around him. He was so cold, he couldn't feel his legs, his arms. He was whittled down to his eyes and ears, taking in any last moments he could.

"Don't normally do this," James said. "You're as good as dead anyway. You wanna go fast, or faster?" He pointed his revolver at Hunter's head, adding emphasis to the last word.

Hunter opened his mouth, struggling to get the words. He didn't feel scared. He'd come to terms with it in the short amount of time listening to James. But part of him just wanted to hang onto that place a little longer.

"F—fast," Hunter sputtered.

James nodded, holstering his revolver.

"Want company for the last few?" he asked.

Hunter managed to shake his head once to the left, then to the right. James was no longer above him and he felt the rain fall against his face again. It was cold, but cleansing. Soon, all he could see were the raindrops crystalize above him when the lightning struck, backlighting them into one of the most beautiful images he could remember.

"Safe travels," James said, his voice like a whisper from across the field.

And then, everything went quiet.

CHAPTER FIFTY-TWO

The rain was relentless. The way it poured down, Elven was worried the roads would be impossible to get through. Even his Jeep had encountered trouble with the mudslides on the road. But somehow, they managed to make it to the field. The one that he'd played football on with Hunter so many years ago. The one that just recently, Hunter had bested him in the quick draw competition.

As soon as they got there, lightning cracked in the sky.

Not a single person stood in the field, and at first, Elven thought he'd made a mistake. That Hunter hadn't gone there, and if he wasn't there, he'd have no idea where to look next.

But just as soon as he thought it, Noah pointed to the center of the field, where a small lump sat in the mud. They both exited the Jeep into the downpour. Elven slid his Stetson on, blocking most of the water from getting into his eyes.

They ran to the center of the field, mud splashing up all around them. As Elven got closer, he saw a leg bent at the knee, sticking in the air. His heart sank at the sight. There was no question in his mind. Noah, however, still seemed hopeful, pushing harder and faster than Elven.

As soon as Noah reached the body, he screamed in agony. As if his leg had been caught in a bear trap.

Elven caught up and looked down at his old friend. Hunter lay with his eyes still open, directed up at the rainfall. He'd been shot in the chest. The blood had run out of the gunshot, seeping into the mud. There was no way to see how much he'd lost by the way the rain watered it down.

Elven squatted down, shoving a finger under his jaw at the neck. His hand was cold, but Hunter's skin was ice. He couldn't feel a single beat against his fingertips.

Hunter was dead.

"No, no, no," Noah said after his wail had tapered off. He stepped closer to his brother, slipping into the mud and falling down next to his body. He grabbed Hunter's shoulders and shook him. "Why didn't you run? Why didn't you do what I told you?"

Elven watched as Hunter flopped in his brother's arms, no life to support him. He was a life-sized ragdoll that Noah sobbed into. "I'm so sorry, brother. I'm so sorry," Noah kept saying.

Elven stood over them, watching Noah rock with his brother for a minute. A wave of emotion came over him, knowing all this could have been prevented. Knowing it was all because of a dumb decision that was fully regretted now.

And it angered him.

Noah looked up at Elven, chin quivering and lip trembling. He opened his mouth, ready to say something, but Elven didn't want to hear it.

Elven grabbed Noah by the jacket, lifting him up to his feet, Hunter sliding from Noah's grip and splashing in the mud. "Elven, I'm sorry. Elven—"

Elven pulled back and decked Noah in the face, sending him tumbling into the water that was overtaking the field. Noah landed on his side, a wave splashing into the air. Noah scrambled to his hands and feet, facing upward. He scurried backward, like a crab. "Elven, wait, Elven—"

Elven worked his way toward Noah, kicking up waves of water, mud, and Hunter's blood into the air with his boots. He reached down and grabbed Noah again, lifting him once more to his feet.

"I'm sorry," Noah pleaded. "I made a mistake. I just—"

"Everyone makes mistakes, but not like this!" Elven yelled in his face. "This was your family. The only one you got, and you did this. Brothers fight. That's what they're supposed to do. And because you had to throw a fit because the way life treated you, Hunter's dead!"

He punched Noah in the face again, feeling the cold hard jaw crack against his knuckles. Noah went down right at Elven's feet. The water was overtaking them so much, he felt as if they were playing a game of Marco Polo.

Noah knelt, reaching up and grabbed at Elven, trying to climb up. Elven hoisted him up to his level, grabbing at his collar and twisting it. He was so angry, he was pretty sure Noah's feet weren't touching the ground. He got in Noah's face.

"Look what you brought to my county!" Elven yelled. "There may be a bunch of assholes, but there's still good people here. These are the people you live with, and you brought all this down on them. Are you satisfied? Are you the big man now? Because let me tell you, all those people who made fun of you, they can't be impressed with you now. I guess you got what you wanted. You've won, Noah. And this is your prize."

He dropped Noah, letting him fall back to his knees in the mud. He sobbed in front of Elven, but Elven didn't feel a bit sorry for him, not anymore. He shook his head, flinging water off his face, off the top of his hat, to the side.

Noah shook his head, but didn't say anything.

"Is this it?" Elven asked. "Are we done? How many more are there?"

Elven hoped there was nobody else. He couldn't imagine having to deal with anyone else. But when Noah didn't speak, he knew that wouldn't be true.

"Who is it?" Elven demanded.

Noah looked up, curling his lip. Fear shone through his eyes.

"I just lost control, Elven. I drank too much and wasn't thinkin' straight. I'm a coward. Who would want me? Not when they could have someone like Hunter. Like you," Noah said.

"Who?" Elven yelled.

"Penny Starcher."

Elven's eyes went wide when he heard the name. He unclenched his fists, the shock settling in. "What have you done?" he asked Noah, his voice strangely calm.

Noah shook his head, but Elven didn't want to hear what he had to say. The anger washed over him all over again, and he wanted to beat the living daylights out of Noah, but it would just be a waste of time. Penny wasn't dead yet, and there was still time to save her.

He turned around and left Noah in the soggy field with his dead brother.

"Ain't you gonna arrest me?" Noah shouted, standing up. "You ain't gonna take me with you?"

Elven spun, trudging back to Noah. He didn't grab him, but he stood so his nose was a breath away from his own. "I don't have time to book you. I've got to get to Penny now that you've put her in the crosshairs. If I bring you with me, there ain't nothin' I can do to keep Hollis from killing you on the spot." He looked Noah over with his eyes. "Even if there was, I wouldn't want to."

Elven turned and ran back to his Jeep. Noah screamed at him. "Elven! Elven!" But he'd already spent too much time dealing with Noah. He was running out of time.

CHAPTER FIFTY-THREE

Elven pulled his Jeep right up to Hollis's front door, digging a trench in his yard with his tires. It wasn't out of spite, but necessity. He'd be able to laugh about the mess he made on Hollis's property once Penny was safe and the hitman was in his custody.

But first, he had to find her and figure out how to get this guy off her tail.

Elven jumped into the cold rain again, not giving his discomfort any notice. Hollis's house was dark, except that when Elven pushed his face against the window, he could see the smallest hint of light filtering out from somewhere deep in the home.

Elven banged on the door with his fist. "Penny!" he yelled. "Hollis, get out here!"

The lights kicked on at the window a few feet down the wall. It was Penny's room. At least she hadn't been found by the hitman. Not yet, anyway. How Elven had made it there first was a mystery he didn't care to unravel, but he was grateful for it.

The living room light turned on and the door opened. Penny stood there, dressed in flannel pants and a night shirt. Her hair was flat, recently blown out with a hair dryer. Her routine hadn't changed much from when he'd spent so many nights at that house in her room, long before his opinion of Hollis had been tainted. Along with the one he held for himself.

She'd just woken up by the bleary look on her face. She wore no makeup, but she was just as pretty as the day he set eyes on her. Her face scrunched in confusion at the sight of him.

"Elven, what's wrong?" she asked. Her eyes traced his body. "You're soaking wet. Come on in."

He held his hat in his hand as he accepted her invitation. He hadn't thought much about how freezing the rain was, about how cold and stiff his hands were, until he stepped inside the warmth of the home and the relief of knowing she was okay settled in.

"Aw, what the hell are you doin' here?" Corbin asked, emerging from the hallway. He wore a ragged shirt that needed to see the bottom of a waste bin. The thing was more hole than cloth.

A dog growled from behind him, and as soon as the pitbull saw Elven, it started barking up a storm. It ran toward him, looking as if it was ready to attack. But Elven stood firm. He loved dogs, but he wasn't about to let one tear him up. He never drew on his gun, though, and instead narrowed his eyes down, holding a single finger up at the dog. The dog let out a whimper and stopped. It still stared at Elven, growling, but never took another step forward.

"Nice dog," he said.

"Oh, Christ," Hollis said, limping his way into the living room. His white tank top revealed his pasty farmer's tan, but he was more alert than anyone else, making Elven think he'd still been awake when Elven got there. "That damn dog is about as useful as a hemorrhoid. Just growlin' around the house, irritatin' the shit out of me."

Hollis held a cane, using it to support himself on his bad leg. Elven had seen it a lot in the past, but only around the house. He never let anyone in Dupray see him otherwise. He thought it a weakness, but Elven thought it as just another way of manipulating the way people thought of him.

"Elven, what's got you all riled up?" Hollis asked.

"Noah Wallace is the one that hired him," Elven said. "Hunter Wallace is dead."

Penny gasped and covered her mouth. "Oh my Lord, what happened?"

Elven shook his head. "It doesn't matter. What does matter is getting you someplace safe," he said to Penny, then pointed to Hollis. "And calling this thing off."

Hollis shook his head. "Elven, what are you gettin' at?"

"Noah put out one last hit," Elven said. He paused a moment, not wanting to scare Penny. But she was bound to figure it out, and time was of the essence. "He put a hit out on Penny."

"Me?" she asked, shocked. "Why would he do that?"

Elven shook his head. "I don't know, I just—"

"You rotten halfwit!" Hollis yelled. Elven had only heard Hollis fly off the handle like this just once before. Penny's being in danger had that affect on him. But what surprised him is who had elicited that reaction.

Hollis cracked his cane over Corbin's back. Corbin dropped to his knees, crying out in pain. "Daddy, wh—"

"Look what you brought down on this house!" Hollis yelled. He smacked Corbin across the face with his open palm. Corbin shielded himself, but Hollis didn't stop. "You're too fuckin' stupid for your own good."

Tanya's head went back and forth between the two men, unsure of whose side she should be on. She let a small growl slip from her mouth and Hollis turned to her, baring his own teeth, and Tanya walked away, circling twice before laying down next to the chair. She was having nothing to do with it.

Elven watched as Hollis frothed at the mouth like a rabid bear, beating his son in a way that wouldn't scar him physically, but emotionally. It would stay with him forever.

"Daddy, stop it, please stop it," Corbin pleaded, his voice cracking. He raised his hands to soften the blows, but even he knew better than to fight back. Corbin was bigger than Hollis, but everyone knew that once that line had been crossed with Hollis, there was no backpedalling.

"That's enough," Elven said, grabbing Hollis's wrist. Elven had to pull firm on the old man's arm, revealing to him Hollis was much stronger than he let himself appear. As much as Elven would normally relish watching Corbin be put in his place, there were bigger things to deal with.

"Can you call this guy?" Elven asked.

Hollis pursed his lips. "James Smith? I sure can call him, but there ain't nothin' that'll get him to change his mind. That ain't the way he works."

"Let's pay him," Corbin said, still panting from Hollis's attack. "Whatever that little twat paid him can't be much. We got enough, and hell, if Elven really wants to be the hero, he sure as fuck can pay."

Elven considered that, but wasn't going to voice it until he knew exactly what he was in store for. For Penny, he would do whatever it took.

"Let the adults talk," Hollis said. "You've already proven yourself to cock up anything you touch."

Corbin hung his head and climbed to his feet. He backed away and sat next to Tanya. Hollis closed the circle until it was just himself, Elven, and Penny.

"That ain't gonna work. Once he gets the money, he does the job. Ain't no amount gonna make him stop. He's got this code, somethin' he'd come up with about work and his daddy. As crazy as it sounds, he lives by it," Hollis said.

"Fine," Elven said. "Then I arrest him."

Hollis put his hand on Elven's shoulder, a touch of genuine care in his voice. "Elven, this guy has his principles because he's got no fear. Anyone stands in his way, he'll shoot them down. Last I heard, he was wanted in at least seven countries. And he still ain't bothered. The only way to stop him is kill him. Now, I know some people that deal in this type of work—not that I have experience in their services," Hollis added, always making sure he didn't incriminate himself. "The problem is, ain't nobody crazy enough to take the commission on this guy. Even if we did find someone willing, ain't nobody better than this guy. Anyone that's ever tried ends up eatin' supper through a tube and shittin' in a bag the rest of their miserable life."

"What do you propose?" Elven asked.

Hollis thought a moment, then turned to Corbin. "Take that damn dog and your sister in your truck. You drive across the damn state up to your cousin Elmer's. Don't you fuckin' stop for nothing. You piss your pants if you have to, you understand?"

Corbin stood, nodding frantically.

"They got guns and the bunker to slow him down if need be. And boy, I tell you, if he catches up to you or gets to your sister, you stop him, you hear?" Hollis said.

"But you just said he ain't gonna be stopped," Corbin protested.

"Then if he gets to your sister, you better damn well be dead next to her. Is that clear?" Hollis shouted.

Corbin swallowed hard. He called for Tanya and grabbed Penny's wrist. "C'mon."

She looked at Elven and he nodded. "We're gonna figure this out, I promise," he said.

The look in her eyes told him she trusted him, even if he didn't have a plan. She left the house with Corbin. When they were gone, Hollis leaned in.

"Elven, I know I said to stay out of this one. And I can't ask anything of ya, but—"

"Things are different now," Elven said.

CHAPTER FIFTY-FOUR

As much as she wanted it, sleep would never come. Two nights of rest and she was right back to the same problem as before. Except this time, it wasn't because of the choices she'd made. Everything she'd done in Dupray had long been forgotten, replaced by new anxiety.

Kurt was no longer some distant paranoia. He was really there. And she so wanted to believe he meant what he said, that he wasn't there for any other reason than to take her back home. To be with her again.

But she just couldn't make the leap.

The curtains were closed. With every strike of lightning outside, a sliver of light was able to escape through the space where the curtain met the wall. The light was harsh against the darkness, casting strange shadows against the wall that tugged at the nightmarish corners of her mind.

The worst part of Kurt being there was that Hollis didn't have her back. Whatever was going on with the professional killer in Dupray had set him off. She should have known that a man like Hollis, family or not, was only in something for his benefit. Whoever this man was, and her not telling him, was far more important than anything she had done—or could do—with her position in the future.

That wasn't the worst of it, though.

She'd never thought about Elven before taking the job. Before deciding to work with Hollis. But over the time they'd spent together, she had really learned to respect and admire him. And there was something else there, too.

She'd never expected anything from him until she knew him. And now, knowing that a good man like him wasn't there for her, hurt more than anything Hollis could have done.

Thunder cracked, rattling the window and door against the frame. She sat up and draped her feet over the edge of the mattress. Staying there was going to do her no good.

She had nobody to help her, so there was no point in staying. She grabbed her suitcase from where it was tucked behind the dresser and threw it on the bed. If Elven and Hollis weren't going to help her, then she had a decision to make.

Believe Kurt, or run.

Either way, she was leaving Dupray.

CHAPTER FIFTY-FIVE

"Yeah," James said, his voice gravelly and hoarse.

Elven looked at the phone that lay on the table set to speaker, listening to the man on the other side of the conversation breathe. There was a hint of a whistle in his breath that Elven could just hear over the rain in the background. He hadn't thought about what to say yet. Only that he had to do something, if only to hear the man's voice. To get a feel for who he was and what he was dealing with.

"You got two seconds—"

"I want to meet," Elven finally said.

There was a pause. "Who is this?"

Elven sat at the kitchen table in Hollis's dining room. The very table he'd had breakfast at in his youth on days he'd come over to spend time with Lyman, or later on, Penny. Hollis, the very man he'd come to loathe, sat next to him, studying Elven's face.

"This is—"

"The sheriff," James said, his voice lifting as if he were smiling.

"That's right. Sheriff Elven Hallie," Elven said. "And I want to meet."

"I'm assuming you got my number one of two ways," James said, clearing his throat. He sounded a little worse for the wear. "That idiot who hired me gave it up, maybe having himself a come to Jesus moment after realizing what he'd done. Or...you're in Hollis's pocket."

Elven grit his teeth. "I ain't in nobody's pocket. Hollis most of all."

James sighed. "Well, Sheriff, I meant no offense by it," he said. "In my experience, anyone workin' with Hollis is either gettin' paid to do so or threatened to do so. And to me, it don't sound like you got a gun to your head."

"You were paid for one last hit," Elven said, steering the conversation to the point. "I want you to cancel it. Whatever it takes, I'll do it."

James let out a gust of air into the receiver, like a breathy laugh from his nostril. "I'm sure you already heard who I am. What I do. There ain't nothin' gonna stop a contract that's been paid for," James said. "Tell me, what's Hollis look like right now? I know it's his daughter. He's sittin' right next to you, ain't he? Is he at the kitchen table, or that recliner that sits in the middle of the room?"

Hollis gripped his cane, knuckles white against it. But Elven held his hand up. Hollis had been given explicit instructions to stay out of it if he wanted Elven's help. A man that could only see rage was bound to mess things up if trying to negotiate with James.

"I was just about to head down that way, but since you're callin' me, I figure that daughter of his is long gone. She's a pretty one. Polite, too. Hollis knows it ain't nothin' personal, but I gotta say, knowing it's gonna kill him on the inside gives me just a bit of satisfaction."

"Why?" Elven asked. He didn't care about the details so much as wanting to keep him on the phone. It sounded ridiculous, but just doing that made him wonder if he could talk him out of it.

"Hollis knows. After that dust-up we got into, well, I ain't never held it against him. But sometimes, life comes around and puts the prize in front of you. Like you was meant to get even all this time. Life's a bag of shit sometimes, ain't it?"

"You piece of shit," Hollis said, breaking his silence. "I ain't got nothing to do with what you think I do." He lifted from the table, positioning himself to smash the phone into pieces.

Elven grabbed him by the shoulders as James laughed. "Hollis, ol' boy. If I'd have known you were on the line, I wouldn't have wasted so much time. Better say goodbye, old friend, 'cause Penny ain't gonna live to see another sunset."

Just before he clicked off, Elven grabbed the phone, turning it off speaker. He put it against his ear. "Wait!"

"Sheriff, I got no time to spend on this anymore—"

"How much?" Elven asked.

"What?"

"How much is your rate?"

James sighed. "Sheriff, I told you that ain't nothin' gonna kill this contract. You're only insulting me and making a fool of yourself by thinking you'll buy your way out."

"Not to kill a contract. To start a new one," Elven said.

James scoffed, but gave pause. "What are we talking?"

"I want it done as soon as possible," Elven said. "I figure two hours? Needs to be done before Penny, but you can do that, right? It wouldn't be breaking a contract just to fulfill one early?"

"And who are we talking about?"

"Me," Elven said.

James laughed. "Sheriff, I'm not sure what you're gettin' at here. This ain't some friendly escort service. I don't get paid to meet, I get paid to kill."

"And if I pay, you'll take the job first, right?"

Elven could hear James swallow over the phone, something hitching in his throat. "It's gonna be pricey. A turnaround time like you're asking, plus knowin' what I'm walking into."

"Name the price."

"This ain't a round of drinks at the bar, Sheriff."

Elven immediately remembered the man at Martin's, drinking by himself at the table. The compliment he'd given to Elven after watching him shut the fight down. "So that's you, is it?"

James didn't answer, but kept on about the contract. "As much as Hollis has his hands in everyone's pocket, deals all over town, ain't no way he's got that kind of liquidity. What you're askin', it's gonna be half a mil at least. And since Hollis and I go way back, add another hundred thousand to it."

"You'll have it wired to you in ten minutes," Elven said. "From what I hear, you're a man of your word."

James paused, as if he didn't believe Elven, but Elven wasn't bluffing. Finally, James spoke. "That's all I am."

"Good. Tonight at the old mine at the top of Basin Road."

"Sheriff, if you somehow manage to do that, you know there ain't goin' back."

"I don't plan on it," Elven said, and hung up the phone.

CHAPTER FIFTY-SIX

Elven pounded on the door of the motel, hoping he could be heard over the thunderous roar in the sky. The rain didn't seem to be letting up any time soon. At the edge of the walkway, the divot in the concrete formed a wash where the water flooded and rushed alongside the building. He began to worry that the road to the mines would be too washed out to reach.

The light was on inside, so he knew Madds was there. He pounded again, this time harder so she would know it wasn't just the storm.

"Madds, it's me, Elven," he shouted.

The door opened a crack, and he was met by a single eye. Once she saw it was him, she opened the door fully. She was dressed in a loose gray hoodie and black leggings that hugged her thighs. She looked stressed and did not greet him with a smile.

"Come on in already," she said, stepping out of the way.

He stepped in, taking his hat off. The motel room was small, just a space with a bed centered against the wall. On the bed, he saw a suitcase, half-filled with folded clothes. Next to it was a pile waiting to be attended to.

"You look worried," Madds said.

"Tank was shot," he said.

"Oh my God," Madds said, dropping her stony demeanor. "Is he gonna be okay?"

Elven nodded. "Yeah, Johnny was there, saw it go down. He was able to get an ambulance and Tank's in the hospital recovering."

"Good," Madds said. "So why are you here?"

"I need your help."

Madds scoffed and crossed her arms. "My help? Fuck off, Elven. I figured I was as good as fired. What happened to this leave you put me on?"

"Hunter Wallace is dead."

"Did you kill him?"

"What? No. I was wrong about him. His brother set it all up," Elven said. "I tried gettin' there in time, but was too late. He was drawn down in the field."

"I'm sorry to hear that. He seemed like a decent guy that you had all wrong. But that seems like something Phil Driscoll should be dealing with right now, not me."

"Madds, I know you're pissed—"

"That's an understatement."

He grit his teeth and glared at her. He was still angry at what she'd kept from him, but he was also angry at himself now. And at the situation he'd found himself in.

"You lied to me when you took the job, so I reacted the way I did. But Madds, now I've got some hitman in my county because some idiots were mean to a kid in high school and he never got the help he needed. And I'm in deep," Elven confessed.

"He was here, you know," Madds said. "Or is here, I should say."

Elven cocked his head.

"Kurt," Madds explained. "He sat right across from me in the booth at Hank's. Says there's no heat on him or me. That I can go back to Arizona with him."

Elven shook his head. "That makes no sense. Is that why you're packing?" He pointed to the suitcase.

Madds shrugged. "I don't believe him. Or maybe I just don't want to."

"Madds, you can't do that," he said. He ran his hand through his hair. "Geez, I cannot deal with this right now."

"Then don't. Go home. Let this hitman blow through town. I get it, he killed Hunter. But nothing you can do now about it."

"I can't do that. He's targeted Penny."

She pursed her lips. "Penny? Why would she have anything to do with this?"

Elven shrugged. "I think Noah had a thing for her, and for whatever reason, well, he paid to have her killed."

Madds sighed. "I don't know what to say to that."

"It's more than that. Now this guy is coming for me before he goes for her."

"What?! Why the hell would he do that?"

Elven bit his lip. "Because I paid him to do it."

Madds stared, mouth open. He waited for her to speak, which she finally did.

"What is with you and her? I get it, you dated in high school and you probably were close. But you don't owe her this, Elven," she said. "You're cocky as hell, but I never thought of you as stupid. And this is the stupidest thing I've ever heard of."

"That's why—"

"You said he killed Hunter," she said, cutting him off. "He was faster than you, and you think you can still beat this guy? And for a Starcher of all people?"

"She's not just a Starcher. There's history."

"Fuck, Elven. I ain't gonna put my life on the line for every ex-boyfriend I had."

"Madds, its been done. There ain't no goin' back now," he shouted. "I ain't wastin' any more time talkin' about it. Are you gonna help me or not?"

Madds chewed the inside of her cheek, staring at the bed and avoiding eye contact.

"No, Elven, I'm not going to help you," she said after awhile. "I'm not going to watch you get yourself killed."

It wasn't what he wanted to hear, but he respected it. He nodded. "I'm sorry," he said. "I'm gonna come back when I finish this, and I hope you're still here when I do."

She shook her head, wiping at her face. She was upset, but she was doing everything she could to make sure he didn't see it.

"I don't have time to get him, but I left Noah at the football field with Hunter. I know you ain't doin' me favors, but he still needs to be in a cell," Elven said.

"Then get him yourself," Madds said. "You can do that after you finish with this guy, right?" Her words were short and pointed.

Elven turned to leave, opening the door. He wanted to say she was right, that he would come off the top of that mountain and get Noah himself.

But as sure of himself as he was, he'd always been a terrible liar.

CHAPTER FIFTY-SEVEN

Elven used his left hand on the steering wheel while his right was holding the phone. The storm was pounding away, and his headlights could barely cut through the constant wash of water. The windshield wipers were on full blast, but it was still not enough. They might as well have been a Dixie cup bailing out the water from a sinking boat.

He was pushing the Jeep as fast as he could. His time was limited, and if he was going to stop James, then he'd need to get his plan together fast. It was going to take some doing, but he was confident he could get it done. His priority was arresting James and getting him into a cell at the station, but if it came to it, he'd draw down on him and kill the man himself.

But he still needed help in whatever form he could get.

The phone picked up and Johnny was on the other line.

"Johnny," Elven said. The connection was fuzzy, crackling in and out at times, but strong enough to hear through. "I need your help. I know you've been through it, but we're gonna arrest the guy that shot Tank."

There were no words from the other side of the conversation. Just breathing that seemed to pick up speed, near hyperventilating.

"I don't know," Johnny said between pants.

"Johnny, I'm headed up to the mines. I don't expect you to take the lead. I just need some back up. I'll handle everything. Look, I know I might be asking a lot, but this is the job we chose, right? It's what we're paid to do."

"El—"

Johnny was quickly cut off, scratching sounds taking over through the speaker. Finally, it cleared up, but it wasn't Johnny anymore. It was a woman.

"Sheriff?" the woman asked.

"Who's this?"

"Bernadette Hensley. Johnny's girlfriend," she said. "I know we ain't spoken much, but that's gonna change right now."

"Bernadette, I'm sorry, but—"

"No, you listen here. What you're askin' of Johnny ain't the job he decided to do. He wants to help people, sure, but not like this. He ain't like you, or whatever you think you're tryin' to be. He's a kind man that stared Evil in the eye once already. You can't ask him to do that again. Dupray ain't equipped for someone like this. If you wanna do it, that's on you, but you can't drag Johnny into it."

"Bernadette," Elven said, but it was no use.

The call ended. He could practically feel the phone slam down from the other side. She might be right, but it didn't change what Elven had to do.

He just had to do it without his deputies.

CHAPTER FIFTY-EIGHT

The way up the long stretch of dirt road to the abandoned mine shaft at the top of the mountain hadn't been easy. The road was slick with mud, but luckily for him, it was all uphill instead of flat. All the water had rushed downward, not pooling or flooding anywhere. The road had been cleared of surrounding vegetation when it had been put in, so there hadn't been any fallen trees or heavy debris in his way.

A couple of old rusted-out trailers still stood beyond the broken fence at the top. Other than them, most of the equipment and machinery had been long sold, scrapped, or stolen since the mines had closed. His parents weren't ones to be wasteful when money was involved.

But it was the perfect spot to bring James. It was completely out of the way from where Penny and Corbin were headed, and there was only one way in and out of the property. James would have no way of ambushing him, if that was even his style. According to Hollis, the man had no problem approaching someone head-on and looking them in the eye.

Hollis was already up there, waiting for Elven. The headlights of his truck beamed a path straight toward the empty mineshaft that had been blocked off with wooden boards. He stood under the small awning of one of the trailers with his hands tucked into his pockets.

When Elven stepped out of his Jeep and into the rain, Hollis lifted his head.

"You sure about this?" Hollis asked.

"If I ain't, would it matter?"

Hollis tipped his head to the side. "Suppose not. Just seemed like the polite thing to ask."

Elven nodded, finding a spot in the mud that was more elevated so his boots didn't sink in.

"Anyone else coming?"

Elven shook his head. "Looks like this is it. What about you?"

"Wade is out of town for business. Lyman is down the road, waiting," Hollis said, seeing the look on Elven's face. "Don't worry, he knows what the score is and what not to do. This is for his sister, after all."

"Make sure he doesn't do anything stupid and get himself killed."

"Elven, I know you and I might not see eye to eye. You got your grudge against me, and I can appreciate it. But I ain't never wanted you dead."

"I know it."

"And I never wanted you to put your life on the line like this. It would be too much, for even me, to ask of you."

"Then it's a good thing you never asked," Elven said. "Besides, I ain't doin' it for you. I'm doing it for Penny."

Hollis walked out into the rain, standing next to Elven. The old guy wasn't using his cane, and he managed to fake it well enough that even Elven wouldn't have known he needed one.

"Everything you've done for her already is more than you owe," Hollis said. "This is a lot more than you've dealt with before. I know you think you're gonna arrest him, bring him down to the station in cuffs, but that ain't the case. The only way to stop James is to kill him."

"I've pulled the trigger before, Hollis. If it comes to it, then I'll do what it takes," Elven said.

"You're gonna have to look him in the eye and pull the trigger," Hollis said. "You'll watch as the life spills out of him, when he looks back at you, knowing it was you that ended it. James Smith might be a rotten piece of shit who's had it coming, but he's still a man. And for good men like you, that kind of thing can eat you up."

Elven stared at Hollis, locking eyes with him. "You and I both know I've done a whole lot worse. I remember what we did all those years ago when I was a deputy that didn't know any better. Just trying to get justice in a way I didn't understand. I think about it every day."

He stared into Hollis's eyes for a moment, both of them silent, letting the storm be their voice to each other as it raged on. After a moment, Hollis spoke first.

"That's assumin' you can pull the trigger before he does, of course."

CHAPTER FIFTY-NINE

"What in the devil are you doin'?" Button asked.

Johnny slid his pants on, one leg at a time, just as he always used to. But he didn't feel like he used to. After having the worst afternoon of his life, he'd found himself in Button's arms and between her sheets. Life didn't seem like he was just bumbling around in it anymore.

He grabbed his shirt from the back of the chair at her vanity. The table in front of it was cluttered with various make-up and skincare products. A small mirror sat in the center.

The shirt was nearly dry as he slid his arms in, slowly buttoning it up. He looked up at Button, unsure of what to say to her. She was beautiful, with her hair down, curling past her shoulders. The back was slightly messy from the activities they'd been up to. He nearly blushed, thinking about them again.

"Johnny, I'm asking you a question," she said, her hands on her hips. She wore a night shirt that was loose and fell below her waist, just barely covering her panties.

He took a deep breath and let it out. "Button, I'm goin' to do my job."

"Your job?" she asked in disbelief. "But I thought you didn't think you wanted to do this job anymore. That seeing the evil in that man gave you second thoughts."

Johnny pursed his lips, never liking confrontation. But he needed to stand up for himself. "Maybe so, but it's still my job. And more than that, Elven's asking for my help. Tank's in the hospital, and Madds is—well, I don't know. But it's the right thing to do."

"He's just your boss," Button protested. "You don't owe him."

"He's more than that," Johnny said. "He's my friend. And he's a good man."

Button opened her mouth to protest, but he held a hand up. He knew she was worried, more than anything. She was a good woman. He recognized that. But as much as she feared for him, he wasn't going to change his mind.

"Button, please don't say anything else. I know we ain't known each other long, but you're the best thing that's ever happened to me. And I think I love you."

"Johnny," she said with a smile.

"And if you feel the same about me, or have any plans on feelin' the same, then you gotta let me do this, you hear? If I don't, then I won't be that man you met in the street the other day. I'll be a shell of myself if I don't do what's right. And bein' on the sidelines while my friend faces down some asshole ain't right."

Button's eyes softened. She put a hand against his cheek and brought his face in to kiss him. He felt the warmth of her lips against his.

"Alright, then. You do what you need to," she said. "Just don't do anything stupid, alright?"

Johnny smiled, probably like an idiot, but he didn't care. He had a woman who supported his decisions, who backed him up and cared about him. And he cared about her.

"Don't you worry none. I ain't the heroic type. I done a lot of stupid things in my life, but gettin' killed ain't gonna be one of them," Johnny said as he strapped his gun to his belt.

MADDS SAT ON THE BED, her suitcase by the door. She was bundled up, her knees lifted up on the bed, making her look like a ball. She wrapped her arms around her legs, going back and forth between being worried about Elven and angry with him.

He was really something, wasn't he?

That asshole had the audacity to practically fire her when she needed his help, and then in return, comes to ask for her help?

And what did she care? She was lying to him, stabbing him in the back, keeping tabs on him for Hollis, and causing him more trouble than he realized. If that's what he was gonna do, then maybe he deserved to face this hit man by himself.

But something tugged at her heart, and she knew things weren't so cut and dry. Hell, she'd been the poster child for that. Running from one criminal to find herself working for a different one, only to become one herself.

Life had a way of turning someone upside down sometimes.

The storm continued on and she turned the lights off, grabbing the suitcase. She opened the door, feeling the temperature shift. She couldn't wait to be done with Dupray.

She stepped into the rain and ran down the walkway toward her car. Thankfully, she'd gotten it back from her cousins just after Hollis had lost total faith in her. She popped the trunk and threw her suitcase in, then slammed it shut. She ran to the driver's seat and got in, starting it up and immediately turning the heater on.

She shifted it into drive and took a deep breath, looking out the windshield. That feeling never went away and she threw her head back.

"God dammit," she said, pulling away from the motel.

CHAPTER SIXTY

He remained focused on the muddy road in front of him. The truck he'd stolen smelled like cigarettes and engine oil, and every time he shifted gears, he could feel the clutch give him issues. It was the newest one in the lot, but that wasn't saying much when it came to a place like Dupray. The gears seemed to be disintegrating, and he gave it a year before the whole thing needed to be gutted and fixed, or just scrapped and replaced.

But tonight, it was doing the job he needed it for.

A bag of tools sat on the floor of the passenger's seat. The radio had been removed and a few wires hung from where it used to be. The heater worked, which was good, and he kept one hand in front of the vent to keep it warm.

He had to admit, he hadn't done much research on this sheriff and thought he was blowin' smoke when he said he'd have the money. What kind of man had that kind of money lying around to wire to someone? Most folks with money like that would have it tied up in investments, maybe have called someone to move it around. And none of those people lived in a place like Dupray.

He drove past a sign that had been weathered, one of the bolts rusted off so the metal plate hung to the side. He squinted through the rain, wishing it would let up already so he wouldn't be cold and wet as he tried to read the sign. It read PROPERTY OF HALLIE MINING COMPANY.

James chuckled. "Go figure," he said. "Some rich asshole wanted to play the sheriff game."

But he wasn't sure he bought that himself. He'd seen this Elven guy deescalate the situation at the bar without waving his badge around or going off on a power trip. But he did use his money to do it, so maybe that was power enough for him—knowing he could buy people off.

Except this was different. He wasn't buying himself out of anything now. He'd actually bought himself into it. The man must have some real stones to do what he did, and for what? The Starcher girl. Maybe he'd find out what that was all about later, if it even really mattered.

He forged ahead up the road, though at this point, it might as well be a slide. The rain rushed down, washing away any semblance of it being something vehicles had ever used.

Lightning cracked in the sky, blasting like a flash bomb. Out of the corner of his eye, he saw a vehicle with its headlights off. But it was too late. The truck slammed into the driver's side door of his truck. The glass shattered, littering shards over him. He could feel the pricks against his face from the jagged edges.

His truck slid off the side of the road, his tires digging into the mud and the entire vehicle's weight tipping. As the water shoved against his truck, he felt it going further and further until he was sideways, then upside down. The glass went everywhere, and James found himself lying on the ceiling of the truck, not having bothered to buckle his seatbelt.

The truck that had hit him was spun around from the force. The front end of the truck was smashed and the engine sputtered as it tried to keep running. James righted himself and kicked at the glass that remained in the frame. The pieces broke away with each kick and he started to crawl out, the running water pouring over him.

Just as he crawled out, he felt a tug on his coat. The man who had rammed his vehicle dragged him through the mud, dropping him in the road. James worked his way to his feet and was met with a fist to the face. He fell to the side and sank his hands into the mud to steady himself. He turned to see the attacker swing his leg at him.

But this time, he was ready.

He brought a hand out of the mud and grabbed onto the attacker's ankle, then wrapped his other hand around it and twisted. The man slid in the mud and landed on his backside, sending a splash of mud into the air.

The attacker let out a loud groan as he rolled along the road. James spotted the man's jacket at the waist, seeing a holster on his hip. He sat up and tried going for the gun, but by then, James was already on it, drawing his first.

"Wouldn't do that," James said, catching his breath.

The two of them were close enough that James could make out the man's features. He had a large gash across his forehead, coupled with a huge bump that was already starting to swell. The aftermath of the accident, most likely. But he also had a look of desperation on his face.

"Take your hand off," James said. "I won't kill ya, but I'll make your life a livin' hell."

The man swallowed. "She's my sister."

James smiled. "You're Hollis's boy? Figured you'd be bigger. You Corbin?"

He shook his head. "Lyman."

"You must take after your momma," James said.

"What is it with you and my dad?" Lyman asked.

James motioned with his gun toward Lyman's hand that still hovered on the pistol grip. Lyman slowly moved his hand away.

"There's some history to get through, that's for sure. But you might say he's the closest thing I got to a brother. At least, he was for a while," James said.

"And you're willing to kill his daughter?" Lyman asked.

"You get along with your brothers?" James asked.

Lyman shook his head.

"A jobs a job, though," James said. "This is the only thing I know."

"So what now?" Lyman asked.

"Tell you what, I'll do ol' Hollis a favor," James said, keeping the gun on Lyman. He walked to the truck he'd stolen that was now upside down and reached through the window. He grabbed the tool bag that had half spilled out and rummaged with his free hand until he found what he was looking for. He held two heavy-duty zip ties.

James motioned with his gun for Lyman to stand. Lyman then followed James to the truck. "Put your hands on the wheel," James instructed.

Lyman sighed, but complied. James wrapped his wrists up around the wheel with the zip ties and holstered his gun. "Now you'll get to see another day standing."

"Elven ain't gonna let you off the top of this mountain," Lyman said.

"He won't have a choice," James said, throwing a punch across Lyman's face. Lyman hit his head against the dash and didn't open his eyes. He'd be fine, just out for a bit. James shook his hand as it ached at the knuckles and took the rest of the road on foot as the rain continued to pour.

CHAPTER SIXTY-ONE

Elven wondered if the storm would stop before the sun rose in the morning, and at the same time, part of him wondered if he would get to see it.

For someone who was normally confident in his abilities, he sure didn't feel it in that moment. It wasn't that he didn't think he was good, but that anything could happen. Even just his hand being wet could cause a split second of his grip to slip and lose control.

He stood underneath the small awning that Hollis had been under before. It was just tucked out of view from the entrance through the chain-link fence that had been long busted open. He wasn't going to stand in the open, allowing James to get the jump on him. He was still the sheriff first. Not some gunslinger killing men because that's all he knew.

That was the other guy's role. His was to take him down, arrest him, and send him to court to face a jury of his peers. What happened after that wasn't up to him, but he wasn't going to play judge, jury, and executioner if he didn't have to.

But deep down, even with all the plans, he knew it would come down to it. A man like James wasn't going to throw his hands in the air and give up. That didn't mean Elven wouldn't try.

"You know, I hate this weather," James said from the gate.

Elven put his hand on the butt of his gun, keeping close to the wall of the trailer. He waited, his heart picking up the pace. He took two deep breaths and let them out steadily, calming himself.

"Sheriff, I know what you're thinkin'," James yelled. "You're thinking that you're still a lawman. You still want to put me in cuffs and haul me down to the station. But that ain't gonna happen. Noble thought, sure, and doin' your job, which I can appreciate. But I still gotta do mine."

Elven pulled out his gun, holding it down as he crept toward the corner. Just a quick step around, and he'd be in the line of sight. He'd have his gun raised and demand that James put his hands up.

"If you're thinkin' of popping around that corner of the trailer with your gun raised, you can bet that you'll catch a bullet first."

Elven froze. Did he really just suss out his location? Or was he just throwing wild guesses out, getting lucky with the first try? He backed away and thought about heading around the other side to see if—

"Ain't no use rethinking your plans," James said. "If you don't come out and face me, I'll head back down that hill and put a bullet in that Starcher boy's kidney. He's got a love for his sister and seems to think highly of you, so maybe you won't like that much."

There was silence for a while as Elven decided what to do.

"Alright, have it your way," James said, his voice growing distant as he turned around.

Elven grit his teeth and stepped out from around the trailer and into the rain. "Wait," Elven called out. He still held his gun, but kept it pointed down by his waist.

James turned around, his own hand on the butt of his pistol. Elven could see through the haze of the rain that he was the man he remembered. The one from the bar he hadn't recognized, the one with the scar on his cheek. He had a large bandage on his neck that had soaked through with red blood.

James's pistol was raised, locked onto Elven.

"You wanna put that gun in your holster? I'll still be able to put a bullet in ya if not, but it would make conversation a bit easier," James said, nodding to Elven's hand.

Elven slowly slid it into his holster.

"Lyman?" Elven asked.

"He's alright. Just restin'," James said. "Tied him up."

Elven nodded. "You can give up now. It doesn't have to go down like this. I'm just here to arrest you. If you give up willingly, I guarantee no harm will come to you." Elven said it with confidence and not a single word wavered, but even to him, it sounded ridiculous.

"You know, when I saw your name on the signs comin' in, I thought maybe you were on some power trip. First, money to put you above the law, then the job to make it your law. But now, seeing you here, I think I got that wrong. You seem to be a good man."

Elven stared him down. What was James expecting? For him to be flattered that a cold-blooded killer had paid him a compliment?

"If it weren't for that Hunter guy, I'd have gotten to Penny before you. That guy could shoot, and I thought for sure he'd be the one to take me out. But he only left me with this here," James said, lifting his head to better expose the bandage on his neck.

"You tryin' to talk me to death, or are we gonna do this?" Elven said.

James smiled. "I guess you did pay me. So you wanna just have it done with, or you wanna draw for it?"

Elven brought his hand up, placing it on the butt of his pistol as he narrowed his eyes.

"Thought so," James said. "You wanna count, or just go for it?"

"How bout we count it?"

James nodded, still holding his gun. "Alright, then." He turned his head toward the darkness. "But first, Hollis, you come on out of there. Whatcha got anyway?" James narrowed his eyes in the dark. "I will put a bullet in that other leg of yours. You ever seen a man with two limps?"

Elven watched as Hollis emerged from the shadows. He was soaked through, just like everyone else. He held a shotgun, pointed toward the ground. His mouth twisted in a scowl at the sight of James.

"A shotgun? That woulda damn near cut me in half, I'm sure. But you know, even with your finger on that trigger, I'd have still beat you to it," James said.

"You're a son of a bitch, James. Comin' after my daughter?!" Hollis yelled.

"That's the way the world is sometimes. Sometimes, you just get dealt a bag of shit," James said. "Now toss it."

Hollis threw the gun in the mud, far out of his reach. James turned back to Elven, slowly putting his own gun in his holster.

"Hollis, why don't you do us the honors, back from three. We pull after one," James said.

Elven breathed deep and steady, nodding at Hollis. He locked his eyes on James, knowing he could do this. He was fast, and he thought about the shooting competition. Lyman had told him then that it wasn't all skill. Sometimes, someone just wanted it more.

And he wanted it more than anything.

Elven strummed his fingers against the grip of his revolver.

Hollis started the count.

Three.

Elven tipped his head, the rain spilling off the edge of his hat.

Two.

Thunder cracked, rattling the trailers around them.

One.

CHAPTER SIXTY-TWO

It happened so fast.

And it wasn't the way he'd expected at all.

Hollis said *one* and Elven felt his hand wrap around the grip of his revolver. He held it so firm that no amount of water pouring over him would have made his hand slip off. At the same time, he breathed slowly, the air thick in his lungs, causing him to work to keep a steady pace.

His eyes remained locked on the man across the muddy lot from him. Through the rain, it he felt as if he were watching a show through the static of an old television. The lightning struck in the background, creating a strobe effect. James's movements were jagged and quick. One moment, his hand was at his hip, and the next moment it was lifted up, the gun pointing at Elven.

Everything seemed to happen in slow motion.

Thunder boomed in the night sky, and Elven swore he saw the flash of James's muzzle. But it couldn't be. There was no way anyone was that fast.

At first, he didn't feel the bite of a bullet, so if James had shot, it must have missed him.

Then lights kicked on from his side, like an explosion from nowhere. Elven didn't risk stealing a glance, though it did cause him to hesitate a second too long. At the same time, James's shoulder arched and his body turned to the side. His left hand went out while he yelled, a war cry or something else. Something guttural.

Elven squeezed his trigger as James narrowed down his barrel toward Elven. He couldn't hear the gunshot with the thunder louder than ever, covering up any other sound. But he knew he'd messed up already. He'd jumped the gun, gotten too excited, and hadn't aimed right, the bullet landing at James's feet, sending a wave of mud at the man's feet. Elven lifted his revolver higher, hoping he hadn't made the worst mistake of his life.

Then the roar of the thunder faded away, sounding like the idling of an engine.

Elven steadied himself, taking aim again, still not feeling the bite of a bullet pierce his own flesh. And before he could fire again, two shots came from his right.

James let his revolver fly from his hands as he spun in place. He caught his footing and teetered in place, his eyes wide and mouth agape. His breathing was labored and he stared at Elven before suddenly dropping in the mud.

The idling sound continued and Elven turned to his right to see where the gunshots had come from. To see what the source of the light was. A white, beat-up truck idled at the fence opening where the road met with the property. The interior cab light was on. Elven squinted down and saw Lyman in the driver's seat. His head bloody and bruised.

What's more, and much to Elven's disbelief, was that the passenger's side door was open, and Johnny stood holding his pistol, one hand on the trigger, the other under the butt of the gun to steady it, as Elven had once shown him. Both feet were planted in the mud and the look on his face said it all.

Johnny had wanted it more than anyone else.

Elven took a moment to pat himself down. He was still alive and he hadn't been shot at all. He let out a long sigh and laughed.

He walked over to where James lay in the mud. The rain continued to pour down and Elven stood over him, offering James a bit of shelter from the downpour as he bled out. James had a bullet in his shoulder and two holes in his chest. Johnny was the reason James had thrown his shoulder back, and Johnny then nailed him twice, center mass. James was still alive for the moment and blood seeped from his mouth.

"I'm gonna call an ambulance," Elven said, turning toward his Jeep, but James grabbed his leg.

"D-don't bother," James managed. "You and I both know it ain't comin' before I go." He let out a loud groan. "Fuck. H-had to die in the cold, didn't I?"

Elven watched as James came to terms with his situation. He wanted to arrest him, to take him down to the station for killing people in his town, his friend included, but James was right. He wasn't long for this world.

"W-w-who did it? I didn't get a g-good look," James said. His breathing was labored and he was hanging on the best he could.

"Johnny," Elven answered.

Another groan came from James as he wriggled in the mud, adjusting his arm. Footsteps approached and Elven looked up. It was Hollis. He chuckled as he looked down at James. "You just got done in by the janitor-turned-deputy, son," Hollis said.

There was humor in it, Elven knew it. But there was nothing to laugh about when someone was dying. No matter how evil that someone was.

James coughed, but it turned to laughter. He sounded maniacal, as if he'd lost his mind. His laughter petered off until it sounded more like sobbing, though James didn't cry.

"Ain't life deal a bag of shit sometimes," James said weakly.

"Must have lost your touch, James," Hollis said. "I ain't never known you to miss someone. Elven's standing without a scratch."

James's eyes were barely open. He was still smiling, his teeth tinted red, but it was slipping away. "Sheriff ain't as good as he thinks." His voice was a whisper, barely audible above the rain. "But I n-never miss."

A rattle came from James's throat, like a zip tie running slow across his esophagus. His eyes rolled to the back of his head and his mouth hung open. The blood ran down across his cheek, filling the divoted scar on his skin like a red river.

James was dead.

"Don't know what he meant by that, cause I ain't—"

"Elven!" Lyman yelled.

Elven spun around and saw Lyman at the side of the truck. Johnny had fallen into the mud, his back against the tire. His head hung forward and Elven saw red blossoming across his soaked tan shirt. Elven widened his eyes and ran toward them. Hollis limped behind him, trying to keep up.

Elven stopped short, sliding in the mud and falling down next to Johnny and Lyman. He didn't care. He needed to see if his friend was okay. But when he looked at Lyman's face, Lyman twisted in a frown.

Elven grabbed Johnny's cheeks and lifted his head up. His eyes fluttered until they opened fully.

"Elven," Johnny said. "I got him. D'you see?"

"Yeah, Johnny. I saw alright. You did so good. So good. We gotta get you up, alright?" Elven said, panicking on the inside. He looked down and saw the blood pouring out of Johnny, but he couldn't pinpoint the location of his wound.

"I'm cold, Elven," Johnny said, his voice weak and raspy.

"C'mon, Johnny, lets get you up," Elven said. He got to his feet and grabbed under him, but Johnny was too heavy. Lyman grabbed the other side, and together, they pulled him up. Johnny groaned from the pain and exertion, but Elven wasn't going to stop until they had him in the truck.

"Hollis!" Elven yelled.

"Already on it," Hollis said from the driver's seat. "Get in the damn truck."

Elven and Lyman managed to lift Johnny up and lay him down in the bed of the truck. They climbed in as Hollis threw it into gear and floored it out of the fenced area, then back down the mud-slicked road.

Elven pulled his jacket off, even though he was soaked and freezing. He draped it over Johnny as he shivered and held it tight against Johnny's chest, trying to stop the bleeding. Lyman held his coat over them, trying to keep them as dry as possible.

The drive was relentless. Slick from the storm, and nearly impossible to navigate. The rain was constant. But Hollis managed to keep them going at full speed, never losing his control of the vehicle while Elven tried to keep Johnny comfortable and awake.

"Johnny, you stay with me, you hear?" Elven yelled. "Keep your darn eyes open, alright?"

Johnny never answered, and as much as Elven pleaded. Johnny couldn't keep his eyes open.

CHAPTER SIXTY-THREE

MADDS SAT IN HER CAR, WAITING IN THE DARK. SHE'D BEEN there for thirty minutes as the rain had pounded away on the roof. Eventually, the rain had slowed down to a small pitter-patter, and then it became nothing. That's when she stepped out of her car.

It was still too cold for her, but at least she was dry. She buried her hands deep in her parka, the hot chocolate stain still there, having never come out in the wash. The clouds had let some moonlight in, but it was still near pitch-black outside, and would be for at least another five hours. The lack of sleep didn't bother her at the moment, though soon she knew it would catch up with her.

She made her way through the puddles in the grass, trying to avoid the deep mud, but doing a terrible job of it as her feet sank in the muck with each step.

She could see Noah sitting in the center of the field next to Hunter's body. Noah shivered, his color pale and blue. He was drenched to the bone. When she was within twenty feet, he looked up at her.

"Did Penny make it?" he asked.

She watched him sit next to his brother, crying over his poor decision. He was a mess, but there was no one to blame other than himself.

Madds shrugged. "Don't know. But if she didn't, then neither did Elven."

He twisted his face, putting together that he would have put himself at risk before letting anything happen to Penny. Madds didn't understand, and maybe it didn't matter anymore.

"I never wanted this," Noah said. "I didn't know. I just thought—" he sighed. "I don't know. I crossed the line and just found myself in over my head. I thought this is what I wanted. And now I just wish I could take it all back. All of them, you know? Just to get Hunter back."

He looked at his brother, hanging his head. "Are you gonna arrest me?"

"Is that what you want?"

"I don't want to go to jail, but I deserve it. Hell, I deserve a whole heap worse. Just look what I did to my brother."

"If worse is what you want, then get in the back of my car. You won't make it to the station, I can guarantee you that."

"Why not?" he asked, wiping his nose with his soaked sleeve.

"You think Hollis will let that stand? Your hiring someone to kill his daughter?"

"You would do that? For Hollis? But—"

"Penny's my cousin," she said. "Hollis is my uncle."

He shook his head, and she wondered if he believed her or not. She really didn't care either way, but somehow confessing felt right. Gave her the briefest moment of relief.

"Why you telling me this?" he asked.

"I guess because I know how you feel," she said. "Making mistakes you wish you could take back. Being in so deep, you can barely breathe, but also so far in that you can't go back."

"Yeah?"

"I killed some people for Hollis and covered it up so Elven wouldn't know. And now I'm having to live with the guilt every damn day of my life. At first, I thought it was necessary, but now, well, how do you go back from that?"

"What am I supposed to do now?" he asked. "I can't run. Dupray's all I know and I don't wanna be anywhere without my momma and brother anyway. Tell me, please, what do I do?"

Madds took a deep breath. She didn't want to say it with her words, so instead, her eyes drifted next to Hunter, a foot away from Noah. In a puddle of mud, his brother's revolver sat.

She locked eyes with him and he nodded, grabbing the gun.

"Will you—" he stopped, sighing. "Just tell Elven..."

She nodded. "I will."

He stuck the barrel of the gun under his chin, his eyes filled with tears. But at the same time, something in them told her that he was thinking straight. In that moment, the decision wasn't made from a place he would regret.

She turned around and by the time she got to the edge of the field, a gunshot rang out through the air.

She got back into her car and drove away.

CHAPTER SIXTY-FOUR

Elven stood in the hospital room, his hat in his hand. He was less soaked now, but still damp from sitting around the waiting room to get word on Johnny. The front of his uniform shirt was stained with Johnny's blood. Even with all the rain, it had stayed in the fabric, unable to wash out.

Hollis had driven them to the hospital in such a rush, Elven hadn't thought the old guy was capable of it. As much as he hated to admit it, the man might have saved Johnny's life. And that was just fine with Elven. The methods didn't matter, or who was involved, as long as it got done. Once they'd pulled up to the hospital, Elven and Lyman had carried Johnny into the hospital in a frenzy.

The doctors and nurses got him a gurney right away and took Johnny to the back, where they spent what seemed like an eternity, but that was probably about three hours, performing surgery. The doctor, some guy Elven didn't know in his early thirties, told him the details of his injuries.

A lot of it went over Elven's head, but the ultimate takeaway was that it wasn't great.

So Elven stood in front of his friend, watching him sleep.

Listening to the machines beep and the ventilation machine next to Johnny pump oxygen in and out, in and out. He had tubes down his throat, tubes in his nose, IVs all over his arms, and wires that stretched everywhere. And there was a large spot in the center of his chest that was bloody, but bandaged.

Apparently, James's reputation had held up. He hadn't worked for free.

Johnny wasn't dead, he was just in a coma.

Elven felt stupid standing there, talking to the man while he was asleep and hooked up to all that equipment. He wasn't even sure Johnny could hear him. But he had something to say, so he was gonna say it.

"You just killed the most dangerous man around," Elven said with a small laugh. "I wouldn't believe it myself if I hadn't seen it with my own eyes. But it's true. And I got it on good authority that he is as dangerous as I say. Coming from a man like Hollis, that should say a lot."

Elven played with his hat, spinning it in his hands. He opened his mouth and ran his tongue against the inside of his cheek, thinking of the words to say, all the while holding back tears that tried to shove their way through.

"You saved my life tonight, Johnny," Elven said. "You're an asset to this department. That's the God's honest truth. I know that Lester might've hired you, with you thinkin' he was desperate or took pity on you. But I'm tellin' you right now, you've earned your position. You hear that?"

Elven pointed at him, gritting his teeth. "You've earned it. You ain't got no reason to second-guess your standing on my team."

Elven felt a tear squeeze past his defenses and pulled up his arm, wiping it away with his sleeve. "Dang it, Johnny," Elven said, sighing. "Oh, and that firecracker you got? Button, as you like to call her? You better hang on to that one, cause she's a real winner."

Elven walked to Johnny's side and patted him on his shoulder.

There was no response from his friend in the bed, just more beeping from the equipment.

"You rest up, alright? When you're able, your spot is always ready for you," Elven said.

He turned and left Johnny to sleep for who knew how long. When asked when he would wake up, the doctors said it could be a day, or it could be never. But Elven had hope that Johnny had fight in him, and that it would be sooner than most people thought.

He closed the door behind him gently and turned to the hallway, where Bernadette sat on a bench. He'd been the one to call her as soon as Johnny had been taken into surgery. She hadn't ripped into him when he'd called, and she hadn't when she'd arrived at the hospital, though she might have been well within her rights to do so.

She just stared at Elven, her silence worse than any words.

"Johnny's a good friend of mine," he said. "I've known him a long time, and if there's one thing he is, it's loyal, and loyal to a fault. Hell, he got himself shot because of it. But you find yourself someone like that by your side, and you might just have life figured out."

She still said nothing. Elven nodded, passing by her in the brightly lit hallway, but he stopped again.

"Also," he said. "You were right to interfere. When he wakes up, I expect you to do that whenever you deem it necessary."

"You got my word," she said, her voice cold.

Elven didn't look back at her, figuring they both understood each other.

CHAPTER SIXTY-FIVE

The night air was frigid, but at least it had stopped raining. Elven stepped out of the hospital in his now-dry coat. Hanging it on the chair while pacing the waiting room had done a good enough job of drying it out. Even if his shirt was still damp, he'd be fine. It was a lot better than he could say for Johnny.

Hollis leaned against the wall, smoking a cigar as he waited. Lyman had headed back to their home and gotten his father a change of clothes so he was dry. Why Hollis hadn't just gone home with Lyman instead, Elven didn't know. But he had a feeling that he'd stayed for Elven's sake. It made Elven hate even more what he had to do.

"Penny's fine," Hollis said.

"Good," Elven replied. At least James had kept his word, though with the speed he'd made it to the mine, Elven hadn't thought otherwise.

"James Smith was the deadliest son of a bitch I ever came across," Hollis said, puffing out a cloud of smoke.

"You're not supposed to smoke so close to the building," Elven said.

Hollis looked at his cigar, then at Elven. He shrugged, snuffing it out against the wall.

"The deadliest?" Elven asked. "'Cause I figured there'd be worse than him. Especially considering you."

Hollis grinned. "I said the deadliest, not the cruelest. He ain't even rank on that list."

"You helped me when I needed it," Elven said. "Thank you."

Hollis raised his hand, waving off the gratitude. "Elven, I know what you think of me, but I ain't never wanted anything other than the best for you. That's the truth. And I may be a lot of things, but I ain't ever wished anything ill upon a good man. That goes for you, and that janitor who took that bullet."

Elven didn't bother correcting Hollis on Johnny's position. Johnny wouldn't care what Hollis thought of him, mostly because Elven didn't care what Hollis thought of anything.

Hollis cleared his throat. "Lyman's out in the truck. We'll take you back home."

Elven wanted to be stubborn and not take the ride, but he was exhausted and needed sleep. Besides, Lyman was driving, and after the night they had, maybe he should just put his beef aside for the time being.

Hollis stepped in close to Elven. He could smell the cigar smoke on his breath. "Elven, to me, this goes without sayin'. But knowing you, I gotta say it anyway. And I know how you'll feel about it, so try not to get too bent outta shape. You stepping into the line of fire like that for Penny says a lot to me. Goes above and beyond your duties. I ain't ever owed anyone nothing in my life. But right here, right now, I'm tellin' you. I owe you one. Trust me, that don't come easy."

"I'm sure it doesn't," Elven said. "But you're wrong about it, too."

Hollis cocked his head.

"You've owed me my entire adult life," Elven said. "For what we did all those years ago. For what you made me do. There ain't never gettin' over that."

He turned and walked away.

"Elven, what about that ride?" Hollis called out.

"I'll find my own way."

CHAPTER SIXTY-SIX

Elven had taken a cab back to his house. Not a lot of cab drivers were around Dupray, but he'd called for one and waited, letting them know he was willing to pay whatever the fare was plus a tip. The driver had been pleasantly surprised when Elven had handed him a wad of cash from his wallet.

Lyman waited for him at the top of the hill in front of his home. After dropping Hollis off, he still had time to make it to Elven's before the cab had shown up. Elven wanted so badly to just go inside and fall face-first into bed next to Yeti, but he let Lyman take him to get his Jeep that he'd left at the abandoned mine. He'd been stubborn to not take the lift back home in the same truck as Hollis, but Lyman was different from his father.

The ride was quiet, nonetheless. They'd both been through a lot that night. But when Elven stepped out of the truck and closed the door, he made sure to thank Lyman for everything.

Lyman, of course, thought nothing of it. "That's what friends were for," he'd said.

Except Elven knew that friends didn't always risk their necks for each other, which made him appreciate the few friends he had even more.

He sighed as he started up the Jeep and knew there was something else he needed to take care of. He just hoped he wasn't too late.

The drive was long, and the night seemed to be even longer. But he made it to the motel, hoping as he approached that she hadn't left yet.

To his surprise, the window was lit up and the curtain was still closed. He knocked on the door, exhausted, but grateful.

The door opened, and Madds stood there, her lips a thin line. She was angry, or at least pretending to be. Her eyes betrayed her, though. They widened, and softened. She was glad to see him, and he knew it.

"It's done," Elven said.

"Bernadette called me. Told me what happened to Johnny," she said.

That surprised Elven as he didn't realize the two of them were all that close. Then again, she had played matchmaker between the two. Not that it mattered. He was glad she'd already heard and he didn't have to give her the bad news.

"He saved my life," Elven said.

She didn't speak, but kept her mouth closed and clenched her jaw. She was a stubborn one.

But it wasn't just stubbornness. She turned around, letting him step inside. He heard her sniffle as she faced away.

"Madds, it's over, alright?"

She spun around, her face twisted in anger, but her eyes were welling up with tears. She smacked him across the face. "That was so fucking stupid. Don't you ever do that again, Elven. If you do, I swear to God, I—"

"Madds, calm down," he said.

She started to pound on his chest. Swinging open hands against him uncontrollably as she lost it. He was surprised by her anger. But it wasn't the kind of anger he expected. It came from a place of care.

The tears flowed down, and she smacked him over and over. He grabbed her and took her into his arms, struggling to keep her from lashing out again.

"I'm alive, Madds," he said. "It's okay. I—well, I didn't know you cared so much."

She stopped swinging and rested her head against his chest. The two stood like that for a moment, and he couldn't help but think it felt right.

"I didn't, either," she said. "I mean, I did. I just, fuck, Elven, I can't lose you, okay? You're the only stable thing in my life right now, and if I don't have that, then I'll just fall apart. I know I sound batshit-crazy right now, but it's how I feel."

Elven looked down at her, the pain in her eyes so out in the open. He felt terrible for everything he'd done to her. For accusing her. For investigating her. For ignoring her. For dismissing her. And now for putting her through the thought of him not coming back.

"Madds, I'm sorry," he said. "Not just for being stupid and putting myself at risk, but for everything. I dug into your past and caused this danger you felt you were in. That ain't right of me, and I had no reason to do it."

She shook her head. "You did, though," she admitted. "I lied to you and gave you cause to not trust me."

He smiled. "It's okay. I understand, and I trust you. You only did what you thought you had to. And now, you've got nothing to worry about, you hear me?"

She opened her mouth, ready to ask, but he beat her to it.

"I need you here. Working with me. I need someone to keep me in check, otherwise I get reckless," Elven said. "Don't worry about Kurt anymore. He's taken care of."

Madds offered a half-smile, relief washing over her face. "Thank you, Elven."

He held onto her as she locked eyes with him. She smelled like body wash, her hair damp from a recent shower. She lifted herself on her toes and didn't wait. She pushed her lips against his, taking him by surprise.

But he didn't pull away. He went with it, their lips interlocking. She was soft and warm. He breathed her in, intoxicated by her essence.

The two of them lingered and eventually pulled away at the same time. He blinked a few times, unsure of what to say. She shied away a moment and wiped her lips with her finger.

"I'm sorry," she said. "I don't know—"

"It's been a long couple of days, hasn't it?" he asked.

She nodded, smiling at him. "I guess it has."

They pulled away from each other, giving a proper amount of space so it didn't happen again. "I tell you what, nobody really tells you how shot your nerves are after a duel. You gonna be okay here?"

She nodded. "Yeah, I'll be fine."

"Good, 'cause I think we both could use some rest. I plan on sleeping for the next week."

"Is that so?"

He shrugged, and placed her badge and gun on the dresser that was across from the bed. "I've got a trustworthy deputy to take care of things if I'm not around. At least, I hope so."

She smiled. "Of course."

He smiled and turned to the door.

"Elven?"

He glanced over his shoulder, half of him hoping she didn't ask him to stay. The other half-hoping she would.

"Thanks for, well, you know," she said, motioning to the room like the moment they'd just shared was a physical object.

He nodded. "Don't sweat it, Deputy."

CHAPTER SIXTY-SEVEN

Elven pulled up to the motel on the outskirts of Dupray. It was so far outside of town, that it was practically in the neighboring county. It had taken him nearly two hours to get there, but he knew it would be worth it.

He'd been wrong about a lot of things in the past few days. About Madds, about Hunter, and about himself. It was time he was right about something instead.

He ran a finger across his mouth, still feeling the warm, soft kiss that Madds had planted on him earlier. He could taste her cherry ChapStick and practically smell the hint of jasmine she seemed to carry around everywhere she went. He told himself that wasn't the reason he was at the motel, and he truly believed it.

He was helping a friend. He was sticking up for what was right.

But the feeling of Madds's body pressed against him didn't hurt, either.

He had to remind himself that the circumstances had been extreme. They were both tired. She'd been without sleep for awhile, worried about the jerk ex-husband of hers, on top of the stress she'd been under in general from the job. They were both emotional. And what he'd done to help Penny had been stupid and reckless, putting them both in even more emotional distress.

Maybe there was something there between him and Madds. Maybe not. Right then, he was truly too exhausted to assess that situation. But he still had one last thing that needed doing.

He stepped out of his Jeep, having parked right in front of the door labeled with a 3. The number was slightly cocked to the side, whatever fastened it to the door having weathered so much, it looked ready to fall to the ground.

He'd made a few phone calls after realizing how messed up he'd made things for Madds. Of course, when he'd hired her, she hadn't told him the reasons why she wanted to move so far from Arizona, and he'd let it be. But he'd also told her he didn't want anything coming back and biting them in the backside because of it, either.

She hadn't kept up her end of that bargain. But then again, it had been out of her control. And the story of her ex-husband, Kurt, had sounded like a desperate situation to get out of. She'd been backed into a corner, so she'd done what she thought was best for her.

And he couldn't blame her. She'd probably been right about Kurt, and he might have done the same if he'd found himself in a similar situation. The cartel wasn't something he would want to mess with— at least, not by himself. And if there was corruption in the department, that was even scarier.

He ran a small operation in Dupray, but if there was anything he felt he had with the four people in that office, it was trust. Any sort of corruption would be out of the question. Or so he thought.

That was the benefit of a small town. He knew everyone in it, and everyone outside of it.

And if he was going to keep that trust and safety, he was going to have to ensure it himself.

The night may have been cold, but Elven's blood felt even colder. The idea of Madds drifted from his mind and he thought again of the night he'd just had. Standing toe to toe with a trained, expert killer wasn't something he would ever forget anytime soon.

Hollis may have been right—facing that sort of thing could change a man.

Elven lifted his fist and banged on the door, his Jeep still running behind him. There was no answer, but he waited a moment before banging again. He knew the man was inside the room. He'd called as many of the motels as he could think of in the county. He'd been given a lot of grief from the owners and managers of the shanty places, who had all been worried that giving up their customers' information would cost them.

It was true—they didn't get a lot of business, and Elven was there to make them lose what little they had. But he also reminded them that he could swing down there any time he liked, going door to door to every room they had, questioning each patron who had decided to stay in the place. He didn't like to threaten, he reminded them. And if they didn't give him the information he wanted, he would make sure it would not be just a threat.

Eventually, they all saw it his way, and this was the one place with a guest who matched the description he'd given them. A blond, nearly white-haired guy who sounded as if he was from somewhere outside of Appalachia, and kind of a jerk.

That's why Elven was at the Road City Motel. Room three.

He pounded on the door again, this time, the light clicking on after he did. The man inside had probably been asleep, but Elven didn't care. The more uncomfortable he could make him, the better.

He pounded again.

"Christ, who the fuck is out there?" the man yelled from inside.

"Open up," Elven growled.

"You're knocking on the wrong fuckin' door, asshole," the man said, just before swinging it open.

Elven saw the white-blond hair, as if the man had seen a ghost. His jawline was strong and he had the blue eyes that Madds had told him about. He wore no shirt, but he'd had the decency to put pants on before opening the door.

But underneath all that description, there were heavy bags

underneath his eyes and he needed a shave. The scary ex was still just a man. And one who appeared to be running from his own demons.

"Who the fuck are you?" Kurt asked, one hand on the door frame, the other behind the door itself.

"I'm your second chance," Elven said.

He scoffed. "You really are messing with the wrong guy right now, you know that?"

"I want to see those taillights of yours heading that way, outside of my county. And you know, it might be best if you kept on heading outside of West Virginia. After that, I don't really care."

Kurt's eyes drifted down Elven's shirt, seeing the badge he wore. "Sheriff, I'm not sure I understand."

Elven had no time for games. Kurt could try all he wanted, but Elven wasn't buying it. "Do I mumble when I speak, Kurt Gormley?"

Kurt grinned at the sound of his name, licking his teeth as if considering what to say next. He found the words fast enough. "I see. She spun a story about me, didn't she? Maybe say I was in deep with the cartel? Something like that? Are you out here being a white knight, protecting her?"

Kurt looked over Elven's shoulder to his Jeep that idled. "Is she out there right now in that Jeep of yours? It's a little dark, and I can't see too well. She watching as you make your big show? Getting her wet because you're here standing up to her scary ex-husband? She is something, I tell you that. I'm sure you already know. A minx in bed, right? I've never fucked anyone that got as wet as she did, especially when things got risky. Danger...she's just drawn to it."

Elven stared him down, not saying a word. He kept in mind Kurt's hand behind the door. He knew what Kurt was holding.

"Wait," Kurt said, "don't tell me that you haven't taken a dip in that pool yet. Shit, Sheriff, you must be some kind of gentleman 'cause she's easier than prom night with a six-pack of wine coolers. You don't know what you're missing."

Elven glared harder, still not saying a word. He wanted to push him into the room and draw on him. But he held back. He was better than that.

Kurt sighed. "Alright, alright. But I mean, after all the driving I did to get here? I get the picture, though." He stepped back, and Elven kept his eyes on the hand behind the door.

Then Kurt stepped forward, swinging his empty hand at Elven. He'd been too focused on the hand behind the door that he hadn't seen the fist coming. Kurt hit him square in the jaw.

Elven stumbled backward, then saw the hand come from behind the door. It held a pistol, just as he'd thought. But before Kurt could bring it down, Elven rushed into him, pushing them both into the room as he grabbed Kurt's wrist. Elven threw a headbutt into Kurt's face so hard, he saw stars for a moment.

Elven planted Kurt's hand against the door frame, the hand still holding the gun. He grabbed the door with his free hand and slammed it against Kurt's wrist. The man let out a scream so loud, Elven wondered if he'd broken the man's arm. But the gun never dropped, so he slammed the door again.

This time, the scream was louder, and the gun fell to the ground.

Elven pulled Kurt's hand behind his back and slammed his head against the wall. He squeezed himself against the man, getting right behind him in his ear.

"Fuck you, you hillbilly with a badge," Kurt cried.

"You can stop with the meet-ups, the notes, the roses. All of it," Elven said.

"What the fuck are you talking about?"

"Not a good time to get cute. I think it's time for you to leave."

"I'm not leaving," Kurt said. "And if I do, I'll just be back. You can't protect her forever. I will find her."

Elven grabbed a handful of Kurt's hair and pulled back. Then slammed his head against the wall, Kurt's nose exploding in a blood spatter. "She ain't hard to find. She'll be right here. But I see you again, I will kill you, you understand that? I won't have to protect her forever if you're dead."

"Bullshit," Kurt grumbled, still defiant.

Elven turned Kurt's head, smooshing his face against the wall, and pointed. "You see those hills out there? I know the places to take someone to make them disappear forever. Nobody will miss you. Nobody will ever think to look for you. Eventually, you'll fade away from every single person's memory, whoever had the unfortunate chance to know you. I don't know how they do things in the city, but this is Dupray, West Virginia. We coined the term for pretty mouths like yours. A place ain't nobody ever cared to know, and if they do, they hightail it out of here faster than they came in. We do things a little different here, you understand?"

Kurt managed to nod his head, leaving a smear of blood against the wallpaper. Elven thought he saw tears running down the man's face. A dog with a lot of bark and very little bite.

"You're fucking crazy," Kurt blubbered. "All of you."

Elven let him go and picked up Kurt's gun from the ground, shoving it in his pocket. Kurt didn't care. He grabbed what little he could off the bed and ran out the door. Elven watched him get into his car, pulling out of the lot, his tired squealing as he did.

Elven had made his point, though he'd had to embellish some things here and there. He wasn't sure how solid Kurt's resolve was to get Madds, but it couldn't be that firm. He had his chance, but didn't take it before. Whatever his end game was, Elven didn't know, though he wasn't sure he needed to know anymore. He hadn't planned on killing Kurt, and now he didn't think it would come to that.

Nobody came into his town and messed with his people.

MADDS LAY her head on her pillow. Her gun was tucked between the mattress and the nightstand, just in case she needed it. After everything she'd had to deal with, it was the only thing that let her mind rest.

Elven being there for her was something, but at the end of the day, he couldn't be everywhere at once. Besides, he was a double-edged sword. She wasn't supposed to be relying on him so much. She was supposed to be keeping tabs on him. Though now, she wasn't sure where she stood with Hollis.

It tore her up inside, but then again, that was the least of the lines she'd crossed since coming to Dupray.

She closed her eyes, letting out a long sigh. She needed to push all the thoughts from her mind. She just needed to sleep. To let the darkness take over, and she could worry about everything the next day. She hoped that eventually, those worries would just vanish on their own.

She could feel herself slipping into a deep sleep. Breathing steadily, and giving into the calmness inside her.

And then, there was a knock on the door.

Her eyes popped open and she stayed there a moment. Almost as if she hadn't actually heard anything. Was her mind playing tricks on her again?

She waited another moment, keeping her breathing shallow and quiet. But no other knock came. Still, something felt off.

She climbed out of bed, grabbing the gun from the side of her bed. The air outside the blanket was cooler, but not cold, as the heater that blared full-blast underneath the window made sure of that. She walked over the carpet barefoot, staying as silent as possible.

Her heart raced, though she wasn't sure why. Someone had knocked on the door, so they expected an answer. It wasn't that she needed to sneak up on them. But it was so late, and she just had a feeling deep in her gut that felt off.

Maybe it was Elven. Perhaps that little kiss she'd shared with him had finally caught up to his senses, and he'd come back for more. That would be a welcome surprise.

"Elven? That you?" she asked, now realizing that perhaps she was being foolish, creeping toward the door with a gun.

But there was no answer.

She took a quick look through the window next to the door, moving the curtain to the side. She saw nothing. It was too dark outside.

She wrapped her hand around the door handle and pulled the door open. The cold cut through the air like a hot knife through butter, but what sent a chill even further down her spine had nothing to do with the temperature.

Nobody stood at the door. No taillights in the distance. No pitter-patter of feet running away.

But there was something there.

At her feet lay a single pink rose. Next to the rose was a card that read:

Always thinking of you.

=GET BOOK 4 in the Sheriff Elven Hallie Mysteries NOW!=

AFTERWORD

Thanks for reading Hunted in the Holler, the third installment in the Sheriff Elven Hallie mysteries.

There were a lot of balls I had to juggle to get this one finished, but I pulled through and it might just be my favorite so far!

I wanted to give a special thanks to my wife and kids for putting up with me missing for long stretches of time to write this, my parents for helping out when I needed them, my author friends Tony and Michelle for putting up with my constant bothering, and my fantastic editor Chelsey for helping me smooth things out.

And an extra special thanks for everyone that has read this book and the previous ones. Your words of encouragement and questions about when the next one will be out have been a serious boost for me! Thank you!

As always, being an independent author, I don't have a huge publisher's budget, so reviews are very important. If you have the time, please consider popping over to Amazon, or your favorite place to leave reviews, and post one!

AFTERWORD

To keep up to date and get some fun freebies, join my reader's list: http://drewstricklandbooks.com/readers-list/

-Drew Strickland

August 26, 2021

ABDUCTED IN APPALACHIA

Get Abducted in Appalachia, book 4 in the Sheriff Elven Mysteries now!

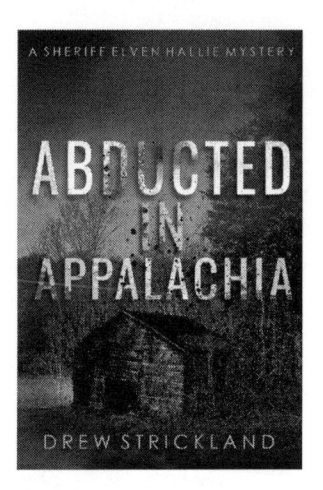

ALSO BY DREW STRICKLAND

The Carolina McKay Series

Her Deadly Homecoming (Book 1)

Her Killer Confession (Book 2)

Her Deadly Double Life (Book 3)

Poaching Grounds (Book 4)

The Sheriff Elven Hallie Mysteries

Buried in the Backwater (Book 1)

Murder in the Mountains (Book 2)

Hunted in the Holler (Book 3)

Abducted in Appalachia (Book 4)

The Cannibal Country Series

The Land Darkened (Book 1)

Flesh of the Sons (Book 2)

Valley of Dying Stars (Book 3)

The Soulless Wanderers Series

Tribulation (Book 0)

Soulless Wanderers (Book 1)

Patriarch (Book 2)

Exodus (Book 3)

Resurrection (Book 4)

Coming Soon! (Book 5)

ABOUT THE AUTHOR

Drew Strickland is the author of the Sheriff Elven Hallie Mystery series, Soulless Wanderers: a post-apocalyptic zombie thriller series, and the co-author of the Carolina McKay thriller series and the Cannibal Country series, both written with Tony Urban. When he isn't writing, he enjoys reading, watching horror movies and spending time with his wife and children.

www.drewstricklandbooks.com